BY RORY POWER

Wilder Girls
Burn Our Bodies Down
In a Garden Burning Gold

IN A
GARDEN
BURNING
GOLD

IN A
GARDEN
BURNING
GOLD

RORY POWER

NEW YORK

Published in the United States by Del Rey, an imprint of Random House, a division of Penguin Random House LLC, New York.

DEL REY and colophon are registered trademarks of Penguin Random House LLC.

Published in the United Kingdom by Titan Books, London.

LIBRARY OF CONGRESS CATALOGING-IN-PUBLICATION DATA
Names: Power, Rory, author.
Title: In a garden burning gold / Rory Power.
Description: First edition. | New York: Del Rey, [2022]
Identifiers: LCCN 2021045608 (print) | LCCN 2021045609 (ebook) |
ISBN 9780593354971 (hardcover; acid-free paper) | ISBN 9780593354988 (ebook)
Subjects: LCGFT: Fantasy fiction. | Epic fiction.
Classification: LCC PS3616.O88317 I5 2022 (print) | LCC PS3616.O88317 (ebook) |
DDC 813/.6—dc23/eng/20211001
LC record available at https://lccn.loc.gov/2021045608
LC ebook record available at https://lccn.loc.gov/2021045609
International edition ISBN 978-0-593-49982-5

Printed in the United States of America on acid-free paper

randomhousebooks.com

2 4 6 8 9 7 5 3 1

First U.S. Edition

Book design by Jo Anne Metsch

Για τον Παππού

AUTHOR'S NOTE

The fictional setting of *In a Garden Burning Gold* is inspired by various parts of the world, but it is not intended as a true representation of any one country or culture at any point in history.

DRAMATIS PERSONAE

* denotes deceased

THYZAKOS

*Aya Ksiga, a saint thought to have lived in the Ksigora

Vasilis Argyros, the Stratagiozi of Thyzakos and father of Alexandros, Rhea, Nitsos, and Chrysanthi

*Irini Argyros, consort of Vasilis Argyros and mother of Alexandros, Rhea, Nitsos, and Chrysanthi

Alexandros Argyros, the second to Vasilis Argyros and Rhea's twin brother

Rhea Argyros, Thyspira, and Alexandros's twin sister

Nitsos Argyros, son of Vasilis Argyros

Chrysanthi Argyros, daughter of Vasilis Argyros

Yannis Laskaris, the Thyzak steward of Ksigori

Evanthia Laskaris, consort of Yannis, mother of Michali

Michali Laskaris, son and heir of the Ksigoran steward

Kallistos Speros, son and heir of the Rhokeri steward

Giorgios Speros, the Thyzak steward of Rhokera

Dimitra Markou, the Thyzak steward of Myritsa

Lambros Tavoulos, a suitor at Rhea's winter choosing

Dimos Vlahos, a suitor at Rhea's winter choosing and brother of Nikos

Nikos Vlahos, a suitor at Rhea's winter choosing and brother of Dimos

Piros Zografi, a high-ranking member of the Sxoriza and Amolovak refugee

Eleni Avramidis, a servant in the Argyros household

Flora Stamou, a servant in the Argyros household

Lefka, a horse

TREFAZIO

Tarro Domina, the Stratagiozi (called Stratagorra in Trefza) of Trefazio

Gino Domina, the second to Tarro

Falka Domina, the second to Tarro

*Luco Domina, a saint and the first Stratagiozi (called Stratagorra in Trefza)

Francisco Domina, cousin of Tarro

Carima Domina, daughter of Tarro

Marco Domina, son of Tarro

MERKHER

Zita Devetsi, the Stratagiozi (called Ordukamat in Merkheri) of Merkher

Stavra Devetsi, the second to Zita

CHUZHA

Nastia Rudenko, the Stratagiozi (called Toravosma in Chuzhak) of Chuzha

Olek Rudenko, the second to Nastia

AMOLOVA

Ammar Basha, the Stratagiozi (called Korabret in Amolovak) of Amolova

Ohra Basha, the second to Ammar

PREVDJEN

Milad Karajic, the Stratagiozi (called Vosvidjar in Prevdjenni) of Prevdjen

Maryam Karajic, the second to Milad

IN A
GARDEN
BURNING
GOLD

ONE

RHEA

A week was too long to be a widow. Even after all her marriages, Rhea had never got used to it. The black, the singing, the veils—it was enough to drive anybody mad. At least no one ever expected her to cry.

She leaned forward in her seat as her carriage rattled up the road toward her father's house, Stratathoma, where it was perched on the edge of a sheer black cliff. From here she could only see the thick perimeter wall and above it the peaks of the stone-shingled roof. Somewhere inside, past the courtyards and double doors, were her siblings. Of them all, Alexandros would be most glad to see her, and she him; it was always strange being separated from her twin, no matter how many times they parted. Nitsos, their younger brother, would have barely noticed her absence, tucked away as he was in his workshop from morning until night. And Chrysanthi would be excited to see her, if only for the stories Rhea brought back from her trips.

Little Chrysanthi—although, Rhea reminded herself, they were none of them so little anymore—gathered up the stories Rhea told about her consorts and kept them in a small tin box by the side of her bed. Sometimes, if Rhea listened closely during the night, she could hear Chrysanthi open the box and munch contentedly on a story or two, leaving crumbs strewn across her bedsheets. Well, she wouldn't be disappointed this time. Rhea had a few stored up with just the right flavor. A flavor: a sweet, spicy autumn sort of crispness. Those were Chrysanthi's favorites.

At last the carriage reached the double doors breaching Stratathoma's perimeter wall, their gnarled surface painted a deep blue, the color most closely associated with their family name, Argyros. Rhea's father was quite proud of their name and insisted that his children and his house bear his colors whenever possible. He was the country's Stratagiozi, her father, in charge of all of Thyzakos, and as his children she and her siblings each had their own responsibilities to contend with. Only hers took her away from home, to some bed in some house in some city that fell under her father's watch.

She had dawdled with this last consort. He'd made the inconvenient mistake of falling a bit in love with her, and Rhea had seen the flicker of it in his eyes and found herself somehow unable to slide her knife under his ribs, plagued by a thing she supposed she had to call guilt. It was only when the time was well past for a chill to dust across the high grasses and olive trees that she had managed, over their morning meal, to ask him to turn away from her and hold still. It had not been a clean death, and so not a clean season. It worked much better when she could get right to their hearts, as she would be sure to with her next consort—winter's, to be chosen in a fortnight.

The carriage continued along the cobblestone path through the grounds and toward the outer courtyard, its studded wooden doors swinging back on their own, operated by a network of chains and gears. Nitsos's design obviously. He was the middle child, slotted between the twins and Chrysanthi, and while Alexandros followed Baba like a shadow, Nitsos was left to while away the time in his workshop. Windup animals with steam-beating pulses, clockwork gardens full of fabric flowers. Tinkering with machines and mechanics to make sure everything operated smoothly, in every corner of the world.

Beyond the doors, the drive straightened out and the cobblestones turned to patchwork flagstone. Rhea pressed close to the carriage window to get a first glimpse of the doors into the private inner courtyard. They were too narrow for carriages, and the lintel hung too low to allow a single rider through. When you entered Baba's house, you entered on your own feet, with no weapons in your hands and no ill will in your heart.

A pair of women were waiting, and as Rhea's carriage came to a complete stop they darted forward, one to fetch the luggage strapped to the back of the carriage and the other to open Rhea's door. But Rhea was too eager to get a breath of fresh air after so many hours bouncing around inside a small box. She shouldered the door fully open, the first servant jumping back to avoid its swing, and hopped down, her boots landing lightly on stones still warm from the afternoon sun.

The grass was well tended here, trimmed short, and the roses that trailed across every wall were fully in bloom, as always. Chrysanthi spent a great deal of time out here tending to the landscape, painting everything in careful strokes, making sure every rose was evenly pink.

"*Kiria* Rhea? Are you ready to go in?"

It was always startling to hear her true name for the first time after a marriage. In the rest of Thyzakos, and across the continent, they called her Thyspira, a title wrought by the first Stratagiozi that passed to whichever child had been given Rhea's particular responsibilities.

She turned to see the two servants clutching her luggage, her bead-studded bags standing out against the plain cloth of their dresses. The taller of the two women looked unfamiliar, but Rhea recognized the other. Eleni, the sister of one of Rhea's former consorts. Usually, Rhea only brought back a few gowns and trinkets from wherever her consorts lived, but five or six seasons ago she'd brought back Eleni. She couldn't quite remember why, only that as she was leaving Eleni had knelt by the carriage and begged, no matter that her sister's blood was still drying under Rhea's fingernails.

They were women sometimes, Rhea's consorts. It depended, of

course, on the selection available. When afforded multiple options, Rhea found she had no particular preference. Lately, though, Thyzak families had been sending mostly sons, apparently judging them to be the most expendable. Frankly, based on her interactions with her own brothers, Rhea was inclined to agree, but it did make for a more boring choosing, both for her and for Chrysanthi, who usually had a bit of fun with the spares.

Rhea nodded to Eleni and the taller servant, and let the two of them walk slightly ahead of her. The servants' dresses were gray and sweeping, high necklines draping into sleeves that hung loosely about their elbows. For the journey back from her consort's house in Patrassa, Rhea had worn a traveling suit in mourning black, snug trousers and coat hidden under a stiff woolen cape. Now she thought longingly of the gowns waiting in her own closet. Gorgeous, vibrant things. Mosaics made fabric, structured shoulders smothered in scrolled embroidery. Red and blue and gold—blood colors, Baba called them.

The cobalt doors swung open, and Rhea sidled through the gap after her servants. In this inner courtyard, too, Chrysanthi's hand was evident, but it was in an entirely different way. Baba preferred the outer courtyard to be orderly and regimented. Here, he let Chrysanthi do as she wished, and she had taken that to heart. More rosebushes, tendrils escaping up the walls and into every crevice, but other flowers, too. Spindly, wild little things, their tiny white buds gathering in lacelike lattices. In the corner, an olive tree stood proudly, its leaves a more vivid green than those growing in the family orchard. Opposite it, a fountain jutted from the wall, water burbling from the mouth of a stylized lion, and the water, too, was far richer in color than anything Rhea had seen elsewhere. The air itself was heavy with sun, gold splashed across every surface. Chrysanthi had exercised none of her usual restraint and let no shadows linger. Rhea could imagine her bent over the fountain, blending her paints on a little wooden palette before daubing at the crest of every ripple, gilding them with glimmer and shine.

"Enough dawdling," came a voice from the far end of the courtyard, and Rhea looked up. Her twin brother, Alexandros—Lexos, for everyday—stood in the doorway to the main house, his blue coat unbuttoned, hands shoved firmly in its pockets. "I'm getting cold out here waiting for you."

"What a hard life you live." Rhea stepped around her servants and crossed to where Lexos was waiting. As she neared him, he held out his arms, and she let a smile snag at the corners of her mouth as she leaned into his embrace.

He smelled of salt and damp, of that musk all old houses got when their stones had sat for so long. Rhea breathed in deeply. It was not a good smell, particularly, but it was familiar. Consorts came and went, but Lexos was always the same.

"Where are the others?" she asked as he released her.

"Chrysanthi's in the kitchen."

"And Nitsos?"

"Where do you think?"

Nitsos's workshop was in what, in another house, might've been the attic. Whenever Rhea visited him there, his worktables were barely visible under the debris his tinkering left behind: gears, finely wrought chains, all manner of pins and screws. Most of his creations were put to use about the house or incorporated into the natural order set working by Stratagiozis past—or if they were somewhat less useful, let loose into the gardens to wander about until their gears stuck.

"Let's leave him be," Rhea said, "and join Chrysanthi."

They found her bent over the kitchen's stone-slab table, a very long thin dowel in her hands as she carefully rolled out sheets of dough. She was a slight thing still, the air of a child clinging to her even though they had all left those days behind nearly a century prior. Rhea would never be able to look at her without seeing the rounded lines of youth laid over her.

Where Rhea and Lexos had been given the dark hair of their mother, Chrysanthi took after their father. All four siblings had straight Argyros noses and a slight downward turn at the corners of their dark blue eyes, but Chrysanthi's hair was the same billowing gold as their father's, her chin the same gentle point. They even walked the same way, with a caution in their steps that belied the steadiness Rhea knew they both felt. It seemed sometimes to Rhea that every one of her siblings had been gifted that steadiness but her. Lexos had his life here, his duties clearly laid out, and no matter how high Baba's expectations rose it seemed he was always able to meet them. And Nitsos was so at home in his workshop, in the worn grooves of his life, that she doubted he ever felt anything but content. No, it was only Rhea who had to go out into the world, only Rhea who had to watch her consorts live and die the way she and her siblings never would.

She'd asked Lexos about it once, when she'd first realized how long the passing years were taking to register on her skin.

"Don't be silly," Lexos had said, sounding vaguely put out. "We're not immortal. It's just we haven't died yet."

That was the way with every Stratagiozi family. You went on until you didn't. Early in her father's reign, Rhea had seemed to age normally, but she looked much the same now as she had when she'd passed into adulthood some eighty years prior. In fact, she thought it might take her another hundred to get her first gray hair.

Chrysanthi looked up as they entered, and the dowel clattered to the ground as she darted around the table, eyes bright, cheeks flushed.

"Rhea!"

Where Lexos's embrace had been a comfort, a moment of stillness in the rush of homecoming, Chrysanthi's was like being shaken awake, with the warm press of her apron, still carrying heat from hours spent in front of the stove, and the tight squeeze of her arms as they banded around Rhea's waist and lifted her an inch or two off the ground. Chrysanthi was taller than Rhea now, and Rhea never remembered until moments like this.

"Goodness," Rhea said as she was lowered back to the ground. "It's almost as if you never get any visitors."

"You hardly count as a visitor," Lexos said from behind her.

Chrysanthi frowned and began brushing off the front of Rhea's jacket. "Sorry. I've got you covered in flour."

"As long as you're making something good, I don't mind." Rhea took Chrysanthi's face in her hands and kissed both her cheeks. "How are you, *koukla*?"

Chrysanthi smiled beatifically. "Better now you're back."

There was nothing in the world, Rhea thought as she undid the clasps to her cape, quite like Chrysanthi's smile. Nobody who held as much light at the heart of her.

"What are you making?" she asked, tossing her cape onto the bench built into the kitchen's rock-slab walls and peeling off her coat.

"Pita, for dinner. I haven't decided what to put in."

"Let me help. I have some stories for you."

TWO

ALEXANDROS

Lexos watched from the doorway as his sisters stood side by side, rolling out dough for the pita. Chrysanthi was chattering away, her hair catching in her mouth as she described her most recent project for Rhea—some special way the sea light hit the olive trees near midnight. He'd heard it before, had been dragged out of his bed to come and look, Lexos, come and see, but Rhea was always better at giving Chrysanthi the smiles and questions she wanted.

Usually, at least. Today he could see Rhea's attention was elsewhere. She was doing her best to listen to Chrysanthi, but every few moments she glanced at the doorway, shoulders tight.

She was safe for the moment. Their father was out, making one of the trips Lexos wasn't yet allowed to follow him on. He would be home before dinner, but with any luck they had another hour of peace.

Rhea and Chrysanthi had finished with a layer of dough and Rhea was carrying it to the end of the table, where the others were waiting. When she'd finished draping the sheet of dough over the rest, she reached for the bell hanging from the wall and rang it once, calling to a servant; one was always waiting nearby, whether Lexos could lay eyes on them or not.

"Someone will bring my bag," she said loudly over her shoulder. "And then we can get started with the filling."

Since they were small Rhea had been the best of them at collecting her words, cupping her hands together as she told a story and watching the seed of it crystallize in her palms. Their mother had taught all of them how, had called it a gift given exclusively to their family line, but of the four children Rhea was the only one who remembered the process.

Kymithi, they called the candies. Not biscuits and not fruit but somewhere in between. Rhea's were all sugar and cloves, crisp on the outside with a soft middle. Lexos's, when he tried, always came out tasting bitter. Sometimes, in the evenings when he was waiting for the stars to burn through the sky, he would try it again. But the kymithi always came out wrong.

Maybe, Lexos thought, Rhea had better luck because she actually had stories to tell. All Lexos could ever tell anyone was that he'd been to a meeting with Baba, and he couldn't say very much more about it, and wasn't that too bad.

Eleni ducked into the kitchen to put Rhea's beaded bag on the counter, and left just as quickly, a harried look on her face. She was probably quite busy preparing with the other servants for Baba's return. There was a sound from somewhere in the house, the scrape of furniture on the stone floor, and Lexos had to keep from flinching. Baba wasn't due home just yet. There was time still.

"What was he like?" Chrysanthi was asking, and Lexos came farther into the room. He drew his coat tightly around him against the chill of the stone and settled onto a bench by the oven.

Rhea began to drop the kymithi, candied with maple sugar, into a ceramic bowl as Chrysanthi hung off her. Under her apron Chrysanthi's yellow gown was an old castoff of Rhea's. Rhea had embroidered the crimson swirls adorning the bodice a long time ago, back when she was still as young as she looked, and you could tell the stitchwork was unsteady if you looked closely. Rhea had tried to throw the dress out, but Chrysanthi had begged and begged until Rhea let her keep it.

His sisters. One lively and smiling, the other with a sharpness to her even as she led her consorts in their wedding dance. He would miss this when Rhea was gone again.

"He was nice enough," Rhea was saying as she poured herself a cup of kaf, the rich, bitter drink Thyzaks favored at all hours of the day. "Brown hair, brown eyes."

"But what kind of brown exactly?"

Lexos could see Rhea struggling not to laugh and got up, coming to lean against the kitchen table. "Horseshit brown," he said, popping one of Rhea's kymithi into his mouth.

"Ftama," Chrysanthi said with a gasp, slapping Lexos on the shoulder, but Rhea snorted and let him steal another kymitha.

"How are they?" she asked.

Lexos bit down and closed his eyes, let the soft center of the kymitha melt on his tongue. It tasted of sweet bread and early morning wind sneaking through a slightly open bedroom window. He swallowed quickly—no need to for the rest of whatever scene Rhea had chosen.

"Good," he said. "If perhaps a bit intimate."

"Well, what did you expect? I have certain responsibilities." Rhea picked through the bowl of kymithi to weed out a few of the undersized ones. They were small and round, each colored slightly differently but all with the same amber sheen. If Lexos looked closely, he could see something flickering at the center of each one.

"You're so lucky," Chrysanthi said with a sigh. Lexos wandered around to the other side of the table. He'd heard this a thousand times before, and would likely hear it as many times again. "Why couldn't I have been Thyspira?"

Long ago, Lexos had wished for Rhea's freedom himself—the lure of the world, the attention, the flowers tossed before your feet—but it had only taken a few trips across Thyzakos with his father to convince him otherwise. Chrysanthi might not realize, but she was lucky to stay at home, wrapped up in her work, in the simplicity of painting a brighter sunlit green onto a single leaf in the garden and trusting that miles away, beyond the walls of Stratathoma and the borders of Thyzakos, a thousand other leaves were beginning to brighten, too.

"Privileges of the eldest, *koukla*," Rhea said absently as she began to lay the sheets of dough at the bottom of a baking dish.

Privileges of the eldest, indeed. Lexos had a few of his own that he would rather not think about.

"Do you think we should fetch Nitsos?" Chrysanthi turned to Lexos. "I don't like to think of him up there alone."

"I'm sure he's fine. We'll take dinner together, after all."

It was true that Nitsos almost certainly preferred to spend his time alone, tucked away in his attic workshop, but Lexos was more concerned with avoiding the workshop himself. There was something about the mechanical tick of everything there, the life that Nitsos could knit out of gears and screws, that made Lexos uneasy. He'd tried, when they were younger, to learn about it, spent days up in the workshop with Nitsos trying look impressed as his brother described how every change he made to one of his creations would ripple out into the natural order of the continent. But his discomfort had never faded. Perhaps it was the artifice of it, though he'd never use that word with Nitsos, that made him anxious.

Their gifts had come to them from Baba, as was true for every Stratagiozi and their children. A Stratagiozi's power could be split apart, untangled and pulled free like strands from a braid. And so, as his children reached whatever he deemed the appropriate age, Vasilis Argyros would cut his palms and mix his blood with the earth. With very little ceremony, he'd press the resulting grime into his children's left palms, darkening the specific lines and whorls in the skin there that corresponded to the particular gift he was giving. They each still bore those marks, vivid and black.

For Lexos, it had started with the stars. The job had belonged first to Baba, but one evening, just after Lexos grew tall enough to see over the veranda walls, Baba took him to the observatory, the highest room in the house, and unlocked a wooden cupboard that Lexos had

never seen before, its doors carved with a series of overlapping circles. From the inner shelves spilled a piece of fabric so slippery Lexos
could barely feel it, so deep a blue it nearly matched the Argyros
family color. It was small enough to gather up in his arms, and yet
when he tried to find the edge it was always just out of reach.

"Sit down," Baba had said, gesturing to the window, where a
cushioned seat was built into the sill.

Carrying the fabric was like trying to grab hold of water, but
Lexos managed it, clutching tightly to one handful and letting the
rest flow where it would. From his seat he watched his father reach
into a small compartment at the back of the cupboard and take out
a spool of diamond-white thread and a long, glinting needle.

"Remember your lessons," Baba said, handing them to Lexos.
"What will you put where? Think."

That was the first night Lexos stitched the stars into the sky. Every
night after, he climbed the stairs up to the observatory, opened the
cupboard, and found the night's fabric waiting there for him, the
previous night's stars gone, no sign of stitching remaining. Every
night after, he pricked at his fingers and bit at his lip as he laid out the
constellations, careful to keep the alignment just right.

After a few years, and when Lexos was tall enough to mount his
horse without a groom giving him a leg up, Baba told him to stitch
in the moon, as well. It was longer work, with more detail to it, but
Lexos liked the look of the fabric when he was done. There was a
wholeness to it, as though he should have been doing it that way all
along.

With the moon came the tides, and with them came a large basin
set on a pedestal in the observatory, full of water always moving, the
patterns shifting as Lexos learned to dip his fingers in and coax them
this way and that. Once he had mastered the tides, had learned to
keep them wild and impassable around the cliffs of Stratathoma, he
earned yet another visit from Baba, this time to tell Lexos that as the
oldest Argyros child, he was to attend every Stratagiozi meeting with
his father and observe. There were other Stratagiozis, of course, one
ruling over each of the neighboring countries, and every season they

met to discuss the state of their federation, and to politely wrest what power and resources they could from one another.

"I never had a chance to learn like this," Baba had said. "So count yourself lucky and make good use of it."

The meetings were always in the same place—a monastery north of Thyzakos, perched on the top of a mammoth spike of stone. The only way to get there was to use a system of baskets and pulleys. A rope stretched from the nearby mountainside across the valley to where the monastery sat precariously, its verandas cantilevered out over the edge of the rock. Hanging from the rope were large woven baskets, big enough to hold a man and not much else. To get to the monastery, one climbed inside, weapons left behind, and used the rope overhead to pull the basket along to the other side, where the monks were waiting with glasses of just-poured wine.

His first trip across the valley had left Lexos nauseated, but now, after more trips than he could count, it felt like nothing to haul himself out over open air. At least for those few minutes his life was in his own hands.

"*Elado,* Lexos," someone said, and he jumped. There were his sisters, each with their hands on their hips, watching him. Rhea was closest—it had been her voice.

"Sorry," he said, giving her his best smile, and Chrysanthi returned to filling the pita with kymithi, but Rhea didn't seem convinced.

"What is it?" she asked. "Has Baba decided—"

"No," he said quickly. "I'd have told you. You know that."

She was asking about her next choosing, the ceremony by which Rhea would select her consort for the coming winter. Long ago, when Baba's seat had been more secure, they'd been dull affairs. Now, with relations in Thyzakos at their most fragile, Baba always had something to say about who Rhea would choose, and given the mistakes she'd made in Patrassa, Lexos thought she was right to be nervous.

He busied himself with searching through his coat for the pocket watch Nitsos had made him, ticking hands pointing to the phases of the moon as they changed, the face of the watch showing the constellations in their current arrangement. Not that he ever forgot, but it was a nice gesture from a brother Lexos wasn't sure he had ever seen as clearly as, say, Rhea, who had not let up and was in fact standing closer than she had been before.

"I'm expecting word from my network," he said, relenting. "There have been some rumblings in the east I'm not comfortable with."

"The unrest? I heard something about a skirmish between Rhokera and another city."

"If that were the only problem, we might have nothing to worry about." Lexos stood up abruptly, mouth going dry as he thought about the reports he'd received from the north—separatist camps, filled both with hatred for the Stratagiozi and with people from every corner of Thyzakos, and other countries besides. "We had better not talk about it now."

There was a clatter as Chrysanthi opened the oven to check the temperature, and Lexos felt Rhea come up next to him. They watched Chrysanthi put the finishing touches on the pita, tucking the last top layer in at the sides and crimping the seam delicately.

"Do you need help, *koukla*?" Rhea asked. Lexos nudged her in the ribs. Rhea had never quite managed to break the habit of looking after Chrysanthi, even though the two were apart so often.

"No, it's fine. It won't need long," Chrysanthi said. "Should we change for dinner, do you think?"

Lexos plucked at Rhea's sleeve, the stiff starched fabric wrinkled from hours in the carriage. "He won't like to see you in this." Nobody had to ask who he meant.

"Oh, come get dressed in my room," Chrysanthi said, beaming. "You can help me choose what to wear. Like when we were little."

Before their mother died, before Baba set his sights on the Stratagiozi title. More than a hundred years ago now.

"You go up," Rhea said. "I'll be right there."

Leaving the pita in the oven—one of the servants would be in to finish the meal—Chrysanthi pressed a kiss to each of her siblings' cheeks and ducked through the low kitchen doorway, heading for the back staircase that led to the second floor without passing Baba's room.

At last, quiet. Lexos hadn't words to express how dear Chrysanthi was to him, but sometimes a bit of peace was even dearer.

"She's tall," Rhea murmured. She was still watching the doorway, one hand idly pressed to her heart.

Lexos slumped back down on the bench. "She's only just taller than you. Isn't that one of your old dresses she's wearing?"

"She must have altered it." Rhea sat down beside him, a grimace on her face as she tucked her legs up under her.

"Sore?"

"I never remember to get out and stretch."

She'd come from Patrassa, a good two days south. Lexos had been there only once, to visit the seaside with their mother when she'd been ill.

Away from the oven, it was cold here in the kitchen. At last, weather fitting the season. For weeks, Lexos had watched as the leaves refused to fall, as the long grasses and flowering trees continued to be untouched by frost. Every day Baba's temper had grown shorter, and Lexos thought of Rhea in some strange house, panic bubbling as she found herself unable, and still unable, to end her consort's life.

It had gone on so long that even Nitsos had noticed. He'd come down from his workshop one afternoon and found Lexos in the courtyard, sunning himself on the baking flagstones.

"She's running out of time," Nitsos had said, squinting up at the sky.

"Don't worry," Lexos replied. "If she needs help, she'll ask for it."

Except she wouldn't, of course. But Lexos thought he might be the only person who knew that.

Rhea sighed and rested her head on his shoulder, and he felt her relax, her hands uncurling from their fists. Her nails were bitten to the quick, the skin around them pink and inflamed.

"You did your job in the end," he said quietly. "He can't ask for more than that."

"He can ask me to do it well, can't he?"

"Hush." Lexos covered her hands with one of his. "Let him say that, not you." They were quiet for a moment, and Lexos eased himself away from Rhea to get a good look at her face. He'd wanted to ask, and now seemed like the only time they might have. "What was it anyway? That kept you?"

Rhea was, he knew, an excellent liar to most people. She had to be, given what she did outside the walls of Stratathoma. But inside them, and with him, the slight drop of her expression was all too clear. She had not wanted him to ask. But better him than their father.

"I couldn't quite say," she told him, and oddly enough, she seemed to be telling the truth. She looked down, frowning. "Do you wonder, ever? About the worth of things?"

That, Lexos thought, was a dangerous road to travel, especially when their father was involved. "What things in particular?"

Rhea let out a little laugh, and leaned her head on his shoulder again. "Lives, I suppose."

"Oh, is that all?"

She waved him off. "Never mind. Call it a lapse in judgment, and let's speak no more about it." At the edges of the house a door slammed and the ease between them disappeared as Rhea jerked upright. "He's early."

"Calm down, *kathroula*." Lexos had called her that since they'd learned to speak. Mirror, it meant. Rhea had never answered in kind, and Lexos had always privately thought it was because Rhea was complete without him in a way he was not without her.

"I should've changed earlier," Rhea was saying as she snatched her coat and cape up from the couch. "This will only remind him."

"No time now, I'm afraid. He'll have seen your carriage out front."

On the floors above, they could hear the scurrying of servants hastening to make last-minute adjustments, and back toward the great room there was the sound of the outer doors closing.

Lexos stood and smoothed his hair down. His shirt was still tucked into his dark, narrow trousers, but there were creases and the collar was folded oddly. He adjusted his coat, hoped it would do something to hide his unkemptness. Rhea, meanwhile, had put the rest of her traveling suit back on and was fussing with her long braid, which was coming loose at the end.

"Leave it," he said as heavy footsteps came echoing down the long hallway to the kitchen. "Better for him to see it like that than see you trying to fix it."

Lexos had the clearer view of the hallway, and so it was he who first saw the silhouette of their father as he strode toward them. He was a tall man—his height had been passed down to each of his children—with slender shoulders and a tilt to his whole body, as if he'd once been knocked off balance and had never quite found his footing again.

It was difficult, sometimes, to remember that to anybody else this man wasn't Baba, but Vasilis Argyros, Stratagiozi of Thyzakos. His title could hardly carry half as much weight to others as "Baba" did to his children. But being Stratagiozi meant something very important to everyone outside Stratathoma's walls: Besides identifying Baba as the country's ruler, it also meant that Baba bore a matagios, a small black dot in the middle of his tongue, and with his particular matagios came death, and the power to hand it out to whomever Baba so chose.

"So," said Baba, stepping into the kitchen. His voice was low, seeming to echo around the hewn stone room. "She returns."

Rhea nodded, barely. "I always do."

There was a moment of quiet as Baba took in the flour-coated counters and the matching white stains still lingering on Rhea's trousers. At last, his gaze settled on Lexos.

"Alexandros. I suppose you didn't have anything else to occupy your time?"

It was always worse when Baba was right. Lexos did have other things he should've been doing, rather than eating sweets and watching his sisters bake. There were documents to read, letters to sum up for Baba, maps to practice drawing freehand.

He said nothing. An apology would do no good. And besides, he wasn't the least bit sorry.

"Well, while you're both here," Baba said slowly, "we can discuss your sister's recent mismanagement in Patrassa."

Lexos saw the color drain from his sister's face, as quickly as if Chrysanthi had taken her paints and brushes to Rhea's skin.

"I know there was a delay," she said, but that was all she got out before Baba raised one weathered hand and her mouth snapped shut.

"You had your marker?" A set of dials from Nitsos, like Lexos's pocket watch, that ticked off the days left until the time for the season was over and done.

"Yes," Rhea said.

"And you knew your responsibilities?"

"Yes."

"And you understand what happens?" Baba stepped closer, his hands clasped behind his back, black coat near the twin of Rhea's save for the gold embroidery weaving down the front. "When the season does not change as it should, as it always has. When people cannot count on us."

"I do."

"Tell me."

They all went like this, these conversations, if they could be called that, when Rhea came home. Even when the seasons changed smoothly she was given a reminder of what could be lost if they didn't.

"Say it," Baba repeated when Rhea remained silent. "What happens when you can't do your job?"

"People begin to doubt."

"Doubt what?" said Baba. "Be specific, *kora*."

"They start to doubt your power. They start to wonder if somebody else should sit in your chair."

"And?"

Crimson spots were flaring on her cheeks. Lexos held his tongue, resisted the urge to take her hand and remind her she was not alone.

"And everything is at risk," she said.

"That's right." Baba glanced at Lexos, to make sure he was watching. "Everything. Our house, our lives, our country. At risk because of you. Tell me."

"Everything at risk because of me."

Rhea had said it so often that Lexos half expected to hear her muttering it in her sleep sometimes when he passed her room in the night on his way to stitch the sky.

"I'm glad you understand," Baba said, eyes soft. "And you'll do better with your winter choosing, yes? You know how much rests on your conduct, yes?" The silence he let stretch on was painful. Lexos forced himself to keep still. "All right. Give your baba a kiss."

Relief melted Rhea's features, and she let out a nervous laugh as she kissed Baba's cheek. Baba didn't give her much back, just a hint of a smile, but it was more than he usually allowed, and Lexos could see a spark light in Rhea's eyes.

He looked away, dried his clammy palms on his trousers. In his earliest days at Stratathoma, he'd been afraid the markings on his palm would wipe away, but they were part of him now, imprinted into his skin.

"Why don't you go and change?" he heard Baba say to Rhea. "You know I don't like to see you in black."

"Of course."

Rhea gave their father one last anxious smile and darted between him and Lexos, avoiding Lexos's eye. She knew how he felt about these conversations, how he felt about the way Baba spoke to her, but she didn't seem to mind it as he did. It was the only thing they ever truly argued about.

"How was your trip?" Lexos said as soon as Rhea was gone from the kitchen, eager to scrub her from their father's mind.

"Too long," said Baba. He'd gone to Rhokera, ostensibly to visit the steward, but Lexos knew it had really been to remind the people there who they owed their allegiance to. Lately the Rhokeri had been reaching for more power than they were owed, and Baba could not bear it. "We'll speak more after dinner." He glanced at the counter, at the mess left behind. "Where is Chrysanthi?"

"Upstairs. She'll be down soon, I think."

"She's well, I trust?"

"She is." Lexos swallowed. "You might ask her yourself."

Baba ignored him and swept by, making for the doorway. Lexos knew it was useless, but he said it anyway: "Nitsos is well, too."

Baba stopped and looked blankly over his shoulder. "I'm sure he is."

When he was gone, Lexos dropped onto the bench and buried his face in his hands. If only Rhea could be like Nitsos, Nitsos who knew his father's heart and had walled himself off from it. Instead she let Baba hurt her and insisted, at the same time, that he had done no such thing. And it was left to Lexos, then, to open her eyes, to show her the scars on her skin. Not a job he'd ever asked for, and not a job anybody wanted him to do.

It was quiet here, at least, and the air was starting to warm from the oven. He'd stay awhile, soak in a few minutes of rest before dinner. After all, he was sure he'd need it.

RHEA

Rhea emerged from the mouth of the kitchen hallway into the great room, blinking at the sudden sunlight tumbling through the high windows. Above, across the whole of the ceiling, was a tiled mural of her father, and his fathers before him, all rendered as traditional icons. Wide, down-turned eyes and interlaced hands, and behind their heads a circle of rich blue. Rhea had spent a hundred years under these faces. She could still remember the workers perched on the scaffolding, scraping plaster across the ceiling while Chrysanthi brushed over the tiles with her paints to make sure they would always catch the light.

Waiting for her by the hearth were Eleni and her other servant. They didn't follow her everywhere—Rhea was very particular about that—but she would need them to help her dress for dinner. She motioned to Eleni as she approached, and they fell in behind her as they made for the back staircase.

Up and up, on steps worn smooth. Somewhere below, Lexos was probably still talking to Baba. Discussing the spreading unrest, discussing the ramifications of her inexplicable incompetence. It was shameful enough to have to face her father, but she knew Lexos was probably making his own judgments about her, even if he'd never say so. He knew what it meant when she couldn't do her job, what it might cost them. And though he never said a thing, there was always a look about him after these conversations with Baba. A pity, almost, and a frustration.

They reached the second floor of the house and turned down another corridor, this one lined with a shaggy, red rug. Rhea could remember mornings when she was small, the rug soft on her bare feet as she paced in front of Lexos's door and waited for him to wake up.

They passed Nitsos's room first, probably locked up tight, and as they reached Chrysanthi's, Rhea rapped sharply on the door and kept going. Chrysanthi would find Rhea when she was ready.

Then came Lexos's room. It was opposite hers, facing the sea, and as she hesitated by the door, just slightly ajar, she caught a lungful of salt air. No matter how cold it left the room, Lexos always kept the shutters open. He said it helped him sleep.

And finally, her own chamber. She and Lexos had got the first pick of bedrooms, and she'd chosen this one, with its view facing back to the mountains. The autumn had stripped the leaves from the trees clustered in the foothills, and had left the slopes scrubbed, the wildflowers curling and browning as though burned.

Stratathoma had originally been built many centuries ago, by the first Stratagiozi of Thyzakos, and its style was rooted firmly in simplicity and spareness. Its bedrooms were equipped only with broad wooden window seats, deep enough for two people to lie close together. Each seat was topped with a cushion barely three inches thick, its cover made of patterned wool that scratched horribly if you left too much skin uncovered while sleeping.

The rest of the room was fairly empty, save for a small table with two matching chairs and a freestanding wardrobe tucked along one wall. That held her clothes—gowns, shoes, coats and capes, and traveling suits like the one she still wore.

Rhea had scarcely taken two steps into the room when Chrysanthi

burst in behind her, hair only half pinned up, dinner gown unbuttoned and flapping open at the back.

"How was it?" Chrysanthi asked. "Was Baba terribly angry?"

Rhea motioned to Eleni, who sidled in behind Chrysanthi and
began dutifully doing up her buttons. Chrysanthi had changed from
Rhea's castoff into a fresh green gown with an explosion of pleats
cascading down to form the skirt, and she'd piled on a handful of
beaded necklaces the way she always had, even as children playing in
their late mother's closet.

"I wouldn't say angry," Rhea answered. "Your hair, *koukla*. What
a mess."

"Eleni can do it."

"Fine. You sit still," she said, "while I find something to wear."

Rhea's other maid—Flora, that was her name—began to undo
Rhea's braid, working a comb through the tangles her day of travel
had left there, as Rhea opened the wardrobe and picked through the
dresses hanging there.

"You're in green," Rhea said. "I suppose I might wear red. We'll
look like a poppy field, but there are worse things."

In a few minutes, Eleni had Chrysanthi's yellow hair tucked up
into a looped knot, and Flora was draping a beaded chain across
Rhea's forehead, weaving it back into her dark curls. Rhea had wig-
gled into a rich red gown, its fabric and silhouette simple until the
broad sweep of the skirts, which were embroidered with gold.

"I've never understood this," Chrysanthi muttered. "It's not as
though we're trying to impress anybody."

"Just Baba," Rhea said, meeting Chrysanthi's eyes in the mirror.
She'd missed it, the preparing. Her late consort's family had dressed
simply, in pale colors and rough fabrics. Nothing like the armor Rhea
was strapping onto her body now.

At last Flora finished with her hair and knelt to pull off the traveling boots that Rhea still wore. They were placed carefully in the
wardrobe as Rhea slid her feet into a pair of thin slippers and brushed
past Chrysanthi on the way to the door.

"Wait, where are you going? It isn't time yet."

"To fetch Nitsos." She couldn't sit around here waiting for Baba to call them down. She'd go mad thinking over everything she'd done wrong with her consort. All the ways she could've been better.

Down the hallway, then, and back out to the staircase. The only way to get to the attic was through an access door at the top of the bell tower, which was in fact empty of any bell. One had hung here once, long ago, to be run in times of strife, but when Baba had taken Stratathoma, he'd had it removed. A symbolic gesture, he said, that there would be no more strife in Thyzakos. Rhea wasn't sure if it hadn't been a bit silly.

She hauled her skirts up to her knees as she began the climb up to the top of the tower. As she reached the final landing, she paused for a moment to take in the view. Mountains and sea stitched together, and if she turned, the country spreading out, farmland and forest. Most of the time, when Baba lectured her about sacrifice and patriotism, she didn't quite understand that bone-deep love he spoke of for land and people. It was as if talking about it made it shrivel up in her chest and hide away. But here, wind cold against her cheeks, Rhea felt her heart open wide. There was blood in this soil. Some of it was blood she'd spilled, yes, but some, too, was her own.

The doorway to the attic was off to the left, a low, curving thing, and from there, another flight of stairs, and another, until at last Rhea was at the very top of the house, higher even than Lexos's observatory. She knocked on the wall as she climbed the last few steps; there was no door to Nitsos's workshop, and they had all learned long ago not to surprise him. You never knew what he might be working on.

"Te elama," Nitsos called, and Rhea took the last step up into the workshop.

In here it was always bright like summer, light rioting through the air, sent ricocheting by the mirrored ceiling. Rhea ducked as a mechanical beetle came whizzing past her head on one leg of its predetermined pattern, and stepped around a small mechanical rose in mid-bloom to greet her brother.

He was still in his leather apron, and his round, ruddy face was smudged with what looked like oil. Rhea could see an indent on his nose from where he'd perched his magnifying glasses, which now lay on the table before him.

"You're back," he said.

Rhea trailed her hand along the edge of the worktable, smiling to herself as Nitsos grimaced when her fingers brushed an incomplete bit of machinery. "Indeed."

"And dressed for dinner."

"Ah, your sharp inventor's eye at work."

"Quite," Nitsos said dryly, and reached to untie his apron. Rhea waited for him to snatch up a jacket from somewhere, or at the very least wipe his hands on the kerchief in his pocket, but Nitsos just folded his apron and came around the table, heading for the stairs in his stained trousers and work shirt.

"You're going like that?"

He stopped and turned, glancing at the ceiling to get a look at his reflection. "Like what?"

"You have grease all over your face." Rhea sighed. "Come here."

Nitsos frowned but let Rhea shake out his kerchief (also dirty, she noted unhappily) and spit in it.

"It's as if you're baiting him," she said, taking the kerchief to his face and scrubbing at the streaks of black there. "You know Baba likes things a certain way."

Nitsos squirmed as Rhea rubbed particularly fiercely at a stubborn smudge. "Maybe with you, and maybe with Lexos, but he wouldn't notice with me."

"You're already testing him." She plucked at the waistband of his trousers. "So let's aim to be tidy at least from the chin up."

She'd barely finished when there came the distant sound of the kitchen bell being rung for dinner. They were due in the dining room as quickly as possible. But Rhea found herself lingering, looking around at the various creatures Nitsos was in the middle of. What animals and plants he made here would serve as symbols for their living counterparts in the world beyond, and any changes or manipulations would take effect across the continent.

It was, in essence, much the same sort of process as the rest of the family's gifts, but theirs had been given to them young, whereas, to Nitsos's great frustration, he'd had to wait until even Chrysanthi had got hers first. And when Baba had finally decided he was ready, it had been this he was allowed: not the creation of natural order, but only the mechanical care and maintenance of it. He could still build whatever creatures he liked inside the confines of Stratathoma, but in accordance with the parameters set on his power by Baba, his machines held none of the bearing on the world beyond Stratathoma that the others did, those built by some other Stratagiozi's child centuries prior. What true importance was left to such a job nobody could quite discern, but what they did understand was that Baba meant for Nitsos to be as far removed from the management of the country as possible.

Whatever it was that made Nitsos's presence so distasteful to Baba was something Rhea couldn't identify. Perhaps it was that he looked the most like what Rhea remembered of their mother, despite his blond hair. Perhaps it was that he was too young, by Stratagiozi standards, to be of much use, although Chrysanthi had never suffered in equal measure.

As it was, Nitsos had taken Baba's tossed-aside gift and welcomed it, exploring and inventing with a vigor that Rhea pretended not to be alarmed by. It might not have left her so uncomfortable if their gifts had been more matched, but where Nitsos was particularly concerned with the inner workings of things, Rhea preferred to give that as little consideration as possible.

Her siblings dealt in symbols of clockwork, of paint and cloth. She was the only one who ever had to confront the real, beating heart of the world. Time passed as it would—managing all that was the domain of some other Stratagiozi, although nobody had ever told her who—but it was Rhea who nudged the seasons along with it. Each one began as she chose her suitor, the next instance of which was looming on the horizon, and ended as her suitor died.

Died, she supposed, was a vague way of putting it, but the alternative was too distasteful to think about just before dinner.

She and Nitsos met Chrysanthi and Lexos on the way to the dining room. Rhea felt something flip in her stomach at the sight of
all three of her siblings together again. Of course, Nitsos looked as
though he'd rather be anywhere else, and Chrysanthi was still asking
all about her last consort. She exchanged a weary smile with Lexos,
and led the way through the double doors into the dining room.

It was set on the back side of the house, with a series of windows
cut into the wall that looked out over the ocean. In winter the servants boarded them up with brightly decorated shutters, but it was
warm enough still that they stood empty, the sea air sweeping
through. At one end of the room, a fire burned steadily in the hearth,
and across the center stood a long stone table, so roughly hewn that
its surface could only just be considered flat.

Baba wasn't there yet, which sent a frisson of relief skittering
down Rhea's spine, so they took their places, Lexos and Rhea on one
side of the table, Nitsos and Chrysanthi on the other. Baba always sat
at the head, and at the foot there was a place setting for their mother,
even though she had died a few short months before they came to
Stratathoma.

"At last," came Baba's booming voice, and the double doors
banged open. Baba swept in, followed by two scurrying servants, one
carrying a pitcher of wine and the other a tray of glasses. "My children."

He had changed out of the black coat Rhea had last seen him in
and put on one that brushed the floor, red and black patterning running across it in stripes. On his fingers were a smattering of rings,
and he smelled different, too, the leather and dust of travel covered
over in spice and amber.

He paused at his chair for a moment, gaze passing from one sibling to the next until at last he gestured for them to sit. Rhea sank
down, smiling tightly at the servant who came to fill her glass.

"So." Baba took a long sip from his and dabbed at his mouth with
the corner of his sleeve. "Which of my children will speak first?"

Chrysanthi opened her mouth—of course, Rhea thought
fondly—but closed it as Lexos shifted, probably giving her a kick

under the table. No, Baba knew who he wanted to hear from, and it was Rhea. She sat up a bit straighter and cleared her throat before she began.

"I've been thinking, Baba," she said, flushing as her voice trembled. "I want to apologize to you."

Baba leaned back and crossed one leg over the other. "Whatever for?"

"I let you down in Patrassa." She could feel Lexos staring at her, but it was the right thing to do. It was the only thing that would really earn Baba's forgiveness. "You've placed so much trust in me. You've given me so much responsibility. I will try to be more worthy of it when next I choose."

Baba's face was solemn as he looked at her with his dark, endless eyes, and then he smiled, wrinkles splitting across his face like lines in the summer earth, and clapped once, startling Nitsos, who had been fiddling with something under the table.

"My girl," he said, beckoning her to him. Rhea got up, nearly tripping over her skirts, and hastened to his side. He took her face in his hands and kissed her forehead. "You need never apologize. You have my trust, my heart, *koukla*."

"Thank you, Baba." Rhea thought her knees might give out, so potent was the relief that washed over her.

"And you'll use them well in a fortnight's time."

She would. Baba would guide her choice, and she would be useful to him, would be part of what held Thyzakos together even as it threatened to break. "I promise," she said, and she meant it.

"You see? How a good daughter treats her father?" He released Rhea, patted her hand once before waving her back to her chair. "Children, you will never know how deeply a father's love runs."

"Indeed," said Lexos as Chrysanthi's stomach growled absurdly. "Now perhaps my father's love might include asking for dinner to be served."

Baba's jaw clenched but he said nothing, only waved at the servants and took another sip of wine. Eleni came in carrying the pita, its scent filling Rhea's nostrils. She had handpicked the kymithi inside—all the best moments, the loveliest stories, and nothing she wouldn't want her father to know about.

Rhea glanced at Lexos as Eleni began to serve. He didn't like the way Baba spoke to her, but it was only that he didn't understand Baba like she did. Baba loved in his own way, and you couldn't expect him to change.

Perhaps it was different with fathers and sons. If Mama were still alive, she might have been able to bridge the gap between Baba and Lexos. But she was gone, buried in the countryside around their old house, in accordance with the old custom she'd loved, with not even a stone left behind to mark her grave so that nobody could steal the jewels draped around her cold, dead neck.

Rhea wondered how much Lexos remembered. He was only a few minutes older than she was, but he always seemed to remember their childhood in more vivid detail. Meals with their mother, outings to the meadows, walks in the meandering forest. And other things. Whispered conversations, and the one Rhea couldn't believe—Lexos and her on a stolen horse, riding away with no thought of ever coming back.

"*Elado,*" Baba said, clapping sharply. Rhea jerked to attention. Across from her, Nitsos did not look up from his plate. "Join hands before we eat."

Baba carried out many of his Stratagiozi duties in private, but this particular one he liked to perform in front of his children. It was nobody's favorite thing to witness, never mind participate in, but Rhea had no intention of ever saying so to her father.

Chrysanthi, on the other hand, had no such reservations and chose that moment to clear her throat. Rhea knew before she even opened her mouth what she was about to ask. It always went the same way.

"Baba, do we have to?" He did not respond, and only stared at her, brow furrowed. "It's just a bit grim for dinner, isn't it?"

Rhea kept her head down, right hand already clasped with Lexos's, left reaching across the table for Nitsos's right. Privileges of the eldest, she'd said in the kitchen earlier. Well, here was the privilege of being the youngest. Questioning Baba like this was the sort of thing only Chrysanthi could ever get away with.

"I mean," she continued into the strained quiet, "that it would be nice to have a meal not preceded by a mourning prayer, particularly one with—"

"Oh, just hold my hand," Nitsos muttered, and smacked his own onto the table palm up, his mark, a trio of black lines at the base of his thumb, clearly visible even in the low light. Reluctantly, Chrysanthi took it, and moments later Baba had joined in, closing the circle. He shut his eyes, and as he took a deep breath, Rhea allowed herself to agree with Chrysanthi. Even she found that this spoiled the meal, and she'd murdered a man over breakfast less than seven days prior.

"Lopon," Baba said, his voice taking on that calm it always did when he began this prayer. Out of the corner of her eye, Rhea could see the servants making for the door, and wished briefly that she could join them. *"Aftokos ti kriosta. Ta sokomos mou kafotio."*

Dutifully, the children repeated it back to him, opening the prayer. Lexos's palm was warm against Rhea's own, and his fingers squeezed once around hers, offering reassurance she hadn't known she needed.

"Aftokos ti kriosta," Baba went on, *"po* Panagiotis Nikolaides. *Ta so-komos mou kafotio."*

There it was. The first name. The first death honored by the mourning prayer. It was the same prayer Rhea recited at each consort's funeral, the same one recited at every funeral within Thyzakos's borders and even beyond, but though she'd heard it more times than she could count, it sounded different when her father spoke it. Foreboding rather than soothing, because whatever name Baba spoke during this prayer belonged to someone who had been alive when it began and would not be by the time it finished.

This was Baba's power. Death, doled out across the continent simply by reciting the prayer. Contrary to the rumors (rumors that the Stratagiozis themselves had long fostered), Baba didn't know where the names he spoke came from. He said they arrived in his head much the same as dreams do, and Rhea had heard enough of these little ceremonies to believe him. The names were never familiar. There were no lists of enemies, no discussions of strategy; the matagios was not a weapon to be wielded. Despite this, Baba's power was certainly among the most coveted, and the most feared by those outside of the Stratagiozi Council, who knew nothing of its limits. Previous holders of Baba's seat had even been murdered for it, but thus far nobody had ever come after Baba. Baba said that was because people respected him; Rhea thought that was because people knew that not even the might of the entire federation could be counted on to defeat Vasilis Argyros's temper.

"*Aftokos ti kriosta,*" Baba repeated now, "*po* Maria Dimou. *Ta soko-mos mou kafotio.*"

Rhea did not know how many names there were left for Baba to say. How many lives there were left to end. But Lexos would listen, as he always did, and tell her if there was anyone important, or anyone they knew, and meanwhile she would close her eyes, lean back in her chair, and think of Patrassa. Of those days when her consort had loved her, and she had never wanted to come home.

FOUR

ALEXANDROS

When the meal was finished and the plates had been cleared, Lexos stayed seated as his sisters left the dining room together, their hands linked. Nitsos stayed, too, rested his elbows on the table and watched their father with a stubborn intensity. Rhea and Chrysanthi knew when they weren't wanted, but Nitsos rarely gave Baba anything without first being asked.

A breath of silence as Baba looked up from his wine and realized that Nitsos was still there. Lexos waited. Maybe today was the day Nitsos would be allowed into these discussions. Maybe today was the day he could share the weight of Baba's expectations with somebody other than Rhea. But no.

"*Figama,*" Baba said, waving Nitsos away. "I have to speak with your brother."

Nitsos's custom, once ordered by Baba, was to obey while making clear that he found said order absurd. But something had emboldened him tonight. Lexos suspected that Rhea's decision to humiliate herself for a chance at their father's mercy sat about as well with Nitsos as it did with him, which was not well at all, and Nitsos remained right where he was, his chin propped on one hand. The idea of Baba looking up to see his younger son still in the room, his order ignored, left Lexos cold.

"I don't mind if Nitsos stays," he said. "In fact—"

"Well," Baba interrupted, "I do. In fact, I believe I have made it clear with whom I wish to share the details of ruling this country. What use do I have for a child and his toys?"

A child and his toys. If Nitsos was so, it was only because Baba would not let him be more. But how was Lexos supposed to say that? Instead he watched as Nitsos rose from the table so stiffly he seemed one of his own early creations, and left the room without another word.

"What an odd boy," Baba said.

Nitsos would remember that for a long time, Lexos knew. They each had their own wounds they refused to let close, except perhaps Chrysanthi, and Nitsos had just acquired another. Further proof, though he hadn't really needed it, that as far as Baba was concerned his family line began and ended with the twins.

As the eldest, Lexos would someday inherit the Stratagiozi seat of Thyzakos, and everything that came with it. While the gifts Baba gave to his children were passed on through ritual, the matagios— the true mark of each Stratagiozi's own power—passed on through the blood. When Baba died, it would go to Lexos, and when Lexos died, it would go to the next surviving Argyros. So on, and so on, until someone who wanted it for themselves came along and ended the entire bloodline, as Baba had done to the Stratagiozi before him. When the last of them had fallen, Baba had mixed their blood with the earth and smeared it across his tongue. This was the ritual from which every other had come. Lexos had not been present, but some days, and some moments, like this one here, with his father caught in the firelight and the empty room pressing in, he wished he'd seen it. He wished he'd been there, if only to stay his father's hand.

But it was done. And he was his father's son, his father's weapon and heir, so he leaned in and said, "What did you want to discuss?"

"I've had word from the others. We're expected at Agiokon after Rhea's choosing."

When things in the federation were running smoothly, as every Stratagiozi was taking great pains to pretend they were, the council met at the end of each season. This particular meeting had been delayed by Rhea's trouble with her recent consort, and it was an embarrassment for Baba, one that Lexos knew he would not easily forget.

"I think now might be the time to ask a favor of our friends." Baba took a long swallow of wine. "After my trip, I think it best."

He'd been to visit Rhokera, Thyzakos's wealthiest city and home to the strongest of the stewards. It was Rhokera Baba was desperate to appease, Rhokera that was best equipped to mount a campaign to remove Baba from his seat. Stratagiozis marshaled no troops of their own, and had always relied on their subjects for protection, but none of Baba's stewards felt much like subjects anymore.

"How was it?" Lexos asked. "Your trip. Fruitful, I hope?"

Baba nodded. "Giorgios agreed to send his son for Rhea's winter choosing."

The Rhokeri steward, Giorgios Speros, had not sent anyone to Rhea's choosings in recent memory—that was the sort of small defiance the stewards had preferred to display until the recent assortment of skirmishes between Rhokera and its neighboring cities. Giorgios's acquiescence now was good news, certainly. And Lexos knew Baba planned to use Rhea's winter choosing as a bridge between himself and the Speros family. Thyspira, functioning as she ought, binding the country together and staving off war, one season at a time.

But to Lexos this trip to Rhokera had been misguided. If it had been his decision (and he had been reminded, quite forcefully, that it was not) Lexos would have sent Baba to appease the Ksigora, a collection of northern territories that were isolated from the rest of the country by a treacherous mountain range. It was there that most of the country's more outspoken dissidents had pooled, forming a movement against the Stratagiozi and the federation, which Lexos's scouts told him they called the Sxoriza. It meant nothing to Lexos— a word from Saint's Thyzaki, from the old language—but it certainly meant something to the Ksigorans. That left him uneasy. Baba had won his seat with battle and blood, and though the years since had made those memories kinder, there was still a bitterness to Thyzakos that Lexos was always worried might take deeper root.

In fact, the Sxoriza so worried Lexos that he'd done something he very much was not supposed to do. The Laskaris family had been the stewards of the Ksigora since Thyzakos's founding, but they had never been regular participants in Rhea's choosings. He had a few weeks back written to the Laskaris steward and asked that his heir be sent to the winter ceremony, with the hope that it would demonstrate the reach and continued strength of Baba's power. Baba, of course, would be furious when he learned that Lexos had disobeyed him, but if he would not acknowledge the northern territory as the problem it truly was, it fell to Lexos to take action.

It would presumably change nothing about Rhea's choosing, though. Baba was set on Rhokera. Rhea's marriages, as short as they were, went a long way toward buying a steward's loyalty. In exchange for the life of whichever suitor she chose, and for the show of deference that constituted sending a suitor in the first place, the suitor's city of origin was given particular wealth for the duration of that season. Its farmers reaped greater harvests, its trade guilds made greater profits. And Baba, the power of death a black spot on his tongue, took fewer lives, a mercy he claimed to provide out of his own generosity, and one Lexos was fairly certain was simply part of the matagios's mechanics, and had very little to do with Baba's disposition.

Still—prosperity for many at the expense of one: It was a lesson every child in Thyzakos was taught, a sacrifice every child believed to be the highest honor. And if there were stories told that Rhea's consorts never truly died, well, Lexos was happy to let them spread.

There was movement in the doorway, and he saw a flash of jeweled hair. "I'm sorry," he said, even though Baba had started eating again and seemed not to require his presence any further. "May I be excused?"

Baba had barely nodded before Lexos was out of his chair and heading for the door. He hastened out of the dining room, stopping short in the hallway to peer into the shadows.

"Rhea?" he whispered.

A scuff against the stone floor, and there she was, leaning out of an alcove where the lamplight couldn't reach. "Shh, he'll hear you."

"He'll hear *me*?" Lexos fumbled for her arm in the dark and latched onto it, dragging her with him away from the dining room. He let go once they emerged into the great room. "What were you thinking?"

"I only wanted to know where Baba's planning to send me."

"I would've told you. I always do."

"I know." Rhea shifted uncomfortably.

"What? What else?"

"I thought maybe he'd say something to you. About Patrassa . . . and me." She looked away. "It's silly."

It wasn't the time, Lexos reminded himself. Rhea never liked hearing what he had to say about Baba, but especially now it would only turn into an argument. "It's not silly," he said as gently as he could manage.

"It is." She shook her head. "I must learn to be content with what he gives me."

He couldn't help himself. "Well, you know what I think of that."

Rhea faced him, her jaw set, shoulders back. "I do. Good night, Alexandros."

As she left the fire guttered in the hearth, and Lexos felt the shadows cling more tightly to him as he made for the opposite staircase. With a frustrated sigh, he bounded up the steps, heading for the observatory, where his duties for the evening were waiting. Thread between his fingers, and the glint of the tidewater in the moonlight, and the weight of the day would vanish. Perhaps only for a moment, but it was all Lexos had ever been able to expect.

FIVE

ALEXANDROS

Morning came quickly, and with it came the sounds of Chrysanthi and Rhea laughing as they went down to the kitchen to make breakfast. One could usually count on Baba being occupied during daylight hours, and when he was, the hush he brought to the house lifted. Lexos knew that Rhea's coolness toward him the prior evening would have long since left her, but still, as he followed at some distance down to the kitchen, the shape of her stuck in his head. The strength of her lines, the unfamiliarity she held sometimes. They had been born together, lived together; indeed, Lexos sometimes thought they would die together. How strange that there should be anything about her not belonging in part to him.

He paused at the kitchen threshold, watching as Chrysanthi took a pitcher of fresh fruit juice from the box Baba kept lined with ice imported from the Ksigora in the north. Rhea was at the counter, piling a tray with slices of bread and a selection of jams.

"Oh, come in," Rhea said, her back still turned to him. "As if we've never disagreed in our lives." And there was enough affection in her smile when she at last did face him that Lexos stole a slice off her plate and pretended not to notice the smear of jam on his chin as Chrysanthi giggled into her napkin.

"It doesn't matter whether I like it," Rhea said to him after breakfast as they strolled through the groves. He'd just finished telling her about Baba's trip to Rhokera and about how Baba presumably meant to leverage her choosing accordingly, the start of which seemed a great deal closer than it had the day before. "What must be done must be done."

Lexos said nothing in response. Rhea rarely disagreed with Baba, at least out loud. After her mishap in Patrassa, it seemed nothing would make her appear anything less than perfectly dutiful.

Underfoot, the ground was shrunken, the sudden frost withering even the hardiest grass, but the sun still held its warmth. Here at Stratathoma, Lexos saw more of it than Rhea ever did.

He peeled off his coat, spread it on the ground, and she sat, her black skirts tangled around her legs, her shirt an old one that Chrysanthi had once stolen and used to practice her stitching. This was the Rhea Lexos knew. Plain, smiling, dirt smudged on her palms and a twig caught in her hair. He reclined next to her and watched the sun move overhead, Rhea humming absently as noon grew closer and closer.

They were disturbed not long after by the distinctive call of one of Lexos's mechanical scouts. He'd developed his network over time, person by person, smile by smile, but when faced with the impenetrable sweep of the northern cliffs, the most reliable creatures available were the ones Nitsos had built for him.

It had taken a lot of convincing to get Nitsos to agree to it. He'd been worried about what Baba might think, and only agreed on the condition that Lexos keep the creatures a secret. But really, Lexos's success had been achieved by insisting that if he was able to pass on vital information to Baba and then reveal that the source was in fact of Nitsos's creation, Baba would be unable to deny his youngest son's value.

As appealing as that had been to Nitsos a handful of years ago, though, Lexos thought it might not carry much weight if he tried to use the same argument now. The Nitsos at the dinner table the night before was not the same boy who'd built Lexos's machines. He was more determined these days. More alive. Different enough, sometimes, to make Lexos wonder what kind of creatures he might build now, if asked.

His creations for Lexos took all forms, but were always small things designed to slip in and out of sight. Lexos's favorite, and the one he had sent north to the Ksigora, was a bird (of course they were the most efficient) about the size of a falcon, with a similar sharpness to its eyes and talons both. It was white, perfect for the sky and the snow, and it watched him now from the branches of one of the olive trees, its head cocked, its particularly chosen call slicing cleanly through the air. Lexos knew if he pressed the bird to his ear, he would hear the gears turning inside where a heart might have been.

"Go and fetch it, will you," Rhea said, not looking up from where she was lazily knotting a circlet out of dried grass. "It won't stop making that noise until you do."

There were other reasons to fetch it than easing Rhea's annoyance—namely, that it was bringing him word of the Sxoriza and the north—but she had no real appreciation of them. Perhaps it was time he shared this with her. After all, he was always telling her she didn't have to bear her duties alone. Why should he?

He would have to take the bird to Nitsos to learn what it had seen. Its mechanics were, as Nitsos had put it, far too complicated for someone with fingers the size of Lexos's to operate. And Lexos had in fact broken a bird or two before this one. But Rhea was here, and her fingers seemed slender enough, and who could say, exactly, how long it would take him to find Nitsos, wherever he was?

The bird didn't move as Lexos approached, nor as he cupped it in his broad palm and carried it back to Rhea. The calling had indeed stopped, and as Lexos approached, Rhea looked up at the creature with a bored sort of annoyance on her face, as though she were considering snapping its head off just for the sake of it.

"Here," he said, holding it out to her. "Will you take it apart for me? I can't get to the eyes."

Rhea seemed to have an innate understanding of Nitsos's creatures that Lexos did not, because she said yes and then quickly found the latch built into the underside of the bird's throat and pressed it. The bird's skull folded outward. Inside, beyond a tiny knot of mechanisms that Lexos couldn't distinguish between, was a piece of polished white stone, slotted carefully behind what passed for the bird's eyes.

"Now what?" Rhea said, looking up at him from where he'd positioned himself between her and the sun.

"The stone," he said, and was reminded briefly of when they'd been children, in the garden of their country house. Of how Rhea had looked up at him that day with the same wide, trusting eyes, asked the same question, and climbed onto a horse behind him, let him run them both away. He tried, sometimes, to remember just what it was they'd been running from. It had been only them in that house. Just the four children, Baba, and their mother. What could there have been to be afraid of?

"Here," Rhea said, holding up the stone between two fingers. He took it, startled by how cool it felt. Nitsos, whenever he showed Lexos the bird's findings, slid the stone into a little metal frame he had built up in his attic workshop, one that caught the light Chrysanthi had left brushed across the air. But going all that way seemed like more trouble than it was worth when there was plenty of sun right here, and besides, after Baba's sharp words yesterday, Lexos wasn't sure he wanted anybody to see this but himself, and perhaps Rhea.

With a glance over his shoulder toward the looming reach of Stratathoma, he held the stone up to the light and watched the images it held scatter out across the ground, faded and shadowy as though they were reflected in the surface of a small pond. There were only two, which Lexos found unusual. His scouts tended to report with a great deal more information.

The first was of a landscape Lexos immediately recognized. He'd had scouts patrolling Thyzakos's northern border with Amolova for years. Ammar, the Amolovak Stratagiozi—Lexos could not remember the word they used among themselves in its place—kept a notoriously tight grip on his people, and by all accounts kept them happy, as well. Or at least, that was the official word. Any Amolovaks with separatist leanings would need to find another home, and it seemed they had found one with the Sxoriza in the north of Thyzakos.

Nitsos's creature had captured a party of Amolovak refugees (although Ammar would never hear of them being called such) passing south across the ridge of mountains that filled the northern territory. This was hardly surprising, but it was worrying nonetheless. Lexos had raised the issue with Baba before, had pointed out that Ammar would be furious to know that the Thyzaks were in any way encouraging dissent among his people. And furthermore, Lexos had argued, Ammar certainly wouldn't hesitate to bring it up during a council meeting, further exposing Baba to the humiliation of playing host to a domestic insurrection.

But Baba, it seemed, would much rather pretend there was no insurrection at all. And for the moment, he still could. This movement across the border was still small, and still unnoticed. Lexos had time to put a stop to this, if he acted quickly.

He turned then to the second of the pair of images. This one seemed to be of a Sxoriza camp. It looked much the same as every other camp Lexos and his scouts had found, with the same ramshackle collection of shelters set against the same steep tumble of rocks. Lexos sometimes wondered if his scouts were only finding the same settlement over and over. There had to be something larger hidden in the mountains—some base of operations the Sxoriza were managing to keep concealed. Lexos gave the image a cursory look, and was ready to pass it off as nothing new when something caught his eye.

A pennant, hanging off the camp's central shelter. It was red. Specifically, Lexos thought, Laskaris crimson, the house color of the family charged with stewardship over the northern territories. He'd had no reports from the Laskarises, no word that they'd captured members of the insurrection. No, this was something else—something Lexos found deeply worrying. A member of the Laskaris family was in league with the Sxoriza.

The Laskarises were by no means the most powerful or well loved of Baba's stewards; the Ksigora offered little in the way of taxes, and the longer harvest, preferred by the rest of the country and put into effect by Rhea, left them with too short a season to properly collect the ice and furs they were known for. But any defection from a steward family would be genuinely damaging to Baba's rule.

Lexos peered more closely at the image. The Laskaris line had dwindled, leaving, if Lexos remembered rightly, only the steward himself, his consort, and his son. Lexos had met Michali, the Laskaris heir, once, had found him intelligent and engaging, if a bit reserved, and remembered thinking that he would be a good steward once the title fell to him. But the banner in the Sxoriza camp was likely his— the steward himself was, and had always been, loyal.

Bad enough that there was any independence movement at all. Worse that a steward's heir should be involved. And particularly, especially terrible that Michali was due to attend Rhea's choosing in a matter of days. Although, he thought, there was perhaps something else to be made of it. Originally the invitation had been extended with the hope of bringing the Ksigora more firmly under Baba's control, of showing the northern separatists that nothing passed in Thyzakos without Baba's notice. It was something else now: an opportunity.

"What?" Rhea said from the ground, startling Lexos. "You've got that horrible look on your face."

"Horrible?"

"Yes. It means you're thinking."

He was. He'd never meant for Rhea to marry the Laskaris heir; for the moment he'd been content to let Baba's focus on appeasing the Rhokeri dictate her choice, content to take careful action with the Sxoriza where Baba would take none. But the situation had changed. A steward's heir in the Sxoriza was dire indeed, and Lexos could no longer afford to defer to Baba's complacency.

There was little use presenting Baba with the images the scout had collected. Baba always saw exactly what he wanted to see, and Lexos was sure that his low estimation of the Sxoriza problem extended to the north as a whole, which provided little to the Strata-giozi in the way of money and material. Even if Baba did accept that the Laskaris heir was working with the enemy, he would likely deem it entirely unimportant. No real threat. Nothing to worry about.

No, Lexos had been right to act alone in inviting the boy, and he would be right again to leave Baba out of whatever came next. Thankfully, he had some idea as to what that might be.

"Kathroula," he began sweetly, "there's something I need you to do."

RHEA

R hea gaped up at her brother. He couldn't be serious. Choosing the Laskaris heir as her consort? In what would surely be defiance of Baba's orders? Did he have no sense of the risk he was asking her to take? She could ill afford to upset their father, especially after her delay in Patrassa.

"Well?" he said. He'd finished explaining his request some moments ago, but Rhea had been unable to find the words to respond. Now they arrived easily at the tip of her tongue.

"Lexos," she said, "have you gone mad?"

"I haven't." There was an odd gleam in his eyes that Rhea did not like, and it only burned more brightly as he knelt down next to her, the bird's pale stone still clutched in his hand. "We serve this family, Rhea. That's exactly why I'm asking you to do this."

This family. What an odd way of looking at it. "We serve Baba," she corrected. "He tells me who to choose. Does he even know you invited the Laskaris boy?"

"Well, no, but—"

"That is disobedience enough. I see no reason to take part in any more." She could picture it—her hand in some northerner's, Baba's stern face gone soft with disappointment, which was the very worst of his punishments.

Lexos scoffed. "Disobedience? How can that matter to you, Rhea? I am speaking of this family's future."

Of course that wouldn't matter to him, Rhea thought. He had never been as afraid of their father's anger. And it wasn't that he had never borne the brunt of it, but rather that he had far more of Baba's trust to balance the scales.

"So am I," she said. "Baba will not have me choose poorly."

"He will," Lexos said firmly. "Any choice but this is the wrong one. I've told you about the Sxoriza. I've explained—"

"You decidedly have not," Rhea cut in. She'd heard bits here and there, to be sure, but Lexos had never done anything that might reasonably be called explaining.

Lexos rolled his eyes, but he held the bird's stone up to the light and told her how to read the images it contained. He told her what his initial plan had been, how he'd only meant for the Laskaris boy to kneel at Baba's feet and nothing more. But things were different now, he went on, and this was an opportunity they couldn't pass up.

It was clear to Rhea that he hadn't expected to have to convince her. After all, though they disagreed as often as she supposed siblings always did, they rarely found themselves truly at odds.

"And Baba really knows nothing of this?" she said when he'd finished.

"He's been kept abreast of the threat," Lexos said. "But he doesn't know the invitation has been extended. Nor has he seen what you and I have."

Laskaris crimson in the Sxoriza camps. Rhea was well aware that this meant more to Lexos than it did to her, even after his attempt to explain, and she couldn't quite find in herself the urgency that pulled at the corners of his mouth. "What have we seen, really?" she asked. "How can you be sure it really was the Laskaris heir in that camp?"

He blinked at her. "Who else would it be?"

"I don't know." She sighed, picking at one of the burrs stuck to her skirts, and Lexos reached out to take her hand in his.

"I am as sure as I need to be," he said softly, "when the risk is this great."

"Risk?" She yanked back her hand. Had he not paid any attention when Baba shared reports from the rest of the country? Even she was aware there were other problems, and she wasn't nearly so deep in Baba's confidence. "Don't you think the Rhokeri present a larger one? They've taken up arms against another city. It must only be a matter of time before they march on Stratathoma."

Lexos sat back on his heels, smiling sharply. This was the Lexos Rhea hated a little: smug, calm, and always in possession of more information than she could ever hope to have.

"I will deal with the Rhokeri," he said. "That's simple enough. But we need to cut off the danger in the north before it has a chance to threaten the existence of Baba's seat itself. He isn't taking it seriously."

"Perhaps," she snapped, "he isn't taking it seriously because it isn't serious."

"It is. There's too much I cannot say, but we cannot afford to be seen housing those against the federation."

Too much he couldn't say. Did Lexos have any idea how pompous he sounded? Rhea was well aware of the conversations she had always been kept out of; she did not need or appreciate the reminder. "Who would really hold us responsible for the separatists?"

"Every other federation member," Lexos said, as though it was the most obvious thing in the world, and Rhea flushed. Perhaps it was. "If you marry the Laskaris boy," he went on, "you will go to the Ksigora. Live there as his consort and my spy. Learn everything you can about the Sxoriza, about their camps, their numbers, their strategies. With that information, we'll be able to pick them apart, and when you kill him they'll be left leaderless. A threat handled, yes?"

"But it's not my job," she said. "And it's not yours, either. It belongs to Baba. He's Stratagiozi."

"And if we leave it up to him, he won't be much longer."

Lexos sounded so certain that Rhea felt every rejoinder leave her head, her mind full of fog in their place. She blinked up at him, at his silhouette caught in the sun. As much as she hated to admit it, Lexos knew a great deal more about this sort of thing than she did. He was the one who went to the council meetings, the one who kept Baba's correspondence. The one who knew what was happening in the farthest reaches of Thyzakos, in places she hadn't even heard of before.

Besides, as much as she professed to believe in Baba's competence as a ruler, his hold was weakening—anyone could see that. And she did like the cold. A winter in the Ksigora . . .

No. She remembered Baba's face at the dinner table the night before. How happy he'd been when she apologized, and how generous he'd been to forgive her. She knew him, trusted him. He would handle things. "Speak with him about it," she said to Lexos. "Change his mind. If anybody could—"

"Yes, yes," Lexos said, waving his hand, "if anybody could. But I don't think anybody can." He ducked down so their eyes met. The same blue as hers, dark like the sea. "I know you're not comfortable with this. But it's me asking. I am your flesh and blood, *kathroula*. Don't you trust me?"

"Of course I trust you," she said, grimacing at his use of that particular endearment, one he knew she hated. "I'm just not sure that has anything to do with disagreeing with you."

Lexos let out a long breath. She could tell he was adjusting his approach, could almost see the gears turning in his head like he was one of Nitsos's creations. "All right, then. Don't decide now. Meet them, see what Baba has to say for himself. But remember: If we leave it to him, Baba will have lost his seat by the close of the season. It will cost us our lives, Rhea."

"You don't know that," Rhea said, but Lexos shook his head.

"I do," he said. "If we do nothing, Baba will be the end of us both."

The pale stone was still clenched in his fist. Rhea wondered how much it had seen that she had not. Sometimes it seemed that every single creature in the world knew more than she did. To be sure, she left Stratathoma and spent every season somewhere new, but she never saw anything beyond the walls of whatever house she had chosen for herself. Whatever house Baba had chosen, really.

"Rhea?" Lexos prompted. "Will you think about it?"

She sighed. "Will you leave me alone if I say yes?"

But Lexos didn't answer, and so neither did she.

SEVEN

RHEA

They had a little more than a week to themselves before the consorts were set to arrive, and Rhea made the most of it by avoiding nearly everybody. She made an exception for Chrysanthi, who spent a few hours here and there teaching her to paint shadows along the undersides of flower petals. While Chrysanthi was able to do most of her work through the ever-changing gallery of landscapes she kept in her studio—what strokes she made on canvas there appeared a hundred miles away, in the gardens and fields of other villages and towns—she preferred to do the housework in person, and Rhea enjoyed watching her nudge the shadows along with little strokes of black paint. It was something simple, and given the decision facing her, simple was exactly what Rhea needed.

At meals Baba was hardly present. When he was, his mind was clearly elsewhere, perhaps in the same place as Lexos's, who, whenever she saw him, seemed to be deeply preoccupied. But despite that shared preoccupation, both men found time to let Rhea know who they thought her next consort should be, Lexos with meaningful looks over the dinner table and pointedly yet vaguely phrased questions about how she was feeling, and Baba with a simple note, delivered to her late in the evening the night before, which read only:

Kallistos Speros, Rhokera

It was not his way to explain, Rhea had thought as she folded up the note and cast it into the fire burning merrily in her bedroom's hearth. At least, not his way with her.

Now, with only a few hours before her suitors arrived, Rhea was wandering down a path that followed the perimeter wall. She was coming up on the small gap that led to a staircase, which carved down the cliff face to a small beach below. In their first few years at Stratathoma, she and Lexos had spent their summers there, burning their feet on the sun-scorched stones and letting the salt spray curl their hair.

She shook her head, determined to chase Lexos from her mind. Whenever she thought of him, all she could see was his face as he'd asked her to trust him. Don't you see, she wanted to tell him, you are asking me to forsake our father. If she married the Laskaris boy, if she committed to destroying the Sxoriza instead of appeasing the Rhokeri, it would mean that she was turning her back on Baba and on her own trust in his judgment. Lexos had done that years ago, whether he knew it or not.

She was still thinking about Lexos's plan when she bumped into Nitsos, stepping onto her path from an adjacent one with his eyes fixed on a book he was in the middle of reading.

"*Elado,* Nitsos," she said, stumbling a few steps into the grass as his shoulder collided with hers.

He looked up from the page, surprised by the sound of her voice even though he'd practically knocked her over only seconds prior. "*Sigama.* I didn't see you."

"Clearly." She ruffled his thick mop of blond hair and gave him a gentle shove until he'd made enough room that they could walk on the path side by side. "Where are you going? I'm surprised to see you out of your workshop."

"I'm going to the garden," he explained, and she hastened after him, past the opening that led to the ocean staircase.

"Nitsos," she said, resisting the urge to lay her hand across his forehead and feel his temperature, "we're in the garden, *kouklos*."

He gave her a look so withering that Rhea suddenly felt all of her hundred-and-some years. "I know. I meant my garden."

His own private one, full of his creations. She'd always known he kept one, but even so she'd never all the way understood what it was Nitsos did with his time, or with the gift given to him by Baba. Now she found herself curious. "Would you mind," she asked carefully, "if I came along?"

He said he wouldn't, or rather he said nothing, only kept walking down the path, a sudden spring in his step as Rhea followed. They soon arrived at a place where another wall branched off from the perimeter and curved sharply around, enclosing a patch of land that was tucked against the house, between it and the edge of the cliff. The way in, Rhea could see, was a small, low archway built into the wall, to which a rickety door had been affixed.

Nitsos hesitated for a moment, his hand trembling slightly on the latch, and it occurred to Rhea that in their hundred-odd years at this house, she'd never been here before. All that time, and there were secrets still at Stratathoma. Parts still of her family that she hadn't laid eyes on.

"Won't you show me?" she asked, prodding as gently as she could, and he glanced at her nervously before jostling the latch and opening the door.

She had to duck to pass through, and so it was the grass she saw first. Brown, crackling, exactly like what grew in the rest of the grounds. She couldn't help but feel disappointed. And then she looked up.

It was snowing. Flakes drifted down from the trees, falling in what seemed like random eddies until Rhea looked closer and saw the patterns, the grooves dug into the ground and the miniature belts that carried the fallen snow out to the wall, where a mechanized pulley system ran it up and back into the gossamer dispersal network that Nitsos had built in and among the leaves.

And what leaves they were. Translucent in the autumn sunlight, bright copper filaments running through them like veins. As she watched, one detached from its branch and came floating down, its papery surface catching the air and slowing its fall.

Some of the trees were tall, spindly things, their trunks white and peeling. Inside, through the gaps in the bark, she could see their clockwork bodies, gears turning, spools winding. Others looked like the ones they had up north. Plane trees, they were called, their trunks so thick you couldn't wrap your arms around them. And in the back corner of the garden, across a carpet of lightly tinkling glass blue-bells, was an ancient-looking cherry tree, fully in bloom. Its blossoms were hand-painted in swirls of white and pink, petals made of wood shavings and paper.

Overhead, a hummingbird was in flight, its gears turning so quickly that it made a high-pitched whir that Rhea could hear from the ground. It had been painted in a deep, Argyros blue, and its eyes seemed almost to have the same down-turned shape she knew from her family's portraits. It seemed so familiar, as though she'd dreamed of it once. But she was quite sure she'd never seen it before, neither it nor anything else in Nitsos's garden. She would have remembered.

"Do you like it?" Nitsos asked, and she turned to see him smiling eagerly, a windup cricket sputtering in the palm of his hand.

"How?" she asked, staring up into the canopy of mechanically fluttering leaves.

"Haven't you heard?" Nitsos replied. "I'm very good."

He set the cricket down and it hopped off into the grass until its windup ran out and it tipped over onto its side. Beyond it, a deer was moving stiffly through the trees, taking three steps before bending to sniff the ground, and then repeating the whole process again. Within Stratathoma's walls, Nitsos's creations still bore the markers of their mechanical origins, but out in the world, they moved and breathed as real beings. It was like that with almost every gift Baba gave—one way at Stratathoma, and another everywhere else.

She crouched down to watch the snow inching along in the grooves in the ground. "What are they? The flakes, I mean."

"Fabric. Here, take one."

She plucked one off the conveyor belt. It glinted softly in her hands, like some kind of metal, but it was so soft, so light. It was even cold.

"It's a stiff silk," Nitsos explained, pulling a magnifying lens from his pocket. "I embroidered it with silver thread to help it keep its shape."

She took the lens, held it over the snowflake. There was the star and its points, the latticework around the edges.

"And then Chrysanthi helped me," Nitsos went on. "She showed me how to paint all of it. Let me use some silver leaf. She thought it added a nice bit of shine."

"It's lovely. Would you . . ." She cleared her throat. "Would you mind if I kept it?"

Nitsos looked so pleased that he might burst, and Rhea felt a pang of guilt for not having asked to see his garden sooner.

"What about that?" she said, pointing across the garden to the cherry tree, which looked almost older than the house itself. "Has it been here long?"

"I made it a few summers ago," Nitsos said, taking her arm. "Come and see."

He led her across the garden, their steps keeping carefully to the narrow, winding path of living grass that led through the carpet of glass flowers. They were making a beautiful, bell-like sound as their petals jingled lightly against the stems.

The cherry tree was unlike the other trees in the garden. While the others seemed to move on their own, their gears turning and operating constantly, the cherry tree was still, its only movement coming from the hummingbird, who paused on its branches once during every round of the garden and looked at her strangely with those down-turned eyes.

"I was trying something new," Nitsos explained as Rhea ran her hands along the trunk. This close, she could see it was made of burnished, beaten copper, with verdigris beginning to creep across it like moss.

She knocked on the trunk softly with her knuckles, and heard a soft, echoing ringing. "It's hollow."

"To leave room for the mechanism." He reached out to where the trunk split in two directions. At the split was a small, stunted branch, and from it stemmed one blossom. He took gentle hold of that flower, and began to turn it. Rhea could hear gears winding, could hear them gathering tension.

"Ready?" Nitsos said, and he let go.

The branches began to move, revealing themselves to be made up of hundreds of smaller segments that adjusted to give the tree the appearance of being buffeted by a breeze, and one by one a handful of blossoms began to fall, suspended from their original perches by tiny, threadlike cables that glittered in the sun. They hung in midair for a moment, and then, as the gears began to slow, the cables retracted, pulling the blossoms back up to their spots on the branches.

"It's not very practical," Nitsos said, stepping back to admire his handiwork. "Well, none of it is. But I do like it."

"Do you come here much?" Rhea squinted up through the branches at a snatch of blue sky. "I always thought you were hidden away in the attic."

"Once a day at least," Nitsos said, heading back the way they'd come. She followed, her hand trailing reluctantly along the lowest branch. "To make sure everything's running smoothly."

She could imagine it very well. The sky gray overhead and Nitsos alone as he walked from the house out into the grounds, never looking over his shoulder to see if anyone was coming along, because nobody ever was. It was absolutely pitiful. But he'd mentioned their sister, hadn't he?

"You said Chrysanthi helped you with some of it," Rhea said eagerly. Nitsos nodded, his eyes still fixed on something in the distance—probably some small imperfection only he could see. "Does she spend much time here?"

Nitsos turned to Rhea, a sort of blank confusion in his expression.

"With you, I mean," she clarified. "It's only the two of you here with Baba when I'm away."

"And Lexos," Nitsos said, which left Rhea feeling a bit silly. Of course. Lexos was here with them, too. But somehow that didn't quite feel as though it counted. If Lexos was anywhere near as distant with Nitsos as Rhea was ashamed to admit she had often been, then his company was probably not worth very much to their younger brother.

Still, it was Nitsos who'd remembered, and that was comforting. She hated to think of any of her siblings left alone. "Yes," she said. "And Lexos."

"Chrysanthi comes out sometimes," Nitsos said abruptly, and Rhea had to think for a moment to pick up their conversation. "Mostly in the spring." He reached down to a nearby leaf, fabric stretched across wire, and adjusted the lie of it. "She likes everything better in spring."

It was the fondest Rhea had ever heard him sound about a person. He was almost smiling, even. If only the other two were here. If only it could be the four of them together in Nitsos's garden with nothing else to worry about.

"I don't know how you find the will to leave," she said. "If I were you, I think I'd spend my whole life here."

"We all have our duties," Nitsos said darkly. "And speaking of yours—"

"I'm not sure that we were."

He smiled, shrugging. "You've just got quite an afternoon ahead of you. That's all."

"Well," she said, tilting her head back to catch the weak sun. "You're right about that."

There was a moment of quiet, and then Nitsos said very evenly, "Do you know what you'll do? Who you'll choose?"

That was odd. He had never asked her anything like that before. In fact, she rather thought he tried to pay as little attention to her choosings as possible. But perhaps he felt the same sort of urgency Lexos did—about Thyzakos, about their father. Perhaps it was only she who'd been ignorant to it.

"I don't know," she said. "What would you do, if you were in my position?"

Nitsos scoffed. "What a world that would be. Come on. Let's get back to the house."

And then, to her great disappointment, he was ushering her through the arched doorway and closing the door behind them. Soon they were heading through the grounds, the high walls of the clockwork garden disappearing behind them. If not for the fake snowflake in her pocket, Rhea might have thought that it had never existed at all.

EIGHT

RHEA

The afternoon came in a wash of gray clouds overstuffed with rain, and with them arrived the first of Rhea's potential consorts. There would be five in total, a notable decrease from the days when Rhea had danced with twenty or thirty suitors before announcing her choice. The rewards on offer, it seemed, were no longer quite enough to merit the sacrificing of one's life.

First came Lambros, from a city near the middle of the country, not far from where Rhea and her siblings had been born, though that was not something anybody was allowed to discuss. Thyspira was eternal, from everywhere and nowhere. She had never been born, and indeed she would never die.

Lambros had been sent to her choosings twice before, and she'd nearly made the mistake of mentioning their shared origin when fishing for topics of conversation. It would not have been a breach of etiquette so bad as, say, telling him her true first name, but it would have been shocking enough that she could picture it now—his eyes widening, his smile turning strained as he took a sip of wine and prepared to tell everybody else present what a blunder she had made.

Since then, Rhea had never forgotten that most important rule: Never mention the real woman who lived inside Thyspira's skin.

Rhea watched through the window of an upstairs storeroom as he climbed out of his carriage and hurried, his head covered with his coat, through the inner courtyard and into the house, out of the rain. He was a nice enough boy, Lambros. Facing down his death twice before had given him a resigned attitude that made him good company, at least for one glass of wine.

Then there were two from what Rhea figured was probably the western edge of the country, near where it butted up against Trefazio, if the veils they wore over the bottom half of their faces, a Trefzan fashion, were anything to judge by. They had arrived together, and Rhea was disappointed to realize, as they removed their veils to reveal similar faces, that they were brothers. Baba had only managed to scrounge up four suitors—five if Lexos's guest counted—and two of them were of the same family at that.

It was the Laskaris boy who came next. Rhea sat forward, watched with some interest as he climbed out of his carriage and attempted to exchange pleasantries with Eleni and Flora, who were stationed at the door to the innermost courtyard. When neither woman responded, the Laskaris boy—Michali, that's what Lexos had said, wasn't it?—quickly looked up and away, scuffing at the flagstones with his boot. He was just turning back to the servants, who were unloading his luggage, when he caught sight of Rhea, perched as she was on the storeroom windowsill. For a moment they simply stared at each other, and then Michali raised his hand and waved. When she did not respond, he turned somewhat awkwardly around, as though pretending he'd never seen her at all.

Could this really be the boy Lexos was worried about? Could he really be such a threat to their family that his death was worth Baba's anger?

Well, whatever his political leanings, Rhea supposed his very presence was danger enough. With Chrysanthi's help in running the preparations, Lexos had managed to keep the fact of Michali's arrival from Baba thus far. Tonight, though, Baba would see him at dinner, and they would have to face whatever came of it. Or rather, Lexos would. Rhea hadn't decided yet whether or not to do as he wished, and was very glad she could yet claim ignorance of the whole thing.

Last to arrive was Kallistos from Rhokera. Baba's great hope, according to the note he'd given her. He looked well enough, Rhea supposed. Hair a touch too long, clothes a touch too brightly colored, as seemed to be the Rhokeri fashion, but would it be so bad to marry him? After all, her marriages never lasted long, and winter in particular was short, as the Thyzak farmers preferred. If it turned out to be awful, she only had to get through eight weeks of it. And Lexos would forgive her for marrying someone else, for not going along with his plan. She couldn't say the same for Baba.

Eleni and Flora would be busy getting the guests settled in the far wing of the house, but there was plenty she could do to prepare without them. She gathered her skirts and eased out of the storeroom, careful not to get any cobwebs on her dress.

She reached her bedroom and ducked inside, heading directly for her wardrobe and flinging it open. There were a number of gowns she kept aside, meant solely for her to wear as Thyspira. In fact, they were so associated with that other self of hers that when Rhea was only Rhea, the gowns did not seem to fit. The laces would not tighten far enough, or the seams would dig into her skin. Today, though, she was Thyspira incarnate, and when she slid into her chosen gown, this one a rich, blackened blue—the unofficial Argyros house color, as Baba's line was not old enough to have laid any official claim—she didn't even need her servants to help her do it up.

The back of the gown was open, and for that, Rhea fetched a handful of long, glittering diamond strands and carefully draped them so they pressed close against her throat and hung down the exposed stretch of her back. She was a winter Thyspira this time, after all, made of deep night and snow.

It would have been easier, perhaps, Rhea thought as she stared at herself in the mirror, if Thyspira had been more different from her. But they were both crisp, both coy, and the enjoyment Thyspira took in toying with her suitors was Rhea's, too. The dresses helped, and the paint they borrowed from Chrysanthi, but even so, sometimes Rhea could not keep her own heart separate from Thyspira's. After more than eighty years of it, they had bled so together that they might never part again.

Before long, Eleni and Flora came rushing in, and both set immediately to work twisting Rhea's thick curls into orderly ringlets. Chrysanthi was not far behind, already dressed in a vivid yellow frock awash in a froth of ruffles.

"You're taking forever," Chrysanthi said, throwing herself down on Rhea's bed and promptly getting back up again, the woolen cushion cover too rough to be at all comfortable on her bare arms.

"You're rushing," Rhea replied tartly as she turned to give Eleni better access to the rest of her hair.

"Did you see them? The suitors?"

"I did. I suppose they'll do."

Chrysanthi plucked at her skirts, frowning. "I wish they wouldn't only send boys these days. It's so much less fun this way."

Rhea laughed. "We must all make sacrifices."

"What difficult lives we lead." Chrysanthi flicked Rhea's back, making her shriek, and then leaned in and gently kissed her cheek. "Good luck tonight, *kora*."

She left, and the two servants followed, their work done. In the mirror Rhea could see that Eleni had taken her curls and pinned them up to better show off her exposed back. Chrysanthi had also done a wonderful job with Rhea's face, using paints to give her cheeks an unnatural flush and darkening her eyebrows so that the woman looking back at her wasn't Rhea anymore. It was Thyspira who would go downstairs, Thyspira who would wind each of these boys around her little finger until they were falling over themselves to pledge horse and soldier to her father. Rhea straightened her shoulders, felt the cool graze of diamonds swinging down her back, and fixed her painted lips into a tricking smile. Thyspira always smiled.

The men were gathered out on the back veranda, and Chrysanthi was probably already out there with them, coaxing a tune worth dancing to from the musicians and needling Nitsos, who would be hiding in the shadows, grumbling to himself at being pulled from his workshop. Lexos met her at the foot of the stairs, his arm extended for her to take. She hesitated for a moment, examining his face for any trace of an agenda—she could do very well without a last-minute lecture, thank you—but he seemed to want nothing more than to escort her, and so she looped her arm through his.

"You look all right," Lexos said, fumbling with his words the way he often did when asked to acknowledge the physical form of his sisters.

Rhea rolled her eyes. "Thank you."

"I've left it to you to think over," he said as they passed through the great room and started along the central corridor, which ran the length of the house and would deposit them on the back veranda. "But you know what I think, *kathroula*. You know how I think this night should go."

She sighed. "*Ftama*, Lexos. You made yourself clear days ago."

"It's not that I don't trust you to make the right decision," he started, and Rhea couldn't help scoffing.

"If you have to say that," she interrupted, "it probably isn't true. Look, can we leave it for the moment?" They were approaching the end of the hallway, the flickering light of a hundred candles reaching through the doorway into the dark of the corridor. "I'm not going to make a choice tonight."

"I know."

"And I'm not convinced Baba doesn't have this all in hand."

Lexos smiled grimly. "Watch him tonight. You'll see. It's up to us now to protect this family's power."

Out on the veranda the air was crisp, the sky still streaked with orange and red though the sun had just dipped below the horizon. The afternoon's rain had left the flagstones damp and glistening, and they were cold through Rhea's slippers. Torches were lit everywhere she looked, and beyond the veranda railing, the sea glittered darkly.

In years previous, when the suitors had come from all over the country in great numbers, there had been four banquet tables set up in a square around the reflecting pool that was built into the center of the veranda. Now the guests all fit at one table, but the servants had made use of the freed space, filling it with potted cypress trees and extravagant bouquets of flowers. Chrysanthi had clearly been to work, too, and had dotted each tree with bright paints so it looked like their branches were decorated with strings of burning candles.

A servant approached with a tray of wineglasses, and Lexos shook his head. He never drank at things like this, but Rhea made a particular point of always having a glass in her hand. She was taking her first sip when one of her suitors noticed that she had arrived, and left the group of men to cross the veranda toward her.

"Have fun," Lexos murmured in her ear before stepping away. She watched him go to the head of the table, where someone— Baba, she realized with a start—was slumped, staring glumly at his empty dinner plate. She pushed down the impulse to go look after him as her suitor neared, his glass raised for a toast.

"*Keresmata, kiria* Thyspira," he said grandly, his voice shaking only a little. He was the younger of the two brothers who'd been sent, and judging by the anxious look on his face, he was probably hoping that she would dispense with him quickly. Everyone in Thyzakos knew that making this particular sacrifice was the highest achievable honor, but that didn't mean they were exactly happy about what it entailed.

She raised her glass, knocked it delicately against his. Like his brother, he had taken off the veil he'd worn upon arrival, and she could see his face clearly.

"What's your name, *koros*?" she asked, inching closer.

"Dimos, Thyspira."

"How lovely." She took a sip of wine and licked a stray droplet from her lips. "And you already know mine."

He gulped. "I do."

Across the veranda, Kallistos was eyeing her as he slouched against the railing. The ocean behind him cast a blue haze about his head, as though he were one of the traditional Stratagiozi icons, like those painted on the ceiling of the great room. Dimos would have done well enough on a different night, but on this one, she handed him her glass and set off instead toward Kallistos.

By the time she reached him he had straightened and, she'd noticed, adjusted the fall of his collar. In Rhokera they dressed lightly, showing their skin to the sun. But for the cooler weather at Stratathoma, he was wearing what passed for winter clothes in Rhokera. Over a pair of thin, loosely draped trousers and a matching shirt, Kallistos was wrapped in a stiff brocade coat, its hem grazing the floor, its color the dark purple that marked him as belonging to the Speros house. The Speros stewards had spent centuries building Rhokera from a simple outpost to the country's wealthiest city, and clearly they preferred to make that wealth apparent in every way possible.

"More wine?" Rhea said as she neared him. "It'll do something to fight the chill."

"Thank you, but I think I've had enough for the evening."

"Already? We've hardly begun."

Kallistos smiled, revealing a set of teeth that were, in Rhea's opinion, obscenely white. She felt her stomach turn, as though she were barely sixteen again. He really was something to look at, all shades of gold and tan, his hair laced through with a crown of olive leaves.

"Some water for my friend here," she told a passing servant. "When I toast to our meeting it won't do for his glass to be empty."

"Is meeting you really such a special occasion?" Kallistos asked idly as the servant hurried off.

Rhea leaned against the railing, her arm brushing his. "I think you'll find that it is."

This was the part of the conversation that had taken her years to master. Even now, her instinct was to remark on the weather and then immediately spill some wine on her dress and flee to the safety of her room. But by now she knew every word, every minute movement that was required. First things first: flattery.

"I've been to Rhokera before," she said, tilting her head so her perfumed neck was laid bare. "It's beautiful. You and your family must do an excellent job of maintaining things."

"Well, we do our best."

It would certainly be strange to spend the winter so far south, Rhea mused. She'd only had a handful of winters without frost in all her years as Thyspira.

The servant returned, carrying a tray on which stood a single crystal glass of water. Kallistos took it, his eyes never leaving Rhea.

"You held a symposium not long ago," she said, "if I'm not mistaken."

"We did. I arranged it, in fact."

She knew that very well, of course. Why else would she have brought it up? She smiled, gritted her teeth—no matter how pretty they were, the men always lost a bit of shine during this next part.

"It sounds fascinating. Do tell me about it."

Kallistos began to talk in a way that suggested he didn't particularly care whether anybody was there to hear him, and Rhea took the opportunity to observe the other suitors. There was Dimos, probably still attempting to regain feeling in his legs after their conversation (if one could call it that), and Dimos's brother was with him, looking bored as he plowed through another plate of cheese. Lambros, the repeat suitor, was seated at the table already and was having a lively conversation with Chrysanthi. Well, at least he was making an impression on somebody tonight.

That left the Laskaris boy, Michali. Not at the table. Not by the reflecting pool. No, there he was, in the farthest corner of the veranda, partially hidden by a cluster of potted trees. And that wouldn't do at all.

She laid a hand on Kallistos's arm and gave him a smile before leaving him adrift behind her. It was impolite, to be sure, but a small slight, and easy to fix. Michali's slight, on the other hand, was not so small. To stand so far away, in such an obvious rejection of her and of this process, was an affront to her, to her father, to the very power of the Stratagiozi. And they couldn't afford any more of those.

Rhea marched across the veranda, indignation simmering with

every step. How could this be happening now, now when her father was watching her every move so closely, when so much seemed to depend on the outcome of this ceremony? Whether he liked it or not—whether she chose him or not, Rhea added, thinking of Lexos—the Laskaris boy would fall in line.

She stepped around the potted cypresses and found herself in a patch of cool shadow overlooking the water. There was Michali, his glass of wine resting on the railing while he picked at a loose thread on the sleeve of his fur-lined coat, a northern style that was far too warm for Stratathoma. She waited for him to notice her, to apologize, but he didn't even look up. Crossing her arms, she cleared her throat.

Michali jumped, turned, and knocked his wine into the ocean.

"I'm sorry," he said, words tumbling over one another. "I didn't mean . . . I'll pay for the glass. To replace it. Or I suppose I could try to retrieve it, although I think the—"

"You should feel free," Rhea said, "to be quiet at any moment."

He was a peculiar-looking boy, she thought. Pale, almost alarmingly so—she supposed they didn't see much sun up in the Ksigora. Thick, inky curls, darker even than her own, and eyes to match, their stare unnervingly calm despite the flush on his cheeks. Most startling was the shape of his face, the touch of gauntness of it. He looked in need of a good meal, or two, or three.

So this was the great hope of the Sxoriza. If she hadn't known of his involvement with them, she might well have guessed. He looked so uncomfortable here in her father's house that Rhea thought he might burst into flames. As it was, he'd been quiet for a long moment, watching her warily, and she realized that he was probably waiting for her to speak. She unfolded her arms and smoothed down her skirt.

"The glass is no matter," she said. "But might I say, perhaps you wouldn't have knocked it over the side if you weren't hiding in the shadows."

"I'm not hiding," Michali replied. "I simply know when I'm not needed."

"Excuse me?"

"Well, it's quite obvious who your choice will be." He looked over her shoulder, to where Rhea was sure Kallistos was still standing, in fact possibly still speaking without noticing she'd left. "I'm only here to fill out the guest list."

"I think I find that a little insulting," Rhea said, ignoring the fact that Michali was right.

"Oh dear," he replied dryly. "Whatever can I do to make it up to you?"

"Tell me, do they find these manners charming in the Ksigora? Has the cold northern air so addled their brains that they find you tolerable?"

She was surprised when he threw his head back and let out a bark of laughter. "Have you been to the Ksigora?" he said, a smile lingering on his mouth.

"No."

"It really isn't so cold."

"And I'm really not very interested." She turned to go before remembering why she'd come over in the first place. "It's customary to show respect when you're in someone's home, especially when that someone is Stratagiozi. If you can't muster the courage to come out from your little hiding place, you should feel free to depart. We can have your horses ready in just a few minutes. Otherwise," she finished, smiling as sweetly as she could manage, "I will see you at dinner."

He did not, in fact, come out, and as the sunlight finally faded and the servants began to light the candles that ran down the center of the dinner table, Rhea waited by the reflecting pool with Chrysanthi and wondered if perhaps he had taken her at her word and gone home. But she was saved from any further worry when the servants announced that dinner was being served and Michali approached the table with the other suitors. He looked out of sorts, his hair askew as though he'd run his hands through it one too many times.

Rhea took Chrysanthi's hand and they made their way past Nitsos, who was sulking by the reflecting pool, to the table, Chrysanthi eventually peeling off to make for her seat at Baba's left hand. There was Lexos, standing at Baba's right, watching her with furrowed brows. Rhea looked determinedly away, focusing instead on the chair that waited for her at the foot of the table. Kallistos was the suitor seated closest to her, which was no surprise.

Everyone sat down, with only Baba remaining standing at the head of the table. Nitsos was the last to take his place, clearly displeased that he'd been stranded in the middle of the table with no family members nearby. Once Nitsos had finally thrown himself into his chair, Baba lifted his glass, and the conversation quieted.

"Thank you all for coming," Baba said, looking directly at Kallistos. "And welcome to our Thyspira's winter choosing. Let dinner be served."

The servants brought in the first course, a salted cheese poured over with oil and fresh vegetables, and the chatter started up again. Dimos and his brother spoke with a slightly different accent, but it was easy to get used to, and she watched as they fell into conversation with Michali, who seemed startlingly more polite now that he was speaking with someone other than her.

Baba had calculated well, putting Kallistos so near. He hadn't taken offense at her earlier sudden departure, it seemed, and resumed their previous conversation without prompting. As the evening continued, she found herself sinking back in her chair, allowing Kallistos's gaze to slink down her body, allowing her lips to curl in a lazy smile. He would be an easy consort, she could tell. Easy to win over, and easy to kill, when the time came.

But by the time dessert was being served, Rhea could tell that something was beginning to happen at the far end of the table. It wasn't much, and indeed she didn't think the guests had noticed yet; still Baba was restless in his chair and Lexos was clenching his jaw so hard that she could see a muscle popping in his cheek. She stood up, waving off Dimos, who, in order to stand with her, had shoved his chair back with such a scrape that it disturbed a flock of sparrows roosting on the roof, and made her way to where Chrysanthi was sitting.

"Might I borrow her for a moment?" she said to nobody in particular, resting her hand on the back of Chrysanthi's neck. Chrysanthi shot up from her chair, relief softening her tense, polite smile, and latched onto Rhea's arm as she hastened into the house.

They bustled in through the open double doors leading to the house's main corridor, and Chrysanthi immediately ducked around the corner into a small alcove, pulling Rhea with her. Two servants approached, each carrying a tray loaded with tiny bowls of mint leaves to refresh the palate. Rhea waved them away, but not before Chrysanthi could snatch a pinch of mint and pop the leaves into her mouth.

"All right," Rhea said, glancing over her shoulder to make sure they were alone. "What is going on?"

"Lexos wishes you were talking to the other suitors," Chrysanthi said, ticking everything off on her fingers, "Baba wishes he was talking to Kallistos, Nitsos is a pit into which all conversations disappear, and there is too much salt on the tomatoes."

"Delightful. Well, the meal's nearly over," Rhea said. There was still a way to salvage everything. "When it's done, I'll bring Kallistos to talk to Baba. That should accomplish something."

"And in the meantime?"

"Excuse me, *kiria*."

Rhea and Chrysanthi both turned to see Eleni waiting a few steps away, her eyes averted.

"Yes?" Rhea said. "What is it?"

"It's your father. I think you'd better come."

NINE

RHEA

The scene, when Rhea emerged onto the veranda, seemed innocent enough. There was Kallistos, still in his seat, the picture of studied indifference, and there was Nitsos, folding his napkin into a bird of some sort. No, the only things different—the only things troubling—were Baba's and Lexos's empty chairs.

They were standing on the other side of the reflecting pool, Lexos rigid while Baba gestured broadly. Rhea couldn't hear them from the steps, but there was a decent chance that anybody at the table could hear whatever argument her family had chosen to have in public. She descended the stairs as gracefully as she could manage, doing her best to not appear in any kind of hurry, and skirted the table, making straight for Lexos and Baba, aware of the suitors watching her and beginning to mutter among themselves.

"Oh, excellent," Lexos snarled as she neared. "Just what we need—more participants."

"I've done nothing to earn that from you," she said, sure to keep her voice low. "I'm only here to ask the both of you what you might be thinking, to conduct yourselves this way in full view of our guests."

"And what, exactly, is wrong with my conduct?" Baba said.

Rhea felt a shiver run through her. "Baba," she said, facing him, "I only meant that perhaps your conversation might be better had in private."

"This is my house, isn't it?" Baba said, his voice rising. "My house, although by my son's behavior you might never know it." He stepped closer to Lexos. "It was reckless. Poorly done. Deceitful and—"

"And what?" Lexos said, a challenge in the lift of his chin. Rhea froze, aware of every stare, every whisper back at the table. Now was not the time.

"And ungrateful," Baba finished. Lexos didn't flinch, and Rhea felt a reluctant swell of pride. "We will have words later, and you will remember your place."

He pushed between her and Lexos, stalking back to the table. Rhea stumbled on her skirts, saved from tumbling into the reflecting pool only by Lexos's steadying hand on her elbow.

"The Laskaris invitation?" she asked. Lexos nodded, and she sighed. "Why you needed to have that conversation here is quite frankly beyond me."

"As if I had any say in the matter." He hesitated for a moment, glancing at her before continuing. "He's angrier than I expected. Perhaps he believes you might choose outside of his recommendation."

"I don't know why he should. I've been speaking with Kallistos all night."

"Well, I suppose he doesn't trust that your talk is enough," Lexos said, and Rhea reeled back, the sting of his words fresh and cold. She waited a moment, sure he would apologize—he always did—but he just gave her elbow a squeeze and nodded toward the table. "Look."

Baba stood by his chair, the guests silent as he lifted his perpetually full glass. "A toast," he said loudly. "To all of our guests. But most important, to my daughter Rhea."

"Mala," Lexos whispered behind her, and as every eye turned to her, Rhea felt her gut twist. Her name was not meant for anybody outside the family. It was near sacrilege, if that still existed without the saints, for these men to be hearing it.

"Isn't she something to look at? She makes quite a bride."

Rhea locked eyes with Chrysanthi, who scrambled to her feet.

"Dancing, I think," Chrysanthi said, her voice shaking. She gestured to the musicians, whose playing had ceased during dinner. "We should have music."

It was a valiant effort, and Chrysanthi had certainly distracted, say, Dimos, who got to his feet eagerly at the mention of dancing. But the others, the ones who mattered, had not been affected, and the damage was done.

"Go," Rhea said to Lexos. Nitsos was already at Baba's side, easing the glass from his hand and attempting to turn him away from the table, and in a moment Lexos had joined them, stepping between Baba and the table. It snapped the tension somewhat, and conversation began to build again, though this time Rhea could tell that most of it was about what had just happened.

Movement at the far end of the table drew her eye, and she watched as Kallistos rose from the table, glancing at her once before turning resolutely away. He couldn't be leaving, could he? It would ruin her, her family.

Rhea abandoned pretense and hurried toward him, hoping to catch him before he could make his departure too obvious to the other guests.

"Sir," she said, and once she was within reach she snatched two fresh wineglasses from a passing servant's tray and pressed one into Kallistos's hand. "To bed so soon?"

"Actually," Kallistos began, but Rhea kept on, smiling relentlessly.

"I do hope you will stay a little while longer. All this talk of dancing has caught my interest. But of course, dancing is most enjoyable with the right partner, don't you think?"

Kallistos narrowed his eyes. "I suppose."

He hadn't snubbed her outright. She relaxed slightly. If she played this perfectly, there was still a chance to save it. "Indeed, a discussion of the right partner is very timely, wouldn't you say?"

"It depends." Kallistos took a long sip of wine, and then stepped farther away from the other guests, drawing her with him. "I think we should speak plainly with each other, you and I."

"Plainly, then," Rhea said, and she had made her choice—not this instant, but long ago, it seemed, judging by how easily the words left her tongue. Baba. Always Baba. She was his child, belonged to him, and maybe Lexos could put that aside, but she didn't think she could. "You are my winter consort. Tomorrow I will send these other men home and I will ask you to put your hand in mine." She took a breath, unable to find any hint of emotion on his face, and added, "I hope you will accept."

She had never said such a thing to anyone before. Her suitors were not permitted to reject her, or to withdraw their suits, not even when the weight of their required sacrifice fell heavily on their shoulders.

"As the arrangement stands," Kallistos said, "I'm afraid I cannot. The rewards offered are not enough to merit my sacrifice."

"Not enough?" Rhea said. She could feel her temper rising—there was Baba's pride, passed from father to daughter. "Your city benefits. A generous season, the wealth of your people, in exchange—"

"Ah." Kallistos leaned in. "In exchange for what?"

She did not answer. Everybody knew her consorts paid with their lives, but it was in poor taste to say so.

"I have heard," he went on, "of consorts who continued on past their season. Consorts so favored by Thyspira that they paid no cost. I should like to join their number."

He was wrong, of course. Her consorts died without fail; there was no other way to close a season. But she and every Thyspira before her had let the rumors continue, rumors of a palace full of living consorts, where the season never changed. And perhaps they had done so for just this reason.

"If I agreed to it," she said, "you would accept me tomorrow?"

Kallistos did not answer and only raised his eyebrows. They were neither of them comfortable speaking in absolutes, it seemed.

"Well," she said, "we have made no bargain. But perhaps we ought to seal it anyway."

Kallistos laughed, and when he leaned in to kiss her, she let him. What was one more rule broken tonight?

They returned to the party, danced late into the night, and when she was at last laid out in her bed, Rhea found that sleep was far away from her. Only one evening, and customs had been left in tatters, words said that had never before been spoken at Stratathoma. And now she would have to get up tomorrow and marry a man she'd offered to leave alive. Would it be as simple as going back on that offer, come the end of the season? Or would that push Baba's already precarious situation with the stewards over the edge? Surely Kallistos would not keep their bargain a secret.

With a sigh she sat up and pulled on a shawl as she slipped out of her room, into the hallway. She wound her way through the house, out to a small balcony tucked over the atrium, and watched as the stars began to shift, the sky taking its proper shape as Lexos tended to his duties, some hours later than he normally did.

It should have felt like a relief to have her decision made. The past few days had been taut with quiet, with expectation, and maybe now she and Lexos could stop negotiating with each other and go back to being only siblings. But she still felt that anxious clutch in her chest, a whir in her head like tiny, clockwork gears. She couldn't settle, and wouldn't, she thought. Not when she knew Lexos would be so upset to learn what she'd decided.

When at last her eyelids began to droop, Rhea took the long way back to her quarters, avoiding the quicker route that took her by Baba's rooms. She was coming down the last flight of stairs when she caught a light from a hallway up ahead.

Lexos, probably, come looking for her after seeing her door open and bed empty. That corridor led to the family quarters, after all.

But it wasn't Lexos she nearly smacked into as she rounded the corner. It was someone else—a man in dark clothing, with a fur wrapped around his shoulders. In the torchlight, all she could see of him was the shine of his skin, nearly translucent, and the hollows in his cheeks. Michali.

"What are you doing here?" she said, her voice coming out more loudly than she'd intended and echoing off the stone walls.

Michali looked as surprised to see her as she was to see him. He lowered his torch, casting his face into shadow, and Rhea had the distinct sense he was inching away from her.

"I'm sorry," he whispered. "I'm afraid I got lost returning to my room."

The obvious question hung in the air—returning from where, exactly?—but Rhea refused to ask it. She had no wish to hear about his midnight piss.

"Your room is that way," she said, pointing behind her. "This way leads only to the family quarters."

"Oh," Michali said, his voice faint. "I do apologize."

"Come, I'll take you back."

She waited for him to raise the torch again, its flame guttering in the breeze between the atrium and Lexos's room farther down the hall, and then together they circled the balcony and started down the hall to the guest quarters. They passed the plainly tiled guest baths in silence and Rhea frowned. What had he needed to come all the way out to the atrium for? Could he really have got lost between the baths and his room? And would he really have come to the baths at all? Presumably he was like other men of his age and needed only a spare pot and a vague nod in the direction of privacy, if that.

Perhaps he'd been on his way back from some dalliance with a servant, then. Normally the suitors would never think of such a thing, but after Baba's display at dinner, she doubted any rules were still in effect.

At last, the hallway opened up onto a terrace, off of which branched several archways leading to the different guest rooms. Rhea gestured to Michali's, which was across the flagstone floor.

"Here you are."

"Thank you. Again, I really am—"

She shook her head. "Please, don't bother. I'm too tired to be as gracious as I should."

The night air had kept hold of the autumn chill, and had a brisk, almost crackling feel to it so late at night. She shivered and turned to go, but Michali mirrored her steps.

"*Kiria* Thyspira," he said, and with the added light of the moon she could make out a smile on his face. "You said you'd never been to the Ksigora."

"I did."

"Well, for what it's worth," he said and shrugged, as though he knew she was thinking it wasn't worth much, "I think you'd like it there."

They watched each other for a long moment. "All right," Rhea said at last, a bit at a loss for how else to respond, and turned again to go. This time, thankfully, he let her.

Back in her room, Rhea settled once more into bed. The sun would be up soon, and she would dress for the choosing, and confirm what everybody already knew—that she was going home with Kallistos. At some point, she would have to tell Baba about the bargain she'd made to keep Kallistos alive. He would be angry, but perhaps he'd recognize the opportunity to create a closer bond between himself and the Rhokeri, and he would sort out how to keep the seasons changing the way they ought, if only by sheer force of will.

But she couldn't pretend she hadn't just happened upon Michali, late at night in the family's quarters. Could he have been up to something on behalf of the Sxoriza? She knew she was meant to be wondering, but she found instead that she was most curious about the word itself, about what it meant to say "Sxoriza" in that saintly accent the old language was rumored to require. It was a noun, she thought—as different as Modern Thyzaki professed to be from Saint's, their grammatical patterns were much the same—but the definition, and even the root escaped her.

Maybe Lexos knew, but she certainly couldn't ask him. In fact there was no need to ask him anything; she could hear his advice already, could hear him telling her to open her eyes, reminding her of what she'd seen at dinner. And maybe he was right. Maybe Baba couldn't be trusted to handle everything. Maybe it really was all in their hands. But it didn't matter. She'd chosen. It was done.

TEN

ALEXANDROS

W hen Lexos woke, the sky outside his window was a pale rose light beginning to reach in from the east. The sea was roiling, a wind picking up from the gulf, and Lexos winced to remember how he'd stirred the tides the night before, with barely a thought to how, across the gulf in Trefazio, one of Tarro's children was twining strands of cloud around their fingers. Long ago the gifts had separated almost into orders, with one family tending to the sea even as another kept care of the sky. Now the bloodlines had broken too many times, leaving each Stratagiozi family responsible for an odd assortment of things, and Lexos had to read the skies along with everybody else, and try to match them as he could. Today, his carelessness meant a storm was brewing.

He dressed quickly, pulling on a shirt and some trousers, his Argyros dagger slotted into the concealed pocket Chrysanthi had stitched into every pair. Rhea would want to talk, and he was anxious to point out that last night had proved him right. He was almost at the door, barefoot and wrestling his arms into a jacket that might have been inside out, when he stopped short.

Would she resent it? Would she feel that he was pressuring her? Of course, he wasn't—he was simply helping her make the right decision—but perhaps she wouldn't be ready to listen to him. No, there was a better way.

Lexos slipped out into the hallway and moved past Rhea's door, past Nitsos's, and stopped in front of Chrysanthi's room. He knocked once and heard a muffled voice from within. When he opened the door, it revealed Chrysanthi sitting cross-legged on the cushioned bench underneath her window, her hair shrouding her face, a paintbrush in her hand.

"What are you doing?"

She reached up and moved a thick lock of hair off her face. "Good morning, Lexos. I'm painting."

He watched as she dipped the paintbrush into the pot of gold paint she had balanced on her knee. Then, in delicate strokes, she began coating the curls of her hair, bringing particular light and shine to a few of the locks.

"Are you allowed to do that?" Lexos asked.

Chrysanthi smiled. "They're my paints. I can do what I like with them."

On her windowsill were a number of other pots, each filled with a different color. There white, there a rosy pink, and there a rich earthen brown. All the colors, Lexos realized as Chrysanthi shook her hair back, that she needed to do herself up.

"You know you're lovely just as you are," he told her gently.

But Chrysanthi only gave him a look and said, "That's hardly the point." She switched the gold paint out for the pink. "Well? What is it you want?"

He watched her dab a flush onto her cheeks. "You saw everything that happened last night. And I know Rhea must have said something to you about the choice she faces today."

Chrysanthi set down her brush, her expression uncharacteristically grave. "She hasn't said a word to me, Alexandros, and you had better not say a word to her. She has enough to deal with without you lecturing her first thing in the morning."

"I'm not going to. I promise." Chrysanthi frowned, unconvinced, and he sighed. "I thought you could."

"Lexos, I know you mean well. But I doubt very much that Rhea wants to talk to anybody this morning."

"Not even you? You're her favorite."

"I am everybody's favorite," Chrysanthi said. "Now get out of my room and go find Nitsos downstairs. He's probably eating breakfast all alone."

"You join him, then."

"We see quite enough of each other as it is," she snapped, and Lexos had a sudden, vivid image of Chrysanthi's delicate paintbrushes clasped in Nitsos's grease-blackened hands. They looked after each other, his younger siblings—he knew that—but it rarely occurred to him to wonder if either of them liked it that way.

"All right," he said, and kissed the top of Chrysanthi's head. "I'll go."

Breakfast was laid out on the veranda, on the same table from the night before, but the candles were gone and where there had been curtains of ivy and nests of brightly colored leaves, there were now sprigs of fresh flowers and strategically placed heating braziers. On the veranda it felt like spring, but Lexos knew that behind the house, the fields would be draped with a thin lacework of frost.

Chrysanthi was right. Nitsos was there at the table alone, with not even a suitor or two to keep him company. Lexos sat down gingerly across from him. It wasn't that they didn't get along—"getting along" implied that they actually spent time together. It was more that Lexos couldn't help but be keenly aware that he held something Nitsos wanted, whether Nitsos admitted that to himself or not.

"Bit chilly out today" was all he managed before Nitsos abandoned the attempt at conversation entirely and began to fiddle with one of the delicate silver melon forks, fishing a foldable pair of pliers from his pocket and using them to bend the tines this way and that.

"Wonderful," Lexos muttered and took a long sip of kaf.

Baba never showed up to the meal, so it was left to Lexos to stand, once it seemed the suitors had all finished, and invite them to assemble beyond the house's main doors, which led from Chrysanthi's wild courtyard into the great room. One by one, each suitor would knock on the doors and ask to be let in, and Rhea would open the door to her chosen consort.

The custom was used, too, for Thyzak weddings, when they had occasion to happen, and was older than Thyzakos itself. It came, if the history books at Agiokon were to be believed, from one of the practices of saint worshippers, and had, like rocks in a riverbed, been smoothed down over time, its origins blurred and worn until they could no longer be quite deciphered.

Compared to the previous evening, the suitors weren't dressed in their finery, Lexos noticed as he led them through the doors and out into Chrysanthi's wild courtyard. Dimos and his brother looked just about ready to depart, and Lambros, who might've still been drunk from the night before, had one of his boot laces undone. The Laskaris boy was at the very least put together, but there was an unease about his mouth that ruined the effect. And they could none of them compare to the Rhokeri, Kallistos, whose splendor was only enhanced by his general dishevelment.

Overhead the sky looked swollen, its clouds bruised with rain. With any luck the coming storm would hold off for a few hours, and give them time to get everyone on their way. Lexos watched as a small, dark blue bird—a hummingbird, maybe, with wings like that—darted over the courtyard wall from the outer grounds and alighted on the top of the fountain. One of Nitsos's pet creatures, judging from the mechanical tilt of its head.

With the suitors lined up, all that was left now was to wait for Baba. Lexos tried not to be worried by the fact that Baba had not already arrived. He'd had what Lexos would generously call a long night, and presumably he was only taking his time in scrubbing the smell of alcohol off his skin. Lexos looked instead to the courtyard beyond this one, where the suitors' carriages were ready for their immediate departure following the end of Rhea's choosing.

The doors between the courtyards stood open, and like the other sets built into Stratathoma's layered courtyards, were a vivid blue,

the passage of time visible in marks worn into the wood, some presumably from the blades of the soldiers Baba had used to batter his
way into the citadel. Lexos had been too young to fight during that
campaign, but he had watched from a ship off the coast as waves of
men broke against Stratathoma's walls, called from every corner of
Thyzakos to rally to the banner of the famous Argyros general. The
stewards had supported Baba's claim, but Lexos knew now that it
had only been under the assumption that once in power, Baba would
be theirs. Of course it hadn't turned out that way, and Baba's rule
had borne the weight of every steward's disappointment since.

A cough drew Lexos's attention back to the five suitors, who
seemed increasingly uncomfortable in the cold and quiet. He could
tell from the way the color was seeping from their faces that the enor-
mity of the sacrifice demanded of Rhea's chosen consort was starting to truly sink in. It was all well and good to dress up in finery and
make speeches, but here they were, putting their lives in Thyspira's
hands, and at least two of them looked very nearly ill about it.

At last, footsteps could be heard coming from down one of Stratathoma's many hallways, and soon Baba was crossing the great
room, dressed in a severely cut black jacket and trousers to match.
The jacket's shoulders were covered in gold stitching that poured in
spirals down the back of it, and at the high collar Lexos caught the
glint of obsidian, a small stone pinned there in a mimicry of the
matagios Baba bore on his tongue.

Some Stratagiozis reveled in their finery. Some wore thin circlets
of gold in their hair, and some wrapped themselves in shifting fabrics
that seemed woven from gemstones. Baba wore his power like
this—in starkness and sharp edges, bare as bones.

"Good morning," Baba said to the suitors, his voice rough. "I
hope you are all well."

Rhea herself was nowhere to be seen, and would not appear until
during the ceremony itself; Lexos knew she was somewhere just inside the house, waiting to be called. Chrysanthi had been right to
keep him from speaking with her, but he wished he had all the same.
He'd asked something of her, and on any other day he could be sure

she would comply, but today Baba had asked something, too. And as much as he loved his sister, loved her like she was his own body built once over, he was not at the moment entirely sure that he trusted her.

"Thyspira has made her choice," Baba declared, beginning the speech he always made, and Lexos tried not to wince. It was, of course, better to pretend the previous evening hadn't happened, but that didn't make it any easier to hear Baba address Rhea now the way he should have then. "As is the law of our land, whomever Thyspira chooses and the city from which they hail will be gifted with good fortune and a bountiful season. Your sacrifice is great, but so is your honor in making it. For this, the most precious of gifts, we thank you; Thyzakos thanks you."

Stratathoma's doors began to close, the creak of wood and pulleys filling the air, startling the hummingbird from its perch, sending it streaking into the air to disappear. Lexos tried to follow its path—anything to avoid Baba's gaze through the narrowing gap between the doors. He had to know, Baba. He had to know that Lexos was pushing a choice on Rhea contrary to Baba's own.

At last, the rattling thud as the pulleys finished their work and the doors shut. Lexos waited, giving Rhea the time she would need to emerge from whatever shadows she'd been hiding in. But he couldn't wait too long, couldn't give Baba the chance to talk to her—as it was, he could imagine the pressure Baba might apply with simply a look. Rhea would have to be stronger than that.

"*Elado,*" he said loudly. "We begin with Lambros Tavoulos, whose suit has been made."

Lambros had done this twice before, and of everybody, even the Rhokeri, he looked the least uncomfortable. After all, Rhea had passed him over twice before. He could be reasonably certain that she would do so again.

"To Thyspira and to Thyzakos," Lambros said, stepping up to the imposing façade of Stratathoma's doors, "I offer the shelter of my house and the devotion of my heart. Let them be hers if she chooses." Raising a steady hand, he knocked firmly three times.

Quiet. Lexos let out a slow breath as Lambros stepped back in line. He couldn't pretend that he hadn't been worried Rhea would, in a fit of panic, choose the suitor most familiar to her.

"Dimos Vlahos, whose suit has been made," Lexos said next. It was up to him what order the suitors went in, and while he supposed he could have simply got the whole thing over with, Lexos knew Rhea, and he knew she needed whatever time he could give her.

Dimos took Lambros's place before the doors and repeated the words Lambros had spoken, faltering a little. His knocks could barely be heard over the wind that was picking up, but they, too, received no answer. And neither did Nikos, Dimos's brother, who Lexos sent up next.

Now it was down to two: Baba's candidate and Lexos's.

"Kallistos Speros," Lexos said, eyes fixed on the doors, "whose suit has been made."

Please, Rhea, he thought. I am with you. Are you with me?

Kallistos sounded almost lazy as he spoke the required words, and his confidence in being chosen wafted off him much as the scent of alcohol had done off Baba last night. Lexos stared through him, willed his entire being toward his twin sister. Do nothing, he thought as hard as he could. All you have to do, *kathroula*, is stand still.

Kallistos knocked. Once, twice, again.

There was no answer. Just silence, stretching smooth and unbroken, and Lexos thought his heart might burst with relief, and with pride. Rhea, his sister, so dear and so strong when she had to be—she was holding firm.

The smug smile began to slide off Kallistos's face. Frowning, he raised his hand to knock again.

"Thyspira's choice has been made clear," Lexos interrupted, and as he spoke he could hear Baba's voice coming from the other side of the door, speaking low and quick. Too muffled to make out, but the sentiment was clear. Lexos had to keep the ceremony moving before Baba forced Rhea to go back on her decision.

"Don't presume," Kallistos began, "to tell me what—"

"Michali Laskaris," Lexos called, looking past Kallistos to where Michali was standing, "whose suit has been made."

Rhea's choice by now was obvious, and Michali had grasped that much, if the look on his face was anything to go by. He had gone pale, but there was a brightness in his eyes that spoke of determination as he stepped past Kallistos and knocked on the door.

"You have to," Lexos began, but Michali shrugged.

"She knows why I'm here."

He'd barely finished when the doors began to swing open, revealing Baba, whose face was luminous with rage, and Rhea, who seemed utterly dazed, her mouth open, her eyes staring at nothing.

In keeping with the season she would be bringing in with this consort, she was dressed all in white. Her gown began as a jeweled band across her shoulders and from there billowed into sheets of white gauze, their volume obscuring her shape. Her hair was bound up in a long braid, and hanging from a chain drawn across her brow was something small and unnaturally bright—almost a jewel, but not one Lexos had ever seen before.

It was at this point in the choosing that she was meant to respond to the words spoken by her suitor. But as Michali had done no such thing, and as Rhea looked about ready to collapse, Lexos thought they might be better served by skipping it.

He came up next to Michali, reaching for Rhea to urge her closer. Over her shoulder, Baba was watching with his jaw clamped shut, and Chrysanthi, who always came with Rhea to these things, had her arm looped through his, her grip tight as though she was ready to hold him back. Lexos supposed he had her, along with pure shock, to thank for the fact that Baba hadn't yet erupted.

"Let Thyspira's choice be sealed," Lexos said. Best to work quickly now. He slid his Argyros dagger from its concealed pocket in his trousers and held it out to Rhea. She stared at it for a long moment before something seemed to reawaken behind her eyes, and Lexos swallowed a sigh of relief as she took it from him carefully. Michali flinched as the blade glinted in what sunlight there was. Did he think Thyspira killed her consorts immediately?

"A generous season to the Ksigora," Rhea said quietly. Lexos felt a rush of pride at her steadiness as she reached for Michali's right hand and turned it palm up before cutting a mirror of her own mark—a long thin line that swept from her index finger to her little finger—into his skin. That finished, she quickly cut the same line into her own hand. It always healed over between seasons, but Lexos had seen the scar there, the raised white tissue on her right palm a match for the black line on her left.

She cleared her throat and clasped Michali's marked hand in hers. "Just so," she said.

Michali looked startled, but he had enough sense left to repeat it back to her. "Just so." She let go, and Michali glanced from her to Lexos. "Is that how you marry here?"

Lexos shook his head. "The marrying is yours and your family's. I suppose you do not have to, but it's what's done."

Rhea swayed gently toward Lexos as the air turned sweet with coming snow. The circles under her eyes were dark and sallow, and there were spots of blood on her dress from the blade of his knife. She needed quiet, Lexos thought, a place to take a breath.

"Well," he said loudly, turning to address the other suitors, "thank you all for coming. You'll find your carriages have been prepared and are ready for departure whenever you should wish it."

In each carriage would be a consolation prize of sorts, a package of goods and fine fabric to soothe those who hadn't been chosen. But Lexos knew none of them would be truly upset except Kallistos, who was staring at Rhea with narrowed eyes. He'd clearly thought that last night had been some kind of contract between them.

Lexos left Rhea standing silently next to Michali and went to his father, who was still clenching his jaw so tightly that Lexos thought one of his teeth might have popped out.

"Do you want to speak to the Rhokeri?" Lexos said in his father's ear. "To smooth it over?"

"I do not think I can speak to anyone just now," Baba gritted out. "Bring your sister to me as soon as this mess is finished clearing up. I shall be in my study."

The other suitors had started to drift to their carriages, leaving Kallistos by the doors, clearly waiting for some kind of explanation.

Lexos made for him, all too aware of the chill coming off the Rhokeri in waves.

"May I be the first to apologize," he said as he joined him. "Thyspira chooses according to her heart." He tried for a smile. "And we all know how fickle women's hearts can be. She doesn't understand what she's done." Rhea, of course, very much did understand. But men like Kallistos were happy to underestimate her.

"If only women's hearts were the only forces at work here," Kallistos said. "Rhokera and I will have no further business with this charade."

Rhea had done her part; Lexos had to do his. "Please," he said, keeping his voice low. "Surely there must be some way I can make up for my sister's mistake. It is of great importance to me, and to my father, that our two families remain friends."

Kallistos pursed his lips, and when he spoke his voice was firm, any vestiges of politeness entirely vanished. "You speak of your father. Mine offered you the life of his eldest son. I was prepared to make the highest sacrifice, prepared to make our two families even more than friends, and yet after a bargain had been struck, your sister has cast me off. What can you do that may repair such a breach, such a sullying of honor?"

Lexos faltered for a moment. Baba had not authorized him to make any real promises. He could not offer a better trade deal with Vuomorra; he could not promise Stratagiozi support of a Rhokeri invasion of one of its neighboring cities. All he could do was try to appease Kallistos with the only thing he had left—Rhea.

"If you were to present yourself again, in another season," he tried, but there was no point in finishing the sentence. It was clear from the look on Kallistos's face that no Speros would ever again offer themselves to be Rhea's consort.

"Tell your father his hold is weakening," Kallistos said. "Tell him to look after his seat, while it still is his." His eyes were cold and his posture stiff as he got into his carriage, and Lexos clenched his fists as it pulled away.

So. Baba couldn't count on Rhokera's allegiance, and a threat to his seat was imminent. It wasn't entirely unexpected—Lexos had taken that risk, sending Rhea to the north. While she worked to silence the Sxoriza and keep the country from fracturing, he would work to keep the Stratagiozi seat in Argyros control. To do that, he would need to find support against the Rhokeri. Support, perhaps, from the rest of the federation.

With Kallistos gone, Stratathoma was at last empty of suitors, and Lexos went back to fetch Rhea. They were expected in Baba's study, where they were probably both due for a scolding, or worse. Leaving Chrysanthi behind to deal with Michali, Lexos took hold of Rhea's elbow and escorted her toward the stairs.

She waited until they were on the second floor, far out of earshot of anyone else, to speak. "How angry is he?"

"Best to prepare yourself for the worst, I think. You made the right choice. I really do think so."

"Of course you do. It was your idea."

"I'm serious." He stopped walking, waited for her to look him in the eyes. "You're saving this family, Rhea. Saving this country. That's more important than anything." She didn't answer, but there was a hollowness to her face that made him nervous. "Don't let him take that away. Don't let him make you forget."

The door to Baba's study was open when they arrived, and Lexos could hear him pacing inside. He hesitated, gave himself a moment to put up the façade he knew Baba would expect—angry, shocked, devastated by Rhea's disobedience, or, as Baba would likely call it, betrayal. With one last squeeze of Rhea's hand, he set his shoulders and barged into the study, dragging her along behind him.

"Ah," Baba said, spreading his arms wide to welcome them. "There they are. My eldest children, my pride and joy."

Lexos's heart sank. Baba was difficult enough when he was explosive, but this Baba, sweet and sharp together, was the hardest of all.

He closed the door behind them as Baba came striding forward and swept Rhea up in an embrace, trapping her arms by her sides. Lexos watched her close her eyes. If she was shaking, he couldn't tell, but her knuckles were white from the tight clench of her fists.

"Good work, *koukla*," Baba whispered. "What a thing you have done. What bonds you have broken." He released her then, pushing her back hard enough that she stumbled, and it was against every instinct that Lexos managed not to rush to her side. "Truly I have raised a singular kind of woman. There is nobody in this world like you, my dear."

When Baba yelled you could appease him with apologies, with open groveling. But with this Baba, with this sugar-spun anger, Lexos had never found the right way to disperse it. Rhea was clearly also at a loss, her mouth opening and closing as she searched for something to say.

"So tell me," Baba went on. "What do we owe this delightful surprise to?"

"I—"

"Perhaps you misunderstood my instructions. Perhaps you misread my letter, in which I told you by name which suitor to choose."

"No, that's not—"

"Or perhaps you simply forgot. Either way, it doesn't seem like there's much of a brain behind that pretty little face, does it, *koukla*?" Baba reached out and grasped her chin, chucking it in a way that might have been affectionate had Lexos not noticed Rhea's head jerk to one side.

"I know what you said," she replied, her eyes almost vacant, as though she was trying to call up the memory of it. "I meant to . . . I'd decided to . . ."

Lexos wished she'd keep quiet. Baba would force an explanation out of her, and she certainly wouldn't tell him the truth, not when she had to know as well as Lexos did that Baba would take it as the ultimate betrayal, a conspiracy to undermine him. He would never understand that they'd done what they had to protect him, not to ruin him. So what was left? Incompetence. Or—

"I couldn't help it," Rhea finished softly. "I think I love him, Baba."

It was one of her better-told lies. But it burned the sweetness from Baba, left bare the unyielding rage beneath.

"Love him?" Baba scoffed. "You have doomed him and your family both." He pointed to the chair behind his desk, which was piled high with parchment and littered with inkwells. "Sit."

Rhea glanced sidelong at Lexos as she passed, but he could give her nothing more than the smallest of shrugs. Baba was watching them both, and any empathy Lexos showed her would be recognized and punished.

She sat in the ornately carved chair with some difficulty, the skirts of her choosing dress too voluminous to handle easily. When at last she was settled, hands clasped in her lap, Baba peeled off one of his black leather gloves and handed it to Lexos.

"I'll tell you when to stop," he said.

Lexos looked for some sign in his face, some relenting, but there was nothing. Just the stone set of his jaw and the empty depth of his eyes. Baba wouldn't say it, not out loud, what he wanted Lexos to do. But Lexos knew.

If he refused, would that reveal his collusion with Rhea? Baba expected him to share his betrayal, expected him to participate. Lexos couldn't afford to do otherwise.

He closed his hand tightly around the glove and picked a spot just beyond Rhea to stare at. Behind her, morning sun was attempting to break through the heavy cloud cover. How strange that it should still be morning.

The first blow landed with a crack against her cheek. A cry, ringing in the air, and Rhea's eyes suddenly glimmering wetly. Lexos took a step forward, let his silhouette cast her face into shadow.

The other cheek, this time. The glove, smooth against his palm, pleasantly weighted as it made contact. Don't look, he told himself. You are somewhere else.

He didn't know how many times he struck, only knew that by the time Baba said, "Enough," his palm was clammy with sweat.

"Go," Baba said. Lexos took a deep, shuddering breath, watched out the window as the sun gave up and the first raindrops began to fall, and stepped aside to let Rhea pass. He didn't think he'd broken the skin. Had he? Had she been crying?

She would forgive him. Probably, she already had.

"She's weak," Baba said as the door shut behind her. "You both are. Don't think I didn't notice your hesitation." Lexos held out the glove, but Baba only stripped off the other one and passed it to him. "Keep them. A reminder of what you did here today."

He crossed to behind his desk and adjusted the chair before sitting down heavily. Lexos took his usual spot opposite him, in a smaller, far less comfortable chair, the gloves clutched in one hand.

"If we might put Rhea aside," he began, and Baba's eyebrows rose. "The situation with Rhokera requires our attention."

"A situation she created," Baba snapped.

Lexos hardly thought that was fair. Rhea's decision had sparked the fire, but the embers had been there for a long while, gathering heat, starting to smoke. Lexos had taken a risk, but if all went as he knew it would, Baba would face the Rhokeri stewards with the backing of every other federation member. No trouble in the north would arise to sever those bonds.

He had done the right thing. There was nothing to do but go on.

"She did," he said. "But it's here now. And we must decide how to resolve it."

Baba watched him for a moment with narrowed eyes before sitting forward sharply. "Yes," he said, and Lexos let out a breath. The worst was over. "We're due at Agiokon in a fortnight's time."

Agiokon, where the leaders of every federation member met. Would word of Rhea's choice have reached them by then? How would Baba present it if they had heard? Surely not as Lexos had intended it—as a step taken to head off their northern problem at the pass. As his own daughter's folly, then? Or perhaps he would simply ignore it altogether.

"I'll present the news to the others." Baba tilted his head, considering. "We'll reassure them we have it well in hand, but should the need arise, we would appreciate a show of support."

Lexos frowned. No, he hadn't been observing council meetings as long as Baba had been attending them, but he knew the other Stratagiozis well enough to worry. Most of the others had held their seats for far longer than Baba, and to ask so bluntly for help would almost certainly invite the sort of extortion and politicking that Thyzakos couldn't afford.

"You don't think we might be better served by a more tactical approach?" he asked.

Baba was already shaking his head, displeasure drawing his mouth into a thin line. "What I think," he said, "is that this country's seat belongs to me, and not to my son."

Lexos could keep pushing. But there was no sense in it. He'd got what he wanted from Rhea, and there was time before the meeting at Agiokon, time to soften Baba's approach. "Of course," he said. "And Rhea? What will you do with her?"

Baba scoffed. "Let her rot in the north. She'll come home frozen to the bone. Some hardship might do her good."

Some hardship—as though Rhea hadn't suffered already. As though she wasn't as familiar with pain as with breathing. As though neither of them were.

With their conversation finished, Lexos found himself wandering up to his room. Rhea would be in hers, he was sure, and though he knew he wouldn't be welcome inside, it would soothe his nerves to know she was close by. She'd be preparing for the trip north she and Michali would take at first light tomorrow. He'd be able to stretch out on his bed and fall asleep to the faint murmur and rustle of Rhea and her servants packing things into her trunk.

Her door was open when he passed. Inside, her two servants were at work, folding clothes, stacking them neatly and tucking sprigs of pressed lavender in between them, but Rhea herself was nowhere to be found. They looked at him blankly when he asked where she was, and Lexos gave a resigned sigh and retreated to his room.

It would be worth it. This distance, this hurt they were passing between them, it wouldn't matter when they restored their family to its full strength. He would be glad of it. He would do it all again.

ELEVEN

RHEA

"It will be simple enough," Lexos was saying, and Rhea had to push through the haze in her head to focus on the movement of his mouth. "Their operation can't be too sophisticated, and no doubt the Laskaris boy will be near the head of it."

They were standing in the outer courtyard, waiting by the carriage for Michali to make an appearance. Lexos was wrapped in his own cloak, a well-draped thing in blue wool, and was very busy doing everything he could to keep from looking at her. In fact, he hadn't since yesterday, in Baba's study. He hadn't spoken to her, either, had seemed to trust that everything between them was resolved. Usually, it would be by now. But Rhea could still feel the sting of the glove on her cheek.

It was made worse by the gap that seemed to open in her memory when she thought about her choosing. She had done what Lexos asked of her, had stayed silent when Kallistos made his suit and chosen Michali, but she wasn't sure she'd ever really decided to. In fact, she'd woken yesterday with another plan altogether, and frankly,

Rhea thought that if she was going to suffer, she should at the very least remember why.

Impulse, maybe, or an eagerness to avoid the bargain she'd struck with Kallistos. But no reason she could come up with explained the oddity of standing there by her father's side, listening as Kallistos made his suit, and being unable to open her mouth to do as she'd been told. She'd felt dazed, somehow less herself, and that clinging, disorienting fog had only dissipated when Lexos's voice had come cutting through, announcing Michali. For a moment, she had known with such certainty.

Michali. Of course, Michali.

"They must have a base in the city," Lexos went on, drawing her attention back. "The mountain camps are too remote to survive without a supply train running up to them. You'll find that base, find out their numbers and supplies, and report to me what you learn. The Laskaris boy's death will leave them in tatters, and once he's out of the way, I'll use your information to finish the job."

"You might as well have killed him the moment he arrived," she said, frowning, "and spared me the trouble."

Lexos looked over her shoulder, to where the Laskaris driver was emerging from the servants' quarters. "My scouts have turned up nothing. Without Laskaris, we have no chance at finding the rest of the separatists. You keep him alive until you get what we need, yes? And you tell me everything."

It was not enough, Rhea thought. Not enough of a plan to warrant the trouble they'd caused with Baba. But here she was. Lexos's spy and Michali's consort, and though she had never really chosen to be either, she couldn't go back now. She thought, briefly, of the little blue hummingbird she'd seen in Nitsos's garden, of how it followed the same pattern from tree to tree, hovering in the same places, over and over. Was that to be her fate now? Following along in the path set for her by someone else?

It was not, she supposed, all that different from serving Baba. Only this time she was serving Lexos. Her twin, her brother, the one person who understood what it was truly like to be a child on whom Baba depended. He wouldn't lead her astray. He had his reasons for asking her to do this, and now that she'd said yes, she had to trust him.

She didn't have to like it, though. She ignored Lexos's worried stare and instead moved to the carriage door where Chrysanthi was waiting to give her one last hug.

"Look after the house," Rhea said, drawing her close. "Make sure everyone is fed and the linens are changed."

"You've gone away before. We'll be fine."

Rhea wrapped her arms around Chrysanthi's middle and pressed her cheek against her younger sister's. "Lexos and Baba have their meeting at Agiokon. It'll be just you and Nitsos. At least try to get him to come to dinner, would you?"

"What a lovely going-away gift," Chrysanthi said as she pulled back. "A fool's errand! I've always wanted one."

"Do you know, I won't miss you at all."

Chrysanthi grinned and kissed Rhea's cheeks lightly. "Away with you now."

"*Apoxara, koukla.*"

Michali was lingering a few yards away, and Rhea knew it was her job to go and fetch him, to look as in love with him as possible in case Baba was watching from some high window—why had she chosen that particular lie to tell?—but she could barely muster the energy to give him a smile, let alone engage him in conversation.

She turned away and boosted herself up into the carriage. The door slammed shut behind her as she settled onto the bench, her smart gray traveling suit a welcome reprieve after days of maneuvering in heavy skirts.

Lexos came to the open window and leaned in, a frown buried deep on his brow. "You'll be careful, won't you?"

She faced resolutely forward. "I always am."

A moment of silence then, and she heard Lexos shifting uncomfortably. "Look," he said at last, "*kathroula*—"

"We have to go." She knew that tone of his, knew that there was no apology attached to the end of his sentence. "And I'm sure you have more plans to make."

"Fine," Lexos said flatly. "Travel safely. Goodbye." And he was gone, his cloak whipping around his knees as he stalked back to the house.

Had he not expected her to be angry? They'd both done questionable things under Baba's instruction, but that had never absolved them before.

The opposite carriage door swung open, and Michali clambered in, carrying with him a large fur and a brazier of coals. It was nearly two hundred miles to the Ksigora. All of it would be spent in the cold, and, as they got farther north, likely in the snow, too. Rhea had more than a week in the carriage with Michali to look forward to, and another day after that on horseback, following the winding tracks that crept through the mountains. She rarely had to travel so far with her consorts—in most cases they were home within a few days, and married by the next night.

"Here," Michali said, handing her the fur. "I won't need it for a while yet."

"Thank you." She swallowed and spent far longer than she needed to adjusting the fur around her legs.

"I realize," he said suddenly, "that this is strange. You don't know me and I only slightly know you. And let's not forget that my death will come at your hand very shortly. So why don't we dispense with any expectation of conversation?"

Her relief was instant, but she couldn't help the heat rising in her cheeks. It was poor manners for him to mention the outcome of their marriage like that. Rhea knew, of course, that all her consorts presumably grappled with a similar resentment of her—that they all, to some degree, hated her for what she had to do—but they'd offered themselves as suitors. Surely they'd known what they were getting into.

She smiled tightly and sat back as the carriage started moving. Rude, and an enemy besides. She was not looking forward to this winter.

The days passed in dream. Rhea watched the landscape ease by out the carriage window—the plains of the middle country, the long grasses and spindly shrubs clinging to the hillsides that began to rise as they traveled farther north. In the evenings, when they stopped at one of the guesthouses that popped up along the road, Rhea was given her own room, complete with creaking cot and lumpy mattress, and she spent the nights awake, stretching her cramping muscles and watching the sky as Lexos's constellations flickered to life. Come morning, she hauled herself into the carriage, Michali silent across from her, and slept as long as she could, eyes closed even when the rattling of the carriage was too much to really sleep.

At last they reached the base of the mountains that separated the Ksigora from the rest of Thyzakos. Snow was starting to show on the ground here, thin enough that it barely lasted the day, but the briskness of the air promised more to come. She dressed warmly the next morning, layering wool stockings under her riding trousers and piling on two shirts under her long, split-tailed coat. She traveled without servants—her consort always provided them when she arrived—and so there was nobody to help her plait her hair and coil it up, off her neck and out of the brutal wind that was sure to kick up as they rode higher into the mountains.

Michali was waiting when she came out of the guesthouse. Already the snow seemed thicker, falling in large, wet flakes. So different from Nitsos's garden, Rhea thought. She'd left that gift from him back at Stratathoma, wrapped up in a handkerchief and stored carefully in her wardrobe. Now she wished she'd brought it with her. It would've been nice to have another piece of home.

"Are you ready?" Michali asked. It was one of the first things he'd said to her since they'd left Stratathoma. Thankfully, after realizing she meant to spend the whole trip in slumber, he hadn't bothered her.

"Am I dressed warmly enough, do you think?"

He took in her outfit, frowning slightly as he noticed her boots, which were well crafted for riding but were thin enough that Rhea could already feel a chill nipping at her toes.

"They're all I have," she explained.

"We haven't got any spares that would fit you." Michali sighed. "We'll just have to be careful. Speak up if you start losing feeling."

Rhea looked up, over the roof of the guesthouse, to where the foothills started in earnest, their slopes covered with trees. It would be hard riding, along trails riddled with roots and pockmarked with stones. Even with more than a century's worth of practice, she was unused to riding in these conditions.

The Laskaris grooms were finished preparing the horses, and they led a roan gelding up to her, his mouth gentle on the bit. He was too tall for her by at least a few inches, and she hesitated, looking doubtfully at the saddle.

"Here," Michali said. "I'll help you up." He braced his hands against his knee, fingers laced together to cup her boot. She rested one hand on his shoulder for balance and vaulted up, his chest pressed against her thigh as she swung her right leg over.

She settled into the seat as he mounted his own horse, a white mare, with the sort of ease she was used to seeing in her consorts, the sort who traveled, who saw the world in more ways than just through a carriage window. The rest of the retinue was already mounted, their horses stomping and snorting as they maneuvered into a long column. Michali was headed for the front, so Rhea nudged her horse with her heels and followed after him.

"Everybody's ready," one of the guards was telling Michali. The packhorses were loaded and the carriages had already left, heading for the long road through the mountain pass far to the east, which would add at least a day to their journey. Rhea had volunteered to stay with the carriages, eager for the chance to have some time to herself, but Michali had said only, "You'd have to sleep next to the horses, you know," and that had been enough to convince her that his company might be endured for a bit longer if it meant she got to sleep in an actual bed tonight.

"Well, then." Michali shifted his weight, and his mare danced to one side, making room for Rhea beside him. "Let's be off."

Within a few minutes, they were in the thick of the forest. The leaves had only just fallen, and they were still vibrant on the ground, Chrysanthi's hand evident in their color. On either side of the trail, moss-covered boulders loomed large.

It must be a very alive sort of place in the spring, Rhea thought. Bursting with green, the sky only just visible through the canopy overhead. Now, with the snow gathering, she knew it was only a matter of time before the whole place turned as white as the gown she'd worn to pick Michali.

Slowly the trail began to narrow, and Rhea fell in line behind Michali. The pitch was beginning to steepen, and she found herself sitting forward in the saddle, her fingers knotted in her horse's mane. Michali was setting a slow pace for her benefit, she knew, but with the sun already reaching its zenith, they would need to make better time to keep from being caught on the mountainside by nightfall.

"Michali," she said, hoping he could hear her over the trample of the horses. "You can go faster."

He twisted in his saddle, and Rhea was struck by the spots of color high on his cheeks, by the sway of his body as he moved with his horse. How different he seemed here. How at ease.

"Are you sure?" he said.

"Yes."

"And your feet—they're not too cold?"

"I'm fine." Thyspira did not get cold, or at least, if she did, nobody had ever told Rhea. She nudged her horse forward, crowding him. "Let's go."

Rhea gave her horse his head as they kept on up the trail, and soon her breath was coming short as the cold air swept by. Around her the landscape was changing, pines growing taller, moss growing thicker, and there was a sweetness to the air that made her want to stick out her tongue and catch one of the falling snowflakes. Every now and then she could spot deer tracks winding between the trees, bark scraped away from the trunks where they'd stopped to eat. That was some of Nitsos's work, a habit he'd built into the clockwork deer that roamed the grounds at Stratathoma to keep their living counterparts from scavenging among farmers' winter crops.

"We're coming up on the river," Michali called over his shoulder. "We'll gather in the tree line before we cross."

The trail took a downward turn, and before long Rhea could hear the burble of water over stone. She sat forward, craning her neck eagerly as her horse slowed to match Michali's pace. Oceans she didn't care much for—that endless horizon made her sick to her stomach—but rivers were another matter entirely. There'd been a small creek on the grounds of their old house, and Rhea had spent her summers up to her knees in it, splashing at Lexos, who preferred to stay on the banks and watch.

There, the glint of water in muted sun, and the trees opened up onto the banks of the river. Rhea took in a sharp breath and drew her horse up short. The water was odd, so clear she could see the pebbles coating the riverbed, and it was an unearthly shade that fell somewhere between green and blue. She'd never seen water so bright—even Chrysanthi's hand had never created a color such as this before.

"What is this?" she asked, her voice full of air.

Michali gave her a sidelong glance. "It's the Dovikos."

Said as though that would explain everything, as though she should know the name of every tiny river in every corner of the country. Rhea eased her horse closer to the water's edge. "Where does it come from?"

"Farther west, up where the mountains start."

Was it something about the source that gave the river its color? Or was it just that Chrysanthi's work looked different in this diffused winter light?

The rest of the party was gathering around them, pulling the horses in tight to avoid the boulders that littered the riverbank. So often Rhea forgot the oldness of things—her own life stretched so long, and it was rare to find a reminder that many things stretched even longer—but here it was inescapable. The boulders left behind by some natural movement thousands of years ago, the trees with roots as thick as her middle that reached far under the riverbed.

The river itself was fairly wide, the opposite shore perhaps forty or fifty yards away, but its water was shallow, its current mild enough that Rhea thought a crossing should be fairly easy.

"Why are we waiting?" she asked Michali.

He gestured to farther upstream, where the ground climbed steeply and rocks hemmed in close, the trees casting them in shade. Snow was still falling, heavy enough now that the world was slightly blurry.

"It's perfectly safe," he started, which meant it wasn't. "But this crossing sometimes attracts a mercenary sort."

Rhea thought of the packhorses, their saddlebags full of food and fresh supplies. But of course there was something else to consider—she could almost hear Lexos screaming about it in the back of her head. This mercenary sort could be the separatists. If they'd heard she was coming, she would be a valuable hostage for them.

"You'll ride between two guardsmen," Michali hastened to add, perhaps seeing some distress on her face. "Nothing will happen to you. It's only a precaution."

It was decided that Michali would go first, flanked by his own pair of guards, and that Rhea would follow. Once they were safely across, they would continue on the trail until they were well clear of the river, and wait for the rest of the party to catch up.

Michali's crossing went surely and swiftly. At its deepest point, the water reached his horse's chest, and Rhea breathed slowly to calm herself. She'd thought it looked shallower, but she would be fine. Really. And after all, Thyspira was never supposed to look something so human as afraid.

"On your signal," one of the guards said to Rhea once Michali was waiting on the opposite bank.

She sat up straight, flexed her numbing fingers. Michali had crossed safely, without any movement from the outcroppings above. Overhead a wheeling hawk let out a cry and her horse, gentle and stoic thus far, spooked slightly, prancing back from the water's edge and pulling at the bit.

"Get him in hand," the guard said, but no matter how Rhea tugged on the reins, she couldn't settle her horse. He was rearing back, stamping at the ground with his forelegs, and it was all she could do to keep her seat.

"Something's wrong," she called, clinging to the saddle. "He won't—"

An arrow landed with a squelch in the eye of the guard next to her. Rhea watched, mouth open, as his body dropped to the snow, blood trailing down his cheek as he stared, sightless, up at the sky. Her hands went loose around the reins and her horse wheeled about, plunging for the cover of the trees. Sharp, humming, the zip of an arrow as it whipped by her ear.

The guards closed fast around her, even as more arrows began to land, thunking into the trunks of trees, finding their targets in the necks of soldiers and grooms alike. She twisted in her saddle to see Michali charging into the water.

"Get her across," he was yelling. "Quickly, across!"

They were regrouping, the guards unbuckling their shields from the backs of their saddles, but Rhea couldn't wait. She gritted her teeth and yanked the reins hard to one side, digging in her heel on the opposite flank and squeezing her thighs as tightly as she could. Her horse balked once, but then she felt him relax, and they were turning, cantering toward the river's edge. Rhea flinched as an arrow hit the thick leather of her saddle, but there was nothing for it— she leaned low, pressed her cheek to her horse's neck, and spurred him on.

They crashed into the water, icy spray soaking through Rhea's boots. Her horse pounded through the surf, the river breaking against his chest, and she found herself speaking in his ear, calling him all the dearest words she knew. They were almost across, Michali knee-deep in the shallows, hand outstretched. Rhea was so focused on his face, twisted with worry, that she barely felt the arrow as it skimmed the side of her neck, the sting bright and fizzing.

Blood seeped down her neck, pooled in the dip of her throat, soaked into the collar of her coat. It didn't hurt much, Rhea thought dimly as her horse careened past Michali and up onto the riverbank.

"Are you all right?" he said, dashing up to grab hold of her horse's bridle, but it sounded so far away. The snow rushing up at her, world spinning.

"Water, get some water."

Her boots hit the riverbank. Rhea tottered against Michali's shoulder, one hand clasping the side of her neck where blood was sticky against her glove.

"I don't think it's that bad," she said, her voice unsteady. Michali ignored her, hauling her almost off her feet as he helped her into the cover of the trees. The arrows had stopped flying, but across the river the rest of their party was still in hiding, waiting for Michali's orders.

"I'll be the judge of that. Here, sit down."

He sat her on one of the boulders, left in the forest as the river changed course over thousands of years. Rhea pulled her coat away from her neck, watched a drop of blood land on the stone. Rich red on bone white. It seemed to her that the blood sank into the boulder, disappearing second by second until all that was left was a coating of snow.

She started as Michali brushed his fingers along her jaw, angling her head away from the wound.

"Sorry," he said. "I just need to get a good look."

One of the guards came rushing back from the river, his helmet upended and filled to the brim with water. Michali had ripped a strip off the bottom of his shirt—cotton, she thought absently, which was really more of a summer fabric—and was pressing it gently to the wound.

"It looks shallow," he said from somewhere near her ear.

"I told you, it's fine."

"We'll see." Leaning back, he bound the strip of cloth loosely around her neck, watching her closely as he slowly tightened it. "How's that?"

"Fine, really. Shouldn't we be moving?" She peered over his shoulder. "Who was that shooting at us? Won't they keep attacking?"

"It's only a single volley," Michali said absently, eyes narrowed as he focused on tying a secure knot. Rhea tilted her head—how did he know that? "We should be safe until Ksigori." Satisfied, he sat back in a crouch. "Have some water."

The guard held out the helmet, and she took it in shaking hands. She felt weaker than she'd realized. A cool drink would do her good, soothe the feverish sweat she felt breaking out on her brow. She pressed the helmet to her lips and took a long sip.

For a moment she felt better—different, really, an unfamiliar clarity filling her—but then it was gone, and she was bracing her hands on her knees and gagging until the water came splashing back out.

"*Mala,*" Michali whispered, scrambling to hold her hair back. "*Kiria* Thyspira? Do you feel worse?"

She straightened, wiped her mouth on her sleeve. "No, just thirsty." The guard offered the helmet again, and she cracked a smile. "Thank you, but I've had enough of that."

They would go on ahead, it was decided, and meet the rest of the party in the Ksigora. It wasn't far, Michali assured her. They would be fine on their own, and the party would travel more safely without her anyway.

It was when they were riding again, the trail climbing ahead of them, that she caught Michali watching her with an odd look in his eyes.

"What?" she asked.

"It's nothing." He shook his head. "I just wasn't sure your kind could bleed."

"My kind?" She frowned, nudged her horse into a quicker trot. "I think you'll find my kind is much the same as yours." And besides, didn't he know? The federation had been built on blood. And most of it belonged to the Stratagiozis. Michali's own would join theirs soon. Every season ended eventually.

TWELVE

RHEA

The sun was low in the sky when they began their descent into the Ksigora, and lower still when they emerged onto the flatlands and joined up with the main road. The farther they got from the mountains, the more the river crossing seemed as though it had happened to somebody else. Rhea could still feel her heartbeat in the cut on her neck, but as Thyspira, danger was not something she ever had much cause to consider, and so all she could conjure as she mulled over the attack was a pointed curiosity about Michali.

Only one volley, he'd said. How had he known the attackers wouldn't keep firing? She could practically hear Lexos now, pointing out the obvious: Michali was in on the attack, and trying to set himself up as an enemy of the separatists. But Michali's concern for her had been genuine, the worry etched too deeply into his face to be false. No, Rhea would reserve judgment for now, but certainly something worth spying on was going on in this northern corner of Thyzakos. It was right that she had come here.

Ahead, Rhea could see the outskirts of Ksigori, the region's capital, beginning to take shape. Small houses, their tiled roofs broken, their doors propped against the doorframes. It all seemed like more damage than a few hard winters could reasonably do on their own, and it made Rhea uneasy to see, made her wonder if there were things Lexos's descriptions of the area had failed to include. But the people who lived inside those houses, who came out to watch them pass, didn't seem particularly bothered, and looked happy to see Michali.

"You carry no standard," she said as they passed a house whose occupants were only a hunched old woman and six or seven dogs. "How do they know you?"

"By my face," Michali said, somewhat stupidly.

That answered that.

Slowly, the small houses turned to bigger ones, and at last they were in what Rhea assumed was the heart of Ksigori. The buildings looked like cousins to Stratathoma, with thick walls and layers of courtyards, but here their roofs were dusted with snow and their windows were decorated with brightly painted iron scrollwork. The streets here were winding, cobbled in a haphazard way that didn't seem to bother the horses, and though Rhea was sure that if left alone she would wind up hopelessly lost, the streets all seemed to be leading to the same place—downslope of the land, into the city, converging on something.

Now and then they would open onto a square of sorts, and at the center was always a plane tree, so old its roots could usually be seen darting in and out of the cobblestones. Old women in black sat on the benches under these trees, their heads bent together as they gossiped in the last of the evening light. Children were playing games, chasing after a ball as they knocked at it with sticks down the long covered walkways that bordered every square.

It seemed lovely at first glance, and Rhea was quite ready to tell Michali so—there was never any harm in good manners, something he could stand to learn—when the truth of life in Ksigori began to peek through the idyllic façade. Here a child barefoot in the cold, there a young woman huddled against the shut door of a bakery.

Rhea didn't have half the information that Lexos's reports afforded him, but she'd heard the Ksigora was faring poorly, and the more she looked for it, the easier it was to see. Was this enough to crumble Michali's loyalty to dust? Surely the unity of Thyzakos was more important.

They took another turn, and soon the city opened up onto what was clearly a main street, bustling with families and lined with shops. Here, too, people recognized Michali (or, in the case of some of the younger children, recognized his horse). As they crested a small rise, Rhea got her first glimpse of what the city seemed to be converging on: the lake.

It stretched out for what seemed like miles, the far shore obscured through the falling snow. With the sunset streaming in from the west, the lake was ablaze, its water catching the firelight. It was ringed by a wide stone promenade, and tonight it was full to bursting with families and children watching the water burn out.

But more than anything, Rhea's attention was caught by the island that dominated the center of the lake, and by the house that occupied it. It was much like the others she'd seen as they passed through the city, but larger and low-slung. In the dim light its stones looked a faded blue, and she could just make out the crimson shine of the house's massive double doors.

It was the Laskaris house, of course. It could be nothing but.

She traced the curve of the shore, looking for a bridge or some way to cross, but as Michali continued to lead them around the edge of the lake, it became clear there was none.

"The stables are on this shore," Michali explained when he saw her looking. "We leave the horses and cross by boat."

Rhea tried to pretend the very idea didn't make her stomach turn over itself and smiled as politely as she could.

One altogether too-long boat ride later, during which Rhea fixed her gaze on the house and did not once let it waver, they arrived at a small dock some ways off from the house itself. Michali helped her ashore, and Rhea was thankful he made no mention of how tightly she gripped his fingers as she stepped from boat to dock.

"This is where we'll live," he said as they started up the path to the house. "My family has had this house for generations."

"Do the people come to see you here? Are they permitted?"

"No," Michali said, looking embarrassed. "But my father spends his days in the city. That's where most of his business is done."

They had reached the house, and Rhea wanted nothing more than to lie down and sleep for a year or two, never mind spy for her absent brother, but there was someone waiting in the doorway, a lantern clutched in their hand. A woman, Rhea thought as they grew closer. A sister? She didn't think there was a Laskaris girl.

"My boy," the woman called as they neared. "My Michali, home at last."

Of course. He had a mother. Rhea's own lack of one often made her forget that mothers were something that existed outside of her memory.

She was tall; that was the first thing Rhea noticed. Broad shoulders and a strong chin, with stark streaks of gray in her dark hair. Michali left Rhea's side with an apologetic glance and approached his mother.

"Hello, Mama," he said wearily, a vein of fondness running through his voice.

"No hug? No kiss? After I carried you inside me?"

"I was getting to it."

Her smile was practically beatific as Michali dutifully kissed her cheeks and embraced her. "You've been gone too long, *koros.*"

"I'm not sure we agree on that." But he was smiling, and when he turned back to Rhea it seemed that some of the care that had settled on his shoulders since the river ambush had lifted. "This is my mother," he said, beckoning her closer. "And, Mama, this is *kiria* Thyspira."

"As if she needed an introduction," the woman scoffed, and came forward, leaving her lantern in Michali's hands. "This is the woman who will kill my son."

Rhea bit her tongue so hard she tasted blood. But Michali's mother offered her no chance to answer.

"I'm Evanthia," she said, wrapping her arms around Rhea and squeezing the air out of her. "Welcome to our home, and to Ksigori."

"Thank you," Rhea gasped once she'd been released. "I'm very glad to meet you."

"Well, let's not just stand about getting cold. Come in, come in." Evanthia looped her arm through Rhea's, her momentary sharpness seemingly gone, and escorted her past Michali into the house. As was the way with most Thyzak houses, the main doors opened onto an inner courtyard, but where the courtyards at Stratathoma were wide and dotted with ironwork chairs and low tables, this one was small, barely big enough to comfortably accommodate all of them, and they didn't linger there, moving quickly instead into the house.

"Michali's father is in the city still," Evanthia was saying as she ushered Rhea inside, "but he will join us later. Well, here we are."

The first room was large, clearly the heart of the house, and a fire burned steadily in the fireplace. Around it were arranged a number of wooden divans, their seats piled high with patterned cushions in bright colors. Off to one side a long table was set up for a meal, its waxed wood gleaming. Rhea could see through a doorway to the kitchen, where two young women were chopping vegetables, and a well-lit passageway cut through the back wall, leading to the rest of the house. Everywhere, the ceilings pressed in. Stratathoma was high-reaching, full of empty space, and when the sun left the air the chill was inescapable. This house, Rhea supposed, was built to trap the heat and keep it close.

"You must be starving," Evanthia said, bustling her toward the dining table before abruptly changing her mind. "Or are you cold? Should we warm you up first? Perhaps you should eat in front of the fire. I think this seat would be best."

Rhea looked helplessly to Michali, but he just shrugged as Evanthia steered her to the divan closest to the fire and began unbuttoning her coat. This close, Rhea could see a mole on her chin and the single hair sprouting out of it, dark and wiry. She leaned back as slowly as she could, hoping Evanthia wouldn't notice.

"Goodness," Evanthia said, touching the bandage at Rhea's neck. "What happened here?"

"Attack at the crossing," Michali answered, his voice muffled as he drew his sweater over his head. His coat had already been discarded and lay draped over one of the chairs around the dining table. "We lost the Drakos boy, too," he added.

Evanthia made a mournful sound as she clutched at her chest with one hand, the other already reaching for the bandage on Rhea's neck.

"It's only a graze," Rhea explained.

"You can never be too careful," Evanthia answered. She called to the kitchen for some fresh herbs and hot water before undoing Rhea's makeshift bandage and tossing it to the floor. "How do you feel? Feverish? Too warm? It doesn't seem infected but goodness knows we should prepare for the worst, especially if it took the Drakos boy."

"Yes, well, his hit him square in the eye," Michali said. "I think we've got a bit of leeway with this one."

That did not deter Evanthia, who only leaned in closer. Rhea tried to shift backward on the divan, but its high back trapped her in place as Evanthia used her fingernail to pick at the wound on her neck and came away with a flake of dried blood. There was an odd silence as Evanthia examined it, and Rhea remembered what Michali had said.

Your kind.

She stood up suddenly. "I'm sorry," she said. She needed a moment alone. She needed air. "It's just I'm very tired."

"Of course," said Evanthia, but neither made to move. Rhea found herself uncomfortably pinned by Evanthia's dark, unnerving stare.

"I'll show you to your room," Michali said. Evanthia blinked, and Rhea took the opportunity to escape, moving toward Michali, who was waiting at the entrance to the hallway.

"Thank you for your hospitality," she said to Evanthia, averting her eyes. Sweat was pooling in the hollow of her throat and her palms were clammy. This place, this room—she had to get out. "Good night."

Michali was quick in leading her to her guest quarters. She'd wondered briefly if she might be expected to share his bed—they weren't yet married, but then that was not important to everyone—but it was her own room with a narrow single bed that he showed her to.

"Your things will arrive tomorrow," he said, referring to the rest of the party, which Rhea had barely thought of since leaving them behind at the river crossing, and the carriages that had taken the longer road. "I know that must be terribly inconvenient."

"Really, it's all right." She couldn't bring herself to be upset about something so trivial as that, especially when her room thankfully had a window and she could feel a bracing draft of cold air sneaking through it. Perhaps in a few weeks she would want something warmer, nearer the center of the house, but at least for now it was refreshing to feel such a chill.

Michali gestured to a small chest of drawers. "There might be something useful in there. I'm not sure, exactly. I don't know what you Stratagiozi ladies require."

She shifted uncomfortably at the bitterness in his voice. She wasn't used to consorts—to anyone but Baba, really—talking to her like this. "You mean, you don't have a nightgown made of rubies and diamonds for me to sleep in?"

"I'm afraid that's in the other guest room," he said without a hint of a smile.

She stepped farther into the room and shucked off her coat, tossing it onto the bed. "Good night, then."

"Good night."

Once he was gone, she sorted through the contents of the drawers, finding a number of woolen nightgowns so long that they had to be castoffs of Evanthia's. Rhea shuddered. She would sleep in her traveling suit before she put on any of those.

Eagerly, she went to the window and threw it wide. The shutters clattered against the stone as the cold came barreling in, bracing and fresh, and Rhea leaned out into the dark, breathing deeply. She couldn't see too much beyond the trees that crowded this island, but across the moonlit water, the ever-present reach of the mountains rose into the starred sky. She was looking forward to seeing what this view looked like come morning, at least. And then she could get started on the work that needed to be done.

It was as she was retreating from the window, meaning to leave it open for a few minutes more, that she heard a snatch of birdsong. Lexos, she thought immediately, before the song had even finished. That had to be a signal from him.

And it was. Only moments later, a white bird alighted on the windowsill. She'd seen it last at Stratathoma, that day with Lexos when he'd suggested the very plan she was currently entangled in, and the sight of it now stoked an uncomfortable fire in her chest. The warmth of comfort, but with something else alongside it. Anger, perhaps. Hadn't she done enough for Lexos already? Did she really need his supervision before she'd even had a chance to try anything alone?

With a bit more force than was necessary, she snatched the bird down from the sill and pulled the shutters closed behind it, before some stray guard at the house could wonder what exactly it was doing there. It went still as soon as she touched it, allowing her to see that there was, as she'd expected, a scroll of parchment rolled tightly around one of its legs.

"Wonderful," she muttered, and undid the twine knotted around it before holding the parchment up to the nearest lantern to read it.

Some information you will find helpful.
Observed this exchange near middle of Ksigori.
Look for enclosed. I'll be watching.

It was not one of Lexos's longer letters, written without the particular endearments he usually included. Rhea pushed down the feeling that she'd done something wrong somehow and reminded herself how busy Lexos always seemed to be. He'd just been in a hurry when he'd written. They were fine.

She turned her attention back to the bird. Lexos said something was enclosed with the letter, but there was nothing wrapped up with the scroll. There was only the bird, and whatever it had seen, stored in the pale stone behind its eyes. That must be what he meant.

The mechanism of the bird's skull opened up just as easily as it had that day at Stratathoma, and Rhea was able to pluck out the stone, its weight familiar and grounding in her palm. The last time she'd looked at a piece of intelligence gleaned from Lexos's scout network, it had changed things entirely, and whether it would be for better or for worse was still being determined. Did she really want to do it again?

No, if she was honest, but she was adrift here, and out of her depth. Any information she could get would be helpful. With a sigh, she held the stone up to the lantern, and watched as the light seemed to pass through the stone itself, creating images that projected onto the opposite wall.

There were two images that the bird had carried with it. One was of a man and a woman, huddled in the shadow of what looked like either a house or an empty storefront. They were dressed warmly, and the man was looking over his shoulder while holding out his hand toward the woman, who was about to place something there. It looked like a coin, or a few of them, but any confusion Rhea had was resolved by the second image, which focused in on what was in the woman's grip.

It was indeed a coin. Made out of some dark gray metal with etchings on it, some that cut through the coin's surface entirely and left neat gaps. Not federation currency, and not anything Rhea had seen changing hands elsewhere on their ride through the city. This had to be something to do with the Sxoriza—or at least, Lexos clearly thought so, if he was sending this to her.

The letter had told her to look for the coin. Well, she would. She was here, whether she'd wanted to be or not, and she would do the job she'd been given.

But she would do it come morning. Right now there was nothing she wanted more than to send the clockwork bird back out the window, lie down, and forget for a night that she had ever left home in the first place. But she supposed for the moment she owed Lexos a response.

She tore a small strip off the parchment Lexos had sent and dug a piece of charcoal out from her coat pocket before using it to scratch out a short reply: *Thank you for the information. Now kindly leave me to my task.*

After tying the message to the bird's leg and shooing it out the window, she went back to her coat and fished again in its pockets for the small tin of kymithi she'd packed for herself. Back when she'd first started her duties as Thyspira, Lexos or Chrysanthi would often sneak a few into her luggage whenever she left, just in case she found herself missing home. It had been a long time since they'd fallen out of that habit, but she was glad she'd thought to bring some for herself on this particular journey.

She climbed into bed and opened the tin. A dozen kymithi were nestled together, amber shells gleaming in the lantern light. Carefully, Rhea selected one, holding it up to get a good look. The surface was cracked and a bit sunken, and underneath she could see a flicker of the dining room table, with Baba smiling at the head. Nitsos's figure was there in the background, halfway to the door, a look of envy on his face so strong that Rhea could see it clearly despite the haze shrouding the scene. Lexos had to have made this one—only he would want to preserve such a moment. She set it back down very quickly, and chose another.

This time it was one of her own. Summer at Stratathoma, Chrysanthi in her wild garden, cupping water from the fountain in her paint-stained hands.

Perfect, Rhea thought and took a bite.

The blankets took a long time to warm all the way through, and there was a breeze still coming in through the shutters. But Rhea fell easily asleep and did not notice at all.

THIRTEEN

RHEA

When morning came the snow was still falling, and Rhea awoke to a weak shaft of sun draped over the bed. She'd had things more important than her surroundings to focus on the night before, but her eyes felt fresh and her head felt clear, and so she went to the window and peered out at her view of the lake and the city where it wrapped around onto the far shore.

It was only the beginning of winter—her palm pressed to Michali's, each with a mark fresh in blood, had started it nearly two weeks prior—and being this far north meant shorter days and snow that lingered on the ground for a few hours before it melted back into the air. As the season set in, the snow would start to collect in drifts that came up to her knees.

How was it possible that in all her years she had never seen the world like this? She'd made marriages as far afield as Chuzha, had traveled to Rhokera and Vuomorra and seen the richest and most beautiful things the world had to offer. But the Ksigora seemed its own world, cut off from what she knew by the mountains. This region hadn't mattered to Baba, and so it had never mattered to her.

Some of her nausea from the night before had disappeared, but she still felt uneasy when she thought about Evanthia and the close, inspecting way that she had watched her. Rhea supposed she was a rarity of sorts, which explained some of it. They didn't see her kind much around these parts, but then again, her kind was the same as theirs. Stratagiozis weren't anything different from other people. Longer-lived, certainly, but that was an effect of the gifts they were given, and hardly her fault.

There was a knock on her door. When she opened it one of the young women she recognized from the kitchen the night before was waiting outside, a bundle of clothing in her arms.

"Good morning, *kiria*," the girl said. "Your wedding breakfast is about to begin."

Well, they were wasting no time.

After so many weddings, Rhea had been part of just about every tradition on offer. She'd worn white, and black, and red, had exchanged promises with her consort at sunset, had locked hands with her consort as the sun reached its highest point on the first day of summer. Breakfast seemed easy enough.

She let the serving girl run her a bath, let her perfume and powder her hair. When her skin was pink with warmth and rubbed near raw, Rhea wrapped herself in the dress she'd been brought. She recognized it as one of her own—her things must have arrived in the night—and was more glad than she expected to see something of home. It was a long white gown made of heavy material that held its own shape. Around her chest it hugged her tightly before flaring out in bell-shaped sleeves that stopped at her elbows. The skirt was draped in wide pleats, which gave it a folded appearance, and the whole thing was covered in white embroidery, nonsense symbols and patterns that vanished into the texture of the skirt if you stood far enough away. It was a wise choice: fancy enough for the occasion (although, Rhea thought, it was only a breakfast) but thick enough to keep her warm.

With the dress settled, folds adjusted and creases straightened out, and her hair wound through with snowdrops, Rhea was ready, and the serving girl led her out of her room and down the hallway, back out to the main room of the house. She expected to see Michali and his family waiting for her, but the room was empty, only a few used dishes on the dining table to suggest that anybody had ever been there.

"It's outside," the serving girl explained.

"What is?"

"The breakfast."

"But it's snowing." The serving girl didn't seem to know how to answer to that, and Rhea sighed, rubbed at her exposed forearms to jolt some blood to life in them, and nodded. "Let's go outside, then."

She saw them as soon as she stepped through the doors. A table had been set up on a stone patio closer to the lakeshore, and it was decorated with wildflowers and ribbons in crimson and white. There was Evanthia, seated at the head, and that was presumably Yannis, Michali's father, at the foot, both of them dressed in mourning black. Of course—this wedding meant the eventual loss of their son.

But Rhea's eyes were drawn to the center of the table, where Michali was standing beside two empty chairs, his coat as white as her dress. He was watching her, the solemn expression on his face clear even from a distance.

Behind her, the serving girl cleared her throat. "You walk down by yourself," she whispered.

They'd given her a sturdy pair of boots, and Rhea was glad for them as she followed the snow-covered path down to the patio. Once she'd reached the edge, she said, "Good morning," as only seemed polite, but nobody responded. She fought the urge to sigh. If there were rules to this sort of thing—and it certainly seemed like there were—it would be helpful if somebody would tell her.

Michali was still standing, and looking rather pointedly at the empty chair next to him, so she gathered her skirts and made her way around the table. His hand landed gently at the small of her back as she took her place next to him, and urged her slightly forward, signaling that it was time to sit.

The food had already been served, all of it cold—fresh fruit and sweet cheeses, and a selection of meat. Wary of making some mistake, Rhea ate exactly as Michali did, serving herself what food he did and taking what bites he took.

They were both of them halfway through their meal when Michali reached across her for the glass carafe of water and surreptitiously tilted his head toward her.

"We're not supposed to speak until we're married," he whispered, "but you have some cheese in your hair."

Rhea sputtered out a surprised laugh, drawing sharp glares from the rest of the family. She didn't recognize the others at the table, but she assumed they were cousins or other distant relatives. As far as she knew, the Laskarises themselves were limited to Michali and his parents. And, technically, her, as soon as this ceremony was over.

When everyone had finished—and that couldn't happen too quickly for Rhea, given how uncomfortable it was to have a meal where the only audible sound was the woman across from her who couldn't seem to chew with her mouth shut—the servants hastened down from their posts near the house to whisk the plates away and refill water glasses here and there. Rhea was starting to feel a chill sneak through her dress, and her hair was damp with melting snow.

At last the table was clear, and Yannis rose slowly. Like the others at the table, he was paying no mind to the snowflakes collecting in the folds of his coat, in the empty water glasses at every place setting, in the lone glass of wine sitting in front of him that he now lifted.

"*Efkos efkala,*" he said. Rhea couldn't help it. Her mouth dropped open in surprise. That was Saint's Thyzaki, which had been outlawed since long before Baba's rule. Didn't Yannis care that a Stratagiozi's daughter was present?

"*Efkala,*" echoed the others, their voices hushed and somber, more fitting for a funeral than a wedding. Rhea was used to a hint of melancholy being present during these sorts of ceremonies—everybody knew what happened to her consorts—but no family had ever been quite so honest about it as this one.

"We are here," Yannis went on, "to bind our son to winter's daughter."

"*Efkala.*"

"May their marriage warm them as does the fire in the winter hearth."

"*Efkala.*"

"May they begin each day with hearts as pure as winter's new-fallen snow."

"*Efkala.*"

She should have been offended by the continued Saint's Thyzaki, but instead Rhea found herself blinking back the tears pricking at her eyes. Next to her, Michali's head was bowed. She'd never heard words like this, but to Michali they must have been familiar, must have meant something. She felt a sudden rush of pity; how it must hurt, to hear these words and know that they were not the beginning of something but rather the end.

Yannis sipped from the wineglass and passed it to his left, to a man who looked so like him that they must have been brothers. He, too, took a sip, and slowly the glass made its way around the table. When it reached Michali, he turned in his chair to face Rhea, and she was grateful for his light tug on her wrist, telling her to do the same.

Carefully, he held the glass up to her lips. She took a sip, and then, when he nodded to her meaningfully, took the glass from him and returned the gesture. Was that it? Were they married? She really didn't see any reason they had to do this outside.

The glass was passed on, and eventually made its way back to Yannis. He raised it, to the sound of another muttered "*efkala*" from the whole table, and then poured the remaining wine on the ground as everyone broke into applause.

"That was lovely," Rhea said to Michali, but he shook his head. They weren't finished.

Their hands clasped, he drew her to her feet, and the whole party followed as he led her down the slope of the island to the shore. Rhea felt dread curdle in her stomach as they grew nearer to the water.

Michali kept walking, closer and closer to the water until it was lapping at their boots. Rhea gasped as the cold hit her, and Michali's grip tightened on her hand, a pained noise slipping from his mouth.

Farther, and farther in, until her chest was swollen with breath and the water was at her waist. Gray waves licked at her as her skirts billowed, and under her feet the lake bed was solid, silt frozen stable. Rhea could hear her teeth chattering as her body began to numb.

Michali stopped walking, reached for her free hand with his. Gently, he placed her hands at his jaw, arranged them so she was cupping his face. She opened her mouth to ask what he was doing, but she had a terrible feeling she already knew. With determination showing in the clench of his jaw, he took a deep breath and, her palms still pressed to his cheeks, plunged under the surface.

Rhea let out a cry of surprise, but there was no time to do anything before he was surging up again, gulping at the air. They stood there for a moment, Michali fighting his breath back into his chest, his face bent close to hers.

She swept his sodden hair away from his face, and as he grinned down at her, Rhea found herself smiling in return, nearly giddy. The ridiculousness of it, the twin chill in their bones, and the snow still falling, catching in his eyelashes. He ran his fingers along her cheek, an almost apologetic look in his eyes, and then he was cupping her face and nodding. Because it was her turn, and she would have to do what he had done.

Quickly, that was the best way. She grasped Michali's wrists, closed her eyes, and dropped.

For a moment she couldn't move, could only feel the cold punch the air out of her in a rush. Her skirts felt so heavy, her hair floating every which way, and she would've forgotten what she was supposed to do if not for the insistent press of Michali's hands against her cheeks.

She found her feet and shoved up to the surface, breaking into the air with a heaving gasp. She couldn't feel her fingers, wasn't even sure that she was really still in her body, but there was Michali, smil-

ing so widely it must have hurt, and she laughed, the sound shatter-
ing the distance between them.

"If only you'd picked me during summer," he said.

"These are your traditions, not mine." But there was no edge to
her voice. "Can we get out now?"

They splashed to shore, Rhea's dress so heavy she thought she
might fall over. The mournful mood of the whole affair had dissipated, and even with Michali's eventual death looming over them,
the family was boisterous and cackling as they congratulated the
newlyweds and wrapped them up with blankets.

He wasn't what she'd expected, she thought as Michali laughed at
something his cousin was saying. There was more to him—more
humor, and a willingness to be surprised that she found vastly appealing despite his continued poor manners.

It was a shame he was a traitor, and doubly so that he was her
consort. She'd have liked to let him live a while longer.

FOURTEEN

ALEXANDROS

Stratathoma felt empty without Rhea in a way it did not usually, so Lexos was more than glad that he and Baba were due so soon at Agiokon. When the time for departure came, he and Baba climbed into their carriage, a sturdy trunk loaded onto the roof, and Lexos braced himself for three days in his father's company. They passed in an excruciating quiet, and by the time they arrived, Lexos was ready to commit all manner of crimes for just a moment to himself. Baba, even asleep, as he had been for the bulk of the trip, demanded every bit of his energy. Luckily, Lexos reminded himself as he stepped, muscles aching, from the carriage, he would have tonight in a room of his own at the Devetsi house.

Agiokon was nestled at the meeting point of three countries, but fell technically within the boundaries of Merkher. As such it belonged to Zita Devetsi, the Merkheri Stratagiozi, which frustrated Baba to no end. The monastery itself was a no-man's-land and housed the Stratagiozis just for the meeting—though it was the only sufficiently neutral territory available, it was too steeped in saint worship to be a place any Stratagiozi was comfortable remaining in for long.

Saint worship was still alive in Stratagiozi country, but only just. Gone were the churches and ceremonies, the name days celebrated every year. Instead, those who worshipped did so in the face of a number of laws forbidding that very thing. According to the earliest books of Stratagiozi history, those laws had been passed on the grounds of protecting the continent from the folly of mindless belief (and the smattering of war that sometimes came with it), but Lexos knew better, and he suspected that most everybody else did, too. The first Stratagiozi had been a saint himself, and had slaughtered his brethren to claim their power for his own—outlawing saint worship was just a means of keeping them dead in the minds of the people who'd loved them. So was the advent of Modern Thyzaki, which used a modified form of lettering and eschewed those words used in prayer.

Of course, none of that did much to deter the truly devout. Lexos's mother had been one of them, part of a small, secret group of worshippers back home. She'd never told Baba, who was known for his particular vehemence in enforcing the ban; Lexos was fairly certain that if he returned home today, those worshippers would have long since been found out and arrested. The Agiokon monks were, of course, exempt from such punishment and continued to welcome the Stratagiozi Council, even though the first Stratagiozi had been the one to murder the saints in the first place. A reluctant kindness, given so that they might continue their worship in peace.

The Devetsi house loomed ahead of Lexos as he waited for Baba to disembark. Inside it somewhere was Stavra, the only Devetsi child. Lexos liked Stavra, as much as he could like anyone whose company left him feeling out of breath.

"Well, don't dawdle," Baba said as his boots hit the cobbled court-yard. "It's cold out. Let's get inside."

It would have been right to wait for Stavra and her mother, Zita, to come and welcome them, but Baba had never had much patience for that sort of thing. And by now, Zita and Stavra were quite used to Baba barging in without being formally welcomed.

The house was well inside the city, but even with the cacophony and filth of everyday life swirling around it, it could hardly be mistaken for anything ordinary. The paint on its smooth, plastered walls was a vivid yellow, unaffected by long years of sun, and the windows were covered in intricate metal grates that glittered even in the dark. Lexos paused at the door—thick, the wood inlaid with precious stones and carved delicately—and hoped that Baba would at least let him knock, but it was no use. Baba shouldered his way past Lexos and pushed at the elaborate gold lion head at the center of the door, opening a smaller entrance cut into it. Unlocked. Clearly Zita and Stavra were expecting them.

"Hello," Baba called, taking off the riding gloves he'd worn during all three days of sitting in the carriage. His voice echoed up into the atrium. Lexos stared at the highest balcony, at the very top of the staircase. That was where Stavra usually appeared, her dark complexion lit by the sun coming through the glass ceiling.

Today was no different. A noise, a scurry of footsteps, and there she was, coiled hair twisted away from her face. "Shut the door," she said, and then she grinned and waved.

Stavra spoke excellent Thyzaki, but in her family's house, her family's country, they spoke Merkheri, her family's language. Lexos had been instructed in Merkheri as a child, at his mother's behest, and over the years he'd nearly reached fluency—it was only occasionally that he said something in an archaic, overly formal construction that left Stavra smirking.

"I trust you're well, Stavra?" Lexos said as she came thumping down the stairs. At last she arrived on the ground floor and clasped Lexos's left hand, her own black mark pressing against his as she ignored Baba, who in turn was very studiously ignoring her.

"I am always well," she replied, grin still lingering. She glanced over her shoulder at Baba, who seemed to be seconds away from clearing his throat impatiently. "My mother will be down in a moment, if you don't mind waiting. I'll take Alexandros and get him settled."

"Yes, thank you," Baba said, frowning, and before he could add anything else Stavra was off, darting through one of the arches ringing the atrium and beckoning for Lexos to follow.

"He's so charming, your father," she said once he caught up to her. She took a hard right turn, and he had to trot to keep up.

"Where are we going?"

"The stables. We're riding tomorrow and I am tired of grooming your horse for you."

Lexos rolled his eyes, but kept quiet. While she seemed as cheerful as she ever did, Stavra also seemed to be in a fighting mood, and he knew from experience that when he fought with Stavra, he did not win.

She was in one of her suits today, cut simply in plain fabrics. At the council meetings she wore gowns like the ones Rhea had stocked in her wardrobe, but outside of the monastery Lexos most often saw her in clothes like these.

The hallway took them past a number of rooms, richly furnished and bursting with color, and out a side door of the house into a dusty back courtyard. Stavra led him across it and into the stables, and nodded in the direction of a stall that needed cleaning.

"You can start with that."

"You said grooming the horses, not cleaning up after them."

"Can you blame me for not passing up an opportunity to see you standing in shit?"

Lexos shucked off his jacket and began to roll up his shirtsleeves. "Oh, Stavra, this hurts me. I thought we were friends."

"We are," she said idly, picking at her fingernails. "Is this not how friendship works?"

"Unless you're in the shit with me, no, I don't think so."

Stavra laughed. She'd always found him funnier than she had any right to. Surprise, she'd explained once, at hearing anything light-hearted come out of that dour face of his.

"So," he said, grabbing a shovel from the far wall of the stall, "tell me. How is Agiokon treating you?"

Unlike Lexos, Stavra went out into the world most days, saw real people, paid real money for real things. She watched lines deepen on people's faces, watched them disappear, watched their children take their places in shop fronts and market stalls. It had surprised Lexos how quickly he'd forgotten age, how easily he'd left it behind. Stavra, though, saw it every day. She made sure of it.

It was, after all, her job. To comb through the pages of portrait miniatures that her mother had compiled, and to every evening add something new. Brighten the flush of the cheeks for a young girl, add a set of wrinkles to the forehead for an old man.

"Agiokon is fine," Stavra said, and when Lexos looked up from his task, surprised at the brittleness of her voice, she was avoiding his gaze, her eyes trained on the shovel in his hands.

"Stavra?" But still she wouldn't look at him. Instead, she stepped out of sight, into the stall next door where a tall stallion was beginning to stomp impatiently. He propped the shovel against the wall and followed after her, knocking his boots once against the wall to get the horseshit off.

She was speaking softly to the stallion, working a comb through its mane, unease pulling her mouth into a tight line. It was one of his favorite things about her, Lexos decided: That despite all her years in her position, Stratagiozi manipulation had never become a habit for her.

"What's happened?" he asked, and watched as her shoulder twitched, as though she were trying to shrug him off.

"Nothing. Just—your house is out of order," she said. "And we are feeling the effects."

He frowned. "I think you'd better explain."

"Grain shortages," Stavra said, a flicker of frustration crossing her face. "Low demand and high prices. My people cannot afford to pay what yours are asking, and yours cannot afford to give it for less."

Lexos had heard of this, the poor harvest in central Thyzakos and the lack of respite given by the stewards' high taxes. But that wasn't Baba's fault. And Rhea had done her best to make the season sweet. "It sounds as though your issue is not with us," he began, but Stavra turned to face him, her anger uncharacteristically obvious in the curl of her lip.

"No? Who else, then, if not your father? I go to the markets, Lexos. I see, and what I see cannot be the worst of it. Your people are suffering, and suffering spreads."

"Suffering?" Certainly Baba would never describe it that way. Certainly Stavra had to be exaggerating.

"Yes," she said. "And I am not the first one to take notice."

That sounded pointed. "Oh?" he asked. "You've heard something, I take it?"

She only waved him off. "It may have reached my ears, but it wasn't meant for yours."

He held back a sigh. Stavra and her rules. Zita had held her own seat far longer than Baba had held his, and so the Merkheri tradition ran strong, inextricable from the tradition of the Devetsi family such that nobody could quite imagine one without the other. The oath Stavra had taken as her mother's second was far more stringent than Lexos's, which could be whittled down to one tenet only: Do not make Baba angry.

"Come on," he said, ducking down to catch her eyes. "Break your rules just this once."

"It is hardly ever just once." But she leaned in, looking resigned. "Your Rhokeri problem," she said, in Thyzaki this time.

"What about it?" There was no reason to be nervous, surely. They'd been planning to tell the others about it anyway. What did it matter if Stavra had already found out?

"Your steward there has been busy lately." She lowered her voice. "He wrote to my mother this morning, inviting her to stay."

Lexos's stomach turned over uneasily. "What for?"

Stavra didn't respond, and only looked at him, her gaze steady as ever. Of course, the answer was clear. The Speros family was reaching abroad, looking to forge connections that might help them oust

Baba. Looking to undermine Baba's alliances and claim them for their own.

"Is there nothing else you can tell me?" Lexos asked. "Anything at all?" The more he knew, the better use he might make of tomorrow's meeting. "Did Zita say yes? At the very least you owe me that."

"She hasn't yet. But I don't imagine we're the only ones your steward wrote to." She looked away, and when she spoke next it was in Merkheri, a clear signal to Lexos that the conversation was over. "Now, come on. Don't think I haven't noticed your attempt to avoid cleaning that stall."

They spoke no more about it, but it was all Lexos thought about during the evening that followed, as he embroidered the sky up on a deck built into the roof of the Devetsi house, and later as he returned to his well-appointed room and its wide bed. It should have been a relief to be in such comfort, considering how long he'd spent trapped in the carriage with Baba, but he could only lie awake and recite the names of every other council member in his head, and wonder which of them would be the first to abandon Baba for the Speros steward.

At last, he shut his eyes, and when Lexos fell asleep it was with thoughts of his sisters, one enjoying Stratathoma without Baba, the other shivering in the north, and of his brother, toiling away in his attic workshop, working for something he would never get.

FIFTEEN

ALEXANDROS

The next morning, the bell rang before the sun was even up. It was a hard ride to the monastery, the narrow, splintering path full of twists and turns as it wound up the cliffside, and they would need to make an early start to arrive by noon.

With sunlight leaking over the horizon, Lexos waited in the courtyard for the others. Baba was first, brushing off the sleeves of his blue jacket, which was studded with a number of gold medallions (meaningless, as he had no troops to command in battle).

Soon Zita followed, a silver circlet woven into her tight coils, her matching dress gleaming like armor against her brown skin. Stavra trailed behind in a gown the color of the evening sky, as if it had been made of the fabric Lexos carried in his own trunk and stitched with thread every night.

They rode out through the city, houses and market stalls silent as if to honor the dignitaries passing by. Ahead of him, Stavra had wrapped herself in a cloak, its hood drawn up to obscure her face, and in front of her was her mother's retinue of servants, their eyes averted as they guided Zita's horse-carried litter through the streets.

Next to Lexos, Baba was tense, his eyes fixed on the point in the sky where, when the fog cleared, the monastery would become visible. Time to ask a favor, he'd said that night after dinner back at Stratathoma. He'd never explained exactly what he meant, and Lexos wished he'd been brave enough to ask.

There was sun in the air when they reached the base of the path. Zita abandoned her litter for a single horse, and by the time they were taking the last of the hairpin turns, the sky was a full blue. This high up, Lexos could see the valley spread out below, the river cutting through it all, its waters now lilac, now silver, now blinding white. And there, jutting out into the sky, was a spire of rock, atop which sat the monastery, with its weathered tiles and stone. From far away, he supposed it looked something like Stratathoma, both houses committed to a precariousness that Lexos had no real love for, but where Stratathoma was massive, its walls thicker than a man was tall, the monastery was small and irregular. Its structure dipped and swerved in odd ways, all to accommodate the cliff it sat on.

Lexos called it a cliff, but that implied that it was attached to something, that it was the edge of some larger mountain. In fact, the tower was just that: a tower of rock, spearing so high into the sky that when you stood at the foot of it, its top was obscured in a corona of sun.

They were approaching the end of the path, and would soon leave the horses behind, crossing to the monastery using the system of baskets and pulleys. Ahead, Lexos could see Stavra shifting in her saddle, adjusting her skirts. Strange, how Stratagiozi customs differed from country to country. He rode ahead of his father, to draw any danger away from Baba, but Stavra rode behind her mother in a show of deference. They even called the Stratagiozi something else in Merkheri—Ordukamat, or at least that was what he'd heard on the rare occasion Zita made mention of her title. Unlike Baba, she wore hers lightly.

Ahead, Zita called the party to a halt. Lexos's horse pulled at the bit and pranced to one side. Lexos had been holding the reins tight the whole way up, careful to keep from crowding Stavra, and it was a relief to pass the reins off to a groom and dismount. He tried to stretch discreetly, aware of his father watching.

When it was at last his turn, Lexos stepped into the basket, its walls reaching a foot or two above his head, and resolved firmly not to look at the knot that attached the basket to the pulley, or at the pulley itself, which ran along a long, thick rope connecting the mountainside to the monastery. Instead, he focused on the rope that ran parallel to the one above, cutting through two identical windows on either side of the basket. The grooms would slowly ease the basket off the cliff, so that it hung in midair, and Lexos would use the lower rope to pull himself along until he got within reach of the monks' long, hooked poles. He wasn't the only one who got nervous when it came to this; Stavra had confided to him once, when she'd been deep into her wineglass, that she still nearly vomited when she thought about it.

First came the scrape, the jerk of the basket being inched toward the edge, and then the voice of one of the grooms, counting loudly in Merkheri. And on three, the lurch and the drop, and Lexos felt almost as if his chest were collapsing in on itself, the core of him suddenly so hollow that he could barely stand. The basket bobbed up and down, pulley squealing under the stress, and Lexos squeezed his eyes shut. If it held now, it would hold until he got out.

And of course, hold it did, as it did every time, and he tugged himself across the sky, one hand over another, eyes fixed on the clasps of his boots. He only looked up when he heard the welcoming cries of the monks waiting on the landing veranda. He felt a slight hitch as they hooked their poles onto the leather loops attached to the basket, and relaxed his grip on the rope, letting them do most of the work of bringing him in.

When he got his feet on solid ground once more—although, he thought, how solid could he really call the top of a naturally formed stone tower?—Stavra, Zita, and his father were all waiting, Stavra with a pained look on her face that suggested she had not fared very well in making small talk with the two Stratagiozis.

"Finally," Baba grumbled, before turning on his heel and stalking off into the depths of the monastery, where their rooms would be waiting.

During the first days of Stratagiozi rule, every meeting had been followed by an afternoon meal, but perhaps two hundred years ago a Prevdjenni Stratagiozi had made a declaration of war that he later wrote off as being the product of unsatiated hunger, and since then it had been Stratagiozi law that every meeting was to be preceded by lunch. It was already served when Lexos arrived in the monastery's plain, sparse dining room. Brickwork arched to create a ceiling with several vaults, and two low wooden tables ran the length of the hall, separated by a row of stone columns. Lexos was used to these plain sorts of trappings—they were, after all, not so different from how he lived at home—but he always delighted in watching men like Ammar, the Amolovak Stratagiozi, attempt to hide their disgust at being forced to use wooden tableware.

He took his seat across from Baba at the near end of one of the tables. Farther along the same table, Ammar was arguing over something with his second, Ohra, a woman with gray hair at her temples. Ammar wasn't the longest serving Stratagiozi, but he was close, and his particular matagios, which made the bearer responsible for shaping the sea, had only changed hands, so to speak, a reported three times before him. There had, however, been enough overlap—that was the word Lexos preferred to use—between Ammar's line and some former Thyzak Stratagiozi that the tides in particular ended up falling under Thyzak power, a loss that neither Baba nor Lexos were at fault for but for which Ammar clearly blamed them.

"*Elado,*" Baba commanded, drawing Lexos's attention back. Baba was waiting, of course, for Lexos to serve. There were two large dishes in front of them, and each table setting had its own smaller bowl. In the first was a dish of cold green beans smothered in a kind of tomato sauce. It was Thyzak food, something Baba took great pride in. The monks did their best to keep the whole affair as neutral as possible, but some things were politicized no matter what.

The second dish held a row of cabbage rolls, the steamed leaves wrapped around a mixture of spiced rice and meat. Merkheri, technically, but Lexos had been eating them all his life. He spooned some of the beans into Baba's bowl, topping them with a carefully balanced bit of stuffed cabbage, and did the same to his own dish, doing his best to keep the food from touching.

"I spoke to Zita last night," Baba said under his breath. Lexos hadn't seen him at all the night before, and had presumed him to be shut away in his rooms, complaining to no one about something or other. "I wanted to feel her out before the meeting."

"And?" Had she told him about the letter from the Rhokeri steward? Would Lexos be exposing Stavra if he brought it up now?

"She gave me her word she would back me," Baba said. Lexos relaxed slightly. No need to mention it for the moment, not if Zita was theirs. "And I take her word to be worth quite a lot."

"That's excellent." It really was, but it left the question of the other Stratagiozis. Ammar hadn't looked twice at them since they'd come into the dining hall, but that wasn't unusual. Lexos couldn't take it as a sure sign that the Speros family had written to him.

"It is not enough," Baba said sharply. "Merkher is central in the federation, yes, but if we are to hold firm against a direct challenge, we need more."

There was only one family he could mean. "The Dominas."

The Dominas were in charge of Trefazio, the federation's oldest and wealthiest country. They were the most ancient Stratagiozi family, so respected by the rest of the council that they used Trefza in all official proceedings as a show of deference. In fact, the Dominas were descended from Luco Domina, the last of the saints and the first of the Stratagiozis. He'd been the one to kill his fellow saints and unite their territory under one rule—Lexos supposed that if Luco's descendants ever had a mind to it, they were within their rights to reassemble the pieces. Tarro Domina was the head of his family at the moment, and had been for so long that nobody, even the monks, could quite remember who had come before.

"Tarro isn't here yet," Baba went on. "When he arrives, I will need your help in finding us some time alone together."

Expressly forbidden, but Baba had no care for that.

"Do we know, is Isotta still his second?" Tarro's second was always changing as his children died at an alarmingly rapid rate. As far as Lexos understood, in Trefazio it had been accepted by Tarro's children that they would never take his seat, and that the highest they could hope to rise to was being his second. Apparently the atmosphere in Vuomorra, Trefazio's capital, was fairly cutthroat as a result. Indeed, Lexos met a new face nearly every time he came to Agiokon, and found himself wondering if Tarro might one day run out of children, and just what lengths he was going to in order to avoid such a situation.

"I'm afraid we won't be seeing Isotta again," Baba said, and they shared a grim smile. "It'll be someone new this time. A son, I think, but I forget the boy's name."

The other two Stratagiozis—Milad, from Prevdjen, followed closely by Nastia, from Chuzha—had arrived and everybody's meal had long since been finished when Tarro finally presented himself. Tarro had taken his seat young, and had been ruling for so long that nobody could quite remember a time when he hadn't, but with the slow, almost invisible way the Stratagiozi aged, his hair was only just beginning to gray. He was dressed in his house's colors, in a sage-green coat that was stitched through with shimmering gold thread. His trousers were a crisp black wool, and with them he wore a billowing white shirt, its buttons embossed with the Domina house crest. It was an outfit fine not in its extravagance but in its quality, and Lexos knew that Baba respected Tarro all the more for it.

"Friends," Tarro said, his voice booming down the long hall. "I see we're all here?"

As always, Lexos was grateful for the education he'd had as a child, for the Trefza he'd retained over the years and all that he'd learned since becoming Baba's second. Baba hadn't had such opportunities, something he liked to remind Lexos about, and so there were occasionally moments during meetings or meals where Lexos found himself leaning in to discreetly whisper a translation in Baba's ear. Like so many things, it was something they never spoke of.

Baba was first to his feet, stepping around the table to clasp hands with Tarro in greeting. Next to each other, they were a study in contrasts. Baba's shoulders were narrow and sloping, Tarro's, broad and well-built; Baba's face solemn and unfathomable, and Tarro's open and smiling. Tarro had the luxury of being open, Lexos supposed. Nobody could take his power from him—what point was there in protecting it?

"Good to see you, Vasilis," Tarro said. "How's your family? Well, I hope."

"Indeed," Baba replied. "My family is quite well. And yours?"

Tarro let out a booming laugh. "Dropping like flies, I'm afraid." He reached out behind him and drew forward the man who'd been hovering just behind him. Well, not a man, really; this was a boy, Lexos thought, looking him over. Blushing cheeks; fair, wispy hair; and teeth so small they had to still be his milk teeth. "This is Gino, my new second."

"I'm sorry," Baba said. "Isotta will be missed."

"By someone, perhaps, but I am not sure who." Tarro looked over Baba's shoulder, and Lexos stood up straighter as their eyes met. "Alexandros, my goodness. Have you grown taller?"

"I have not, sir."

"New shoes, then? Alexandros, I wonder, will you look after Gino for me today? He's a little nervous," Tarro said, clapping Gino on the back firmly. Lexos was surprised when Gino did not simply disintegrate into dust. "It might be easier to just kill him now and have done with it—I do hate training a new second—but I suppose we must let due process run its course."

Gino was growing paler by the second, but Lexos was familiar with this way of Tarro's. After so many years, his children were to him like the blink of an eye.

"I'd be honored to look after him, sir." This was exactly what Baba had wanted, and Gino would be wildly easy to lead astray.

"Excellent." Tarro let go of Gino. "Shall we?"

The rest of the group stood up, benches scraping on the stone floor, but there was a pause, the silence deeply awkward until it was broken by a delicate throat clearing. Lexos hid a smile. Stavra.

"Ah, yes," Tarro said. "Pardon me. I must eat before we begin." He stepped past Baba and Lexos and bent to examine the food left in the serving dishes. "Nothing Trefzan, I see."

"Maybe next time, sir," Lexos said.

"Very well." He snatched a green bean out of the serving dish, pinched between two fingers, and took a bite off one end before tossing the other into Lexos's empty bowl. "That will do. Come along, everyone."

They followed Tarro and the increasingly wan-looking Gino out of the dining room and down a long corridor that ran up the center of the monastery like a spine. When they reached the end, a veranda stretching out into the open valley air before them, Tarro took a sharp right and together all six Stratagiozis and their seconds descended a steep staircase to the lower level. This was where their rooms were, in the narrow chambers branching off the corridor, but Tarro led them onward, back down toward the double doors at the hallway's end.

As they reached them, a monk stepped out from each side and held the doors open, allowing them into the room. It was a round, windowless room, set into the tower of stone so that the back wall was a single, roughly hewn piece. It was empty of tables or chairs—another product of more volatile times, when one Stratagiozi had murdered another with a broken-off chair leg—and the wooden plank floor sloped down slightly toward the middle, where a small hole acted as a drain for any blood that might be spilled. Of course, the meetings never came to that anymore, but Lexos still carried with him his dagger stamped with the Argyros crest. Just to be safe, that was what Baba had said when he'd given Lexos the dagger. But as the years went on and peace continued, Lexos thought it was rather that Baba wanted the opportunity to be the first to strike.

Tarro and Gino led the way inside, choosing to stand on the opposite side of the room, and once they were settled the rest filed in. Baba and Lexos took a spot near the door, as Baba always preferred to be near the exit, and Lexos watched as the others passed. Ammar and Ohra, their severe, uniform-like suits in matching dark colors. Nastia and her son Olek, Nastia's jacket and trousers plated with metal stripes. Milad and his daughter Maryam, neither looking like they were in the least bit happy to be there, and finally, Zita and Stavra, who wore matching smiles.

"Let's get started," Tarro said as the doors slammed shut behind Stavra. "I think we would be remiss to begin without addressing the delayed nature of this meeting." He looked at Baba, his stare level and grave. "And the cause for that delay."

Lexos had expected that Tarro would mention it, but he had not expected to feel quite so responsible. It was Rhea, after all, who had failed to bring in the season on the regular schedule. But what was Rhea's was his, both good and bad.

"For that I must apologize," Baba said. It was clear to Lexos that Baba was holding back an explanation; they both knew there was nothing for it but to apologize and accept responsibility, which Baba would make sure to once again pass on to Rhea as soon as he next saw her. "I know a great many things depend on the regularity of the seasons. Thyzakos will not fail you again."

Thyzakos, Lexos thought, and not Baba himself. It was splitting hairs, to be sure, but it was a difference that would matter to Baba.

"That is all very well, then," Tarro said, "and let us speak no more about it." Of course, speaking no more about it could not keep the other Stratagiozis from thinking more about it, which they certainly would.

Tarro turned to Gino, who as his second was supposed to keep an agenda for the meeting, compiled from notes on the one before. Isotta, Gino's predecessor, had always kept it inscribed neatly on a scroll in perfectly readable Trefza. Gino, it seemed, had not followed her example.

Hurriedly, he fished out a scrap of parchment, its edges ragged, and then after a moment snatched it back from Tarro and exchanged it for a different one. The whole while Tarro simply stood with that impassively genial look on his face, his hand patiently extended. Tarro rarely saw sense in truly getting angry, which at the moment, given the mention of Rhea's mistakes and what Baba was planning to ask for at the close of the meeting, Lexos was particularly grateful for.

"Ah," Tarro said as Gino nodded, confirming it was the right list, "it seems the first item to discuss is the renewal of the northwestern trade agreement."

This particular agreement did not involve Thyzakos—it concerned the export of grain from the fields that covered the eastern half of Chuzha into Prevdjen and Trefazio to the south—and so Lexos allowed himself to drift slightly. When the agreement had first been raised some decades ago, he and Baba had discussed ways in which they might manipulate it in Thyzakos's favor, but they'd realized that disrupting Chuzha's supply to Prevdjen and Trefazio would only place more pressure on Thyzakos as an alternative supplier. While Thyzakos produced its own grain, it was not nearly enough to compete with Chuzha's sheer size, nor enough to meet needs both domestic and foreign. The farmers were restless enough already. Lexos could only imagine how tangled things would have become had they meddled with the agreement.

Tarro finished his negotiation with Nastia and Milad soon enough—negotiation was probably a generous term for it, given that Chuzha and Prevdjen were at the moment both dependent on a series of loans from Trefazio's well-stocked banks—and discussion turned to the Vitmar, the second item on the agenda.

The Vitmar crisis (though nobody in the meeting would ever refer to it as a crisis) had been going on for even longer than Lexos had been Baba's second. The Vitmar was a piece of territory that ran along Chuzha's eastern border, where it bumped up against Amolova. The harder Ammar cracked down on his people in Amolova, the more refugees began to flood into the Vitmar, which lived under Nastia's rule. According to Ammar, that population made the region rightly his, and he and Nastia had been fighting over the Vitmar ownership, explicitly and implicitly, for nearly two hundred years.

There was little progress to be made—Ammar had yet to temper his request, or to even suggest joint ownership of the territory, which Nastia would never agree to, and Nastia was holding her ground. But every meeting, they brought up the Vitmar, and every meeting, Lexos had to listen as Nastia and Ammar made speeches and pleas to the other Stratagiozis.

At least Lexos could respect Nastia's arguments. Ammar, meanwhile, was still pretending to be motivated only by the wishes and welfare of his people. Maybe those things did matter to him—who was Lexos to say?—but if refugees were his true concern, Ammar would've been eyeing the Ksigora for annexation as well, given how many Amolovaks seemed to be finding their way over the border. Ammar had yet to show any inclination, though, and Lexos couldn't be too upset about that.

The meeting slowly drew to a close, thankfully before Gino collapsed in on himself, as he looked dangerously near to doing, and Tarro cast a glance about the room, allowing the customary moment for any last-minute additions before officially ending the meeting.

This was what Baba had been waiting for. Lexos watched nervously as Baba cleared his throat, the sound drawing every eye.

"I have some news," Baba said. "And not all good, I'm afraid."

"Oh dear," Tarro said dryly. "What have you got on your hands, Vasilis?"

"Let me be clear," Baba started, "that everything is under control."

That, Lexos thought, was not a particularly inspiring beginning.

Baba took a breath. Lexos noticed the slight shift in his weight from one foot to the other. "You may have heard the news regarding my daughter's most recent choice of consort." He was speaking slowly, and to the others Lexos knew it would sound as though he was choosing his words carefully, but Lexos knew better; Baba was nervous.

"It has led to some slight unrest among my stewards," Baba went on, "particularly in Rhokera, and while I am confident I have it well in hand, I would be remiss if I did not address you now about the possible ramifications of any further conflict. Our livelihoods are intertwined, yours and mine." He cleared his throat again. Lexos braced himself. Baba had described the situation as carefully as he could. Now for the most important part. "Should open war break out in Thyzakos, one can only assume it will not be long until it spreads past our borders. That's why I'm asking you today to pledge your countries' forces to the cause."

The quiet was stifling. Lexos could feel sweat beading on his brow as he scanned the room, taking in every raised eyebrow, every slight frown. Zita hardly looked surprised—after all, Baba had already spoken to her the previous night—but what about the others? What about Tarro? These other Stratagiozis generally gave Baba the respect his position warranted, but Lexos knew that was because of the power he held—the deaths he handed out every day—and not because it was he who held it. They had no loyalty to him. Surely Baba knew that, and had considered that in his plans.

"You know we have no forces to call our own," Tarro said, a smile catching on one corner of his mouth, and Baba nodded a bit too quickly.

"But your influence cannot be overstated." If Tarro asked his stewards to go to war, they would do it in a heartbeat.

Tarro's smile widened. "That is true."

"I am only asking that you consider lending your support," Baba said, breaking his gaze from Tarro to entreat Nastia, Milad, and Ammar, who scoffed.

"It's ridiculous," Ammar said. "We are supposed to pay for your weakness?"

Of course Ammar would respond that way. He had the most at stake; he actually did have forces to call his own, something they were all pretending not to be aware of.

"It is unlikely," Baba responded coldly, "that I will need your help, but should I ask, it's in your best interests to provide. If I fall, who might be next?"

Baba looked to Zita, clearly hoping she would step in, tell the others that her support had already been pledged, but Zita looked back calmly and very decidedly did not say anything.

Tarro cleared his throat. "I have seen a great many people in your seat, Vasilis, while keeping my own, but thank you for bringing this to our attention. We will, I'm sure, give it our consideration."

There was color rising in Baba's cheeks, fury simmering in his clenched jaw, but he swallowed hard and said, "Thank you," sending a cool wash of relief through Lexos's veins.

"Is that all the business for today, then?" Tarro asked. "Anybody have any other pleas for aid?"

Baba opened his mouth, and Lexos could imagine it—the veiled (or worse, not so veiled) insult, the poorly checked anger. He tugged discreetly on his father's belt loop and did something seconds never did: spoke.

"No," he said, aware of every head turning to look at him. "Thank you all for coming. We appreciate you taking the time, and of course look forward to helping you and your people in any way that we can."

The contrast between his Trefza and Baba's was shameful, but that was the least of what anybody would care about. Lexos could see Stavra's eyes just about bulging out of her head.

"Wonderful," Tarro said. "Why don't we adjourn?"

The doors opened promptly, and most of the Stratagiozis streamed out, heading for their rooms, or perhaps to the upper levels to take in the views. As he passed, Tarro nodded to Lexos.

"Your Trefza, Alexandros. It's quite good."

Lexos was caught off guard, and so he forgot to hide his smile as he said, "Thank you, sir."

Baba was watching. From the look on his face when Lexos turned back to him, he was not pleased.

"I'm sorry," Lexos said to Baba in Thyzaki as soon as Tarro was gone. "I shouldn't have spoken out of turn, I know, but—"

"I thought," Baba replied, "that it was only your sister who behaved so carelessly. But I should have known. Twins in everything, it seems."

It was for your own good, Lexos wanted to say. But he found he could barely open his mouth. "Do you still want to speak to Tarro alone?" he managed.

"What good would that do me now?"

Baba stormed out, perhaps intending to ride for home at this very moment. Lexos hastened after him. Didn't Baba understand that Lexos had just saved them both?

Baba was rounding the corner at the end of the hallway, and Lexos could hear him pounding up the steps to the main level. He made to follow, but a hand on his arm brought him up short. Stavra, her eyes blazing, already in the midst of a sentence so peppered with what he thought must be Merkheri profanity that he could barely understand it.

"What?"

"How," she said slowly, enunciating clearly so as to convey that she thought he was an idiot, "could you let your father make such a fool of you both?"

"Let him?" As if he had any control over anything Baba did. "I had nothing to do with it."

"He's your father. Your family, your country. You cannot distance yourself from it."

"I've had enough scolding for one day, thank you," Lexos said, and he tried to step away, but Stavra snatched at his jacket and held firm.

"I am trying to help you, Alexandros. I gave you intelligence. I broke Merkheri law."

"I didn't ask you to." He sounded like a child, he knew, but didn't he have enough expectations placed on him? He had no need for Stavra's, too. "I didn't ask for your help."

"Unfortunately, you have it. And you obviously need it, given that you seem to think the best way to handle the situation is to break protocol and speak during a—"

"What do you care?" He yanked free. "What's your stake in any of this, Stavra? If Thyzakos falls it's only more land for the taking."

"I would never think like that," Stavra said, shoving him back. "You go too far."

She was right, he knew, and the thing to do was apologize, but Lexos had asked for forgiveness too often already, and he stayed silent as Stavra gave him one last disgusted sneer before leaving him behind, alone in a dark hallway that seemed darker by the second.

SIXTEEN

ALEXANDROS

Chrysanthi was waiting at the door when Lexos and Baba arrived at Stratathoma from Agiokon. If Baba had a favorite child, it could be reasonably said that it was she, but he passed her as though she weren't there and disappeared into the dark of the house.

"Oh," Chrysanthi said to Lexos, who remained in the courtyard. "All right."

Lexos wished he could cheer her, but the trip from Agiokon had required every bit of good manners he possessed. All he had left was a small, strained smile. "Thank you for welcoming us."

"Has he been like that—"

"Yes." It had been worse when they'd left Agiokon. This, compared to that first day in the carriage, was nothing. "Might we go inside now, do you think?"

Chrysanthi turned and flounced into the main hall, the skirts of her long blue gown trailing behind her. It was, Lexos thought, very like something Rhea might wear to entertain her suitors. In fact, when Rhea was away from Stratathoma, Chrysanthi tended to dress in her clothes. Lexos couldn't understand it. Did she not realize that the safest thing to be in Baba's company was anything but his two eldest children?

He supposed it would have been more polite of him to follow Chrysanthi, to ask about how she'd spent her time while they'd been away, but all Lexos wanted was a moment to himself, perhaps in the bracing sea breeze. He made for the staircase that led to his room, abandoning the luggage to the servants and Chrysanthi to her own devices.

But his room was not empty, as it should have been. Instead, inside was Nitsos, sitting on Lexos's bed by the window and looking very much like he had no intention of leaving any time soon. He was barefoot, dressed in his nightclothes, and some of his hair was standing straight up, which made him look so young that for a moment Lexos could have sworn they were back in their country house, Nitsos still small and scared of sleeping alone. He'd been only a few years old when they'd left that place to come here, Chrysanthi even younger. Lexos knew that of the four siblings, only he and Rhea really remembered their lives as they had been. Before Stratathoma. Before their mother passed.

Did Rhea think of her much? She never said, and whatever stories she told of their childhood, Lexos recognized as ones he'd told her first. Perhaps she missed Mama too much to dwell on it. After all, it gave Lexos no pleasure to think of those days, of his sister clinging to his back as he urged the horse forward, away, away, away. Of the guards herding them home. Of the pyre that never burned for their mother. Why had they never mourned her properly?

"Well?" Nitsos said, and Lexos blinked. "Do you have plans to do anything other than stand in the doorway?"

Lexos cleared his throat and came farther in, shedding his jacket. "I can do what I like in my room, thank you."

Nitsos had already turned away from Lexos. "I suppose," he said, drifting and absent. Spread in front of him on Lexos's bed were various bits of machinery, glinting silver in the midmorning light that came in through Lexos's always-open window.

"What's all that?" Lexos asked. Some parts seemed assembled in a way that looked familiar.

"Your scout." Nitsos frowned down at two tiny gears, which he was attempting to slide into place on a rod so thin it disappeared in the sun. "Something's not working as it should."

The white bird, which Lexos had sent to carry word to Rhea, had returned, and now lay in pieces. Lexos swallowed a rush of indignation that it should be disassembled without his permission. Nitsos had built it; Lexos supposed he was therefore allowed to take it apart.

"Thank you for fixing it," he said. He knew, after Agiokon particularly, how it felt to be given no gratitude for one's work. "Will it fly again, do you think?"

Nitsos scoffed. "Of course it will. I may be good for nothing else, but I am quite able to fix my pet projects."

That gave Lexos pause. It was no secret what Baba thought of Nitsos's particular gift. He'd given it to his younger son to keep him occupied and out of the way, and it was true that in essence it required very little work. All Nitsos had to do was keep the creatures that lived on the grounds at Stratathoma running. They'd been built by previous children of previous Stratagiozis, hundreds of years ago. Nitsos was little more than a caretaker, as far as Baba was concerned.

But Nitsos had made more of it. Lexos knew that, even if he didn't quite understand how. And to hear his brother refer to his own work the way Baba did—well, it left Lexos unsettled.

"*Kouklos,*" he said, ignoring the way Nitsos grimaced at the childish endearment. "Are you quite all right?"

Nitsos slotted two larger pieces together, the bird's wing taking shape. "Why should I be anything otherwise?"

There was little sense pushing. Lexos had never had the way with his siblings that Rhea seemed to, and even she was often left bewildered when it came to their brother. "I don't know. Never mind." He nodded to the bird. "Did that come with any response from Rhea?"

"Is that where it went? The Ksigora?"

"It is. A response, Nitsos?"

Nitsos shook his head. "Nothing I saw."

Lexos allowed himself to worry for a moment before taking a long breath. What was there for Rhea to say in answer anyway? He'd sent her the image of the coin and told her what to look for. He'd given her everything he could. It was on her shoulders now.

"So this went to the Ksigora, and you went to Agiokon." Nitsos had looked up from the bird and was watching him closely. "How was *your* trip?"

"Mine?" That was startling. It had been a number of years—maybe even a decade—since Nitsos had last asked him anything like that. When they'd been younger, back before Baba's distaste for Nitsos had become entirely clear to all of them, Nitsos had tried often to become more involved, begging to be allowed to manage some aspect of the business Lexos handled for Baba. But all that had stopped, and Nitsos had turned away, sinking into his work with the creatures around the grounds. It had been a trial to even get him to build the number of mechanical scouts he had.

That said, the memory of Nitsos at dinner before Rhea's departure lingered in Lexos's mind. How he had refused to leave, insisting, at least for a moment, that a place at the table was his. Maybe Nitsos was changing. Maybe he was returning to the fold, in a sense. Lexos would welcome him back, if that was true.

"Agiokon was . . . tolerable," he said. "The meetings are never my favorite, but the city is beautiful, at least."

"You're lucky," Nitsos replied fervently. "I've seen paintings, but never—" His voice cracked. Lexos looked away, flushing with embarrassment for him. "Is the monastery really that high up?"

"Higher," Lexos said. "We'll go one day." Nitsos said nothing, but his eyes were hungry and wide. "In fact, maybe Baba will let you come next time. You can go out into the city while we're stuck in our meeting, and I'll be very jealous."

He expected some kind of reply. Perhaps not the show of enthusiasm Chrysanthi might give in a similar situation, but at least a smile. Maybe even a thank-you to Lexos for thinking of him. Instead, Nitsos's expression seemed almost to fall for an instant, before he looked down at the bird wing in his hands, and said, "Right. Well, I won't keep you."

Lexos stared blankly for a moment. There seemed no point in arguing that Nitsos could hardly dismiss him from his own room. No, this was probably the best ending anyone could hope for from a conversation with Nitsos. "I'll see you later, then," he said. "Try not to get any grease on my bedsheets."

He left Nitsos there to finish fixing the scout and retreated to the high tower, where a servant had left the bowl of tides perched on its pedestal and the drape of the sky folded neatly in the cupboard. Lexos wasn't sure how it was that anyone else managed to handle it. Whenever he touched it, it seemed too fluid to ever sit on a shelf.

This could have been the entirety of his life. The tides and the stars, and nothing else. No worry over whether Baba would embarrass them at the next council meeting. No scouts sent to Rhokera to watch for coming war. But he was the eldest child, and so it all fell to him. Baba, the family. The future. All in his hands.

Lexos stretched out on the stone floor, sea air soft against his brow. He quite thought he deserved a rest.

SEVENTEEN

RHEA

Michali didn't ask her to share his bed on their wedding night, or on the next, or on the one after. In fact, more than a week after their wedding, Rhea was both relieved and somewhat miffed that he seemed content to cross paths with her occasionally during the day and then, once dinner had finished, disappear.

Even without Michali's company, she was rarely left alone— Evanthia was her constant companion—and so she'd barely had a chance to do any of the spying Lexos wanted. Michali, she knew, was her best possible source. As the season continued and his death approached, so her chance of wringing any information out of him dwindled, but it was difficult to work a person who wasn't there.

That was why, at the moment, she was sitting in the main room of the house, adjusting the cuffs of her trousers as she waited for her boots to warm before she put them on and crossed the lake to the city. Michali was at the building his father kept in the busiest district, where he conducted all of his business as the region's steward, and she was meant to meet Michali so that he could take her to a shop that, according to him, sold the best eel in all of Ksigori. Rhea was, to say the least, not looking forward to trying the eel, but time alone with Michali would give her a chance to poke and prod at him a bit, and she'd be able to explore the city, look for signs of the base in Ksigori that Lexos was sure the separatists had. After all, while she still couldn't think of her choosing without enduring a wave of confusion and guilt, she was here, wasn't she? She had better make the most of it.

The trip across the lake was uneventful. Rhea was sure to keep her eyes on the horizon, hoping desperately she wouldn't accidentally catch a glimpse of one of these famous eels. Back on solid ground, she began picking her way along the crowded promenade, its cobblestones packed with sellers offering goods nobody seemed to have the money to buy. She had wondered if perhaps the Ksigora's isolation would have kept its residents from recognizing her as Thyspira, and it seemed that it had, or that without Michali by her side to mark her as somebody important, neither Rhea nor Thyspira mattered very much to anyone at all.

It wasn't long before she arrived at the spot where she was supposed to meet Michali, across the promenade from the building that housed Yannis's study. Even late in the day, the entrance was busy with people. Something about the sight of them, so earnest, so genuinely hopeful that someone inside might be able to help them, kept her from going in. Instead she wandered to the railing and looked out toward the island she'd left. There were good people everywhere, she knew. She met them in the house of every consort, even married them sometimes. Why was the sight of them now affecting her so much?

She was just hungry. That was all. She'd barely eaten all day, and now that she was paying it any mind, her stomach burbled so loudly that she was quite sure anyone within a few yards of her could hear.

Most of the food stalls were concentrated farther down the promenade, nearer, Rhea supposed, to the dreaded eel shop, but there was

one cart set up nearby from which drifted the smell of sugared chestnuts. She picked her way toward it, skirting a trio of young men who
seemed to be competing to see which of them could spit the farthest.

Aside from a pan of chestnuts keeping warm over hot coals, the
cart was also selling glasses of something that smelled deeply alco-
holic. Rhea ordered a serving of each from the young woman shivering behind the cart. As the young woman piled chestnuts into a paper
wrapping, she nodded to the glasses lined up, waiting to be filled, and
said, "Help yourself."

Rhea poured herself a glass from the pitcher. It was mulled wine,
rich and ruby and lingering as she took a sip, a brief flare of heat
bursting through her veins. But it was gone too soon. Even with the
chestnuts to look forward to, the cold felt inescapable.

"I don't know how you all live like this," she said. "I can barely
feel my fingers."

The young woman raised her eyebrows, glancing at Rhea's thick
coat with a frank judgment that made Rhea flush.

"You've got money, I think," the young woman said, "so you
might try one of these." She reached under the cart and pulled out a
jar full of amber spheres. "They're the best for the chill."

If she said anything next, Rhea didn't hear. She bent down in front
of the jar, reached out with a shaking finger to tap the glass. Those
were kymithi. The food that her mother had taught her to make out
of stories and sugar, the food that her mother had said belonged only
to the Argyros family. Here, in Ksigori, miles and miles away.

"What are they?" she asked. Maybe she was mistaken. Maybe it
was only wishing that made them look like a piece of home.

But the young woman said, "Kymithi," and opened the jar, fished
one out, and held it up in the weak sunlight. "They've got heat in
them. Should warm you right up."

They couldn't be the same as the ones she'd brought with her
from Stratathoma. Surely they wouldn't have that same feeling, of
being wrapped in somewhere else, of tasting words on your tongue.
"I'll take one," Rhea said. "How much?"

The number given to her was not something Rhea could attach

much value to but from the look on the woman's face she supposed it must have been high indeed. "Here," she said, dropping the counted coins into the young woman's hand.

The kymitha, when it was placed in her own outstretched palm, felt different. Denser, heavier. There, Rhea thought. Not the same at all.

"Thank you," she said, unable to keep a sliver of snide satisfaction from finding its way into her voice, and took a bite.

It was like standing in front of a fire. No, not in front, Rhea thought, gasping as the heat worked through her bones. Like standing inside one. Like feeling it burn every inch of your skin without ever reaching the point of pain. She could see it, the bonfire this kymitha had been spun out of, the story that had been crystallized and captured inside.

"That should last you another hour," the young woman said. "Price goes up if you want another."

"No, thank you," Rhea said, and she was embarrassed by the hoarseness of her voice, the dryness of her mouth. Kymithi were barely half as strong as that the way she made them. Perhaps her mother had forgotten to teach them some crucial step in the process. Or perhaps it was that Rhea had never felt anything as vividly as whoever had made this kymitha had. Not heat, and not cold, and not anything else, either. "That will do perfectly well."

The young woman grinned. "Nobody makes them the way we do."

And that was the question, really—how they knew to make them at all. Rhea's mother had said it was an art only their family knew. A lie, clearly, but Rhea couldn't understand why it had been told.

Had her mother learned here before she married Baba? Had her mother been from the Ksigora?

"I heard they only had these in Stratathoma," she said carefully.

The young woman's face crumpled into a frown, and she shook her head quickly. "I don't know where you've been," she said, "but you heard wrong. Ksigorans have been making these for longer than those *mathaki* Stratagiozis have been here."

Rhea recoiled. She'd never heard anybody curse so strongly, least of all about her. It was one thing to know that there were separatists in the north, to know that some of them probably hated her family more than anything in the world. It was another entirely to hear that hate in person.

She wanted to leave. To get back on the boat and hide herself in her room for the rest of the season. But she knew what Lexos would do if he were here. She could practically feel his grip on her shoulders, nudging her forward.

"You must not be pleased," she said, glazing over her voice with sympathy, "with your lord's son marrying that girl, then."

"Oh," the young woman said, her eyebrows raised, "Thyspira? I am anything but. Do they really imagine it to be a fair trade? A life—a life such as that boy's—in exchange for what?"

A generous season, Rhea thought immediately. That was how her promise went during her choosing. But that did seem awfully abstract. It had in Patrassa, with her last consort, the poor boy so in love with her he couldn't see straight, and it did now that she was confronted with the practicality of living here in the Ksigora. "Is he so beloved?" she asked. Rhea knew she was clearly not from the area, and decided to give up any pretense of being local. "Michali Laskaris?"

"He's not like his father," the young woman said. "He actually seems to still have life in his body. Though not for much longer if Thyspira has any say in the matter."

"Have you ever seen her?" Of course she hadn't, or she would've recognized Rhea by now, but it was what someone else would ask. "Now that she lives here."

The young woman shook her head. "I don't think she's left that house. I'm not surprised. I wouldn't expect her sort to mingle with ours. Maybe we'll get lucky and she'll deign to throw us some of that Stratagiozi wealth come Meroximo."

Rhea thought of Stratathoma, of the bare stone walls and the sparely laid table. What wealth? she wanted to ask. How do you think we live? But then, she supposed that was Baba's choice, and there were no such choices here.

"Let's hope," she said wryly, and backed away, leaving her glass of mulled wine on the counter, still half-full.

There were plenty more sights to be seen along the promenade; Rhea's taste for them, though, had soured. Of course she'd always known how different life must be outside Stratathoma, but being inside it came with such a particular set of difficulties that in truth she'd never given it all that much thought. It felt bad, she thought absently, leaning against the railing and looking out over the lake. Bad, but better than feeling worse. Which wasn't a particularly nice thing at all.

"There you are," she heard from behind her, and she turned to see Michali jogging across the promenade toward her. He looked tired, and his hair was out of sorts, as though he'd run his hands through it a number of times.

"Here I am." She smiled as prettily as she knew how. Michali was a mark, a target, and most of those warmed to the same things. "How was your day?"

He shrugged, and they began walking into the city, toward the dreaded eel shop. "Well enough."

That wouldn't do at all. "You seem tired. Do you not enjoy your father's work?"

"It is not a question of enjoyment," he said crossly, before sighing and letting some of the tension leave his shoulders. "We are responsible for these people. I only wish my baba would let me take more part."

He sounded like Nitsos, Rhea thought. Which wasn't promising, as she'd never been able to reach Nitsos the way she had her other siblings. "I am sure he is only waiting for the right time," she said, aiming for gentle reassurance.

"He had better hurry," Michali said darkly. "I am your consort, after all."

Rhea grimaced and kept silent as they passed through a particularly crowded stretch of the promenade. She had better hurry, too, if she meant to make good on Lexos's plan before the season required Michali's death. Perhaps one of Thyspira's sly flirtations would draw him out, would encourage him to trust her. But then he hadn't particularly liked her much at Stratathoma, when she'd been wearing Thyspira most completely.

"What precisely does your father do?" she said instead.

"Oh, you know," he said. "Settling disputes, managing the treasury, tabulating the harvest. The sort of governance you expect from a leader." His voice had grown tight, and now Rhea watched him pretend as though it hadn't and paste a smile onto his face.

"Is it really so bad?" she asked. This was not the sort of information Lexos had asked her to gather. No, it was something she wanted for herself.

Michali looked askance at her. "To be without one's freedom? To be at the mercy of those who care nothing for you? I should think so."

"A strange thing to hear coming out of the mouth of a steward's son." She reached over and plucked at the sleeve of his finely woven coat, ignoring the odd little choking noise he made. "You seem to benefit quite a lot from this thing you hate so much."

"I know," he said, and when she looked up his jaw was clenched so tightly she could see the twitch of his muscles. "Believe me, I am well aware."

If, even after the river crossing, she'd needed confirmation that Michali was with the Sxoriza, she had it now.

The eel shop, Michali told her as they kept walking, was practically at the other end of the promenade, set back from the water by a square in which fishermen gutted their catch. But rather than take the promenade there, which was starting to become clotted with people waiting to watch the approaching sunset over the lake, he suggested instead that they cut through the city.

The buildings they passed were softened by the snow, and wreaths hung on every door, made from the last of the living leaves. Alleyways opened up into inner courtyards, off of which branched a handful of houses. Everything here was small, much smaller than Stratathoma and nothing compared to the great open streets of Rhokera. Rhea expected its overall smallness to make her feel closed in, trapped, but as they wound their way into the city, instead it felt easier to breathe somehow. The sky open wide above her, the breeze whipping through the streets in great gusts. She stopped walking for a moment, turned her face up to what sun there was left, caught a whiff of spice, felt the cool graze of snow against her lips.

Michali cleared his throat, watching her with raised eyebrows.

"What?" she asked.

"Nothing."

"No," she said, "out with it."

"I'm only surprised you still find pleasure in things after a hundred years in this world."

"I believe it's impolite to discuss a lady's age."

"I wouldn't think age in any sense applies to you." He tilted his head. "You look no older than twenty."

Rhea frowned. "I'm not sure how old I look. That is not the sort of thing a Stratagiozi finds important."

They were nearing what functioned as the main square of the city, which Rhea had only seen a glimpse of during their initial arrival. Michali escorted her to the side of the street, joining a number of other people standing aside to let a carriage pass, and then they were walking again, Michali matching his pace to Rhea's despite his longer legs.

"I suppose you are quite disgusted," she said mildly, "being married to a woman your grandmother's age."

"Disgusted, certainly, and envious of the advantages your long life has afforded you." He slowed, considering her. "Although you are an odd sort. For everywhere you must have been and everything you must have seen, you still remind me a great deal of a child."

"Yes," Rhea replied flatly, "much of my charm is wrapped up in my helplessness and naivety."

Michali let out a loud bark of laughter, startling Rhea so that she choked briefly on her own spit. "I'm not sure I would have chosen those words to describe you."

"Oh?" It wasn't what she had expected, and nothing she'd heard before from the mouths of her brother and father. She went on without thinking. "I am, after all, the woman who passed up a winter in Rhokera to spend the season here with you."

It was rude, but more than that, it was reckless to invite further scrutiny of her choice, which she knew had been a surprise to Michali. But he just shook his head and gave her a confiding smile.

"I am sure," he said, "you had your reasons. And I did make a wonderful impression on the veranda that night."

"That is true. I will have to break a glass of yours to pay you back in kind."

"Have at it," he said, "but I think you will not find my mother as forgiving as you were. We do not have so many fine things here as you do at Stratathoma."

"I don't exactly consider Stratathoma to be the height of luxury, actually," Rhea said, unable to keep herself from sounding a bit snide. "You must never have been to Vuomorra if that's what you think wealth looks like."

"I don't need to cross an ocean to know there are things a Stratagiozi can afford that other people cannot."

Lexos, Rhea knew, would have held his tongue. He would've let Michali win, and filed all this away for later, for another conversation. But she was not as practiced in this sort of thing, and besides, Lexos had not seen what she had. For all his talk he had never set foot this far north.

"Was my house really so terrible?" she said. "I think you are the first of my consorts to have been so offended by their time there."

Michali did not answer right away, and when he did, it was with his eyes fixed on the cobbled street ahead of them. "Perhaps the first to tell you so," he said, "but I very much doubt I am the first." She had no idea how to respond, and it seemed her silence prodded him to continue. "Your consorts are just another season to you," he said, shaking his head. "Yet to them you are the final and highest point of their lives."

"You say 'them,'" Rhea pointed out, "as if you were not one of their number."

Michali blinked and for a moment the composure was gone from his face, baring a grim sort of sorrow underneath. "You are quite right," he said. "Forgive a man for not facing his death with as much grace as you seem to be able to muster. In this as in so many other things, you must remember we are not equals."

They kept walking, but Rhea could not forget his words. Her other consorts had never been so forthright as to mention that most fundamental difference between them—in short, that they would die, and she would not.

At last, the street opened up onto the square, and Rhea stayed close to Michali to avoid getting swept up into the crowd that nearly filled it. It was bounded on all sides by buildings a level or two taller than the houses she had become familiar with. Most of them held shop fronts at the bottom, with a handful turned so they were facing an adjacent street. Market stalls were lined up in rows in the center of the square, some of them in the process of being folded up and carted out for the evening. Elsewhere, some of the kafenios that served kaf and hot meals were spilling out across the flagstone, their tables occupied by clusters of young people who seemed to have no care for the bracing cold.

"Aside from the fish market," Michali said, his head bent close so he might be heard over the din of the crowd, "this is the center of Ksigori, and of the Ksigora."

On the opposite side of the square, there was a gap in the line of the buildings, a spot where it looked like something else should have stood. She made her way toward it, keeping her head down and slotting herself between knots of people. The air was heavy with the smell of cooked meat and roasted vegetables, and Rhea found that her mouth was watering. Anything here would be much preferable to the impending eel.

Was this where Lexos had observed that coin changing hands? If only she were alone, with none of these people watching, putting the name of Thyspira together with her face as Michali accompanied her. She would have to try to come back sometime to look around further without him, and hope that on her own her anonymity remained intact.

The stones began to look different under her feet, the texture rougher than the smooth flagstones that made up the rest of the square, and as she got closer to the other side of the square, she realized why. This had been the site of the church of the Ksigora.

Like most every other Thyzak church, it had been torn down, and only a small portion of its ruins near the back had not been cleared away. There were no memorials or plaques, either, to commemorate what had once been the heart of the city. But something had been done after the church had been torn down. The stones used to pave over the old foundation were lighter, exposed to fewer years of sun and storm. Rhea had a feeling that if the people in the square vanished, she would easily be able to trace the outline of the building.

"How long ago?" she asked Michali, who was standing a pace behind her, as if to give her a moment alone with the church. "When did it come down?"

The correct answer would have been, "Nearly a thousand years ago." The Thyzak churches had been destroyed under the reign of the first Stratagiozi, and their continued existence was technically outlawed.

But Michali said something else. "A hundred years back. When your father took his seat."

His anger was obvious in the stiffness of his posture. Michali hadn't been alive then, but the destruction of the Ksigoran church was personal to him, as it probably was for every person up in the mountain camps.

It would make sense, she thought, for the church to be at the heart of the separatist movement. The demolished church, a symbol of so-called Stratagiozi oppression, a reminder of what they thought of as a freer age. Rhea thought that if they would just give the situation a hard look they would realize how similar what they idealized was to what they were rebelling against.

Could this be the city base Lexos had mentioned? There was clearly nothing left aboveground; there appeared to be a few crumbling piles of stone just at the edge of the square, but those were barely up to her hips, and they couldn't house anything bigger than a bag or two of supplies.

She turned, hoping to ask Michali a veiled sort of question that might help her discover more. Instead, she found herself face-to-face with a young man.

"Thyspira?" he asked, and she nodded, too startled to think better of it. He had narrow shoulders, a sweep of dark hair, and a small, nastily curled mouth that had started saying something in Saint's Thyzaki that Rhea could not quite understand.

"Excuse me," she said, "I'm not sure I—"

"It should be you," he interrupted, leaning in close. "Laskaris is the one dying, but *mathakos ala*, it should be you."

No, the Saint's Thyzaki she had not understood, but she understood very well when he cleared his throat and spat in her face.

The uproar was immediate. Rhea heard it, heard the lift of voices, saw Michali yank the young man back from her by his jacket and knock him to his knees. But it seemed far away, blurred as if by a great fog, and the only thing she knew for certain was the cold spread of thick saliva on her cheek.

She reached up to wipe it away and found that her fingers were numb. Trembling, too. How silly.

"Are you all right?"

Rhea jumped, feeling rushing back into her body. The world around her, so muffled and distant a moment before, now seemed too bright. Too loud. She squinted up at Michali, whose hands were pressed to her shoulders, her hair, her forehead, as he tried to make sure she hadn't been hurt.

She nodded. Her neck felt loose, as though her head were about to topple off it. "He barely touched me."

Michali bent down to catch her eyes with his. She blinked against the sun. "You're sure?"

"Yes," she said. "I'm fine."

He'd hated her. That young man, the purity of his disgust—she'd been entirely unprepared for it. Michali's feelings were clear enough, and she'd only just spoken to the woman at the market, but still, she had never expected anything like this.

"We should go back to the house," Michali said. She was surprised, really, that he'd shown so much care. Perhaps he assumed that any harm that came to her would come to him tenfold from Baba. Rhea nearly laughed.

"No," she said. "I'm quite all right. And I'm eager to see these eels."

"That, I think, is something nobody has ever said before," Michali replied, raising an eyebrow, "but I suppose I can't deny you. Come on. We're nearly there."

EIGHTEEN

RHEA

Michali left her mercifully alone for most of the evening once they returned to the Laskaris house, and Rhea spent it in her room, peering out of her window and feeling quite like a fool. She had known, of course, how little attention Baba paid to this part of the country. It could give him little in the way of either leverage or wealth, so as far as he was concerned, he owed it little in return. Rhea had understood this way of thinking, even shared it sometimes. But she'd seen its true impact now. How could she not have expected this? Of course, neglect like Baba's would breed exactly this sort of discord. She knew that only too well.

There had to be a better way. Not just to rule, and to provide, but to maintain one's power. Baba didn't realize what a threat he was fostering here. The Sxoriza were dangerous, yes, but it was not just the fighters in the mountains who hated Baba. It was everyone. The whole of the north, eager to see Vasilis Argyros lose his seat.

She had to do something. Michali, the Sxoriza—she wasn't sure it was enough to get rid of them, the way Lexos wanted. But what else was there? What would it take to keep her family safe?

Whatever it was, she needed more information. And in that much, Lexos was right—she needed Michali.

Dinner was served late in the evening, and included the eel she'd purchased (of which she ate practically nothing). When they'd finished with the meal, Michali stood from the table and, determinedly avoiding eye contact with his mother or father, offered Rhea his hand. His meaning was clear, as evidenced by the blush that suddenly appeared on Yannis's cheeks and the approving nod from Evanthia.

It was bound to happen sometime, Rhea thought and took his hand.

He dropped it as soon as they were out of sight of his parents, and Rhea felt a swoop in her stomach—relief or disappointment, she wasn't sure. They were silent as they continued down the hallway, passing her bedroom, and another, and another, entering a large parlor much like the one at the front of the house only to cut through it to a door at the opposite side.

It seemed the house had been built to hold a great deal more people than currently lived inside it. Everywhere she saw the remnants of what must have once been a sprawling, thriving family: a nursery, a second kitchen, and an open-air atrium with a firepit.

At last they came to a well-lit portion of the house, the floors padded with rugs, the torches burning brightly in their sconces. Michali opened a narrow door and gestured inside.

"This is it."

It was, Rhea decided as she entered, nice. No, more than nice. It looked comfortable. There was a fire burning in the hearth, and settled in front of it were two armchairs, both worn and cracking with age. The bed—and she did have to acknowledge it eventually—was similar to the kind she'd left behind at home, only instead of a thin cushion on a window seat, it was a slightly thicker cushion on a raised platform. Michali had covered over the scratchy wool of the cushion with woven blankets and a fur lay piled at the foot of the bed, for the deeper cold. The stone walls had a blue flush to them, as if somebody long ago had attempted to paint them and then changed their mind, but they were only visible in bits, covered as they were by a collection of paintings and old maps.

"What's all this?" Rhea asked, crossing to get a better look at them.

"I guess you might call them relics." He paused, tilting his head. "Have you never seen anything of their sort?"

She shook her head. They were renderings of the Ksigoran countryside in varying degrees of skill, some so well done she could imagine herself there, and some so poor she couldn't make out whether the subject was land or sea. Here and there, sketches of the city itself were tacked to the wall, the bustling cheer depicted familiar. And in each one, a church, the one whose ruins she'd visited earlier in the day, its spire rising high above the other buildings.

"Quite the collection," she said, tracing one with her fingers.

When she turned, he was watching her with a closeness that made her wonder if this was some sort of test. "I imagine you must find them terribly offensive."

Well, she wouldn't take the bait. "Not offensive," she answered. "Interesting. You know my father's stance against saint worship to be quite aggressive, but for all that we never heard much about it."

Michali raised his eyebrows. "Really? Nothing about bands of heretics in the north?"

"If anybody cares about that, it's Lexos," she said, the words slipping out before she'd thought them through. A mistake, to let Michali know how distracted her father was when it came to the Ksigora. "Anyway," she went on quickly, hoping that Michali wouldn't realize what she'd given away, "you must remember that just as you did not choose your father, I did not choose mine." She looked back at the sketches. "Did the saints have fathers? Did their titles pass through the blood?"

"You don't know?" He came up next to her and pointed to a sketch of a small chapel. "They say the saints roamed the countryside until they found a place that called to them. Someplace holy."

Rhea had never heard that word before. It hardly sounded like it belonged to Modern Thyzaki. But then, she supposed, it didn't.

"And they wrested the power from the earth, and never died until they met the edge of the first Stratagiozi's blade."

She tilted her head. "One person ruling over the land, holding its people in thrall. Your saints sound familiar."

"My saints," Michali said hotly, "did not take their power with blood."

"Who was that first Stratagiozi, then? Luco Domina killed his kind, and he was a saint," she said, jabbing her finger into Michali's chest. "By rights, as power has passed from his family to mine, so am I."

"Oh, and what a saint you make. What worship we owe you, Aya Thyspira, for gifts we never needed given to us before."

"I don't—"

"Do you think the seasons never changed on their own?" He leaned in, his eyes narrowed, and Rhea felt a flicker of fear. "Do you think we've always paid for them with the lives of our children?"

"No," she said, fighting to keep her voice steady. She couldn't let him know he was affecting her at all. "But it was the saints who first stripped those powers from the earth. It's the saints with whom you have your fight."

"Well," Michali said, "according to you, saint, Stratagiozi—what difference is there?" He sighed, rubbed wearily at his eyes. "I have had enough for the night, if you don't mind."

Rhea was left with her mouth hanging open as Michali ambled toward the bed, one hand working at the muscles in his opposite shoulder. Was that it? Was their fight over? She was an Argyros, and in her family fights buried themselves in your bones for days afterward, but Michali seemed entirely unbothered as he bent to fish a nightgown out of a basket at the foot of the bed. He tossed it to her and she caught it, fully expecting that at any moment he would call her to join him, his expectations clearly written on his face.

Instead he only grabbed another nightshirt from the basket and said, "I'd leave your stockings on if I were you. It's colder in this part of the house."

He was toeing off his boots and pulling his shirt up over his head before she realized what was about to happen and looked quickly away, her eyes squinted shut. The nightshirt in her hands was too big, clearly one of Michali's, but the thought of going back out into the dark hallway to find her own things wasn't very appealing. She snuck a glance over her shoulder—Michali's form was obscured by his own nightshirt as he slid it on—and bent down to undo her own boots.

Michali, now changed, went about the room and tidied up his discarded clothes, and Rhea took advantage of his turned back to throw on her nightshirt, hurrying out of her clothes a bit awkwardly underneath. With him still across the room, fussing with the fold of his jacket, she marched to the empty side of the bed and threw back the blankets. And watched as Michali continued to struggle, the hang of the fabric bulky and twisted.

"The sleeve," she said. Though her younger siblings were very much grown, she had never quite lost that impulse to take a problem out of their hands and unknot it for them. "It's still inside out."

"I know," Michali said stiffly, but this was clearly news to him, and she watched as he sheepishly reached in and pulled the sleeve back. "See?" He draped the flattened coat across the bottom of the bed, carefully tucking one end under the mattress. "My feet get cold," he explained when he saw her raised eyebrows.

"You could get another blanket."

"This does fine."

She frowned. "They're right there. In that basket just a few inches from where you're standing."

"And my coat," he said, straightening, "is even closer."

"Yes, but—"

"Coats keep you warm. It's keeping me warm."

She could imagine Nitsos saying much the same thing, could imagine him clinging so tightly to the notion of practicality that he didn't notice as it turned into something ridiculous instead. Well, if Michali was even the slightest bit like Nitsos, she would have no luck changing his mind.

"At least empty the pockets," she said. "Or every time you move you'll make noise."

"Oh." Michali looked genuinely surprised—she remembered suddenly that this was his first and only marriage—and hurried to gather a handful of change from the breast pocket of the coat. Small coins, for the most part, federation currency, and a few things that he presumably thought were coins but would discover, come morning, were spare buttons for his coat. And something else, too. Dark gray, with bold markings she could only just make out in what light was left.

A coin just like the one Lexos's scout had seen. Thank goodness for his letter. She wasn't sure she would have recognized it as anything out of place if not for that.

But she still didn't know what it was for. Just that there was indeed some use for it, just as there was something waiting for her in the middle of the city. She would simply have to find out what.

"Good night," she said and curled up on her side.

In the amber dark of her closed eyes she heard him move about the room, blowing out the last of the candles. When he joined her in bed, he was far enough away that all she felt was the dip of the mattress. No body heat, no graze of skin against skin.

Small gifts, Rhea thought, and waited for Michali to fall asleep.

RHEA

I t took until well past midnight. Hours of lying there next to Michali, the both of them painfully awake as the moon rose higher and higher, until at last a long, ragged snore broke the quiet, and Rhea knew he was asleep.

She wasn't sure exactly what she meant to do with the coin, and with the knowledge that Michali had it. Only that something did in fact have to be done.

She rose quickly, quiet on her stockinged feet as she slid back into her clothes. She'd kept mostly to her traveling suits since arriving in Ksigori, and she was glad of it now. She could only imagine the noise she'd make trying to do up the back of one of her dresses by herself.

Michali didn't stir as she crept around the bed to his low nightstand. Carefully, she ran her fingers across the top of it, catching against the base of a candle and the prick of a knife blade before finding the shape and curve of the coins. It was easy to find the one she was looking for, its weight unfamiliar in her palm, and then she was out of the door and heading down the cold, empty hallway, low-burning torches throwing strange shadows through the dark.

The main room, when she reached it, was empty save for the fire burning in the hearth as it did all winter. Someone was probably awake somewhere. A servant, perhaps, although Rhea had yet to see any of them, or Evanthia. But they weren't there to stop her from pushing open the main doors, bracing against the gust of icy wind, and stepping out into the night.

The guards at the dock—and there were guards, because it did not do in Thyzak country to leave your door unwatched—were so startled by her arrival that one of them nearly pitched headfirst into the lake, and they hesitated when she told them what she wanted. But she was still their master's consort, and a Stratagiozi's daughter besides, so they untied the rowboat from its moorings and helped her in, the boat dipping as the wind picked up.

"I'll be back before morning," she said once she'd sat down, doing her best to sound as dignified as she could while rocking gently back and forth. "If your steward's son asks where I have got to, you may tell him I'm taking a walk." She swallowed. "In the boat."

She had never rowed a boat before, which became abundantly clear as she struggled her way across the waves, but she made it to the promenade still mostly dry save the sweat freezing at her brow. After tying a knot she hoped would keep the boat moored, she set off down the web of streets, making for the center of the city, and the space left there by the church. She could hear Lexos in her head, telling her it wouldn't be there, telling her the separatist movement had nothing to do with worship, with the saints, but he hadn't heard Michali. He hadn't seen the space the Ksigorans still made for the echo of what was gone.

The streets were empty this time of night, save for a few staggering groups of young men who stank of alcohol and something else Rhea preferred not to think about. She kept her hood drawn up as she walked, taking care to shield her face. Most people probably wouldn't recognize her—alone in the city earlier, she'd barely drawn a second glance—but her excursion with Michali had certainly attracted attention, and she would have to be more careful from now on if she wanted to go unnoticed.

The coin felt heavy in her pocket as she kept going, footsteps echoing off the cobblestones. Past one shop and another, past an alleyway that housed a trio of scraggly stray dogs, until at last she neared the outline of the church, set into the flagstone, brushed free of snow as though somebody had come by not long ago with a broom. With the square practically empty, Rhea could see it clearly, could take in how massive the building had been. She could only imagine what a blow it had been to Ksigori to lose it.

Well. She was here. Now what?

She'd supposed the church might be a meeting place of sorts, and that when she arrived she'd see someone immediately conspicuous to whom she could show the coin she'd taken from Michali. It had seemed like a token, after all, when she'd seen it passed from hand to hand in that image Lexos had provided. A badge, perhaps. But of course there was nobody here. Just the square, and the drunks, and her.

Rhea started across the church outline. On the opposite side of the square there was a crumbling wall, the only church stones left in the city. Most of the wall was still in ruins, but bits of it had been wrestled into order. And any sign of order was a sign of something else.

She traced a path down the stretch of the wall, peering closely at the warren of broken stone, trying to make out any hidden figure or sign. There was no way that the Sxoriza would gather in Ksigori and not build their movement around what was left of the church.

She'd nearly reached the end of the wall when it opened up into a small archway, the fine relief carvings in the lintel still showing. Lines still deep, still deliberate, forming letters she recognized but could not read. Well, read or not, Rhea knew a door when she saw one.

She ducked through, expecting to find herself in some tiny, cob-webbed alcove, but instead stepped into what would have very nearly been a complete room if not for the missing ceiling. The stonework was well put together, and some of it looked fresh, as though some-body had been tending to it and making repairs. But it was empty.

Rhea turned slowly, examining the walls for another archway, maybe one hidden by the snow that had begun to fall. From the square came a shout and a burst of laughter—men, it sounded like, leaving the tavern at the corner—and a ripple of torchlight spilled through the archway, spreading across the back wall.

There. A small slot in the stone. At first it looked like nothing more than a natural gap, but as Rhea stepped closer, she saw there was something inside. A mechanism of sorts.

She pulled the coin from her pocket and held it up against the slot. It wasn't exact, wasn't perfect, but it fit. A lock, and the coin was the key.

It slid home, and she felt the click as its ridges and dips caught on the right gears. There was just room to grasp it between her fingertips, and after a few tries she managed to turn it. Once, and then again, and again, and the gears began to shift, the mechanism spinning until she heard the thunk of a dead bolt sliding back. She felt a draft gust against her cheek as a tiny gap opened in the wall.

She was right. The Sxoriza were here.

But she knew too well what disappointment looked like on the faces of the Argyros men. This wasn't enough proof for Lexos. He would want more. He would want as much information as possible.

Carefully, listening for any sound from the other side of the wall, Rhea wedged her shoulder against the stone and shoved. A section of the wall shuddered and slid back just barely, opening a gap less than the width of Rhea's little finger. Still. She was close.

At last she got what proved to be a door open, and stepped through. On the other side, there was another almost-room, this one in worse condition than the one she'd just left. In the middle of the floor, a section of the ground had been brushed fairly clean, revealing a warped wooden trapdoor, its handle coated with rust. The snow fell constantly enough these days that Rhea could be sure someone had been here recently to clear it, but there were no footprints left, and enough of a dusting covered the trapdoor that it had to have been left alone for at least a few hours. Enough time, she decided, that she could go down there herself.

She heaved the trapdoor up, revealing a poorly lit stone staircase that was, at least, free of cobwebs. At the bottom it opened into what looked like a long hallway, with enough light at the far end to spill into view. No sound, just the drift of stale air, wonderfully warm against Rhea's flushed cheeks.

Carefully, she set one foot on the first step, and when that didn't crumble under her weight, continued down, lowering the trapdoor shut behind her. A torch was in the slow process of burning out in a sconce at the bottom of the staircase, and its light showed her a pale stone floor coated in straw, and walls of the same lifeless color, their surfaces worn smooth from time, stained in patches from the steady drip of water from above.

She made her way along the passage, eyes fixed on the low opening at the other end. There was a room beyond, full of firelight, and with her skin beginning to thaw from the chill, Rhea was feeling much more at ease, until she noticed the skulls.

They were set in the bottom of the walls, fit together like tiles in a mosaic, their gaping eyes and mouths packed full of dirt. She let out a cry and stopped short, her heart ricocheting in her chest.

The dead were supposed to burn. That was the way in every Stratagiozi country. But of course, she reminded herself, this was a church, from the days of the saints, and the dead then were buried as her mother had been, returned to the earth from which the saints had taken their power.

How unsettling, to see bones just lining the pathway as if they were nothing more than a border some craftsman had made for decoration. In all her years, in all her consorts, Rhea had never seen anything like it.

There was a word for this sort of thing. She'd learned it once, and though she couldn't quite remember where—her mother, probably, as she was the source of all strange knowledge she couldn't explain—the word still sounded like a bell in her head. The catacombs.

The shock had worn off, leaving absurdity in its place, so she smothered a laugh and continued on until the end of the hallway, where she stepped through a low doorway and into a larger chamber. Alcoves in the walls housed a slab of smooth stone each, and she could picture it: the bodies laid out on the slabs as mourners lit candles and sang prayers for the dead. Or at least, she presumed that's what they'd done during the time of the saints. Nobody had ever really told her.

There were crates stacked in each alcove, some open so that Rhea could see the supplies stored inside. Bags of wheat, of unmilled grain, and a few cartons that looked full purely of the sort of glass bottles Rhea had seen merchants selling mulled cider in on the promenade. In one corner a pallet of straw had been made up with ratty bed linens, and they were slightly mussed. Someone had slept here recently. But otherwise the room was empty, and Rhea—Rhea was disappointed.

Was this it? There had to be more. More people, more secrets. Otherwise what would she tell Lexos? That the separatists were really just an empty room in the ruins of an old church? Had they brought down Baba's wrath for this?

On the opposite side of the room, a door opened onto another winding passage like the one she'd come down. Rhea stepped toward it, determined to keep going until she found something worth reporting.

"I wouldn't do that," someone said behind her. A rough voice, dryly amused. She flinched. Michali.

When she turned, he was leaning in the doorway through which she'd come, wrapped in a long coat, still wearing his nightclothes underneath.

"We haven't had a chance to clear it yet," he said before she could respond. "Plenty of spiders. And who knows what else."

"Michali," she said, immediately embarrassed by the nervousness that had put a tremble in her voice. She had been in far more dangerous situations before, though at the moment she couldn't remember any. She would handle this as she did everything else. "How did you get here? I took the rowboat."

"Well, there's another one," Michali said. He came farther into the room, plucked an apple from a nearby carton, and took a bite so loud that the crunch echoed. "Did you think we only had one?"

"I didn't—"

"A steward's family," he said, his mouth still full, "trapped on an island in the middle of a lake because one girl ran off with our only rowboat." He shook his head. "You really don't learn much of the world at Stratathoma, do you?"

She could still salvage this. Michali might have caught her here, might have discovered she'd stolen the coin from him, but she had told more difficult lies before. A pretty smile and a look of confusion could cover almost anything.

"I just wanted some air," she said, fussing with the ends of her hair, "and to see the city without the crowds. You really didn't have to come after me."

"Yes, I did," Michali said. "You're wearing my trousers."

Rhea looked down. Oh. So she was. One piece of black clothing looked much the same as another in the dark. "Sorry."

Michali tilted his head, swiped at the bead of apple juice that was running down his jaw. "To get some air, you stole a key from my pocket and found a secret door?"

Rhea swallowed hard. "Look, I—"

"Why are you here, Thyspira?"

"Here underground?"

He shook his head, smiling with bared teeth. "Here in the Ksigora. Although I suspect the answer for one is much the same as for the other."

They were both of them on the edge of it, of saying exactly what they meant. How odd, Rhea thought. She'd never done that before. And she wasn't about to start now.

"You," she said warily. "You know I'm only here because of you."

"Because your heart leapt when you saw me?" He grinned. "Because you fell in love?"

"Why did you go to Stratathoma anyway?" she shot back. She was not the only one here with ulterior motives, after all. "Why offer yourself as a suitor if you have the problems with me and mine that you seem to?"

"Your brother wrote to ask—"

She rolled her eyes. "As if anything my family asks of you has any real bearing."

"I did not expect you to choose me." Michali's expression was calm, an infuriating little smile lingering at the corner of his mouth. "And I made no effort to encourage you to. You cannot deny that."

"No," she said, "but you came to Stratathoma for a reason. If I'm lying, so are you."

Michali said nothing for a long moment, only considered her and took another bite out of his apple. Finally, he sighed and sat himself on the plinth opposite her, his boots swinging gently, a strip of bare skin visible between the tops of them and the bottom of his night-shirt.

"I think," he said, "it might be best if we're honest with each other."

She nearly laughed. "How honest?"

"I'm the head of the Sxoriza, the resistance movement here in the Ksigora, and I came to Stratathoma with the hope of laying groundwork for the eventual assassination of every last member of your family." He raised his eyebrows and took another bite. "That honest."

Rhea blanched. Her family, dead. Chrysanthi, who had never done a thing to harm anyone, with her blood spreading across Stratathoma's stone floor. Nitsos, Lexos. Even the thought of Baba, sightless eyes and pallid skin, left her shaking with guilt. What had she told Michali? What had he learned at Stratathoma that he might use to his advantage? She hadn't heard any ill news since she'd left. The citadel was near impossible to breach by an enemy force, and Baba so rarely allowed visitors that any newcomer would be under immediate suspicion. No, everything was safe. It had to be.

"Why?" she said. "What has my family done to—"

"Are you really asking that question?" He didn't sound angry. Instead it was something else, something disappointed.

"I suppose not," she said, thinking of the woman she'd met in the square, of the children and families she'd seen on her travels to the

Ksigora. Of the neglect her father had set to seed here. She could try to call it only Baba's doing, but the truth, if she could bear to look it in the eye, was that she and Lexos had been so focused for so long on their own safety that they had never had time to think of anyone else's.

"Well?" he said. "I have been honest with you now. It's your turn."

Rhea swallowed hard. She wouldn't be her father's daughter if she didn't try, one more time, to twist this entirely in her favor. "Just because you've been lying to me this whole time doesn't mean I have been, too," she said, but he was shaking his head before she'd even finished.

"You're a good liar," he said. "Really. It's just that so am I. I know what to look for. And you're here, after all." He ate the rest of the apple in one bite and tossed the core into the corner.

"You'll get ants," Rhea said before she could stop herself.

"Too cold for that," Michali said. "Come on. Just say it, Thyspira. You'll feel better."

She sighed. Her chances of getting what she wanted out of Michali were all but gone. He would never give her the information she'd come here for. And could she really risk angering him now, when he might well be holding her family's lives in his hands?

"Very well," she said. "You didn't expect me to choose you, and I didn't expect to, either. But I did so that I might come here and dismantle your Sxoriza before you could pose a real threat to my family." She cleared her throat delicately. "And. Well. You're one of my consorts. We've discussed what happens to those."

Michali nodded, his feet still swinging idly back and forth. "We have." She glanced back at him, expecting some of the bitterness he'd shown during their earlier conversations. And it was there, certainly, in the steady coolness of his gaze, but he seemed to shrug it off, and went on, only saying, "Thank you. That's about what I expected."

She let out a long breath. It was done with. Her mission here over, ruined. It was almost a relief, to feel the weight of Lexos's expectations so suddenly removed. "I guess there's nothing left in this for me, is there?"

"Not according to the lie you told your father." Michali leaned forward, smiling wryly. "He doesn't know, does he? You're not doing this on his orders."

She shrugged. Michali could figure that particular part out on his own. "And your father? Your mother? Do they know what you do here?"

"My mother does," he said easily, none of the worry that she'd felt over disclosing all of this information to an enemy evident in his manner. "She's one of our number." He got up, crossed to one of the plinths, and drew out a flask of something—wine, she hoped—from behind it. After taking a sip, he handed the flask to her. She waited for him to swallow, and a moment longer, watching him closely to make sure he wasn't hiding any ill effects, and then, once satisfied, took a sip of her own. Water.

"But my father," he went on. "Well, it isn't that he opposes the cause, exactly. It's more that he's of a different time."

"That," Rhea said, "is a terrible phrase."

"Oh?"

"It excuses all manner of things."

"Ah," Michali said, pursing his lips. "Well, in this case, it excuses a general apathy and an inexplicable loyalty to the Stratagiozi seat."

"To the seat, and not to my father?"

He took the flask back from her. "I think so. But then I've never asked him."

"You tell me all of this very freely, you know," Rhea said. It was disconcerting, and left her checking the shadows in the corner of every room. Perhaps Michali was sharing this on the condition that she not remain alive very much longer. "Should I be expecting a knife in my back? You came to Stratathoma to murder my family, after all."

He waved a hand dismissively. "I said I came to lay the groundwork. To see what might be done once we're ready to strike, and make good use of the chaos that will follow. I'd have been a fool to do it then, alone in a house of your father's allies, with myself the only one with any real cause to draw blood. I'd have died before I could finish the job."

He sounded so sensible, so calm. Rhea wanted to rip that calm right out of him. "This must be a great improvement, then," she snapped. "I am in your headquarters, rather than you in mine."

"These aren't our headquarters," Michali said. "We keep this as a way station, for anybody passing through the city. No, if you had discovered our headquarters we would be approaching this conversation very differently." Rhea could tell from the steely glint in his eyes that he meant it. But it faded as he went on. "You are right, in a sense. I've got what I wanted: an Argyros alone, and at my mercy."

"Who's to say you aren't at mine? I could kill you if I wished," she said, sounding much more confident than she felt. That was what Lexos would do—she was sure of it.

"You're already planning to, aren't you?" Michali said. He tilted his head, pointed to his chest. "Consort, remember?"

Rhea felt her cheeks go hot. "I meant right now."

"Well, all right." Amusement tugged at one side of his mouth. "Have at it."

She'd had almost a century of practice, had spent season after season face-to-face with people she was bound to kill. It should have been easy; she should have already been done with it.

"Perhaps," Michali said when she didn't move, "we might do away with these threats. I'm worth something to you alive, Thyspira. And so are you to me."

She hated the catch in her heart, a traitorous thing that twisted at the pity she could hear in his voice. "Am I?" she said. "What am I worth, exactly?"

"Presumably quite a lot of money, were we so inclined to consider you a hostage," Michali said. "Although reports indicate such a ransom wouldn't be paid."

Rhea held her tongue. She knew as well as anyone how little her father would care were she to ever be held captive. She would die;

her gift would return to Baba, and he would simply pass it and the duties attached along to Chrysanthi; that would be that.

"But I think there is some other value, too," Michali went on. "Everything I heard said Rhokera was as good as promised. It was why I felt safe making the trip. Who else would you possibly choose? And yet here you are."

His implications were clear. She was not entirely her father's daughter, not the loyal sort of puppet Thyspira had always seemed to be. She had disobeyed him; never mind that it had been for his own good, to disarm a threat he refused to acknowledge. Michali probably saw that as a gap in her armor, a weakness he might exploit. And Rhea couldn't work up the strength to tell him he was wrong.

Instead she ignored him and glanced away, up at the ceiling. It was carved, she realized, with a form of writing she didn't quite recognize. Almost the Thyzak alphabet, but not quite.

"What's that?" she said, pointing up. If Michali recognized her blatant attempt to change the subject for what it was, he had the courtesy not to mention it.

"That," he said, "would be a prayer. It's in Saint's Thyzaki."

Saint's Thyzaki, like the speech Yannis had made at her wedding, his words heavy, ancient, imbued with meaning. She'd never seen it written out before, and found that she could only read parts of it. Here and there roots of the words were the same, but the endings were different.

"Can you read it?" He nodded but said nothing. She sighed. "Can you read it to me?"

"Feels a bit strange to read it in front of a Stratagiozi's daughter."

"Fine, I'll try. You can correct me." She cleared her throat, went to stand on the opposite side of the room so the text would be right side up. "Aya Ksiga, that part's easy enough."

"Oh, well done."

She rolled her eyes and continued. "Aya Ksiga. And then something about a body, held in ground."

"Here interred," Michali corrected.

"She's buried here?" Rhea looked around wildly, and Michali smiled.

"Her body was never found. It's a memorial."

"All right." She went back to reading. "There's the root for love, but is that . . . a verb?"

"Noun. Saint's Thyzaki declines its nouns."

"All the more reason to speak Modern."

"But look." Michali came to stand next to her, and pointed to the word in question. "From the ending we can tell that 'love' here is specifically referring to the love of the people for the saint. In Modern you would have to use a whole other phrase."

She couldn't help smiling. He was still staring up at the carving, reading it so intently he was mouthing the words to himself. "Where did you learn Saint's?" she asked. "Your mother?"

"And some from tutors, but mostly her."

"Does she still worship?" Rhea tilted her head. "Is that why she supports your cause?"

"No, it's not about worship for her." He stepped away, looking slightly embarrassed.

"And you?" They'd been dancing around this question, she thought. All this talk about the resistance but nothing about what seemed to lie under every part of it.

"I believe the saints existed," he said with an air of frustration that she felt sure wasn't aimed at her, and gestured up at the words carved into the ceiling. "And I have seen what your sort can do—that must have come from somewhere."

"But you wouldn't call yourself a believer?"

"I suppose not."

"Then why do this?" She could hear the weariness in her voice, the frustration. "Why fight against my father at all? What is any of it for?"

"Haven't you seen this city? Haven't you seen the poverty, the need?"

"Of course," Rhea said, and she had, she had, "but doesn't that happen everywhere?"

Michali looked so stunned she could have knocked him over. "Excuse me?"

"I mean that people are suffering everywhere. Suffering in Stratathoma, too," she added sharply, "albeit in quite a different way, and nobody else seems to think it's that important to move for independence."

"Perhaps they might," he said slowly, emphatically, "if they had the choice. I can give them that."

"Ah yes, Michali Laskaris come to save the people. You sound quite like my father, you know." Like Baba had when he'd taken the Thyzak seat. She'd been very young then; even so, she still remembered how he'd spoken about his predecessor, how he'd raged about inaction and weakness, and promised to be better.

"It isn't like that," Michali said.

But she had heard enough. "You claim to be so different from him. You claim to hate everything he stands for, enough to tear it apart. But you and your separatists—I don't understand it. What is independence from a federation if you let the federation stand?"

"We won't," Michali said eagerly. "To call us separatists is incorrect. It's not enough. Do you see? Yes, I want to break with Thyzakos. Yes, I believe the Ksigora deserves its own rule." His words were fervent, his eyes bright. "But I want that for everyone. That is what we believe. We will move against every last Stratagiozi seat until the whole federation is in ruins and the continent is left to choose for itself." He let out a laugh. "Do you hear yourself? You make my argument for me."

No, what she heard was the worst parts of her father, spilling out of another man's mouth. She and Lexos would fix this. They would return Baba to who he had been, would keep their family safe and in power. But she needed time. And more important than that, she needed to make sure she got out of this room alive.

"I suppose I do," she said, careful to seem as reluctant as possible. Let Michali think she was changing her mind. Let him think he'd won some part of her over. If she was truly honest with herself, he almost had.

She watched the breath fall out of him, his shoulders dropping. "Really?" he asked. He sounded as exhausted as she felt. "Could you possibly be beginning to see reason?"

"You spend all this time arguing," she said, "and you mock me the moment you make any progress?"

He laughed, short but genuine. "We are not so polite here in the Ksigora as you seem to be in Stratathoma."

Rhea felt her smile turn fixed. He had no idea, truly, what it meant to live as she did. How it formed a person to be so examined, so scrutinized, protected only by what armor the politeness he derided could give her. "No," she said. "Indeed."

"If I have hope of convincing you," Michali said, more seriously now, "I will take it. And give you peace for the moment, if you will have it." He held out his right hand, the mark she'd carved there gleaming in the torchlight.

"I will," she said, and she reached out with her own marked hand and clasped his.

Peace for the moment. But that was all.

TWENTY

RHEA

Rhea spent the night in her own room, sleep a distant beacon on the horizon. Michali had promised her peace, at least for the time being, but that did very little to keep her from feeling on edge as she dressed for the morning. More unnerving even than her conversation and changed situation with Michali was the prospect of having to write to Lexos soon. What could she say? That her purpose had been discovered? That she was as useless to her family as she had always feared?

Best not to think about it now, she told herself as she made her way through the chilled hallways toward the main room of the house. She had Michali—and his mother—to contend with.

They were waiting at the dining table when she arrived, a breakfast spread laid out between them. Evanthia had her back to the door, but Michali was watching as Rhea approached, his eyes narrowed, brow creased.

"There she is," he said. "Our escapee."

Evanthia twisted around to face Rhea, smiling bemusedly. "I

hope you were warmly dressed, the pair of you," she said. "Out there so late, and in such weather."

"She was." Michali poked at a stack of rolls, still steaming from the oven. "But I wasn't. She had my trousers."

"You have others," Rhea said stiffly. "I thought perhaps I might go into the city again today. There's so much I haven't seen."

It was, they all knew, an excuse to be away from Michali, and Rhea had expected him to be grateful for it. After all, she thought that the easiest way to preserve their peace was to spend as little time together as possible. But Michali shook his head and stood up, brushing crumbs from his plain gray jacket.

"I'm afraid you'll have to put that off," he said. "You and I have business this morning, of the official sort. We're expected in Paragou."

"Paragou?"

"It's a village up the road," Evanthia said as she began stacking a handful of rolls and stuffed grape leaves in the center of a large kerchief. "Or rather, up the road into the mountains. You'll want a snack for the trip."

"Mama," Michali said, sounding already exhausted, "it's an official visit. I don't need a food parcel from my mother."

"Fine," Evanthia said. "That's just fine. All I do for you, giving you life, and this is the thanks I get. It's just fine."

"Mama—"

"I suppose we all outlive our use." She sighed heavily, looking away and dropping her head into one hand. Michali shut his eyes for a moment, seeming to gather his strength, and then went to her.

"I'm sorry," he said and kissed the top of her head. "Please, will you make up one for Thyspira, too?"

"I already did." Evanthia smiled, pinched his cheek, and got to her feet before bustling into the kitchen. "Here," she said when she reemerged bearing in her hands a bundle tied up in a floral scarf. "Off with you both now. Have a lovely trip."

That trip began with a painfully quiet journey across the lake. As they had the night before, Rhea and Michali said nothing, but in the daylight she could spot the slight frown that never left Michali's face. She could see how his hands flexed every now and then, as though he was readying himself to reach for a weapon. If she hadn't known better, Rhea might have thought he was afraid of her.

Paragou was high enough in the mountains that there was no sense in taking a carriage. Instead she was ushered to the family stables and loaded onto a sweet gray mare called Lefka. Lefka, the grooms told her, was used to inexperienced riders.

Well, Rhea wanted to tell them, she was used to men underestimating her. But then, here she was, finally with the chance to help her family, to really be of use and to do the sort of thing Lexos did, and she'd ruined it all. Broken her cover and told Michali everything. It hardly mattered that he'd done the same.

The road split as they left Ksigori proper, one branch stretching north to the true heights of the mountains, the other winding west into the foothills, and that was the branch they took, the ground rising quickly as Rhea urged Lefka along the path behind Michali's horse. They were traveling with a handful of guards and a standard-bearer, though to Rhea's eyes the standard looked much less like a house crest than it did like a plain field of crimson. Just as she'd seen in the report from Lexos's scout.

"What exactly are we going to Paragou for?" she asked Michali when the path became wide enough to allow them to ride side by side. The trees were growing more thickly here, pine and oak with slender trunks that seemed like needles compared to the plane trees that dominated the squares in Ksigori, and the snow had lingered here, no city heat to steal it from the ground, save for around each tree, where a ring of bare earth spread. Above, a cluster of starlings settled on the branches before swooping into the sky in a blurring cloud, tumbling like the pour of black beads.

"Official duties," Michali said.

"Official duties could mean all manner of things. I don't even know if I'm properly dressed."

He spared her a glance and shrugged. "You look all right to me."

"That doesn't answer my question."

"It's just a visit," he said, looking more frustrated at having to explain this to her than Rhea thought he had any right to. "Shaking hands, saying hello, wishing them well. Doesn't your family do anything like this?"

No. No, they didn't. Baba visited his stewards sometimes, but she had difficulty imagining him shaking hands, let alone wishing anyone well. Some leaders, she supposed, ruled with charm and persuasion, but Baba had taken the seat with pure force, and all of his power now rested in the memory of that, and in the promise that if he had to, he would do it again.

She said nothing, and let Michali's horse edge ahead of hers. Another difference between her father's rule and decency, she supposed. But was there any room, really, for decency when dealing with power?

She knew what Michali's answer would be. She was still figuring out her own.

They were in Paragou before she knew it. One moment they were still in the thick of the trees and the next a cobblestone path had opened up ahead of them, and pressed between two swaths of forest was a village so small and neatly kept that Rhea half expected it to be a child's thing, made of paper. The houses were like those in the city, but here their walls were thicker, their courtyards larger and layered, doors opening onto doors just like at Stratathoma. Rhea allowed herself a brief thought of her siblings. What would Chrysanthi think of a place like this? Rhea was sure her sister had never so much as seen snow. This sort of life might break her in two. And Nitsos would simply wander through the streets, looking for some place to build his next windup garden. She thought of the look on his face that day, the fondness with which he'd watched his creatures at work, and felt a pang in her chest she never really had before. Was it possible she had never missed Nitsos until this very moment?

The farther they rode into the village, the more people began to realize they had arrived. Voices piled on top of one another, filling the air, and Rhea was astounded at the sheer number of people that began to spill out onto the street, their eyes bright, cheeks startlingly thin. As had been the case in Ksigori when they'd run into that group of children in the street, most people seemed only to care about Michali. It was his name they shouted, his horse they reached to touch as the party rode toward the main square.

It had never been like this elsewhere. Whenever Rhea arrived as Thyspira in the home of her consort, she had always been treated as if she were Baba himself. Although, she supposed, perhaps she would have been ignored in much the same way if she'd ever bothered to go out into the actual public.

Michali pulled his horse to a halt by the village's plane tree, this one so old and spreading that Rhea thought it might take a good handful of people to make arms meet around the width of its trunk. He was greeted by a weathered old man wearing loose black robes and a strange tall hat, its shape squared off. His beard was pure white, and his hand shook as he reached out to help Michali down from his horse.

"Please, Patreou Simonos," Michali said, swinging out of the saddle easily. "Don't trouble yourself. Come, let's get out of the cold."

Patreou? That had to be Saint's Thyzaki. It sounded a little, Rhea thought, like a word in Modern that she'd only heard once or twice— the one Lexos used to describe the monks at Agiokon.

She got down off Lefka as Michali began to wade through the growing crowd. He was headed, it looked like, for a nearby taverna, and she supposed she was to join him there. But he hadn't looked back. Not even once. And if he wasn't going to make her, she certainly wasn't going to stand by his side and play the doting bride.

She lingered by the plane tree, dusting the snow from Lefka's saddle and straightening the fall of her own hair. The guards who had ridden with them seemed uncertain, one hurrying after Michali, the other two watching her with hesitation written across their faces.

"I'm just going to look around," she said to them. "You go with Michali. Nobody will harm me here."

She tried not to be offended at how quickly they obeyed.

Much as she didn't want to follow Michali inside, as the crowd had done, she did want to get out of the cold, and out of the snow that seemed to fall without ceasing. She turned slowly, examining the buildings that surrounded the small square. Houses, for the most part, and what looked like a shop front, long since closed.

But there. On the other side of the plane tree, its arched doorway coming to a point, a spire reaching above the tree at the top. Rhea recognized that shape from Michali's drawings. It was a church. Exactly the sort of building that was supposed to have vanished from Thyzakos a thousand years ago. Outlawed. Forbidden. And still standing.

She moved toward it, her boots crunching through the thin layer of frost that covered the cobblestones. Lefka snorted and stamped impatiently, but Rhea ignored her and kept going until at last she was standing at the threshold, the church waiting before her. Its stones were strangely dark, stained in reaching, flickering patterns. Ash, she realized as she reached out to touch it. Somebody had tried to burn it down.

The roughly hewn door was unlocked, she could tell, but she hesitated. Would Baba know? Would he sense it, across the whole of Thyzakos, when his daughter stepped inside a saint's church? It was a betrayal, no matter how she tried to excuse it—just curious, just unaware—but honestly, Rhea found herself too exhausted to care. She'd failed in her mission; she'd been found out by her consort and then dragged up into the mountains before being left stranded in this ridiculously tiny town square by that same consort. Going into the church in defiance of her father's edict might make her feel a little bit better, a little bit more in control of this situation she'd found herself in. At the very least it might offer a place to sit down.

The latch lifted. The door opened easily, hinges smooth and well oiled. Rhea took a deep breath, checked over her shoulder to make sure nobody was watching, and slid inside.

A long, narrow room lined with wooden benches, the air thick and close, scented like cloves and pine and clouded with smoke from a wilting cluster of candles burning at the other end. The walls rose high overhead, stones dappled with shadow so heavily that Rhea could barely make out the timber rafters that reached across the cavernous space in pairs.

Tentatively, she moved down the aisle, brushing her fingers over the benches as she passed. Arranged in rows, they were the red wood of cherry trees, and in the blue dark they seemed to glow. This place could have held the whole town ten times over, Rhea thought. How many people had prayed to the saints in those days? Was it anything like the power the Stratagiozis commanded now?

Forward, past the benches, past the candles that burned in offering, in memory, in prayer. At the back of the church a small window let the sun through, and as if in a folded curtain it fell, shielding the wall with a bright haze. There was something propped against the stone, a portrait perhaps, and Rhea drifted toward it.

Painted icons on the walls stared down at her with their great sorrowed eyes as she passed, their rich colors faded, their long-fingered hands extended in accusation. Like the ones on the ceiling in the great room at Stratathoma, the icons of her father and every Stratagiozi before. Watching, always watching as she and Lexos tried to make anything out of what they'd been given. It was like that now, familiar eyes looking out of unfamiliar faces. She avoided their gazes and kept on.

At last, she reached the cushions in front of what must have been the altar. She remembered that word from those days with her mother in that small room, remembered how it had been a stone pillar topped with a small portrait of a young man with close-cropped hair. And she remembered how Mama had knelt there before it. Had murmured a soft refrain in the quiet before kissing the portrait in supplication.

It was everything forbidden to her, everything wrong, but nobody was watching. And Rhea needed all the help she could get.

She knelt, head bowed. Palms to the floor, breathing deeply. Now, she supposed, was the time for prayer. But how did you pray to the dead?

Please, Rhea thought so fervently she nearly shook with it. I must be worth something.

There was no answer. Of course there wasn't. She wasn't sure what she'd expected. Best to get out of here before Michali caught her like this.

She got to her feet, squinting against the pure light of the sun that streamed through the window, and leaned in toward the portrait set atop the stone pillar of the altar. It was a tiny thing, the paint so oiled and smoothed by the touch of a thousand lips that the face it depicted was hard to make out at first. Whoever it was, a streak of shadow had brushed from ear to ear, the paint thin enough that Rhea could make out the shape of the eyes underneath. They were familiar. Down-turned like her own, she thought, and then, there it was—the line of the jaw, the straight slope of the nose.

She stumbled back, shock rattling through her. That face. She recognized that face.

Her mother.

No, Rhea's memories had never been as clear as Lexos's. She had never been able to trace the line of her mother's smile without closing her eyes, without thinking hard. But she knew. Gooseflesh rising on her skin, a thunder in her heart. She knew.

The text across the bottom of the portrait's thin frame was in Saint's Thyzaki, but she could read enough of it to make out the name: Aya Ksiga. Aya Ksiga and her mother, and Rhea shut her eyes, shook her head, tried to fit these two things together in her mind.

It was true: They had never known where Mama had come from. Rhea had wondered, of course. She'd picked through every memory she had of their lives back before Stratathoma, scoured every fleeting image she had of her mother's face. Even asked Baba before she'd learned what a poor idea that was. But she'd never imagined this.

She stared at the portrait, trying to calm herself. Did the others know? Nitsos, Chrysanthi?

Lexos?

Baba?

And if this was true, if Mama had been a saint, how had she survived the massacre? The first Stratagiozi had been one of the saints, and had killed all of his kind. To have survived that, and a thousand years more, all to have died in some small house in the countryside—it was almost cruel.

Crueler still was that the Sxoriza had almost more of a claim to Rhea's mother than she did herself. They operated in the remains of Aya Ksiga's tomb. They fought, or at least some of them did, in her name. Did they know that she'd survived? Had a family? And did they recognize Rhea for what she was?

She didn't think they did. This portrait was very old, the image of Aya Ksiga somewhat distorted by wear. She supposed that if she was caught here side by side with it, someone would spot the resemblance, but if this was all most worshippers had to go by, she doubted that she would ever be identified as Aya Ksiga's daughter beyond these walls. And besides, Aya Ksiga had died a thousand years ago, as far as they knew. It had likely never occurred to anyone to wonder if she had family, just as it had never occurred to Rhea to wonder too much about who her mother might have been.

But they knew her still. All of the people who'd ever worshipped here, who'd ever kissed that portrait—they knew Mama in a way Rhea could never claim to. She belonged to them, and they to her, and Rhea felt a longing unfurl in her chest. To have a place like that waiting for her.

She knew what Lexos would say. That place is Stratathoma; that place is our family. The most important thing, and she'd given up her chance at protecting it when she told Michali everything. Given up now, when the family was more in danger than ever from the very person she'd confessed to. She had seen proof of how people felt about Baba here in the Ksigora. She had seen proof of Michali's devotion to the cause, of the threat to her family. But fighting those threats hadn't worked. At least not the way she'd tried so far.

Rhea sat down on the first pew, still staring at the portrait. Lexos was right that their family needed protecting. But just as Baba's strategy had not worked, neither would Lexos's. Even if she reported everything back to him, and even if Michali died at the end of the season, there was nothing she or Lexos could do to really dismantle the Sxoriza, not when she felt certain that the ideals moving them were something like those that had moved people to kneel at her mother's portrait.

They would continue. She could kill Michali and someone else would take his place. Lexos could send some other steward's soldiers to raid the Sxoriza camps, and more would spring up elsewhere. Michali had come to Stratathoma meaning to kill every last Argyros; someone would whether he was alive to see it or not. She was sure of that.

No, there had to be some other way. Not Lexos's plan and not Baba's. One that would work, one that would guarantee that no matter what came to pass, no matter what bloomed from the unrest sown here in the Ksigora, her family would survive. Here was her mother, after all, with her name written in Saint's Thyzaki. Her mother, who had cast off that name to become a general's consort. Who had done what she had to, allied with who she must, just to stay alive. The most successful Argyros of any of them. The most loved.

I have tried to be Baba, Rhea thought. I have tried to be Lexos.

A shaft of light fell across her mother's face, and Rhea shut her eyes.

This time, she told herself, she would try to be Mama.

TWENTY-ONE

ALEXANDROS

It wasn't that he had expected Rhea to make too much progress right away, Lexos thought, standing at the window in the observatory as he watched another day close, sunset turning the gulf between Thyzakos and Trefazio a brilliant gold. It was just that he had expected her to at least make some. And yet he'd had no word from her since she'd left for the Ksigora, not even a reply to his own message simply to confirm she'd received it. He was trying not to fret, because, after all, Rhea had never failed before. But then hadn't she come a bit too close for anyone's liking with her time in Patrassa? Hadn't she let the season linger too long?

He shook himself; that was Baba's way of thinking. It did not have to be his.

Lexos turned and made his way downstairs, the house whispering around him. Snatches of conversation between servants, the steady drip of a leak coming from somewhere above. It had always been like this—he knew that—but it felt unsettling now. He was too aware of everything beyond Stratathoma's walls, pieces moving and shifting like parts in one of Nitsos's machines. He doubted it would stay quiet here for long.

Chrysanthi was likely in the kitchen, so that was where he went, eager for some company, even if her particular sort usually left him feeling a bit made fun of. When he found her, she was leaning against the stone counter, her hands dusted in flour as she stared at the oven, where a pita must have been baking.

"Chrysanthi?" he said tentatively. She jumped, and he was startled to see that her eyes were red, as though she'd been crying. "Are you——"

"Well, don't just stand there," she interrupted. Her yellow hair was swept back in a simple braid, and she was wearing a warm winter dress, the fabric an unusual cornflower blue. "Come and make yourself useful, if that's something you are in fact capable of doing."

Whatever had been bothering her, it was very clear that she had no wish to discuss it. Still, as the two of them began to clean up the kitchen, Lexos wondered if perhaps he wasn't the only one feeling less at home than usual.

"It smells delicious," he said after an uncomfortable period of silence. "The pita, I mean."

"Of course it does."

She sounded like herself, but she seemed to be deliberately avoiding his eyes. Lexos sighed. What would Rhea say, if she were here? She was always able to get nearer to their siblings than he was, although there were some gaps neither of them could ever fully close.

He was about to try again with Chrysanthi when somebody cleared their throat from the kitchen doorway, and both he and Chrysanthi turned to see Nitsos there, his hands shoved in his pockets, his brow furrowed in its usual expression of deep thought.

"Yes?" Chrysanthi said.

"Chores," Nitsos said. "Baba wants us to sort correspondence before dinner."

"He told you that?" Lexos couldn't help sounding slightly alarmed. It was strange enough that the other two siblings be involved in a duty that was usually his alone, but to have the order come via Nitsos? Was Baba that upset about the council meeting that he would give attention even to Nitsos before he gave it to Lexos?

"Oh, don't worry," Nitsos said, a sharp bitterness clinging to his voice. "A servant passed on the message."

"Let's go, then," Chrysanthi said, brushing vigorously, and unsuccessfully, at a flour stain on her dress. "I'm sure there's plenty to get done."

Plenty, unfortunately, turned out to be something of an understatement. The pile of correspondence waiting for the three siblings in Baba's study was at least a foot high off the desk, assembled haphazardly and half-covered in dust, as if each letter had been dug out from some hidden corner of the room and dumped there without a second thought. Just the sight of this many letters was enough to make Lexos uneasy. Baba always passed on whatever he received to Lexos to be sorted: messages from the stewards or other Stratagiozis, petitions from people both home and abroad asking Baba to spare someone or undo someone's death (which of course he never did). Then, once Lexos had read everything and determined what required an answer, he would return the letters to Baba, and file them somewhere in the study. These, however, had obviously never been touched. Had Baba been hiding them from Lexos? Or had they simply fallen by the wayside?

Chrysanthi went about lighting the lamps while Lexos approached carefully and plucked the top letter off the stack. It had no date, and so it was difficult to be certain how long, exactly, it had gone unanswered, but if the cracked ink and curling parchment were anything to go by, it was at least a year old, if not two or three. Please, he thought as he folded it open. Let this just be a stack of old petitions and nothing important.

But the first letter was a report on grain stores in central Thyzakos. And while the second was indeed a petition, this time from someone out of a lesser family in Trefazio, the third was a report from one of Lexos's old scouts, a source he'd long since retired in favor of Nitsos's creatures.

"Mala," he said, scrubbing one hand through his hair.

Nitsos let out a snort of laughter. Lexos turned, just in time to see Nitsos attempt to compose himself.

"Laugh all you like," he snapped. "You have no idea—"

Nitsos waved him off, looking so self-assured for a moment that Lexos nearly swallowed his tongue. "I know, I know. Do you want our help or not?"

No, if Lexos was being honest, but Baba had included the others for a reason, and he would certainly hear about it if Lexos refused their help now.

"Fine," he said. "Both of you, sit at the desk and start sorting through. If it's a petition I don't need to see it. Otherwise, just hand it to me."

Nitsos grumbled something on his way past—Lexos caught only the word "inefficient"—and Chrysanthi was already complaining about the ink that was sure to stain her fingertips. Lexos closed his eyes for a moment, his nerves beginning to fray. Be patient, he reminded himself. Be patient like Rhea would.

Luckily, the top half of the stack didn't hold many other surprises. The few reports and letters from abroad that were languishing there were the sort that did not require an answer, and while some of it was information Lexos would've liked to see upon its arrival, he'd had most of it confirmed from other sources. If this was what the whole pile was like, maybe there was nothing to worry about.

Of course, no sooner had he begun to relax than Chrysanthi found the first letter from a Thyzak steward. This one was from Dimitra Markou, whose family held a territory near the center of Thyzakos where the farmland was rich and varied. It was odd to hear from Dimitra at all, which made Lexos snatch the letter from Chrysanthi's hands before she could even begin to read it. Dimitra kept to the edges of things, paying her taxes on time and sending one of her less desirable children to one of Rhea's choosings every now and then. She rarely ever came up in discussions of which stewards were well in hand and which were not; Baba and Lexos both felt that her support was a given, if not in itself particularly fervent.

"Lexos?" Chrysanthi asked as he held the letter up to the light. "Is everything all right?"

He waved her off and paced away toward the lamp by the window. Dimitra had not dated the letter, but the ink was fresh, and the parchment seemed to be in good enough condition that it likely had not sat through a winter prior to this one. Recent, then.

> *Vasilis,*
>
> *You will have to pardon me, I am afraid, for writing to you without your solicitation, and for being as frank as I feel I must be. I have just returned from a journey to Rhokera, where Giorgios Speros was gracious enough to host myself and my consort for a number of days. We were there at his invitation, which I accepted believing it to be a social visit— our families, you see, have a long history, and in fact I believe a cousin of his was once married to a niece of mine, although—*

Here a sentence was crossed out, and the letter resumed again a paragraph later.

> *I have nothing specific I can offer as proof to lend weight to my words, and as such you may well believe this letter to be nothing more than an attempt at subterfuge, but I would be neglecting my duty as your steward if I did not say to you now: Your time, I think, is running short. There are plans being made in Rhokera.*
>
> *Your rule has been kind to my family, and to our people, and while I have no indication that Giorgios's rule would be otherwise, the up-heaval that goes along with a transition like that is something I have no wish to endure. If there is anything I can do to help keep your hold on Stratathoma, you have only to ask.*
>
> *Yours,*
> *Dimitra*

So—a warning and an offer, hidden here in a stack of parchment, with no attention paid to it. Had Baba simply never gotten around to reading it? Or, worse, and perhaps more likely, had he seen this and discarded it, the way he did with some of Lexos's own reports? Lexos could imagine it all too well: Baba's confidence souring to arrogance, a sneer tugging at his mouth as he read Dimitra's offer of help. He would have been too offended by it to accept its implication.

But Lexos was not. Stavra had told him at Agiokon that Giorgios Speros had invited Zita to stay. A steward making inroads internationally was dangerous enough, but if Giorgios was soliciting support from other stewards in Thyzakos, it wouldn't be long before he made a move against Stratathoma, to take the seat for himself. And should that happen, after that disastrous council meeting, Lexos could no longer be sure that Zita, or any of the other Stratagiozis, would be on Baba's side.

He shut his eyes tightly, the letter crumpling in his clenched fist as he ignored the sound of Chrysanthi calling his name from across the room. It was not enough, anymore, to go along with Baba's plan and simply send Rhea out to resolve the situation in the Ksigora; that was no longer the only threat. Something had to be done, and quickly. He had no more favors to call in, though. Nobody else he could send out to fix things—well, there was Nitsos, but Nitsos didn't count. This had to be his job.

"Enough," he said, turning to his siblings. Chrysanthi had risen from the desk, and was wringing her hands, her dark blue eyes wide. Nitsos, of course, hadn't even looked up from whatever letter he was reading. "Thank you for your help. You can both go."

"Are you sure?" Chrysanthi asked. "You seem—"

"Fine. I'm fine." Lexos looked to Nitsos, who had finally lifted his head. "Go. I'll see you at dinner, yes?"

Nitsos got up stiffly. "Looking forward to it."

Dinner with Baba, and no Rhea there to draw his attention. "Yes," Lexos said flatly. "Aren't we all?"

Once the others had gone, he pulled Nitsos's vacated chair closer in toward the desk and sat before digging through the drawers to find a clean sheet of parchment and a sharp quill. Who could he ask for help? And perhaps more important, who would Baba even let him travel to see? Going to visit one of the other stewards might rouse suspicion in Rhokera, and the council meeting had not left him feeling very welcome in most places except—

Vuomorra. Tarro's city. Tarro liked him, and might even respect him someday. Surely he would welcome Lexos. And a perceived friendship with Tarro would go quite a ways toward reinforcing Baba's position with the rest of the council.

He wrote the letter to Tarro quickly, announcing his intent to visit Vuomorra and his hope that he might pay Tarro a visit while in town. With any luck, Tarro would respond and say that of course, Lexos had to stay with him at the Domina house. And that was all Lexos needed.

Across the house, the kitchen bell rang for dinner, the resonance carrying through the stone. Lexos sat back from the desk and pressed his palm to the folded letter. He needed Baba's permission to go, of course. But waiting even an hour was wasting time.

Gritting his teeth, Lexos rose and slipped out of the office, carrying the letter onto the attached balcony where a nondescript clockwork scout waited to carry messages. The letter would go to Tarro immediately, and if Baba refused to send Lexos to Vuomorra after it, well, that was a problem to be solved then.

For now, he was late to dinner.

He thought it was lucky, at first, that Baba was not at the table when he arrived. But then two servants carried the pita out, and another began to pour wine, their unease palpable as they passed on the message from Baba: He would not be attending. The children should eat on their own.

That alone would have been enough to make Lexos nervous, but once the meal was finished he received no summons from Baba to come up to the study, and that was worse still, particularly after the council meeting. No, Baba would never replace him as his second, not when the other options were such, but Lexos much preferred knowing Baba needed him to wondering whether or not he did.

It was some hours later when, on his way downstairs after finishing the night's work in the observatory, Lexos spotted one of the servants carrying a tray loaded with wine and sweets toward the main hall. That had to be for Baba—he couldn't remember the last time Chrysanthi or Nitsos had opened a bottle this late—so he followed, lingering behind the servant as they wound toward the great room. There, he found Baba in a tall-backed armchair by the fire, with Chrysanthi in the chair opposite and Nitsos watching from behind her. Between Baba and Chrysanthi was a low, round table, the top of which was colorfully inlaid with long, narrow triangles that came spiking out from the edges. Placed at different spots on some of the triangles were smooth round coins, the sort that were rarely seen at Stratathoma—nobody here had any need for federation money.

It was a game, called Soldier's Teeth by those who most often won and Saint's Grave by those who most often lost. Lexos remembered playing it as a child, with river pebbles instead of coins, but he'd seen it since, in Agiokori taverns and Rhokeri alleyways. Whoever won would keep every coin that had been played.

At this rate it looked as though that would be Baba. Chrysanthi had her legs drawn up underneath her and was very nearly asleep, only opening her eyes to make whatever move Nitsos told her to make. Baba, of course, wasn't nearly so relaxed. He never lost if he could help it.

"Nitsos," Lexos said as he came into the main hall, "I hope you are advising our sister well."

Chrysanthi jerked upright, her hand flying to her chest. "*Mala,* you startled me."

"It's a good thing I did. Attention must be paid." He leaned on the back of Baba's chair, pleased when Baba reached up to pat his hand in greeting. "You're losing quite terribly."

"I was working on it," Nitsos grumbled.

"Not very well."

Baba let out a gruff snort of laughter. It was cheap, perhaps, to attempt to reestablish his position with Baba by taking aim at Nitsos, but it was sure to work, and after Agiokon, Lexos needed something sure.

"Let's call this game a surrender," Baba said, leaning forward to sweep the coins toward him. Chrysanthi did not protest. No doubt they had never been hers in the first place. "And let's have another."

Chrysanthi yawned. "Let's not, Baba. I'm tired."

"Not you." Baba turned in his seat, his eyes coming to rest on Lexos, hooded and stern in the firelight. "I'd like to see my boys have their turn."

Lexos hid his grimace. This could only end badly. Either he won, and Nitsos's resentment found yet another thing to call its own, or he lost, and paid for it dearly with Baba.

"Perhaps another time," he said.

But Baba was already on his feet, gesturing for Lexos to take his place. "Perhaps now." There would be no arguing with that.

Chrysanthi's mouth was tight as she got up to make way for Nitsos. In her place, Rhea would have been smiling, calling for more wine and doing her best to make sure nobody would be in a position to remember much about whatever was about to happen. Chrysanthi, though, for all that she was used to running the household, was not used to running Baba.

Lexos and Nitsos sat down, watching as Baba bent over the table and swept the coins into the palm of his hand. There were too many, some of them clattering to the floor, but he ignored them, and only shoved his handful into his jacket pocket.

"What will we play with, then?" Lexos said, trying to keep his voice light. If he had no interest in using money, maybe Baba didn't mean for it to be a true competition.

Baba slid open a drawer built into the table. The shadows were too long for Lexos to see what was inside, but he hated the look on Baba's face—the triumph there, the excitement.

"Here," Baba said. "I think these will do." Out of the drawer he lifted a silver tray, cluttered with Nitsos's creatures.

There were all sorts. Hummingbirds like the one Lexos had seen in the courtyard at Rhea's choosing, their dark blue eyes built from little miniature mosaics. A field mouse, a green-brown beetle, a trio of butterflies. Each and every one taken from Nitsos's attic work-shop.

It must have been years of work, there in Baba's hands. And Baba had always made it clear what he thought of that work, of everything it wrought. Lexos went still, clutching the arms of his chair tightly, as if one sudden movement would make Baba cast every last creature into the fire.

Nitsos said nothing. His eyes were wide and his face had gone ter-ribly pale, but still he said nothing. It was only Chrysanthi who moved, straightening from where she had leaned against the back of Nitsos's chair.

"Baba," she said softly. "What's all that for?"

Baba ignored her, and began placing the creatures around the rim of the board, each at the base of one of the colored triangles. They were not moving—they would not, removed from Nitsos's care—and they glittered in the firelight, gears and clockwork visible here and there where Baba's carelessness had damaged them.

"You'll play," Baba said. "Let's see if Nitsos can win back his toys."

Nitsos stared at Lexos, and Lexos's heart clenched painfully. Nit-sos was his to look after, his to protect. How could he have let it come to this? The two of them, on opposite sides, and it was only a game, but it came with consequences, and Lexos could ill afford to lose now. Not when he would need all of his influence with Baba to turn things to their advantage after Agiokon.

"All right," he said. "First move to the eldest."

It was not a surprise when, with every piece Lexos claimed, Baba laid it on the floor and ground it to breaking under his heel. It was not a surprise when Nitsos bore it without complaint, playing and playing with no question of forfeit even as the board cleared. It was not a surprise, either, that Chrysanthi left partway through, sounding suspiciously close to tears as she said she was too tired to continue watching all this nonsense.

Rhea would have stayed, Lexos thought as he made his last move.

The board was empty. He'd won. Every one of Nitsos's creatures had been shattered.

"Well done," Baba said, clapping him hard on the back. Across the table, Nitsos shut his eyes.

Moments later, when Nitsos had gone, Baba drew Lexos toward the fire. He looked strange, Lexos thought. Nearly frantic with delight, and somehow too young.

"That poor boy," he said, leaning in close to Lexos. "Did you see, he—"

Lexos couldn't stand it. It had been hard enough, making each move at his own brother's expense. He refused to rejoice in it. "Enough," he said, knocking Baba's hand off his shoulder. "Why would you do that? What point were you trying to make?"

Baba looked baffled. "Point?"

"Nitsos has only ever tried to serve you. And you punish him for it."

It was a testament to how oddly Baba was behaving that rather than handing Lexos his own punishment for speaking such, he waved him off absently. "He's young," Baba said. "He needs to learn."

They were all young compared to Baba, but they'd lived so many years. Seen so much come and go. And yet, in Baba's house, they were children still. They would always be children.

"We have more important things to speak of, you and I," Baba said, serious now. "You know we cannot let things stand as they are with Tarro and the Dominas."

Lexos thought of the bird already winging its way to Vuomorra and sighed, relieved. Now he could do what he'd already intended to, but with Baba's approval, and Baba never need know the truth.

"Tarro thinks well of you," Baba continued, grimacing. Lexos hid a smile—well of him, and not of Baba. "If you go to Vuomorra, it's possible you may get the promise of support that we need."

"I will be happy to go, if that's what you want."

He sounded smug, he knew, and Baba knew it, too. He looked at him for a long moment, something close to a sneer curling at the corner of his mouth. "Rejoice all you like, boy. You do my bidding and you carry my name." He nodded to the game table. "And you win only when I tell you to."

He left then, and Lexos waited until his footsteps had gone quiet before he moved, slumping down in one of the armchairs. Baba was wrong. Tarro's good opinion? He'd won that himself, in defiance of both the council customs and Baba's orders. And when he got what he was after in Vuomorra, he'd win that himself, too. Let Baba see how well he could protect the family. Let Baba see what he could do.

TWENTY-TWO

RHEA

I t had all seemed so easy that day in the church. Standing in front of her mother's portrait, the room around her dark and cloistered, one shaft of light cutting through the window above, Rhea had felt different. Separate from herself, ancient and young in the same breath. It had taken nothing at all to look into her mother's veiled eyes and say, "I will do what you have done." And then she'd left the church, got back on her horse, and ridden here to Michali's house, all the while realizing that doing as her mother had done was, in fact, going to be rather difficult.

Survive, really: That was the point of it. Mama had lived as a saint and only died some thousand years later, long after her very existence had been outlawed. She had seen a shift in the world coming, a new order beginning to take hold, and she had changed, let go of herself so completely that even these worshippers in the mountains who loved her so dearly had no idea she had not died like the others of her kind.

Mama had married Baba for protection—that Rhea understood. He'd been a general in a steward's army back then, a position above scrutiny but not high enough to draw too much attention. As his consort, Mama would have been removed enough from sainthood by time and status that she could live safely. But there were still so many years before their marriage that Rhea had to account for.

It had taken her a number of days to understand the breadth of it, something she was a bit embarrassed of now as she sat, wrapped in layers of blankets, on the bed in her room at Michali's house. Of course Baba had not been the first. Of course there must have been consorts before him, families found and then forgotten. Still, even knowing that, even understanding that Mama would have had to make her way somehow, it seemed impossible to Rhea that there might be other children she had left behind, strewn across the continent like bits of broken pottery. It was true that Rhea remembered very little of Mama, but she couldn't imagine her as a mother to anyone else. Surely, when Rhea and Lexos had arrived, and been cradled against Mama's chest, their little fingers linked together, they had been the very first.

And if they hadn't been, well, those other children were long dead by now. That, at least, was some comfort.

The question now, though, was how far to follow Mama's example. The more Rhea thought about it, the more nervous she became. If she did exactly as Mama had done, and allied her family with the side of those most dangerous to them in the service of self-preservation, that would mean taking the side of the people in the Ksigora, joining Michali and even the Sxoriza itself if she had to, so that she might protect Baba and her siblings if and when Thyzakos and later the federation came crashing down.

But Michali wouldn't take kindly to that. No, for all his practicality, Michali held closely to his ideals, and that was a bit worrisome because Rhea was not sure she had any of those. She would have to be very convincing, and even if she did win Michali over, there was still the rest of her family to contend with. Lexos, who would hate this plan, partly because it was too big a risk and partly, she thought snidely, because it was not his. And Baba, who would take it as a betrayal, no matter how she explained that she'd done it to protect him. She'd considered writing to him to explain, and even to ask his advice, but he'd never even wanted her in the Ksigora in the first place, and his response would almost certainly be to bring her home, disrupting the already precarious balance that held the Ksigora, Rhokera, and the rest of the continent at bay. And while it would collapse eventually—every day without an update from Lexos made the confidence with which he'd sent her here seem more and more misguided—there was no need to hurry it along.

The easiest thing was to keep the plan to herself. To never let her family know what she had done until it was over, and to never let Michali know exactly why she'd had her change of heart. She would bargain for her family's lives, but he couldn't be allowed to know the truth of it. Men, she had found, did not take kindly to being used. Well, really nobody did, but everybody else seemed a great deal more accustomed to it.

With a groan, she rose from the bed, keeping one of the blankets around her shoulders, and went to the window to look out over the trees. There was no scout from Lexos waiting there with a message, as there hadn't been since her first night here. Was this a sign of his trust in her? Or was it rather that he had no intelligence to help her? Or worse, perhaps things were so dire at home that he wasn't even thinking of her at all. No matter the reason for his silence, she couldn't wait for him to break it. She had already delayed long enough, begging off every official visit and ceremony Michali mentioned to stay here in her room. While he seemed happy for now to leave her to her own devices, she knew things couldn't stay like that forever, especially after their conversation in the catacombs. This peace, like every other, was bound to break, and soon.

So she would have to speak to Michali. Tonight. Convince him that she'd seen the error of her father's ways, which was the truth to at least some degree, and that she wanted to join his fight against the Stratagiozis. His speech in the catacombs had moved her, she might say.

Furthermore, she would have to make herself useful, provide real information and real opportunity for the Sxoriza to move against

Baba. That was all fine. As long as, when the time came, she could protect him and her siblings. And when the Sxoriza moved against Stratathoma, there she'd be. An Argyros, still in power.

Outside, the sun was already low—it set more quickly now that they were into winter, and Rhea supposed that was the responsibility of one of the other Stratagiozi children, though she truly had never considered it for more than a minute or two—and so the house's corridors were closely held by the dark as Rhea made her way through, heading for the great room. Usually with spare hours like these she occupied herself with whatever divertissements were to be found in her consort's house. There was nothing of the sort to be found here. And besides, she had a task to accomplish.

Michali was sitting at the table reading from a stack of parchment as, across the room and through the kitchen doorway, Evanthia was checking on something in the oven. Rhea lingered in the mouth of the hallway. Loath as she was to admit it, she liked watching the two of them when they were quiet, liked seeing them use the same little gestures without thinking. It made her wonder what of Mama she carried without realizing it, if anything at all.

Clenching one hand in a fist, she cleared her throat and said, "Michali?" Evanthia poked her head quickly out through the kitchen doorway, her eyes so intent that Rhea almost lost her nerve. Michali, meanwhile, simply looked up at her, as calm now as he had been every day since finding her in the catacombs. "I . . . if you would join me . . ."

Evanthia let out a bark of laughter, and Michali's mouth dropped open. Rhea realized too late what it sounded like.

"I didn't mean," she added, words tripping over one another. "That is to say, it wasn't a proposition."

"Quite," Evanthia said. She bustled over to Rhea and snatched the blanket from around her shoulders, quickly replacing it with one that had been warming by the fire. "If you mean to proposition my son, kindly do it with a bit more grace than that."

"And perhaps wait until my mother is out of the room," Michali added.

Evanthia shrugged. "That, I care less about."

Rhea shut her eyes. If she couldn't keep her cheeks from blushing, as she was sure they were, she could at least keep from having to look at the cause of it. "Truly," she said, "I just want to speak to Michali alone."

"Take pity on the poor girl," Evanthia said, and soon enough Rhea felt Michali's hand, his skin cold and dry, brushing her own. She startled, jerked back so hard that she stumbled into one of the divans by the hearth.

"Come on," he said, stepping past her. Rhea followed, taking care to steady her breathing as they neared his bedroom.

It was still in the same state of mild disarray it had occupied the last time she'd been in here, with the bed unmade, the fire banked and low, and a few of the sketches Michali kept tacked to the wall hanging askew. There were only two servants in the whole household, and both of them were primarily occupied with keeping out of Evanthia's way. Rhea wondered if, like Lexos, Michali forbade the servants from coming into his room. Men, she thought, crossing to adjust the linens before she could stop herself.

"You wanted to speak with me?" Michali said.

"I did." Rhea went to sit in one of the armchairs in front of the hearth, waiting until he had joined her in the other to lean forward, her hair falling loose from its braid. "I've been thinking about our conversation."

"Have you?" He examined her, and she wondered what it was he saw. Did she look as nervous as she felt?

"You said something," she started. "That I made your argument for you."

Michali raised his eyebrows but did not answer. If he had any idea what she was trying to say, he did not show it.

She cleared her throat. Push on, she told herself. This is the worst of it. "And all of this. It's been picking at me. The boy in the square. You."

The boy who'd spat in her face and hated her, hated her more than she'd ever expected. Michali, determined to end the lives of her family, steadfast and unafraid of whatever Stratagiozi power she might bring down on his head. Let him think it had all moved her to his cause. He didn't need to know that really, it had made her afraid.

"What about me?" He asked, tilting his head. "We have been honest with each other before. I think it's time we were again."

Very well. She sat up straight and put on her best smile. Being Thyspira had been practice for exactly this—a hundred years of convincing people she wanted them enough that it was worth the eventual cut of her knife.

"What you're doing," she said. "This war you mean to fight against the Stratagiozis. I think I'd like to fight it with you."

She watched closely as surprise flashed across Michali's face, drawing his brows into a frown. But it was gone quickly, smoothed over with a careful blankness, his expression lit only by the slight spark of resentment in his eyes.

"Oh," he said, settling back into his chair. "Would you, now? How very like a Stratagiozi's daughter to think this is hers to claim."

That was not the answer she'd been looking for.

"I think you're right," she said, trying again. "Everything you said about my family, my father. You've opened my eyes." It was the truth, taken at an angle. She had to hope it would be enough.

Michali scoffed. "I haven't opened your eyes to a thing. What's this about, Thyspira?"

"I told you," she started, but he shook his head.

"If this is some ploy to keep yourself safe here, you needn't worry. You can leave now. Go back to your big empty house and never set foot in the Ksigora again. I won't stop you."

Rhea wasn't sure if she really believed that. Michali himself might not stop her, but there was nothing to suggest one of his Sxoriza wouldn't put a knife in her throat before she made it out of Ksigori. But even if she did go home and abandon her duty both as Thyspira and as an Argyros, it would be for nothing. When the Sxoriza came for Stratathoma, she would meet her end there, along with the rest of her family. Michali had all but promised her that.

"No," she said. "That's not what I want."

"What, then?"

"I told you."

"To join me, yes," he said. "Where was this zeal before? You were very adamant when we discussed this last. What could have changed so much between then and now?"

She supposed it didn't have to be a secret that she'd seen her mother's face in that church. But there had always been a danger with her family that she would give something to them and only afterward realize she had wanted to keep it for herself.

"It was hardly all at once," she said. "But last week, when we went to Paragou . . . I went into the church. You must understand, we don't have them in the west country. I'd never seen anything like it before."

Michali scoffed. "Your family rules this country and has done for a hundred years. Do you expect me to believe that any corner of it remains unknown to you?"

"Yes," she said. "You are mad if you think I ever saw a single thing my father didn't want me to."

"Until now."

She ignored the mocking slide of his voice and went on. "I saw a portrait of your saint. Aya Ksiga. There was an altar, and I prayed." She met Michali's eyes, willed him to let her leave it at that. The Ksigorans already had such a claim to Aya Ksiga—let her keep her mother as only hers.

But Michali only shook his head. "You were converted? How beautiful."

"What answer are you looking for, then?" she said, irritated. "What would convince you?" She had expected him to be cautious. That was simply good sense. But there seemed to be something more to his reluctance. Something deeper and more fundamental—an unwillingness, perhaps, to believe that a Stratagiozi's daughter could be more flesh and blood than stone.

"I am looking for honesty," he said, leaning forward. "You're willing to forsake your entire family because you saw a portrait in a church? You're lying to me."

"Let me prove my use to you, then."

He frowned, staring into the flicker of the fire. "Your use is not in question, Thyspira. I am speaking of trust. They are not the same thing."

It startled Rhea, running cold through her veins. Had she always held those two things together? How much of that was Baba's doing, and how much her own?

"Oh," she said, somewhat embarrassed.

"What changed your mind?" Michali asked softly, resting his elbows on his knees. "Tell me the truth. All of it."

Would he understand? She thought her siblings might be the only people who really could, but they were in a house across the country, in a house she might never be able to really call her own again. She'd made her choice—this was how she'd keep them alive. So she had to tell Michali everything.

"I recognized the portrait. Or the woman in it," she amended. Her stomach twisted anxiously, and Rhea pressed her hands against it, shut her eyes against the glow of the firelight. She couldn't bear to see Michali's inevitable disbelief. "Your Aya Ksiga is my mother. It was her on that altar."

There was silence for a long moment. Just the slow hiss of Michali's breath as he let it out.

"Are you sure?" he asked finally.

Oh, she'd hoped he wouldn't ask that. No, she wasn't, but that was her business, not his. If only Lexos were here. He was the one who remembered their mother so well. He would have been sure.

But she had to do without him now. That was the choice she'd made. He would live. He would never love her again once he learned she had helped the Sxoriza, never call her his sister, but he would live. No matter what, they all would.

"I know," she said, burying her head in her hands. "You think I must have lost my mind, or inhaled too much incense. But it was her.

I remember her face, and it was there in that church. And it doesn't make sense, not really, but the more I think about it—"

She jumped, eyes flying open, when his fingers brushed against her bare wrist.

"Rhea," he said. "Rhea—"

"You're not meant to call me that."

He smiled, and it was full of something she couldn't identify. Pity, maybe. Or something close. "And you're not meant to change your mind as you have. I think perhaps we can dispense with certain formalities."

"You believe it, then? That she was my mother?"

"I believe that you do," he said, shrugging. "I believe that that's what matters, in the end."

"How can you be so calm?" She stood up and paced away from him. The relics on the walls felt so close, pressing in on her no matter where she looked. There were so many questions that moment in the church had not answered, no matter what else it had given her. How could Mama have kept this from her children? And what did it make Rhea now to be half saint, half Stratagiozi? She herself had said there was no difference, so why did it feel so strange? "Is your saint not worth less to you now? She married my father, after all."

Michali sat back. "I think we all do what we must to survive," he said, his voice measured. "If being your consort has taught me anything, it's that."

He was, she noticed, quite carefully avoiding any outright agreement with her—he probably thought she'd hallucinated in that church—but he was right. How many times had Rhea stepped closer to one danger to avoid another? It was what she was doing now. For herself and for her family.

She stopped in front of Michali's collection of church sketches. Holy, that's what he had called them. Was that the word for what she'd felt, kneeling in front of that portrait?

"She lived as a saint," Rhea said, reaching out to brush her finger along the outline of one of the sketches. That church, that memorial she'd snuck into—that had been Mama's. "But she died as my mother. That's the version of her I'm doing this for." Mama had left her old self behind in exchange for another chance at living, and perhaps another chance at power, too. And now Rhea would do it— would take up the mantle her mother had forsaken, for those same things. She turned, met Michali's shadowed eyes. "Is that enough?"

He got up, and for a moment Rhea felt her skin flush with heat as he considered her.

"Yes," he said. "For now."

TWENTY-THREE

RHEA

I f Michali kept up this pace, Rhea was likely to break her neck. He was ushering her down the staircase to the island dock, his hand firm at the small of her back, and the glare of the sunlight was so bright as it bounced off the ice that it was no use trying to step carefully. She thought it might have been just as effective to shut her eyes and hope for the best.

"What's the hurry?" she asked, clutching at Michali's arm as one of her feet slipped out from under her.

He hoisted her upright, pausing for only a moment before urging them on. "We're meeting a friend of mine. He is always either very early or very late and there is no telling which. I would rather not miss him if it's the former."

They'd ended their conversation the night before with the understanding that Rhea would need to be questioned by another member of the Sxoriza. She had expected that much, but she hadn't expected it to be so soon, or so early, and so she'd gone back to her room—that one night they'd spent in the same bed seemed like centuries ago now—and buried herself in blankets, only to be roused mere hours later by an already dressed Michali.

She was still yawning as they boarded the boat, but the winter breeze did much to wake her, and by the time they reached the promenade, her whole body was alight with shivers. Soon they were tracing the steps Rhea had taken alone through the city that night, searching for the Sxoriza hideout with no idea that Michali was barely half an hour behind her. This time he was at her side, his pace matched to hers. Rhea knew too well the feeling of hurrying after her father, or her brother, and allowed herself to be just the slightest bit grateful.

It was easier, this time, to spare a glance for the people crowded into the square, for the tight hunger she saw on even the brightest of faces. When she'd first arrived, she'd thought surely her father had no idea that these people—his people, the ones he'd sacrificed blood and body for—were suffering so.

But of course he knew. Her father knew every inch of his country, and it was only that he did not care. He'd got what he wanted. Stratathoma and the seat inside it, and when he spoke about Thyzakos with all that love and heart, it was for the land but not the people living on it. Baba cared for what he could own, and it would undo him. Undo all of them if she did not succeed.

Michali opened the secret door using the coin, which he'd taken back from Rhea as soon as they'd left the catacombs, and held open the trapdoor to allow her down first. They passed through the corridor together, Rhea keeping to the middle as much as she could and looking everywhere but at the skulls.

"I may have changed my mind," she said, eager to break the silence that had persisted since leaving the Laskaris house, "but I don't think I will ever be persuaded to change my customs. How you all live with these bones is beyond me."

"It's a reminder of what waits for us all." Michali looked over his shoulder at her as he ducked through the doorway into the room under the church. "Well, almost all of us."

"I take it your friend is not here," Rhea said.

"Any minute, I think," Michali said, running his hand through his hair to shake out the snow.

The room was much as they'd left it, with only a few signs that anybody else had been there. The linens on the pallet in the corner had been changed, some of the water drunk.

She hoped they wouldn't be here long. It was strange, standing in what she now knew to be a memorial to her mother, looking up at a prayer written to her. It left Rhea too wanting, too much alone.

Soon enough, she could see torchlight nearing the mouth of the corridor. Footsteps echoed toward them, a shadow filled the doorway, and a man stepped through. He was tall, tall enough that he had to duck his head a bit to stand in the chamber, and his dark eyes were barely visible under his thick, heavy brows. When he smiled, Rhea was taken aback by the white glint of his teeth.

"So Michali was telling the truth. We do indeed have a Stratagiozi's daughter among us," he said in accented Thyzaki. Amolovak, she thought, or perhaps Chuzhak. "Welcome to our little hideaway." He bent to kiss her on each cheek, and she tried not to wince as his beard scraped her skin.

"It's lovely," she said, stepping back. "Very homey. Have you thought about doing a touch of decorating?"

"Well, with your help, hopefully we will not have to be underground here much longer," the man said.

"We don't have much time, Piros," Michali said, and came around Rhea to stand by him. "We should get right to it before our guest changes her mind again."

Rhea glared at Michali and was satisfied to see him recoil involuntarily. "Please forgive him," she said to Piros. "He thinks he's very funny."

"I wonder what could have ever given him that idea," Piros said, knocking his elbow against Michali's with a wide smile. "Come, let's sit."

Piros directed them to one of the plinths and dragged three cartons out from the corner of the chamber, arranging them around the plinth like seats at a table. He spread his cloak on one for Rhea, waiting for her and Michali to sit before he joined them.

"I will start by welcoming you heartily to our cause, Thyspira." He removed a folded piece of parchment from his coat. "With your help we will bring independence to Thyzakos. And then Amolova and the rest of the continent in turn."

Amolova was held tightly by Ammar, its Stratagiozi, and dissidents there, who according to Ammar's official reports did not exist, were often killed, or kept in remote prisons. Anyone who wanted independence was wise to find refuge elsewhere, as it seemed Piros had done.

"I admire your dedication," she said, feeling slightly ashamed. If the other Sxoriza were like Piros, her motives for being here would only continue to pale in comparison. It was selfish, what she was doing, but did that really matter, as long as she succeeded?

"My dedication?" Piros raised his eyebrows. "It's Michali's we should be commending. Not everybody is willing to die for the cause."

Was that really still his plan? Yes, in marrying her, Michali had sworn himself to die. Only a few nights ago, the prospect of his death hadn't bothered her at all. But sacrificing him now, when she was depending on him to be her tether to this new side, left her uneasy. What would her life look like in the Sxoriza alone? Would she still be able to wield the influence she needed to in order to protect her family?

"Perhaps," she said, "he doesn't have to."

Michali scoffed. "We aren't here to discuss nonsense. We're here to verify whether—"

"If what you want in the end is the dissolution of the Stratagiozis," she said, careful to sound as relaxed as she could, "would it not be wise to take advantage of a chance to rid Thyzakos of its Stratagiozi entirely? You might kill my family, of course, but if you don't take Stratathoma itself, a steward will march on the gates before the day is out."

"Perhaps," Michali said, shrugging, "but we would use that moment of transition to claim our independence here in the Ksigora."

"And then what?" Rhea pressed. "You have your fledgling nation for a fortnight, and then a steward—or Ammar himself—comes and snatches it out from under you?"

"We have plans," he replied. "Forgive me if we don't share them with you just yet."

"And forgive me if I don't believe that your operation can withstand an assault." Rhea looked between Piros and Michali, hesitating for a moment. If she did nothing, and if she let the Sxoriza follow these plans they professed to have, her family would die. A steward would take power again. The Argyrosi would fade into obscurity, their deaths not a price paid for a new order but just more blood left in the earth.

She had to help Michali. Make him and the Sxoriza into something lasting, something powerful, because at least this way, she and her family had a chance to survive.

"Michali said he went to Stratathoma to investigate an assassination," she said to Piros, "but that he could not strike alone without certain capture and, ultimately, failure. In truth, I see no reason for any bloodshed. If you promise me my family's safety, I can help you do more than trade my father for whichever steward would replace him. I can help you sack the citadel. I can help you take Stratathoma."

"Is that possible?" Piros asked, his voice low and alight with hope, even as Michali said, "Your family's safety?"

"Yes," she said to Piros, "with some complications." She refused to look at Michali. She couldn't let him see how important this was to her. He couldn't realize this was the only reason she was here. "I can get you and a small force in through the walls, and you can have your independence while leaving my family alive. You could take Stratathoma in one go, and hold it yourself to keep the seat from being filled in my father's stead."

She was, of course, leaving something out. Baba's matagios and the powers that came with it would never fade while he lived, and even if he did die, they would only pass to Lexos, and so on down through the blood. Perhaps Michali knew that, and that was why he'd wanted the life of every Argyros.

But perhaps he didn't, and he would see no real threat in leaving the Argyrosi alive. She put on a smile. "You must think about the future. Holding my father hostage will do far more for your continued success than killing him."

"Your father," Michali began angrily, but Piros rested his hand on Michali's shoulder.

"You should listen to her," he said. "I don't think we can expect every advance we make to be at the point of a dagger. Thyspira here has far more experience in negotiation, and a hostage could be useful."

"It doesn't matter," Michali said. "We have no force large enough to breach the walls. I saw as much when I was there. No, we bide our time until we can get one man in. Then we strike from here, claim our right to rule and get our defenses in place before a steward or another Stratagiozi can take the seat."

Rhea knew there was quite a lot about the Sxoriza's full working operation that was being kept from her, but she couldn't imagine it had the forces necessary to prevent reoccupation by one of the stewards. Perhaps there were places beyond the continent where it was easier to claim independence, but the federation's grip was tight, and had been for a thousand years. Even Thyzakos, the newest of the continent's nations, had been carved out of Trefazio only a decade after the saints' massacre. Rhea was not sure where the Sxoriza had got the idea that their independence would be in any way tolerated.

Michali was right, though, that the citadel at Stratathoma would be impossible to conquer without significant strength. The walls were near impenetrable, the doors thick and easily defended. Baba had needed an army, its forces wrested from the grasp of every Thyzak steward through sheer intimidation, to take it. But there was another way, one that could guarantee the lives of those she loved.

"You have no need of a force that large," she said. "If I got you in through Stratathoma's outer walls, you could take it with twenty well-trained soldiers. Perhaps fewer. I can give you the heart of power in this country. You will not have to protect your independence from anyone."

"How?" Piros asked, leaning in.

Rhea swallowed hard, resisting the urge to fuss with the ends of her hair. Once she told them this, it couldn't be undone. Baba would fall. They all would. But it would be in a manner she could control, and she would be there, waiting to protect them. It was for the best— she was sure of that.

"There's a beach," she said. "On the north side of the cliff. My brother and I used to swim there in the summers. But once Baba gave him the tides, he brought them in close to the cliffs. To defend Stratathoma, he said."

"So what use to me is this?" Michali asked. "If I cannot get my soldiers to the beach, that's hardly any help."

Rhea sighed. Michali had no siblings, had no bonds strong enough between him and his parents that they could bear the weight of any sort of leverage. This was exactly her sort of work. "I can get him to open the tides again. It will leave the beach vulnerable, and from there your soldiers can climb the cliff path. It'll take them into the grounds, with access to the servants' entrance."

"And that's enough?" Piros asked. "To take the citadel?"

He sounded doubtful. "My father has no troops of his own garrisoned there to defend it," Rhea said, meaning to reassure him. "He's not like Ammar."

"Well," Piros said, "that may not hold for much longer. I have reports that your father has sent your brother to reach out to Tarro Domina."

Of course he had. Baba had always wanted what the Dominas had. Legacy, history, and absolute control. It was only natural that Baba would look to Tarro for help shoring up his weakening position. But Lexos, sent alone? That was interesting. What had passed at the council meeting that left Baba reluctant to see Tarro again?

"Tarro's influence cannot be overstated," Piros continued, looking grave. "If he promises your brother troops, his stewards will comply, and we will be wildly outmatched."

Michali shook his head. "Tarro has never promised troops to a foreign leader before. The Argyros boy cannot be as persuasive as all that. Besides which, we have Falka there to work against him. He won't get what he's after." He stood up, brushing down the front of his coat as though he was ready to leave. "There is no sense in taking such a risk. I don't believe we are strong enough yet to take Stratathoma, and I don't believe that Tarro will come to Argyros's aid."

These boys. Even Piros, with gray threading through his beard, seemed so young compared to her. They had no idea that Baba's best weapon had always been her brother.

"Listen," she said. "You don't know what being an Argyros means. If Vuomorra doesn't give my brother what he wants, he will try somewhere else next."

Michali opened his mouth to reply, but she wasn't finished.

"You don't understand," she said gently, looking up at him. It wasn't his fault, exactly. Just that there were some things only the Argyrosi could know. "We have lived a hundred years watching everything else fade. We have been each other's only constants. Us, and Stratathoma, and this country. You are fighting for your lives, but they mean nothing to my brother. Protecting our family is the only thing that does." She swallowed hard, the weight of her own choices pressing down on her shoulders. He was trying to do good, Lexos. He was. But it wouldn't work. He couldn't see that everything he did was just Baba all over again. "Alexandros will do whatever he must. You would be foolish to assume otherwise."

"So?" Michali said, but instead of the challenge she might have heard in her father's voice, or in Lexos's, there was only curiosity.

"So this is your chance," she said. "My father is vulnerable now in a way he never will be again. Take him hostage now, and look to the long term." The family, alive and well. That was the most important thing. They would survive. But so would Michali. He couldn't suffer the same fate as every other consort. Without him, what assurance could be had of her own safety? Of any influence over the Sxoriza's actions?

"And you, leading the Sxoriza from Stratathoma." Michali shook his head, but she couldn't let him say a thing. She barreled on. "Did you truly mean to die here at the end of the season, and leave the Sxoriza leaderless?"

"If it serves the cause best," he said. "If it buys us the time and cover we need."

Piros looked grim, as though this was an argument the two of them had had before, but he did not contradict Michali. Rhea wanted to smack their heads together.

"I can spare you," she said. "I can. But if I do, the season will not change, and soon enough my father will see what I've done. When he does, my father will see I am disloyal. He will ally himself with the Dominas, and his power will strengthen; you will lose every chance you have."

"Exactly," Michali said, but he was watching her with narrowed, curious eyes.

"So this is why you must strike now. Why you must let me help you take Stratathoma. The end of the season will come. I will pretend to carry out my duty, word of your reported death will spread, and I will return home. My father will believe I am loyal, believe he is safe. He will realize the truth eventually, when the season doesn't change. There is nothing I can do about that. But before then, you'll have perhaps a fortnight. Enough time to take Stratathoma and take my family hostage."

Piros looked to Michali, mouth crooked in the beginnings of a hopeful smile. Good—if she had him, he could help reach Michali, and keep him from dying for the cause when it would do nobody any good.

"*Elado,*" she said, leaning in. "Know when you're beaten. This is everything you want, Michali, and if you let this chance pass, it will never come again. This is how it must be. We fake your death at the close of the season. I go home to Stratathoma, get my brother to open the beach, and let you in."

"And then," Piros added, "we tear the whole federation down, seat by seat. Think what we could do from Stratathoma, Michali, with Vasilis Argyros under our thumb. We can use his power to protect our independence, to protect the Ksigora. We might even set the whole of Thyzakos free at once."

"And I suppose winter will just continue?" Michali asked.

Rhea caught the flash of worry that crossed Piros's face, and reached out to lay a comforting hand on his arm. Winter, forever. She knew enough to know it would have consequences she couldn't predict now. The harvests, trade . . . It made her ache to think of. People would starve. Families would die.

Not hers, though. That was what mattered. Michali would take Stratathoma. The Sxoriza would win, and her family would live.

"It isn't what I would choose if I could," she said. "But I can think of no one so well prepared for the season as you and yours. You might even say this is what Ksigorans were built for."

Piros laughed, covering her hand with his and shaking it heartily. Across the table, Michali sighed, resigned, and nodded.

There. Concession. She'd won. And he was watching her now, a fresh appraisal in his eyes that Rhea couldn't look away from. It lingered there even as Piros closed the conversation with a set of pleasantries, even as he wrapped himself back up in his furs and tramped down the main corridor, promising to write to Michali soon to sort everything out.

The air felt colder with Piros gone, the chill from the stone reaching farther in. Rhea looked to Michali and raised her eyebrows as she pulled her coat up higher around her neck.

"Well?" she said. "Are we going, too?"

She hoped he would say yes. It had been easy enough to ignore while discussing their plans, but now the weight of her mother's presence clouded the air, leaving it thick and waiting like a storm was about to break.

"Not yet," Michali said. He was still looking at her with that spark of consideration, and a sort of fondness that Rhea didn't want to examine too closely. "There's something I want to show you."

He led her down a corridor opposite the one they'd come in through. Ahead she could see rubble blocking the passage, just like Michali had said that first night she'd come here, but he turned sharply into the dark, ducking through a low gap in the wall that she wouldn't have spotted herself.

"Don't worry," he said, reaching back through to offer his hand. "I was lying about the spiders before."

She'd followed him this far. What was a little farther?

His hand was warm against hers as she took it, and she gripped it tightly, let him draw her through the gap. The air here was black and close, clinging to the inside of her lungs, and she could taste dust, dry and sweet, with every breath.

"Hang on," Michali said. She heard the strike of flint and then a torch flared to life. Mounted on the wall, it lit everything in wavering gold. Rhea blinked, looking around at the collection of items filling the room.

First were the books. Stacks and stacks of them, their pages wrinkled and covered in mold, each labeled in the slightly altered Thyzaki lettering Rhea recognized now as Saint's. Some of them looked like the same book—in fact, most of them did. The text the same, the letters shaped almost identically, as though they'd been copied from book to book by the same hand.

Tucked between the stacks were piles of cloth—black and essentially shapeless—and odd assortments of containers made from what she supposed had once been silver. They were all tarnished now, some turning an odd shade of green, and their delicate latticework had snapped in spots.

"What is all this?" she asked, picking up what must have been an incense burner and lifting it to her nose. The smell was still there, and still strong. Sweet and spiced, with a touch of something that made her feel a bit ill. They'd burned something close to it back in Mama's makeshift church, before Stratathoma, and for a moment Rhea's memory of her was clearer than ever—Rhea's own hand, reaching up to twine a lock of Mama's black hair around her finger.

"They rescued these from the church before it fell." Michali was close, his head bent to avoid the low ceiling, and she could practically feel his words before she heard them, could feel the shape of them in his body where it brushed against her own. "Patreou vestments, burners. Prayer books."

"All for my mother?" The effort to save these things, to preserve Mama's memory—Rhea could not imagine anybody doing that for Baba.

"For Aya Ksiga," Michali said.

"What a lovely bit of equivocation," she said, but there was no bite to her voice. How could that bother her when she was here, so much of her mother within reach?

She began to pick her way through the piles of clutter, fingertips leaving streaks in the dust where she trailed them across the tops of books. Maybe she could take one back to the house with her and ask Michali to translate it for her. She would really have to get better at Saint's Thyzaki now that she was the daughter of one.

Near the back of the room, where the torchlight only just reached, stood a pedestal similar to the one she'd seen in the church in Paragou. But there was no portrait. Nothing to worship, no likeness of her mother to offer comfort. She turned in a slow circle, scanning the stacks for anything like it.

"What are you looking for?" Michali asked. "I'm afraid most of the altar burned along with the church."

"Oh." Her shoulders dropped. "I just wanted to see her, really."

Michali turned, one hand braced on the ceiling. "There might be something down here, but we don't have one of the true portraits, like the one you saw in Paragou. Only a few have survived this long, and they're all kept up in the mountain churches, along with most of the records we were able to salvage."

Rhea took another step into the clutter and knelt by a stack of books, on top of which balanced a small silver box. "Is she like that in all of them?"

"Like what?"

"Veiled."

He was quiet for a moment. "I don't know," he said, almost embarrassed. "I've never seen the others."

She sat back on her heels, staring at him. He'd only ever laid eyes on one portrait, and yet he still felt that he was in any place to doubt her when she called Aya Ksiga her mother. "Why not?"

"Because your father would burn them to bits if he found out where they were," Michali said sharply. "Most people who worship have knelt in front of a portrait like the one in that church, and nothing more." He gestured to the books and vestments around them. "They've never seen this. But now you have. You, of all people."

"I'm not sure you get to sound so bitter about it when you're the one who brought me here."

"Yes, but I—" He broke off, running one hand roughly through his hair. "I brought you here because I want you to understand. I want you to realize what you're claiming when you say that you're her daughter."

Rhea shrugged. "I don't mean to claim anything."

She didn't know what else there was to say, or what, in fact, Michali wanted to hear from her. And it seemed he didn't, either, as he let out a small noise of frustration and dropped his chin to his chest.

Well, while he sorted himself out, there was quite a lot for Rhea to do. She turned back to the silver box, the hinges creaking so loudly as she opened it that she feared they might snap.

Inside were a trio of necklaces, each hung with a large pendant painted in colors that, unlike so many of the other objects collected here, were still fresh and bright.

She picked one up and turned it over. There was a latch on the side, small and easily mistakable for a crack in the paint. Carefully, she slid her thumbnail underneath it and worked it open until the pendant split and the front of it lifted away. Not a pendant, really. A locket.

This one was damaged inside, but there were enough streaks of paint left over to suggest that some design had been created there and then scraped away, hard enough to crack the very shell of the locket. Rhea peered closely, trying to pick out each color—blue, red, and some gold, but on one side, there were bits of black, and a curve that could have been meant to be a shoulder, or an arm.

She set it down and reached for the second locket. It opened more easily than the first, but was in even worse condition inside, and offered nothing to help Rhea reconstruct whatever image it was that had been destroyed.

"What's all that?" Michali asked, but she didn't answer as she picked up the third necklace, the pendant fitting just so in the palm of her hand.

Of the three, it seemed most intact from the outside, and that held true when Rhea opened it. The paint was largely preserved, with only a few chips missing from the blue and red stripes that ran across one side. And while the other side had cracked, it did very little to obscure the portrait there, done in miniature. A woman with dark hair like Rhea's and a smile so full of sorrow even the worst painter could not have missed it.

If she'd had any doubt before, it was gone now—that was Mama. Aya Ksiga and Mama.

She'd want me here, Rhea thought. Here with her. She would understand why Rhea was doing all this.

"*Mala,*" Michali breathed, and Rhea jumped. She hadn't realized he'd got so close. "Is that her?"

"I think so." She stood up slowly, and held the locket out into the light so that Michali could see it better. "It's different than the one in Paragou. No veil, and she looks—"

"Young," he interrupted. "She looks so young." He shook his head. "This isn't Aya Ksiga as she's worshipped. That must be why it's down here, why it's . . . I don't know. But it *is* her."

"Now do you see?"

Gently, he took the locket from Rhea's hand and held it up alongside her face. "You really are hers, aren't you?"

She nodded. "That portrait—that's how she looked when I knew her," she said. "I mean, not exactly, but she was never a saint to me." She wrapped her fingers around his wrist and brought it down until the locket was between them. "I'm not trying to claim your saint, Michali. I'm trying to honor my mother."

"I understand," he said. But he was looking at her strangely, and there was a thoughtfulness to his voice, one she was not entirely sure she liked.

"What is it?"

"Nothing," he said. "It's just, now that I know what to look for, you really do look like her. And with the veil . . ."

She frowned. "What about the veil?"

He rested his finger underneath her chin, turning her face up to what light there was. Rhea fought the urge to shiver as he studied her. "It could be you," he said. "We could tell them it's you."

"Tell who what?" She stepped back, and he let his hand fall away from her.

"The mountain camps," he said. "It's been hard to keep up morale since we married, and I can't tell them all we mean to fake my death, can I? We can bring you up there to give them a blessing. Show them the Sxoriza have a real saint to count among our number. If people hear that Aya Ksiga is walking again, they'll come flooding from every direction. Another step toward breaking the Stratagiozi hold."

"I'm not sure," she said. "Does it have to be me?" After all, she'd been traipsing around the Ksigora for weeks, and nobody had noticed the resemblance yet. "I know nothing about your saints. How could I impersonate one correctly?"

Michali smiled. "Wasn't it you saying how similar my saints and your Stratagiozis are? I'm sure you can do it."

Rhea shifted uncomfortably. It was nice, she supposed, to be believed in. To have Michali trust that she could accomplish the task given to her. But it wasn't as simple as all that. Her mother had been worshipped without reservation. She had been holy.

"I'm not one, though," Rhea said quietly. "A saint, I mean. It would be a lie, to let people worship anything less."

"That isn't the point." Michali ducked down to meet her eyes. "It's not who they worship, but that they worship at all."

She shook her head. Such a malleable pragmatism at the core of him, one that seemed to slip in and out of sight behind the soft shine of all his ideals. "I don't think that's true."

He seemed taken aback, and for a moment he did not answer. At last, he sighed and stepped back, holding out the locket for her to take.

"When you are Thyspira," he said, "is it not the same thing? Isn't the symbol more important than the woman inside it?"

She knew what answer Baba would have her give. But being someone's symbol hadn't suited her then, and it didn't feel any better now. Was this really the truth of the choice she'd made? Had she simply traded one mask for another? Did she always have to be someone other than herself to serve her family?

But could she really afford to say no to Michali's proposition? Her place in the Sxoriza was delicate, even if she'd won over Piros, and her family's lives were in her hands now.

"Tell me you will." Michali's face turned solemn. "They will see the saints are walking again. They will know the world is changing."

It didn't matter how it made her feel. It was important. And besides, Michali was asking, his voice low as it had been the night before, when he'd said her own name. He wanted her help. He wanted her here, in a way nobody else ever had.

"All right," she said, taking the locket from him. He shut his eyes in what she supposed was relief, and she didn't look away, only kept watching, kept tracing the fan of his lashes with her own gaze, kept wondering how close she'd have to get to hear the beat of his heart. "Yes, all right."

TWENTY-FOUR

RHEA

It was decided that Rhea would travel with Michali to the Sxoriza camps as soon as possible, which was how, only two mornings following her second visit to the catacombs, she ended up sitting on the bed in his room with him crouched in front of her, his bottom lip pinched between his teeth.

Her hair was already in the appropriate loose spirals that her mother seemed to prefer. All that was left before she dressed was to give her the veil that Aya Ksiga wore in her portraits—well, in most of them, Rhea amended, thinking of the locket she now kept tucked in the tin on her nightstand alongside her handful of kymithi. She and Michali had discussed having her wear something out of fabric, like the sort of thing that was in fashion in Vuomorra, but they'd eventually agreed that a stripe of kohl across her temples would look more accurate, although Rhea's concern was not so much that the veil be accurate but rather that it make it more difficult for anyone to discern that she was not exactly Aya Ksiga come back to life.

Michali being the more familiar of the two with Aya Ksiga's general image, it was his responsibility now to apply it, something he seemed uncomfortable with as he turned a stick of kohl over in his hands.

"I'll press too hard," he said, sounding so genuinely worried that something unhooked in Rhea's chest.

"You wanted to help," she said, coating her voice in a layer of snide nastiness—anything to keep that warmth in her chest from spreading.

"So I did." He set his shoulders. "Shut your eyes, then."

She did, waited a moment in the close dark, and then felt a brush against her jaw. Michali's hand, holding her still, steadying her face, his fingers sneaking into her hair.

"You'll tell me if I hurt you," he said.

Rhea flushed, knew her skin was warming against his. "I will."

For a moment, nothing, and then slowly, there came the drag of the kohl across her eyelid. Gently, carefully, but still Rhea startled, jerking back until Michali urged her forward again.

"Easy," he said.

"I'm not a horse."

"Thank you; I am well aware."

She flicked her eyes open in time to see him swallow an exasperated smile. Quickly, she shut them again, feeling strangely as though it had been rude of her to see him like that.

"Why did they paint her that way?" she asked, hurrying to break the quiet. "Or this way, I should say. With the black across her eyes. Did she really wear a veil back then?"

"It depends on who you ask," he said, and the kohl pressed again against her eyelid. "North of Ksigori they say it's something she wore herself; south of it they say it's something a painter must have added after she died. A mark of mourning."

"And you? What do you think?"

"I think it—"

"I know, I know," she said, leaning back from him, only to be gently repositioned. "You think it only matters that it's there at all."

"Actually," Michali said, but she could hear the smile in his voice, "I think she wore it as a mark of her gift."

And yes, Rhea had forgotten—as a saint, Mama would have held a gift in her blood just as Rhea herself did.

"What was it?" she asked. It didn't matter. Still, she wanted to know.

"The night sky," Michali said.

Rhea opened her eyes, her lashes brushing against his fingertips. He was so close. It was a wonder she was not more alarmed. "My brother has that," she said. "He got it from our father, who got it from his predecessor. It couldn't have belonged to my mother."

He shook his head. "Not the stars. The sky behind them."

The spread of dark. Emptiness and waiting. Rhea supposed there was nothing else so suited to the mother she couldn't quite remember. Maybe, if things had gone differently, that gift would have been hers now, passed down from Mama. Instead, when Mama died without the proper rites, it had seeped back into the earth, just as the other Argyros gifts would have if Michali had got around to killing them all, as he'd originally planned. She was here now, to protect her family from that, but she spared a thought to wonder if perhaps that wouldn't be such a bad thing: for the matagios to disappear and for the lines to fade from her palms. If only that were possible without offering her own life up in exchange.

"And so," Michali went on, "the kohl." He began to smudge the black he'd drawn at her temples. "Your mother must have had a penchant for the symbolic. Seems to run in the family."

"I think I far prefer the resemblance," Rhea said. Lingering too long on the question of the symbolic made this whole endeavor feel even more uncomfortable.

"You don't really look as much like her as I first thought," Michali said. "Enough for our purposes, certainly, but there's something else."

He tapped her nose with one finger, and Rhea blinked.

"My nose belongs to my father, I think," she said. "As far as my eyes, they are said to be very Argyros, but I confess I don't know whether that means they are my mother's or my father's. Recent discoveries aside, she was as much an Argyros as him."

"I have met your father," Michali said. "Close your eyes, please. I have met him and I think I see quite a bit less of his face in yours than you do."

"Only one of us has had the dubious privilege of looking at the faces in question for a hundred years, so you will forgive me if I take my assessment a bit more seriously than I take yours." She met his gaze briefly before retreating again into the dark. "But thank you."

It was odd, she thought. He was touching her eyelid so carefully, but the hand he kept cradling the back of her head was firm and steady, fingertips pressing into the ridges of her skull. She supposed Lexos would say she had left herself too vulnerable. That with the twitch of his wrist Michali might break her neck, and leave Vasilis Argyros's daughter wide-eyed and empty on his bedroom floor.

But she was not vulnerable to the same things anymore, she thought as Michali shifted slightly and began to work the kohl toward the opposite temple. No, she was rather afraid she was becoming vulnerable to something else altogether.

"There," Michali said a moment later, and his hand left the back of her head, the dark behind her closed eyes brightening as, she presumed, he stood up. "Now to the rest."

There hadn't been many indications as to what the saints preferred to wear in the portrait she'd seen, and Michali could offer no real advice. With a strange tightness in her throat, Rhea rose from the bed and went through her things.

She pulled out a jacket and its matching trousers. Black, with gold edging, scrolling silver embroidery looping around the buttons and sweeping up to curl along the high collar. She was here because of what Baba had done with his seat, because of the danger his actions had put his family in, and she never wanted to be as hated and feared as he was. But everything she knew about power, about the home it made in a person, came from him—from the image of Baba, the black of his jacket sharpening his narrow shoulders, drawing out the shadows under his eyes, the gold thread glinting even in the darkest room.

Michali turned away while she dressed, and didn't look back until she said his name, her jacket buttoned up to under her chin, her trousers tucked neatly into her boots.

"How does it look?" she said.

He blinked slowly, and said, "Come and see."

He stood aside as she stepped in front of the warped mirror that was tucked in the corner of his room, aimed at nothing in particular. In the painting, her mother's eyes had been glowing like coals through the shadow. So now were hers, that Argyros blue, that down-turned shape that she had thought was so specific to her family, the shape she had started to recognize on the faces of the Ksigorans around her.

"I heard a word for this once," she said, tilting her head to one side. "For what I'm doing." The kohl carved hollows into her face, stretching up past her brows and out to her temples, where it faded into her unbound hair. It was more than her mother had worn in the portrait, but it obscured the particular sharpness of her features, left her softened and looking as though she could belong to an age thousands of years gone.

"Oh?" Michali came to stand behind her, his eyes meeting hers in the glass.

"Heresy."

He smiled. "I think that's a luxury nobody can afford anymore. Back then they could argue over the right way to worship. Now we barely have the breath to do it at all."

"You told me you weren't a believer, but you sound like one."

"Perhaps," he said, tilting his head to one side, "I was only waiting for the right sort of saint."

He didn't seem nearly so young to her these days. Their wedding couldn't have been more than a month prior, but looking at him now, Rhea would have called it another lifetime. They'd begun this marriage with only fear and secrecy between them. Now there was resolve instead, a shared determination.

It had never been that way with Lexos, or Baba. And of course there were still things about the Sxoriza she didn't know, and things about her that Michali didn't in turn. He thought his ideals had moved her, become her own, and he would be disappointed, she knew, when the time came and her loyalty to her family made itself clear. But for now she was here. Doing something only she could do. Finding something that was only hers.

When they left the house, it was early still, light just tingeing the sky. They crossed the lake, the stillness in the air broken by the gentle splash of the paddles as the servants rowed steadily, taking surreptitious glances at Rhea with every stroke, a reverence in their eyes that left her shaken.

At the heart of her, she was only Rhea, she reminded herself. Still the woman inside the symbol. She'd had plenty of practice as Thyspira. This was no different.

They found the promenade empty in the new morning. Michali dismissed the servants and led Rhea quickly toward the Laskaris stables, where she found herself paired once again with Lefka, whose livery was not the now-familiar Laskaris crimson but black instead.

There had been grooms and stable hands when she'd been here last. Today they were nowhere to be found. Neither were the guards who had accompanied them into the countryside, to Paragou. Instead, when Rhea and Michali left the stable, they rode out alone, the clip of their horses' shod hooves echoing mournfully in the deserted streets. Michali led them away from the center of the city, and slowly the road under them began to climb, the buildings thinning out until at last they left the city behind and reached the base of the cliffs.

Their path was following a narrow, well-worn shepherd's track that picked its way through the hillside scrub before disappearing into the distance. Here the wind was strong, unhindered by the buildup of the city, and what trees remained grew at a slant, the result of years' worth of buffeting from gale after gale. Farther along the path, Rhea knew the forest would return, would enclose them in its thorned and twisting grip, but out here in the brush it seemed impossible that the world could contain anything more than this— yellowing grass and stone whipped clean.

"Are the camps on the clifftop?" Rhea asked, drawing Lefka level with Michali.

He shook his head. "It's too open up there. The wind would tear the camps apart. We're headed round to the back side."

It was hard riding, much harder than crossing the mountains that first day coming into the Ksigora, harder than their trip into the countryside. It made Rhea particularly thankful for Lefka, who knew the path and ignored the nervous clench of Rhea's thighs as they picked their way through the rocks that littered the track.

The wind that Michali had mentioned was making itself felt, too. While the trail was hidden from the city by sheer distance, it was very much out in the open, and Rhea's eyes were streaming, carrying streaks of kohl down her cheeks. She could only be thankful it didn't seem quite cold enough for her tears to freeze.

Ahead, the path veered to the left, following the bare hillside up to curve around onto the clifftop, but Michali kept them moving forward, off the path and into the shelter of an outcropping of rocks. If she looked closely, she could make out faint markings on the rocks as they wound their way between them. Symbols to line the trail, she supposed.

The sun was bright overhead when Michali at last drew to a halt and pointed to the vista ahead of them. The back side of the cliffs tumbled down, a vast mountainside cluttered with trees, marked clearly by the beds of ancient rivers. They formed a deep gorge, its floor narrow and winding—an old river gone dry—before climbing back up as the cliffs continued north for miles. Once, this had all been one plateau, but time and water had created this massive split, fractures jutting off it in every direction.

"This is the back basin," he explained. "It's practically Amolova out here, even though Ksigori's just over the rise."

"And the camp?"

"In one of the dry riverbeds off the main gorge. These all used to be offshoots of the Dovikos, but they dried up ages ago." He hesitated, and then went on. "The saints could not keep them flowing."

"Ah."

The Stratagiozis had stolen their power from the saints, but nobody seemed to remember that the saints had stolen their power, too.

They'd taken it from the earth. The currents in the water, the motion of the sun—one by one, these things had been stripped from the world and clutched tightly in the hands of man. How exactly they'd done it was lost, burned along with every church when Luco Domina had murdered his fellow saints and turned himself into something else. Rhea supposed it was something like what Baba had done, like the bloodied earth he had swallowed after murdering the family before theirs, the earth that had left the matagios on his tongue.

But she kept thinking of the river crossing, of the color of the Dovikos that day. And for the first time, she wondered if some of that power was slipping back to where it had come from.

Michali set off again, and she followed, gave Lefka her head and let her choose her own way along the path. The trees were bare and snow was heavy on the ground, and it should've been all stillness and muffled silence like it was at the Laskaris house, but instead, here there was a sense of motion, almost, a crackling, crystalline restlessness that she could practically hear. It reminded her of Nitsos's garden, of the clockwork snowfall and the delicate whir of that little blue hummingbird, although nothing from that garden would survive long out here.

She had almost forgotten where they were going when a branch snapped ahead. She yanked hard on Lefka's reins, bringing her up short, and ducked low, protecting herself. She'd learned her lesson. But Michali just twisted in his saddle and waved her forward.

"It's only the guards," he said, "letting me know they're here."

They continued on, Rhea glancing nervously around her, but nothing happened, and eventually they arrived at a place where the ground dropped off in front of them. Michali dismounted and left his horse, coming to hold Lefka's reins while Rhea got down.

"We leave them here," he explained, gesturing to the drop. "Don't worry. Someone will look after them."

Rhea rubbed Lefka's soft nose—for goodbye, for good luck—and then followed Michali to the edge of what looked like a narrow ravine. A path wound down to the floor, so treacherous that it couldn't have fit two feet side by side, and when it reached the bottom, it disappeared among the boulders there, all made of the same white stone she recognized from the Dovikos and all perhaps as tall as a man on horseback.

"Stay close," Michali said as he started down the path. "The ground is loose here."

She was sweating by the time they hit the bottom, and her vision felt blurry from staring intently at her footsteps, avoiding the places where the collecting snow had obscured the trail. The path had led them into the bed of a gone river, and they now followed it what must have been upstream, away from the main gorge that ran like a snake between the cliffs. The boulders had been worn into strange, twisting shapes by since-vanished water, and as Rhea walked between them, she felt her breath tight in her chest. No man could make something like this. Not her, not Nitsos, not Chrysanthi.

"Almost there," Michali called. Rhea narrowed her eyes at his back. He'd said that nearly twenty minutes ago.

At last, he slowed to let her catch up. "It's ahead," he told her, "just around the bend." Then, carefully, he reached out and swiped his thumb along the curve of her cheek. "There." He held it up, and it was coated in stray kohl from her eyes. "The rest of it looks all right."

"High praise," she said dryly, but she could hear her own nervousness. So could Michali.

"You'll be fine." He checked over his shoulder to make sure they were still alone. "You know what to do. And she was your mother. If anybody can do this, it's you."

"Are you sure?"

"I am." He stepped in closer. "Remember the good you will do. Remember the hope you'll give them."

Hope. Rhea had never given anyone that before. Thyspira, for all her pretty dresses and sly smiles, for all the gifts being her consort came with, never left a place happier than she found it. She arrived in a flurry of false joy, and left only grief in her wake.

This was better. However strange it felt, however uncomfortably this sat on her skin, it was better.

"Let's go," she said, smoothing back her hair. "Before I lose the rest of my nerve."

Michali didn't answer, only lifted one corner of his mouth into a half smile and turned, continuing up what Rhea supposed someone out of their right mind might call a path. The camp, when they arrived, was only visible in glimpses and snatches. Here a tent, three young men looking out from it with hungry, deep-set eyes. There two children darting behind one of the rocks, followed by an older woman, presumably their mother. A stack of wooden cartons filled with produce tucked in a tiny bit of flat space between boulders. Another tent, farther up, and next to it a makeshift lean-to, a fire crackling underneath it.

It looked quite like what she'd seen from Lexos's scout, but she'd expected only the outposts to seem so ramshackle. Had she been wrong? Were the Sxoriza not the threat she and Lexos had assumed them to be?

"There are others," Michali said, in response to the surprise Rhea knew she hadn't been able to keep from showing on her face. "Many, scattered through the gorge. We can't risk gathering all together, not until we have a stronger position. As long as men like Ammar and your father don't know exactly who or where we are, we're relatively safe from attack."

Strategy, then. Rhea could appreciate the value in seeming weaker than you were.

They passed the first tent, the three men inside eyeing her with evident shock, and Rhea grasped Michali's outstretched hand to vault up over one particularly large boulder to where the trail picked back up. Ahead, the fire under the lean-to glittered warmly. She longed to sit down in front of it and work some feeling back into her fingers but Michali was still moving. He was heading, it seemed, for a larger swath of flat ground farther up the ravine, where the snow draped more thickly and a collection of more permanent structures had been built.

Here there were more people, most of them young, their bodies whittled away by hunger. Voices drifted through the air, chatter and the occasional laughter of children, of whom there were a surprising number. Rhea adjusted her fine woolen coat and looked away, conscious of how well and warmly she was dressed.

Michali led her toward a different firepit, this one lined with blackened stone and dug into the center of the camp. Rhea heard whispers as they tramped through the snow, felt the stares of a growing crowd. A saint, she reminded herself. Walking where none had set foot for a thousand years. Had her mother been here? Had she blessed generations of these families back then? Or was Rhea simply looking for a connection where none could be found?

Well, whether her mother had been here or not, it was her turn now to bless the people gathered behind her. The exact rite had been lost, but the monks at Agiokon performed a version of it that had made its way to the Ksigora. Michali had shown her last night, and the knife strapped to her hip was a reminder of what she had to do. Almost like what Baba had done to become Stratagiozi.

"Now?" she whispered to Michali, and out of the corner of her eye, she caught his slight nod.

When she turned, she was faced with a throng of perhaps fifty people, knit tightly together between the climbing walls of the riverbed. It was at once too many and not enough, and she found herself searching each face, waiting for someone to look familiar, to recognize her. But they only looked back at her, their hands clasped, heads bent.

"My friends," Michali said, his voice echoing in the ravine. "You have dedicated yourselves to our cause for so long. You have sacrificed so much. Today I can tell you it has been worth it."

He looked over his shoulder at her, reached out to draw her level with him. For a moment Rhea felt as though she were back at Stratathoma, coming down the stairs as Thyspira with Lexos waiting at the bottom. She'd worn that name then, let it cover her over, let the evening break against it like waves. She could do it again now.

"You have heard the saints were slaughtered," Michali went on. He sounded the way she'd always expected a leader to sound— steadfast and full of faith. "You have heard our Aya Ksiga killed herself rather than submit to a Stratagiozi blade. You have heard lies. Stratagiozi lies, told to keep you from learning the truth: that Aya Ksiga lives."

There was no answer, just a rising murmur from a few of the children, each quickly hushed by their parent.

Michali kept going. "Indeed, she lives. And I bring her to you, to bless our cause, and to bless our people."

Now, she thought. Just like Mama. Do what she would.

"*Keresmata,*" she said to the crowd, lifting one hand in greeting. The crowd stared. Hunger on their faces, stripping the meat from their bodies. Rhea felt something catch in her throat and swallowed hard, let the light glancing off the snow blind her.

All these people, living and dying and wanting, and she was trying to protect her family from them. From the consequences of what Baba had done. What they had all helped Baba do. It was a sham. Her, hiding behind her mother's face and pretending she felt that same helpless rage that these people did.

But didn't she? Hadn't she always wanted better from Baba, only to find herself let down again and again? Didn't she feel used and left behind? It wasn't the same thing, not nearly, but Rhea took it like a hit all the same. What was she doing here? Standing between her family and ruin, and for what? So Baba could be disappointed in her all over again.

Michali cleared his throat, startling her. "Aya Ksiga?" he said.

"Yes." She took her knife from the pocket of her coat and held it up into the sunlit air, its bared blade glinting gently. A gasp from somewhere in the crowd, and Rhea fixed her eyes on the knife and refused to look. Whatever she saw in these faces—whatever worship, whatever resentment—it would be more than she could bear.

Instead she focused on the next step in the rite. There were no specifications, as far as she knew. Right palm or left—Michali had said it wouldn't matter. But there on her left was the black pattern that marked her as her father's daughter. And on her right, the matching scar that bound Michali to her, and her to him.

Of course it mattered.

Rhea gripped the knife tightly in her right hand, gathering her will. She could almost feel Lexos's eyes on her from off in Vuomorra. What a mess they had made, the two of them together. But she would fix it, she promised, and she sliced open a cut down the center of her palm, wincing as it tore her black Stratagiozi mark in two. She would fix it, even if she didn't quite know what that meant anymore.

She clenched her hand to a fist, blood winding between her fingers until it fell to the snow below. Red spreading like ink through water, and Rhea watched the gathered crowd shape itself into a line, the first of them coming to kneel at her feet. It was an elderly woman, her white hair drawn back under a ratty handkerchief in widow's black.

"*Efkala*, Aya Ksiga," she murmured, her head bowed.

Rhea watched, pain throbbing in her left hand, as the woman took a pinch of bloody snow, touched it once to her lined forehead, and then laid it on her tongue. Her mouth was open for a moment, and Rhea could see the snow melting, could see the blood running, before the woman swallowed.

She stood up slowly and stepped aside. Behind her, more and more people were each waiting their turn: parents and children, strangers shoulder to shoulder, old and young alike with cheeks pulled thin and hollow. Rhea squeezed her fist, sending another thread of blood onto the snow. All of these people kneeling. All of them thanking her. And for what? She wasn't doing this for them. She was here to protect the very thing that had done them such harm. She was here to keep their enemy alive.

It's not right, she thought. None of this is. Pain fizzed up her forearm, and the cloak of Aya Ksiga slipped away, inch by inch. Rhea felt herself sway, the world around her blurring and fractured. Michali's hand was steady at her elbow, the only thing keeping her upright.

"*Efkala*," they said, and she said it back, her Saint's Thyzaki still uncomfortable. Her accent wasn't quite right; when Michali spoke Saint's, it sounded so much looser, its shapes smoothed and sanded down. He'd said it would get easier, said she would get better. The line was nearly ending and she hadn't yet, and she wondered if she ever would. After all, she'd lived a hundred years and hadn't changed. Not like these people. Not like Michali. Lives the length of one heartbeat, and still they pushed, and pushed.

At last, the ground empty before her, snow dappled with blood and sunlight. Rhea took a deep breath. Over and done, and she would never have to step into her mother's skin again. How had Mama done it? Had she really believed herself worthy of that sort of worship? How could anyone be?

"If you would," said a voice, and Rhea blinked slowly, looked down to where Michali was kneeling before her. He looked almost nervous, his throat bobbing. "I would like your blessing."

She wasn't sure why she did it. Perhaps the haze of the winter, perhaps the look on Michali's face, the red, wet shine of his open mouth. But she uncurled her fingers, looked at the dark, clotting blood on her palm, and instead of letting it fall to the snow below, she reached out.

"Aya Ksiga," he said, his eyes depthless and charged. She said nothing. Only tilted her palm toward him.

Michali took her hand in both of his, the icy graze of his fingertips sending a shiver up her arm. He swept his thumb across her palm, gathering the fresh well of blood, and she knew, she knew he was watching her, but her knees were weak, and the air was stinging in her lungs, and she closed her eyes.

"No," he said. "Please, look at me."

People were still gathered a few paces away. Their faces shattered in the winter light as Rhea opened her eyes. And there was Michali, his hand tight around hers, his dark hair tumbling in the breeze. Slowly, he lifted his thumb, coated in blood, and pressed it to his forehead, leaving a red print in the center.

"*Efkala*," he said.

"*Efkala*," she replied, but she could barely hear herself, could barely pay attention to anything beyond the way Michali's snow-spangled hair was sticking to her blood on his forehead.

It was too much. All of it. Michali was looking at her like she was more than a saint, when really she wasn't even that. She was only Rhea. Only selfish, only scared, only someone's daughter.

"I can't," she gasped, ripping her hand from his. Above her, the ravine walls teetered at the edge of her vision. She stumbled past Michali, ignoring his surprise, ignoring the way he called after her, and pushed through the crowd. Away. She had to get away.

It had been a mistake to come here. A mistake to think she could bear it, a mistake, a mistake, and Rhea searched the bank of the riverbed for the path she'd climbed down, but there was nothing. No way out, no changing her mind. No getting back to the life she'd cast off when she'd let that portrait of her mother change everything.

Behind her she could hear Michali calling, her saint's name ringing out. Aya Ksiga, Aya Ksiga, but she wasn't her mother. Mama had worn that name and served these people with her whole heart, and here she was, treating it like something to slip on and off, like something she could use however she pleased. Like it was the same as calling herself Thyspira and doing what Baba told her to.

She dropped to her knees, snow soaking through her trousers. The pain in her hand was refusing to ease, and she cradled it to her chest, hoped perversely that some of the Sxoriza had followed them. Let the people see her like this. It would do them good to see what she really was.

"Come on," Michali said, and she heard his footsteps approaching, the crunch of them as they broke through the snow. She felt him crouch next to her, drape one arm over her hunched back. "Let's get you up."

He lifted her to her feet. He was saying something to her, but it sounded strange, the words roaring and distant like the ocean at Stratathoma. Rhea stopped listening, and let him guide her along the ravine. He found the path up the bank easily, and ushered her up it, one arm on either side of her, pointing out where the ground was safe. At last, the comfort of the trees, shelter and dark, and Rhea thought she might cry with relief to see Michali's horse and Lefka waiting, each munching contentedly on a carrot.

Never again. She could never face those people again. They must have seen it on her face, the falseness of all of it. Rhea wasn't sure she'd ever done something true in the whole of her life.

"Well?" Michali said. She flinched. Here it was: the inevitable reprimand, the scolding for not wearing her name the way she ought to.

She sighed, turned to face him even though she had no idea what to say. His cheeks were red, and the print of blood on his forehead had started to flake off in the wind.

"Well what?" she asked wearily.

He came closer, frowning when she edged slightly away. "Will you tell me what happened back there?"

"Nothing." A twinge in her palm, and she took the corner of her coat and dabbed at the wound, the black of her Stratagiozi mark revealing itself once more. Perhaps there was no escaping it. Perhaps she should leave Michali, go back to Stratathoma, and hope that when he took the citadel, he left no Argyros alive. "We should be getting home."

"Rhea," he said, and the sound of her name—not Thyspira, not Aya Ksiga, not anyone but her—was like a shock running through her body. "I'm asking."

"You shouldn't," she snapped. Maybe he really did want to know, but that didn't matter, because what could she tell him? Not the truth. Not that she was still loyal to her family. He would hate her for it. And he would be right to.

Somehow she always ended up here, wearing someone else's name in service to her father's. Nothing ever changed, did it?

"I just wonder sometimes," she said, looking up at last to where Michali was standing. "What I would do if it were only me deciding."

"Isn't it?"

"Of course not." How simple it must be for him. No other will to balance against his own, no worry that this decision would destroy his family. He was here because it was right. "Aya Ksiga, Thyspira. Sxoriza and Stratagiozi."

"And you," Michali said. She was caught off guard by the sharpness of it, by the break it carried hidden inside. "All of it comes back to you," he went on after a moment, sounding noticeably more controlled. "You're the one who changed your mind about all of this. You're the one doing what's right."

"I'm not."

"Then—"

"You can't really have believed me," she said. It was too much, Michali treating her like she was better than her family when really she was just the same. She had to tell him. Stay silent, a voice like Lexos's told her, but she'd done that long enough. "What did you think? That I came to the Ksigora and somehow became a better person?"

"Is that so preposterous?" Michali asked, but he was watching her, amusement tugging at his mouth, and she didn't understand. He'd trusted her and she'd betrayed him. Didn't he realize that?

"Yes," she said. "I'm getting you into Stratathoma, and I'm here, but I was lying about why. I—"

She broke off as he began to laugh. "Excuse me," she said, astonished. "Is this funny to you?"

"A little. Of course you lied. I expected that."

He said it without condescension, but it rankled all the same. Like that night in the catacombs. Her plans come to nothing, found out in a heartbeat. "Wonderful," she said flatly. "So glad I could meet your expectations."

"You've been loyal to your family all your life. I would have lied, too, in your position." He gave her a broad smile, a little sheepish. "And I wouldn't have confessed to it." He leaned into her, and Rhea felt a flicker of anticipation in her gut, sweet and translucent. "You're more honest than I am, I think."

"You're teasing." Cruelly, too, whether he knew it or not. There had never been any way to be honest and useful at the same time. She'd had to choose one. She and Lexos, and the others, too. They'd done what they had to, to live in their father's house.

"I am, a little," Michali admitted, stepping closer. "Look, you said you wondered what might happen if it were only you deciding."

"So?"

"So, I think we just found out. You didn't have to tell me the truth."

She shook her head. "It's not that simple."

He kept on as if she hadn't spoken, inching toward her all the while. "You could have let me go on thinking you really had a way into Stratathoma. I like to think I would've discovered your plan before it killed me, but you certainly didn't have to help me do that."

"What plan?"

He raised his eyebrows. "Your route into Stratathoma. Setup for an ambush, no doubt?"

Rhea's mouth dropped open before she could catch herself. Is that what he thought? Yes, she'd lied, but all she wanted was her family, alive and well. None of that meant he had to die.

"No," she said, feeling both foolish and relieved. If Lexos had been in her stead, Michali's death would be inevitable. But he would live, he would live, and she felt, all of a sudden, like the surge of a fire freshly lit, that he deserved to. "No," she said again, "you were never in danger."

The Argyrosi had done enough. What Thyzakos needed was something she didn't know how to give. But Michali did. He had been chosen by these people. He had plans, even if he hadn't shared all of them. And he was here, looking at her with a strained sort of expression on his face.

"What?" she said.

"Nothing." He shoved his hands in his pockets. "It's . . . if you would only let yourself be good."

She bristled. "What is that supposed to mean?"

"Really, it's nothing." It clearly wasn't, though, because Michali shifted from foot to foot, his lips pursed, and Rhea did what she'd learned to do—waited, because if she gave him enough quiet, she could wring it out of him. Sure enough, only a few moments passed before he let out a sharp breath. "It just frustrates me, that's all."

"What does?" She tilted her head, watching as he kicked at the drifting snow. "That I'm a Stratagiozi's daughter and yet still somehow capable of doing the right thing? It must be vexing to have your preconceived notions dismantled."

"Enough," he snapped. She couldn't help recoiling. His earlier patience was gone, leaving an intensity in its place that Rhea understood, even as it frightened her. "I am frustrated because yes, you are capable of doing good, but still you don't. Still, you—"

"I'm trying," she interrupted. "We're here, aren't we? What's that if I'm not trying?"

"Try harder, then." He met her eyes, his own earnest and wide. "I know, I know. You've lived your life as you had to. But at some point, Rhea, all that stops mattering, doesn't it?"

She stared at him. None of it made any sense. He knew everything now. The way in, the route to Baba. Whatever use she'd had to him, she'd outlived it. He could leave her here in the woods and let the snow bury her. "Why would you care what I do? Why would you care what sort of person I am?"

"Because," Michali said with a sigh, "I didn't expect to like you, you know. For a while, I didn't much."

"How nice."

"And there are still," he went on, "things about you I can't sort out. But what I do know is enough." He shrugged. "I suppose it's selfish. To want better from someone so you might love more of them."

Rhea's stomach dropped. Quiet swelled for a moment, Michali's face calm where she knew hers must have been slack with shock. She'd felt it, noticed an ease blooming between them lately, and caught herself tracing the lines of his silhouette since before that. But she'd been Thyspira for so long. It had never occurred to her that this might be anything real.

"Well," he said, when she stayed silent. "You asked. That's why I care."

He said it so easily, like it cost him nothing. Like he didn't know he was showing her how to hurt him, if she wanted to.

She didn't want to. She wanted to be the person he thought she could be. She wanted everything waiting for her here: a wrong she could make right. A consort she could keep.

Every choice she'd ever made had been a bargain—something done not for the right of it but for what she could get in return. And she loved her family. She loved Chrysanthi, and Nitsos, and she loved Lexos, too, in a way that hurt more and more, like it did when she thought about Baba. How much was that love worth? The suffering of an entire country?

No, Michali would take Stratathoma, but it was no real change at all as long as Baba remained. As long as there was any power for him to wield, especially power over his children. That had always been the most dangerous kind.

"Rhea?" Michali asked. His hand brushed her elbow tentatively. "Are you well?"

She had come this far, changed this much. She could do more. She had to do more. Chrysanthi, Nitsos, even Lexos—they all deserved a chance just as Thyzakos did. To live. To rule themselves. It would never happen as long as Baba remained.

She could protect him, or she could do what was right. But she was sure now that she could not do both. And it was a gulf opening up between her and her home; it was standing at the edge of the cliffs at Stratathoma, so high above the water she couldn't hear the waves, and jumping.

She would do it. Drown, and hope Michali could help her find the surface again.

"You promised me my family's safety," she said, and she was surprised by how steady she sounded. "And I want it still. But not for my father."

Michali blinked, and his grip on her elbow tightened. Rhea felt a spark light in her chest. "You don't? Are you sure?"

She had jumped, she had jumped, and here he was. It would be all right.

She didn't answer him. Instead, there was snow on her lips as she pressed her mouth to his.

For a moment he seemed too startled to do anything. But then he was gathering her to him, one arm wrapped around her shoulders, his marked hand catching at her jaw with cold, clumsy fingers.

"I hope I am allowed to be proud of you," he said softly once she'd pulled away and rested her forehead against his chest. She nodded, couldn't help smiling into his coat as she traced the symbol of their shared mark on his shoulder.

She'd hated it once, that mark. Hated every time she'd had to carve it into the skin of another consort, hated every time she'd seen it bright with blood. And it would be a while yet until she truly liked it, if she ever did, but she was a sight closer now that it was not a brand to bear but a choice she'd made.

She hadn't made very many of those before, she thought, leaning back to look up at Michali. This, though, was a good start.

TWENTY-FIVE

ALEXANDROS

Vuomorra made Stratathoma look like a shithole. He'd only been here for half a day and already Lexos had seen more finery on display than in all of Stratathoma's history combined. Vuomorra seemed to grow by the second, more and more richly dressed people spilling out of the high-reaching buildings, their faces obscured by the partial veils that were apparently the current fashion.

Lexos was quite dreading the prospect of presenting himself to Tarro, despite the warm reply his message announcing his intent to visit had received, and so he'd spent his morning wandering through one of Vuomorra's many plazas. This particular one was packed tightly with market stalls. Come sundown they would fold up their tables and disappear for the night, but now the air was rattling with shouts and perfumed with bright spices, and he was relishing the feel of solid ground under his boots. The sail across the gulf to Vuomorra had been too short for him to get his sea legs and too long for him to do without them. He was only glad none of his siblings had been there to see him throw up over the side.

Most cities in Thyzakos had grown up organically, their edges ebbing and flowing, but here in Trefazio Tarro had planned Vuomorra before its construction, and so the streets met at perfect angles and were broad enough to accommodate carriages traveling in both directions. Flags flew at regular intervals, the Domina house crest visible wherever you turned. From what Lexos remembered, the Domina palace sat at the city's center, with the main thoroughfares spreading out from it in all directions, like spokes on a wheel. He eased past a pair of arguing men and turned onto the nearest street, following the traffic.

In this part of the city, fairly close to its center, the canals were wide and well planned. Like the streets, they intersected at right angles, and their waters were clean, or at least as clean as could be expected considering that at the moment Lexos could see no fewer than four men urinating into this particular canal. Their walls were built in two levels, so that they formed a narrow but walkable promenade along each side that boatmen and fishermen could use. Did Tarro ever come out here, Lexos wondered, leaning forward to watch a large, oddly shaped fish pass by. Did he ever make use of this city, which had so clearly been designed as a public space? Or did he prefer to wait in his palace for the people to come to him, as Lexos was doing now?

He was getting closer, that much was obvious—where the plaza he'd left behind had been paved with gray stone, here the street was done in patterned mosaics, smooth, rounded pebbles serving in place of tile. Black-and-white patterns stretched ahead of him, contrasting with the bloom of color along the side of the street, all shop fronts and houses decorated with draped fabric in burnt oranges and rich blues. Now and then the buildings were broken up by sections of columns, marbled and gleaming white in the sun, and through them he could see smooth lawns, could hear the burble of carved fountains.

He brushed down the front of his green coat, tugged at the hem to straighten the creases. He'd sent his trunk along to meet him at the Domina palace, but this particular coat he'd purchased upon arrival that morning. Was it a bit obvious to arrive at Tarro's house wearing

Domina colors? Of course it was, but Lexos had never pretended to be above it.

There, at last, the crest of a domed building, and Tarro's house was ahead of him. It was a massive thing, so big he thought Stratathoma could comfortably fit inside it two or three times over, and unlike Stratathoma, it had only ever belonged to Tarro's family. While Stratathoma passed along the line from each Thyzak Stratagiozi to the next, this building—this city—had been built with Tarro at its heart, and so even the building was wearing Domina colors, its mammoth copper dome long since turned to a green patina.

The palace was surrounded by a vast fenced-in garden, the plants shaped in ornamental designs, the hedge-lined walkways paved with pale gravel. There were people wandering along the paths, and if Lexos remembered rightly from the last time he'd been here—right at the beginning of Baba's rule, and only for a few days to pay Tarro their respects—the garden was open, to some degree, to the public. He followed the fence around the palace until he reached a small, unassuming entrance, complete with a guard booth and a bored-looking watchman.

"Is this—" he started to ask, but the watchman, who couldn't have been older than sixteen, muttered something Lexos couldn't understand and waved him through without a second glance.

It was probably a very different experience arriving here, Lexos thought, when someone inside actually cared that you'd shown up.

At last he found another guard booth, this one with its own gangly limbed guard, and said that he was Lexos Argyros, frowning when the guard asked who that was.

"Stratagorra," he said in Trefza. This earned him a slow, lazy look up and down, and then finally the boy waved over another guard and asked that Lexos be shown inside, to Tarro.

Just as the public was allowed into the gardens, so were they allowed into the palace. Lexos saw all manner of people as the guard led him toward the throne room, and they seemed to be conducting their own business. There was a man selling roasted nuts and fruit juice; in another hallway, Lexos could hear somebody singing.

"We clear them out for the night," the guard explained when Lexos asked. "Otherwise the Stratagorra doesn't seem to much mind."

They skirted a gaggle of children—to whom they belonged, Lexos couldn't tell—and arrived at a massive archway. It opened onto a long hall, its ceiling perhaps three times higher than the corridors leading to it, windows ringing the top and letting light stream in. The sides were lined with columns, creating a slightly secluded colonnade that ran down each side of the hall. He felt his jaw drop. It was even larger than he'd remembered.

Overhead, tapestries hung from the ceiling. On one, Tarro knelt over the prone body of one of his children. On another, he was presented as a traditional icon, with a blue ring behind his head. The ceiling itself was patterned with square inlays of pale green, each one with a gold ornamental carving at its center.

In the colonnades, Lexos could see a number of paintings had been hung on each wall. Old men tottered the length of the passages in pairs, discussing the artwork. A young woman sat in front of a particularly striking portrait, sketching a version of it on a scrap of parchment. Farther down the hall, a boy was posing mockingly in front of a different portrait, to the great delight of his friends. This palace, Lexos thought, belonged to the people as much as it did to Tarro.

And speaking of Tarro, there he was, at the far end of the hall, standing on a raised dais with a number of other men who must have been his advisors. Above the dais, the ceiling was scorched and blackened with ash—this must be where bodies burned—and beyond the cluster of people there was something that might have been a throne, but Lexos could tell that it hardly mattered to anybody. He couldn't imagine Tarro sitting here and holding court.

"Thank you," he told the guard. "I'll go alone from here."

Tarro was engrossed in conversation with a man who looked as though he must have been two hundred years old (although, really, Lexos wasn't one to talk) when he approached the dais. If it had been

Baba, Lexos would've waited to be addressed, but things were different here. He had to be different here.

"Good afternoon," he said loudly, jogging up the steps to join Tarro on the dais.

Tarro turned, eyebrows raised, and for a moment Lexos was afraid he'd made the wrong choice, but then Tarro's face broke into a jolly smile.

"Alexandros," Tarro said. "How wonderful to see you. Did I know you were coming?"

"I thought I would surprise you," Lexos managed, caught off guard as he was. He hoped he didn't look as embarrassed as he felt. Of course—the reply he'd got from the Dominas had not been from Tarro himself. Presumably Tarro's second had answered that letter, just as Lexos managed Baba's correspondence at home.

"Delightful. And how long will we have the pleasure of your company?"

"As long as my company remains a pleasure."

Tarro laughed as though that were the funniest thing he'd ever heard. "You will be welcome for quite a while, then, I expect. And your father, is he with you?"

"I'm afraid it's just me."

"What a pity," Tarro said, but he was smiling. "Come, we must find someone to get you settled, and then I will look forward to seeing you at dinner."

"Thank you, I'd be glad to join you."

Tarro led him to the far edge of the dais, and cupped a hand around his mouth. "Gino. Look alive, my boy!"

So Gino had survived, after all, even in the murderous company of his Domina siblings. He was pressed against a column, his eyes darting every which way, and Lexos could see the sweat beading on his upper lip. When he heard Tarro calling, he jumped, hand flying to his dagger where it sat in its concealed pocket.

"Give him a minute," Tarro said confidingly to Lexos. "He's got to work up the courage."

They watched as Gino took two deep breaths, closed his eyes, and then, with a stricken look on his face, dashed across the open space between his column and the dais, darting up the stairs so quickly that Lexos was afraid he might trip.

"Yes, Father?"

"You remember Alexandros, I'm sure. Would you see that he gets settled?"

Gino seemed to sway with relief at the prospect of getting out of the open, away from any sibling who might be trying to steal his position as Tarro's second. "Of course, Father."

"Wonderful. Off with you both." With a glance at Gino, he gave Lexos a smile and turned back to his advisors, who had been waiting with increasing impatience.

The room Gino led him to was deep within the palace. Its floors were made of patterned, inlaid wood, glowing a burnished bronze in the midday light, and they contrasted sharply with the pale yellow walls and the lush white carpeting that surrounded the bed. The bed was shadowed by a canopy so liquidly draped and so richly vibrant that Lexos thought it might actually have been plated in gold leaf.

"Nobody's used this in years," Gino said apologetically as he adjusted one of the bed pillows, which was ever so slightly crooked.

"It's no trouble." At Stratathoma, an unused room would've been draped with dustcovers and locked up tight. But everything was always perfect in the Domina palace, even if nobody was ever there to see it.

"Someone's brought your things," Gino went on, politely averting his eyes from the trunk in the corner. It was a sturdy thing—canvas and leather, built specifically to protect the tidewater bowl and silk sky that Lexos had brought from Stratathoma—but in this room it looked as though somebody had left behind a pile of garbage. "Dinner's at eight o'clock. We dine in the aubergine room. It's down the stairs, and then you take a left at the . . . I'll send someone to fetch you," Gino finished, heading for the door. He turned back to Lexos, stepping aside so Lexos could see the three sturdy padlocks fused onto the door, looking about as part of the room as his trunk. "The code for these is written down in the bedside table."

"The code?" Lexos came closer, inspected the locks with their tiny dials and whirring parts.

"Sorry. I forgot. You can actually sleep easily here." He sighed, and then straightened his shoulders, putting on an attempt at a brave face. "I'm off."

"I'll see you at dinner, then."

"Yes," Gino said, smiling without humor, "provided I last that long."

Lexos slept until the evening meal, grateful for the mattress that put the ones at Stratathoma to shame. When the city's clock— a mammoth thing, its gears and mechanics so complex that Lexos imagined Nitsos might pass out if he ever laid eyes on it—chimed seven, he rose and dressed in the second of his green coats.

As promised, a servant was waiting outside to take him to the aubergine room. They passed empty sitting rooms, galleries full of landscape paintings, glass doors to wide patios that overlooked the ornamental gardens. At last, the servant was holding open a pair of elaborately carved doors and ushering him through, announcing his name with such terrible pronunciation that Lexos couldn't keep from wincing. Trefza and Thyzaki were very similar, but they placed the emphasis so differently in so many of their words.

The aubergine room must have been named after its vegetable counterpart and it was decorated accordingly. The whole place was done up in shades of purple, from the lilac carpet to the amethyst shine of the curtains. The effect was jarring, and nowhere near approaching pretty, but Lexos supposed this was what happened when you were as rich as Tarro was—sooner or later, you ran out of reasonable ways to spend your money.

Tarro and an assemblage of the Domina family were already inside, standing at the far end of the room where it opened up to a large window. Gino, of course, had his back all but pressed to the wall, and those of his siblings in attendance were marked by the glint in their eyes as they watched him closely. Tarro was oblivious to it all, or rather, Lexos amended, it was more correct to say that he did not care. He was drinking merrily from a large wineglass that was perhaps not filled with wine but something stronger, and speaking with an older man who Lexos recognized from the main hall earlier that day.

"Alexandros," Tarro called, waving him over. "So glad to see you've found us."

"Hello," Lexos said, picking the most formal version of it he knew in Trefza. They shook hands firmly, Tarro's grasp unwavering despite the flush on his cheeks and the glaze over his eyes.

"This is my cousin," Tarro said, gesturing to his companion, "or at least he's related to me somehow."

"I'm descended from his brother's line," the man said, reaching across to shake Lexos's hand. "Francisco. Lovely to meet you."

The long life that every Stratagiozi and his children were given passed through the blood. It did not extend beyond direct lineage, not even to brothers, or sisters, or consorts. If Lexos's mother had lived, he would've watched her wither away. As it was, he'd seen something else, even if he couldn't quite remember what.

"Likewise."

"Well," Francisco said, "shall we sit? I believe the first course is about to be served."

Some thoughtful member of the Domina house staff had placed Lexos at Tarro's end of the table, but Lexos held back, allowing the rest of the family to find their seats before arriving at his own. It was important Tarro not think him too desperate—this was, after all, only his first day in Vuomorra. There was time later for the real work. Tonight was about reminding Tarro how much he liked Lexos.

Aside from Francisco and Gino (and of course Tarro), the others at the table were strangers to Lexos, but for all their unfamiliarity they were easily identifiable as Domina children, all with the same hard, unsmiling mouths that the Dominas seemed to breed for. And truly, they were children. Of the four boys and four girls, the youngest was perhaps nine—Lexos had never been very good at guessing ages, age as a concept having been struck from his experience some time ago—and the oldest couldn't have been more than seventeen. With their soft round faces and ruddy cheeks, they made Gino look like a wizened old man, but they had the sharpness of expression he was in such desperate need of.

Still, Gino seemed, at least, to be getting through the appetizers in decent shape. Every time Lexos took a break from the conversation between Francisco and Tarro and glanced Gino's way, he was sat with his arms firmly crossed and his plate of food untouched. That was probably the safest approach, but, Lexos thought as he took another bite of cheese-smothered eggplant, Gino was certainly missing out.

The main course arrived—fish, with an assortment of vegetables that the youngest Domina pushed off her plate and onto the floor—and with it came another story from Tarro about how building this particular room had cost quite a bit of money and taken quite a bit of time. By the end of the dinner, Lexos expected to be quite familiar with the floor plans of the palace. Across the table from him, Francisco was nodding eagerly, his mouth full, as Tarro explained which tree the wood of the chairs had come from.

If he was honest, he'd expected something a bit more exciting from Vuomorra instead of this conversation (which was so boring that he was ready to pluck out his own eyes, just for something to do), but after the matching disasters of Rhea's choosing and the council meeting, it was so important to make a good impression that he could ill afford to stop paying attention even for a moment.

Lexos had just taken a bite of his meal when there came a crash at the far end of the table and a broken cry. He nearly choked, found himself bent over and coughing wildly as Tarro thumped his back.

"Come on, now, there's a good fellow," Tarro was saying as he whaled away, and with one particularly forceful hit Lexos hacked up a mouthful of partially chewed fish. "Are you quite all right?"

"I'm so sorry," Lexos said fervently. "I was only startled. What happened?"

"Just my children arguing, I'm afraid." Tarro gestured to the far end of the table. "Carima, would you apologize, please? Look what trouble you've caused."

Carima was the smallest Domina, and when she stood the table came up to her chest. "I'm very sorry, Papa," she said, her voice small and reedy. "I was only speaking with Marco and I got carried away."

"About what?" The whole room had fallen silent, cowed by the reprimand evident in Tarro's tone.

Carima blushed. "A private matter."

"Well, settle it. I have no patience for this nonsense."

"I will." She glared sidelong at her brother, who must have been a good five or six years old than she. "See, Marco? Papa says."

"At least wait until I've finished eating," Marco muttered.

"You're taking too long," Carima said with a peremptory sniff, but she sat back down, and conversation resumed, the matter presumably done with.

It was not. A server approached the other end of the table, the fresh cups of wine on his silver tray drawing everyone's attention, and Carima was immediately out of her seat. Lexos caught a flash of steel as she fussed with something in the folds of her skirts, and then she was marching toward Gino, a tiny, delicate knife clutched in her hand, wrists still puffy with baby fat. Gino only had time to push his chair back from the table before Carima grasped his yellow hair, yanked his head back, and slit his throat.

The blood went everywhere. There was so much, and it came so fast, soaking into the lilac carpet, into Gino's pale green coat, into his crisp white shirt. Lexos jumped to his feet, staggering back.

"My goodness," Tarro said, laughing, "but you're a frightful little thing, aren't you, Carima?"

Spatter had landed on her cheeks, and when she turned to face her father, there was blood even on the whites of her teeth. "If he'd only eaten his food, I wouldn't have had to make such a mess."

"It got on my fish," Marco complained, dabbing at his meal with his napkin.

"Why don't we take dessert in the garden?" Tarro said, standing, and the rest of the dinner guests rose with him. "We'll leave the servants to clean up. Although we may no longer be able to call this the aubergine room if they can't get that stain out."

They filed out through a pair of glass-paned doors, and Lexos followed dumbly. It wasn't as though he'd never seen blood before—he wasn't exactly new to this sort of thing—but death had never been so casual for him as it seemed to be for the Dominas.

The veranda outside might've reminded Lexos of home were it not for the view, the looming of other buildings and the regimented sprawl of the ornamental garden so different from the sweep of the sea. Some servants were waiting, passing out silver cups of shaved ice, and he found himself unwilling—or perhaps unable—to keep up conversing with Tarro. He drifted to the railing, hoping nobody would approach, and for the most part he was left alone until a tiny figure materialized out of the thickening dark.

"Good evening, sir."

Lexos looked down with a start. It was Carima staring up at him, a smear of dirt on her forehead. She had pushed up the remarkably frilly sleeves of her dress and had her skirts tucked into her long lace drawers, revealing a nasty scrape on her knee. Now that he was listening, he could hear shouts coming from the garden—the younger Domina children, playing at some game or other (or possibly slaughtering one another).

"Good evening, *kiria*," he replied. What could she want? She wasn't Tarro's new second, not by a decade or two, but perhaps she was here to rope him into a plot to kill the new one. She had a conniving look about her, after all.

"Can I have that?"

It took him a moment to realize she was pointing at his hands, where he was clutching his untouched shaved ice. It was starting to melt, the flavoring leaking out into a pool of red.

"Certainly," he said. The word had barely left his mouth before she snatched the ice and darted away, crowing to her siblings about having seconds.

They were still only children.

And he had a job to do.

He reapproached Tarro and Francisco, put on his best smile, and drank more than he'd planned to. It was as the party was breaking up that he finally asked Tarro what he'd been wondering.

"Who does this leave as your second now?"

Tarro shrugged. "I suppose someone will come and tell me sooner or later. I usually find out at the funeral tomorrow."

Gino's funeral. It would be not so much a chance to mourn the dead as a chance to see who was still alive.

"Will you come?" Tarro was saying. "You must. They're such dreary affairs, but the food is wonderful."

And what else could Lexos do, really, but say yes?

That night he managed to tend to the tides and stitch a fresh night sky before collapsing into bed, and the next morning he woke with a pounding headache. A knock on the door stirred him, and he hastened to answer, suddenly panicked that he'd missed the funeral and ruined his chances all in one go. But no, it was still early, and the funeral wasn't until the afternoon.

"What is it?" he said, opening the door.

"You don't sound very happy to see me," said Stavra, and it *was* Stavra, the hood of her long green coat still drawn up, her hair braided tightly in cornrows underneath. There was a crackle in the air about her, and Lexos suddenly felt more awake.

"I'm not," he replied, but he hugged her tightly even though her coat was still cold from outside. "What are you doing here?"

"I came for the funeral." He released her, and she walked in, scanning the room with pursed lips. He'd left things a mess coming in the night before—there were his trousers, there one shoe, and yards away the other.

"You traveled fast," he said, scrambling to gather his underthings from where they were bundled under the side table and hoping she hadn't seen them. "How did you hear about it anyway?"

"You're not the only one with scouts, Alexandros."

"Of course."

"And I was in Legerma. It's only a few hours' sail down the gulf."

He didn't ask her what she'd been in Legerma for—she'd never tell him anyway—but it was unusual for a foreign representative to attend a funeral for a second. Never mind that Lexos was doing the same.

He watched as she ambled across the room to his trunk and bit back a protest as she picked through his clothing. She cut a more severe figure than the last time he'd seen her. Sharper, darker clothing, and the stubborn clench of her jaw that never seemed to relent.

"I'm glad to see you," he said, and he found that he meant it.

"Of course you are," Stavra said. "I'm wonderful." She held up a pair of his trousers. They were patterned in green and white, and he'd never worn them before, but if there'd ever been a right place for them, it was certainly the Domina palace. "These are horrible. Put them on immediately."

He sighed, snatched them from her hands, and went to the washroom. Perhaps the funeral might be bearable now.

TWENTY-SIX

ALEXANDROS

The Dominas wore red to funerals. Red for blood, obviously, Stavra had explained, which Lexos had not packed for, and so he was left, less than an hour before the funeral, staring at a red dressing gown and a white coat with a single red epaulet while Stavra adjusted her scarlet gown in the mirror.

"Just wear your mourning black," she was saying. "And say you're expressing your respect for Gino through your own country's traditions. Besides, Gino's dead. He can't see what you're wearing."

"I don't care about Gino," Lexos said, burying his face in his hands. "It's Tarro I want to express my respect for, and unluckily for me and my mourning black, he is still alive."

"Stand behind me, then."

"You are a bevy of helpfulness."

"I do try." She finished picking a loose thread from the cascading sleeves of her gown. "Whatever you're going to do, do it quickly, before you're late *and* poorly dressed."

He chose the all-black suit and hoped that Stavra's provided explanation would be enough to satisfy Tarro. When he was finally dressed, Stavra hustled him out of the room, her fingers clamped so tightly around his upper arm that Lexos was sure he would have bruises there come the next day.

In the main hall, a transformation had taken place. Red draperies hung between the marble columns, obscuring the portraits of other dead Dominas. Half the city, it seemed, had turned out for the occasion, dressed in their funeral scarlet and calling to the vendors of salted snacks and commemorative handkerchiefs that meandered through the crowd.

"It's barbaric," Lexos whispered as two children ran by, red paint striped across their throats in a mockery of what had happened to Gino.

"To you, I suppose it might be," Stavra replied.

"Where's Tarro?" Stavra, in her heeled slippers, was a good inch or two taller than him. "On the dais?"

"I don't see him. Maybe he's skipping this sham and sleeping late."

They elbowed past a family, the daughter sitting on her father's shoulders to see over the crowd, and stepped into the colonnade, which was freer of people. Lexos was making for the dais, where a cluster of Domina children were gathered around the pyre that would soon be Gino's, when Stavra yanked him to a halt.

"Not so close," she said. "You don't want to be up there for the bit with the body."

"They're only burning it. It's not as if I haven't got the stomach for it."

"I know," Stavra said crossly. "But it does get rather hot."

"Ah."

"And there's the bit where they eat him."

Lexos nearly choked on his own spit. "Pardon me?"

Stavra shook her head, grinning. "Oh, Alexandros, you are good company." It was when she spoke next, Merkheri lilting smoothly, that Lexos realized they had been speaking Thyzaki from her arrival. "Your sister," Stavra said. "I heard she is enjoying her new consort."

Lexos switched to Merkheri along with her. "I've heard nothing of the sort."

"Well, that's a shame. I'd hoped she'd found something to make a winter in the cold worthwhile." Stavra sent Lexos a sidelong glance. "It was an odd choice she made. Surely her winter might have been better spent somewhere warmer."

Rhokera. Lexos bit his tongue. Stavra didn't know everything he did regarding the Sxoriza, and he was not about to share it. "Perhaps you might advise her next time," he said. "And speaking of your advice." He took hold of Stavra's wrist and led her farther away from the crowd. "Why did you give it?"

"What do you mean?"

She was all innocence, but even in the dim light Lexos could tell she was keeping something from him. Whatever that was, it would stay kept. Stavra did not lie—she only refused to tell the truth.

"I asked you at Agiokon. Why would you want to help my father keep his seat?"

"And I told you at Agiokon," she answered, eyes narrowing. "Did that conversation really go so well that you'd like to repeat it?"

"Truly, I don't mean to make you angry," he said quickly, "or to insult you. You know I think the world of you."

"I'm not sure I do." But there was no anger in her gaze as she considered him, and at last she spoke again, quietly and evenly. "I am not helping your father. I am helping you."

"But—"

"If that is not enough of an explanation for you, Alexandros, I think you had better get out of your father's house while you still can." She glanced over his shoulder and stepped away, back toward the crowd. "I'm going up to the dais. It's good form to let the body's ash show on your clothing. You," she finished, eyeing his black suit, "should stay here."

"I've offended you."

"You haven't. You've only made me sad, and you are hardly the first person to do that."

She disappeared into the crowd, and Lexos lost sight of her until she reappeared on the dais, at the front of the crowd around the pyre. Among the Dominas she looked out of place, their laughter slamming headlong into her grave silence. For Stavra, whose hands were stained nightly with the paint of age, none of this was anything she took lightly.

If it truly was a custom to let the ash of the body stain your clothes, then Stavra was right—he was better served near the front of the crowd, but not up on the dais. He chose a spot that gave him a good view (and would give Tarro a good view of him), and waited for the ceremony to begin.

It started with Tarro's arrival. Trumpets blared suddenly, playing a simple, mournful phrase, and the crowd began to split, shifting sideways into the colonnades. Up the aisle formed in the middle came Tarro, dressed in a red coat with a train so long that three men had to carry it. Behind Lexos, one woman whispered to another that Tarro added a foot of fabric for every second killed, but that couldn't be true—the train would've reached out the door and practically into the sea.

Lexos had expected that he would walk slowly, in some sort of processional, but for Tarro this seemed to be an afternoon stroll. He waved to his people, smiled, laughed when they began to cheer. Any moment now Lexos thought he might snatch a baby out from the crowd and smack a kiss to its rosy cheeks. When he at last reached the dais, Lexos was surprised to realize that, in the commotion of Tarro's entrance, Gino's shrouded body had quietly been laid out, with none of its own fanfare.

According to Thyzak customs, now was the time when Tarro would turn to the crowd and say a few words about Gino, about the kind of boy he had been and the man he might've become, about the people who loved him, about what he'd left behind. But instead Tarro stopped at the bottom of the stairs up to the dais and simply waited.

And waited.

Lexos searched for Stavra on the platform, but she didn't seem concerned. Maybe Tarro was just winded from carrying the weight of that massive coat.

In the knot of Domina children, someone began to move, but the movement was quickly cut off, and Lexos heard, over the glassy silence of the crowd, a gurgling cry, and the thud of a body hitting the floor. Next to him, one of the onlookers elbowed his friend with a muffled cry of delight. Whoever Tarro's new second had been, Lexos suspected they had just passed on the title.

From the ranks of red-clad children came a young woman, her dress a column of scarlet lace, her dark hair swept up into a knot at the base of her neck, one artfully curled tendril hanging loose to brush her cheek. She had olive skin and delicate features that seemed built expressly to direct attention to her eyes, which were a color so dark Lexos might have called them black if not for the simmering glow at the center of them. Though she surprisingly had nothing of Tarro in her face, there was an unmistakable Domina quality to the way she moved: fluidly, as though nobody had ever stood in her way.

"That's Falka," someone behind Lexos whispered. "I knew it. I've won twenty off Gianni."

Lexos had never heard anyone mention her—not in the reports his scouts returned, nor at any of the council meetings. But then, there were so many Domina children in existence that nobody could be expected to know them all. Lexos watched as Falka came down the stairs, her gait smooth and assured, and approached Tarro, who looked surprised in a mild sort of way.

"My dear," he said, reaching out to draw her close and kiss both of her cheeks. "I was expecting someone else."

She smiled prettily. "He was otherwise occupied, I'm afraid."

This poor unnamed sod would apparently not get a funeral of his own—he had never officially accepted his new post, and so he had never officially relinquished it to Falka.

She turned (unlike Gino, she seemed to have no qualms about showing her back to her siblings) and took a torch from the hands of a waiting guard. Raising it high above her head, she said something in Trefza, and the rest of the crowd responded with a rousing cheer. She'd announced herself, but she'd spoken using so formal a construction that the closest Lexos could get to a translation was that she was, having been the second of the children of the man whose name was Tarro, now currently the first of the children of the man whose name was Tarro, and that this now currently made her Tarro's lieutenant, or captain, or admiral.

Tarro took the torch from her and climbed the rest of the steps up to the body. It was draped over in a fine red cloth, but the shape of Gino was still clear, from the point of his nose to the buckle of his belt.

With no ceremony, Tarro lit Gino's pyre. It wasn't long before the flames were burning thickly, turning the air to a shimmering haze. The smoke was viscous and gray, and as it rose Lexos looked up to see the ash mark on the ceiling, directly where a thousand bodies had burned before Gino and a thousand more would burn after him.

Was this it? Was this all a father's son was worth?

The body would burn for hours, but nobody stayed to watch. As soon as the whole pyre had caught, Tarro was peeling off his coat and striding into the crowd, Falka following close behind. They had people to greet, adoring citizens to favor with their smiles and handshakes. The rest of the Domina children left together, but Stavra remained, her eyes fixed on Gino's outline inside the fire. It was her job, she had told Lexos once, to bear witness, and he could see that same determination on her face as she stood her ground, so close to the pyre that the heat was surely scalding her.

Slowly, Tarro made his way through the throngs of people, and Lexos pushed to the front, anxious to be seen paying his respects. He was not looking forward to meeting Falka, but he would pay that price to make the right impression on Tarro.

"Sir," he said loudly to be heard over the noise of the crowd, and Tarro looked up, his face brightening when he noticed Lexos.

"Alexandros," he said, maneuvering around a woman clutching a crying infant to join Lexos. "So good of you to come."

"It is my pleasure, sir."

"What a good young man you are. You needn't have stayed." Over his shoulder, Falka was approaching, her polite smile unchanged as she made eye contact with Lexos. "You haven't met my daughter yet, I don't think," Tarro went on. "Or at least, not this one."

"No," Falka said, sidling in front of Tarro. One of her eyebrows lifted slightly. A question, perhaps, or a challenge. "I don't believe we've been introduced."

"It's my honor," he said, bowing his head as he held out his hand. Her fingers were startlingly cool when they landed delicately on the mark he bore on his left palm. She seemed to know him, or at the very least recognize his face in a way that left him uncomfortable. Had they met before, and he simply didn't remember it? No, surely not. It was only his reputation as an Argyros that preceded him.

"This is Vasilis's boy," Tarro said. "His second, in fact. You'll see him when we're at Agiokon next. He can tell you what to expect during the council meetings."

"Oh," Falka said airily, "I think I'll manage fine on my own." Looking back at Lexos, she nodded to his black jacket and trousers. "How interestingly you're dressed, sir."

"Oh, yes. I'm so sorry, sir," Lexos said. "In Thyzakos we wear black to mourn our families. I meant no disrespect."

"And I took none." Tarro tossed his arm around Lexos's shoulders and gave him a friendly shake so strong that Lexos stumbled to one side. "Now, I'm afraid I must be off, but, Falka, look after Lexos, will you? Get him some water, or some fresh air. He looks about to expire."

"I do?"

"It's the black, I think," Falka put in. "Doesn't do much for your coloring."

She was a few steps away before Lexos realized he was supposed to follow and hastened after her. She was a real second, not the wilting flower Gino had been. Perhaps there was room yet to get what he wanted from the Dominas—support, full and unflinching, to bring Thyzakos back under control.

They took a different path through the palace than the one Lexos had taken with Gino, and Falka kept up a run of polite remarks about the palace's history and design as they avoided the interconnected sitting rooms and galleries, keeping instead to the colonnaded hallways that bordered lawns studded with fountains. At last, they broke from the outline of the palace and stepped through a large, scrolled archway onto the first of a number of descending terraces, the vista one of the countryside and its assorted villages, their sunburned roofs toylike in the distance.

The gardens themselves were walled in by tall, sternly cut hedges, and behind them grew orderly rows of cypress trees, their shapes more structured than their Thyzak cousins. At the far end of the terraces, a lawn was laid out, and some of the Dominas were there, already having changed out of their funeral red, playing a game that involved a number of brightly colored balls and a striped pin.

Falka stopped at the top terrace and waved to her siblings. "This is our family's private garden," she said, turning slightly toward Lexos, her hands folded at her waist. "As our guest, you are of course welcome here at any time."

"Thank you. That's quite generous."

She began a slow stroll around the perimeter of the terrace, skirting the sloped ground that led down to the next level. Lexos followed at her side, his hands clasped behind his back, matching his steps to hers.

"It's a lovely garden," she said. "Much like the rest of Vuomorra, don't you think?"

"Oh," Lexos said, feeling out of his depth as he did when any conversation turned to the aesthetic. "Yes. Quite."

"Do you find Vuomorra very different from your own cities? I confess I have spent little time beyond my father's borders. I don't know how it might compare."

"It's certainly different," he answered, "but equally enjoyable."

"I do wish I had more opportunity to travel," Falka said, her words as weightless as if she were simply remarking on the weather. But, Lexos realized, she'd spoken in Thyzaki. Was she worried someone nearby might overhear?

No, more likely, this was a demonstration of sorts, a warning that Lexos had little hope of keeping any secrets from her.

"Now you are your father's second, you may well find it," he replied. He felt more at ease speaking his native tongue, but he had a feeling any sort of comfort in this situation was a mistake.

"Indeed." Falka sighed, wistful and soft. "Your sister is very lucky. All those trips, so far afield. She must be enjoying her time in the Ksigora."

Lexos looked at her sharply, but Falka only kept walking, one hand trailing along the top of the hedge that bordered the terrace.

"Although," she went on, "I think we can agree that what you might find here is a great deal more valuable."

"You are right," he said carefully, "that Vuomorra has much more to offer."

At last she stopped and turned to face him suddenly, leaving them close enough that he could feel her breath prickling the skin along his jaw.

"I can help with what you came for," she said, her Trefzan accent softening Thyzaki's consonants and rolling them together. "You as well as anyone know how a second may influence the Stratagiozi they serve."

In fact, Lexos wasn't sure he'd ever truly influenced one of Baba's decisions. But he nodded nonetheless, and did not break his gaze from hers.

"I will require, however," she went on, "something from you in return."

"Of course."

She smiled, and the softness it lent to her face was disarming. Lexos felt his own mouth turn up in response before he could stop it. "Tell me about your sister," she said.

He blinked. "That's what you'd like from me?"

Falka's hand brushed against his hip, the barest pressure inching him closer before her touch disappeared and Lexos was left swaying forward, the garden blurring around him. She was beautiful, certainly, but here in her family's garden, in her family's house, she was more than that: dizzying, her complete ease sparking a fizz of envy in his stomach.

"Call it curiosity," she said with a half shrug. "We don't have many twins in the Domina line. Or if we do, one of them dies so quickly it barely counts. I suppose you are the elder twin, being your father's second. Even a difference so little as a few minutes means something to a Stratagorra father."

"Yes, I was the elder," Lexos replied dryly. "In fact, I still am."

Falka laughed prettily and stepped back, breaking the closeness between them and continuing on their tour of the garden. "And your mother?"

"What about her?"

"Did she care about the difference between you and your sister?"

"I don't think she did." He was silent for a moment as a gust of breeze—warm, even in winter—ruffled his dark hair. "I don't much remember, though."

"How did she end up paired with your father?" Falka gave him an embarrassed smile. "I confess your family fascinates me. The Argyros line is so short, so clean, and the Domina one so tangled."

"I never knew how he found her," Lexos said. "Or I suppose, how she found him."

He'd never known much about Baba's family, but he at least knew what his grandfather had been called, and where the Argyrosi had lived before Baba became a general in his steward's army. Mama, meanwhile, was a mystery entirely. She had never mentioned any family of her own, or at least not that Lexos could remember.

"Fate, perhaps," Falka said, with a coquettish tilt of her head. Fate had died with the saints, died by the sword of Tarro's forefather (or just father, if the rumors were to be believed). It was odd, if not impolite, for her to mention it now.

Falka looked over his shoulder and signaled to one of the waiting servants, who came rushing down, a tray of sparkling glasses of champagne balanced perfectly on his palm. "Well," she said, "I think we have spent quite enough time dwelling on such things. Please, drink. It's quite refreshing after all the smoke at that awful funeral."

Strange, Lexos thought. For all Falka's professed curiosity about Rhea, he didn't think he'd said very much about her at all.

Lexos took a glass for himself and watched as Falka raised hers in a small toast and drank. He'd expected her to be like Gino, to perhaps have a taster waiting nearby, or to just pour the glass out onto the grass, for fear of an attempt on her life. Instead she closed her eyes briefly and made a small, appreciative noise before taking another sip.

"How is it you are unafraid?" he asked. "Gino could barely touch a glass of water for fear of poison and here you are, out in the open, drinking from a glass handed to you by nobody knows who."

"Well, it was that man, actually," she replied, "so I do know who, but your point is well-taken. I will tell you a secret."

"And what is that?"

"There is a natural order of things," she said conspiratorially. "Sometimes it only takes a reminder of that." She took another sip of champagne, and then set the glass down on top of the hedge, its branches so tightly wound that it did no more than quiver slightly under the added weight. "Well, I'm sure you'd like some time to yourself. I will leave you. But I'll be seeing you again quite soon."

She was leaving before he had a chance to reply, and she made her way down the stairs from one level to the next, until she'd reached her siblings at the lawn, where they were still playing their game. Lexos watched her kick off her heeled slippers and take the pins from her hair, grab fistfuls of her skirts and run across the lawn to one of her sisters—Carima, the young girl who had so efficiently dispatched Gino at dinner the night before, and who now shrieked delightedly and leapt into Falka's arms.

Had she killed Gino's original successor at the funeral herself? Or had she got one of her siblings to do it, the way he was sure she'd got Carima to kill Gino? She was clearly something fearsome, but there was none of the brittleness to her that he might've expected, that he saw in some of the other Domina children. Falka, he thought, was so suited to this kind of life that it hadn't hardened her at all.

Lexos left his glass next to Falka's and went back inside, returning to his chambers as quickly as he could without drawing undue attention. Stavra would surely have left the funeral by now, and he could talk all of this over with her.

TWENTY-SEVEN

ALEXANDROS

Stavra was in her dressing room when he arrived at her chambers, changing out of her ash-stained gown (now ruined, she said from behind the closed door) and into something more suited to the season. Vuomorra was not nearly as cold as anywhere in Thyzakos or Merkher—they would never dream, for instance, of snow—but there was still a chill in the air that was unexpected given the stark sheets of sun that fell through every window.

"Tell me about the new second," she called over the splash of bathwater. Lexos felt heat rise to his cheeks at the thought of Stavra in a state of anything but full dress. "I saw you leave the hall with her."

"Her name is Falka." Lexos threw himself down on the bed, this one done up in blue where his was in gold. "Have you met her before? Heard any talk?"

"I've never heard anyone speak of her, but that may be what she prefers." The door opened a crack, and through it Lexos could see Stavra wiping steam from the mirror as she peered at her reflection. "I take it she's not like Gino?"

"No, no, she's something else entirely. She doesn't even seem to fear her siblings the way the other seconds have done."

Stavra came out of the dressing room in loose goldenrod trousers and a matching shirt, which set off the rich brown of her skin. Her hair was still dry, twisted up into a knot on top of her head.

"She's probably spent her life making treaties with her siblings," she said, dropping onto the bed next to Lexos and bending to pull on a pair of boots. "To be honest, I've always wondered why someone hadn't yet."

"Well, she'll be the first to try it, and I suspect the last." He shook his head wonderingly. "I don't think I've met anyone like her before."

"Oh, Lexos. Of course you have." Stavra sat up and glanced at the open dressing room door before looking at him with a hopeful smile. "Will you show me? I never get to see."

"I'm tired."

Lexos groaned as she dragged him up off the bed, laughing. "Quickly," she said, "before somebody comes to empty my bathwater."

The tub was set in the middle of the dressing room, a great copper thing full of grimy water. There were still some suds left from Stavra's bath, during which Lexos supposed she'd had to scrub quite vigorously to remove the ash of Gino's burning from her skin. He crouched next to it, Stavra standing over his shoulder and bouncing on her toes as she watched.

Idly, he dipped his index finger into the water, drawing a circle that deepened, pulling more and more of the water into its spiral the longer he stirred. The current sucked the water away from the washtub until its walls were bare, gleaming freshly. He'd done this in the reflecting pool at home once, and Rhea had shrieked, gone running to the veranda railing to make sure the ocean was still as it should be, but of course it was. Like the other Stratagiozi children, it was only using the right tools that he could set his designs on the world.

"I wish we could trade," Stavra said wistfully. "Yours is so much nicer than mine. What am I supposed to do, add wrinkles to people just for fun?"

He drew his hand from the water, let it slosh ungracefully back into place. "Even if you could have any fun with yours, you never would. You take everything so seriously."

"There are rules, traditions for these things, Lexos," she said, solemn even as she continued to watch the last ripples in the bathwater. "They've held the federation together for a thousand years. We cannot all break them as easily as you do."

"Quite," he said, "except in this instance I wonder if perhaps we're exaggerating the consequences. It's only bathwater." Stavra snorted, hiding a laugh. Lexos felt a bloom of fondness in his chest as he stood, wiping his hand on his trousers. "Now," he went on, "why don't we leave the palace for the evening? If I see another Domina today I may well scream."

Stavra rolled her eyes, but didn't protest when he led her out of her room and to his own chambers, or when he made her wait while he changed out of his own mourning clothes. They were on their way out of the palace, heading toward the nearest exit when a servant caught up to them, red-faced and breathing hard.

"For you, sir," he said to Lexos, holding out a piece of parchment in his trembling hand. "I am to wait for your reply."

Lexos snatched the letter from the man's shaking hand and held it up to the light. There was no mistaking the handwriting on the front. This was from Rhea.

Stavra stepped away, drawing the servant with her. She couldn't have recognized Rhea's handwriting, but perhaps she knew the look on Lexos's face, the anticipation and dear hope he was sure he wasn't managing to hide.

Lexos slid open the envelope and pulled out the letter. It was brief, and the bottom half seemed to have been ripped off, as if to preserve the unused material.

Lexos,

 Hoping you are well, and that the weather in Vuomorra is fine. How unfortunate to hear of our father's displeasure, but as you are certain of your eventual success with the Dominas, so am I. I confess, brother, I

find myself searching for words to fill the empty space, so that I might
avoid delivering poor news, but there is nothing for it. I must tell you
there is nothing to be found in the Ksigora. The Laskaris boy has noth-
ing to offer—no contacts, no information. I have done what I could, and
I trust that were there any secrets to be revealed, I would know them by
now. I wonder if your intelligence can be true. I can find no confirmable
connection between Michali and the Sxoriza. Instead I count him among
a number of staunch supporters of our father, of our family. A shame to
have chosen him, to have married him and so robbed the Ksigora of such
a leader, and ourselves of such an ally.

I await your instructions. May your time in Vuomorra prove more
fruitful than my own venture here.

Ever your kathroula,
Rhea

Lexos felt the parchment crumple in his fist as he looked up from
Rhea's words, Stavra's figure registering dimly. No confirmable connection? What was Rhea doing up there? Certainly she had simply
not looked hard enough for information. The Laskaris boy had performed some trick, muddled her mind somehow.

"Your sister?" Stavra said, and he nodded. "How is she enjoying
her time in the north?"

He scoffed. "Too well. I knew she would fall prey to that boy."

"If that were true, you would not have sent her in the first place."
Lexos looked at her sharply, and she widened her eyes with a deliberate innocence. "Which, of course, you did not do. Funny, how the
heart—"

"Oh, enough," Lexos said. "It's pointless now anyway."

"Why? What does she say? If there is anything you can tell me."

He unfolded the parchment, smoothing the creases he'd left, and
scanned it again. The opening pleasantries, the bad news about Michali.

Michali. That was odd. Rhea didn't usually refer to her consorts
by their given names. In fact, when confronted with her history of
consorts, Lexos would have been hard-pressed to name a single one.

Further proof, Lexos thought, that she'd fallen for her consort, that she was blind to who he really was.

But there was something else still nagging at him, and he kept reading. Down to the bottom, where she'd signed her name. She'd signed off as his *kathroula*. His preferred endearment for her, but not one she ever used to describe herself. It reminded him of something, and it wasn't until he'd stared at it for a long moment, the quiet weighing oppressively down on him, that he was able to place it.

This letter was almost how she'd spoken to Baba when they were younger, when she wanted something. He could hear it now, that wheedling tone of voice, the sweet words she scattered through her speech so that Baba might smile and relent and let her stay up later into the night, or eat another helping of dessert.

Rhea wanted something from him, whether she was saying so or not. And he had a feeling it had something to do with the consort whose name she was suddenly familiar with.

"Sir?"

Lexos looked up, past Stavra's expectant face to the servant, who was waiting, shifting from foot to foot.

"What?"

"Your response?"

"Tell her," Lexos said, "that she's lost her mind."

The servant's eyes widened, and his sallow skin went pale. "I'm sorry?"

" 'Dear sister, you have lost your mind. Your brother, Alexandros.' There, you have your response." He spun on his heel, Stavra following as he stormed back toward his chambers. Rhea always did know how to ruin his mood.

"What was that?" Stavra said, catching up with him. "What's she done?"

He shook the crumpled letter under her nose. "She's going to let the Laskaris boy live."

Stavra's jaw dropped. To her, Lexos thought, such a blatant violation of the rules would be an even greater affront than it was to him.

"She can't possibly—"

"This letter," he said, "is her asking me to support her in that choice. Perhaps she doesn't know what she's doing, but I do. I have always known her mind better. Always." He pushed his door open with a bit of extra force and resisted the urge to throw himself onto his bed. "What can I do? I cannot ride to the Ksigora and handle this myself—my work here is too important."

"I think," Stavra said archly, "you may at last be required to do what you are always saying you do, and trust your sister."

Lexos frowned. "That's a bit of a terrifying thought."

"Perhaps one better faced with the help of alcohol." She clapped him on the back with one hand and snatched the letter away from him with the other. "Put this out of your mind. I know a place where the drinks are cheap enough. Or they were, last I was here."

The drinks, it turned out, were not so cheap anymore, but that didn't stop them from consuming a great number of them. Lexos's last complete memory of the evening was Stavra hauling him away from the edge of one of the canals as he attempted to remove his shirt and dive into the water, but there were fragments of others collected alongside it, too. The guard's disapproving look as they staggered back into the palace. Falka, waiting outside his door in an altogether ridiculous nightgown, and the warmth of her embrace as she bid him good morning and good night before slipping down the hallway into the dark.

Lexos recalled it now from where he was sprawled, just awake, on top of his bedcovers in the harsh light of the morning, his trousers half off, one of his shoes still on. Stavra was gone—thank goodness, he thought fervently—and there was the distinct smell of vomit in the air. He dreaded what he might see when he looked in the washroom.

He wrestled to his feet and staggered into the washroom, pointedly avoiding the bucket in the corner that seemed to practically ooze with a noxious smell and instead bending over the pitcher set up in front of the mirror. The water in the pitcher had long since lost its heat, and so it snatched the breath from his lungs as he splashed it onto his face and scrubbed the bleariness from his eyes.

He'd let his stress over Rhea's letter take hold of him, had drunk deeply and quickly last night, but no more. It was a new day, and he would keep his focus on his own task. Let Rhea do what she would; he could control only the outcome of what he did here in Vuomorra.

Sluggishly, he dressed in more shades of Domina green, pausing every now and then to wait for the churning in his stomach to settle, and then rummaged on the floor, looking for his trousers. He never went anywhere without his Argyros dagger slotted into the hidden pocket, and the blade was probably still lounging in yesterday's.

Except it wasn't. The pocket was empty. And the dagger wasn't in the drawer of his nightstand, or packed haphazardly in his luggage.

In the hallway, he could hear the stirrings of motion—voices approaching, and tramping heavy footsteps—but he ignored it and ducked his head under the bed, peering into the shadows. No dagger there, either.

Dread began to coil in his stomach. Lexos shut his eyes and stood up, swaying slightly. It was nothing. He must have lost the dagger on the way back into the palace, and it was out there somewhere, on the floor of some tavern, or in the grubby hands of some canalman. Certainly it had not been slipped out of his pocket by someone else. By an unexpected visitor at the end of a long evening.

Outside, the voices were drawing closer, and Lexos was startled by a knock on his bedroom door. It was polite, almost delicate. Stavra, maybe, coming to see if he'd recovered yet. She would know what had happened. She would put him at ease.

"Yes?" he said, swinging the door open, expecting Stavra's smug smile as she took in the stale odor he was sure was wafting off him.

"Good morning." It was Falka, and beyond her stood a phalanx of armed guards. She was smiling, her face lit up with what Lexos could only call exhilaration, and her cheeks were flushed, her eyes bright. She looked entirely unlike the version of her he had encountered last night. She'd been shy, then, almost embarrassed at herself for waiting at his door, and he'd been embarrassed for her, too. He'd allowed her embrace out of pity and had allowed himself to pretend it wasn't happening.

That, he knew now by the sight of her, had been a mistake.

"Good morning," he replied. The guards were watching him, their faces impassive, and though nobody was aiming a weapon at him, the tension in the air left him sure they weren't far from it. Still. He could not let his unease show. "To what do I owe the pleasure?"

"I'm afraid," Falka said, "that this is not a pleasurable occasion." She reached to him, palm up. "Join me."

He would have much preferred to shut the door in her face. But instead he ignored her proffered hand and stepped out into the hallway, squinting at the bright light that flooded in through the windows laid across the far wall. His head began to pound, his mouth dry and sticking. There, waiting a few paces beyond Falka, was Tarro.

He'd been wrong to leave the palace, to lose track of his task. And he was about to pay for it.

"Alexandros Argyros," Falka said, "in the name of Tarro Domina, father of his house, father of Trefazio, I bid you stand and face the charges laid against you."

Charges? Of what? They had to be serious, given the presence of so many guards and of Tarro himself.

Lexos looked to Tarro, but his face was blank, and he was watching not Lexos but Falka, who in turn was smiling triumphantly in a way that left Lexos doubtful that he would find any way out of this.

"I will hear your charges," he said, because something of that nature was required of him, but he looked then to Tarro and spread his hands to show he was unarmed. He had to make an appeal—Tarro's support was everything to him, and to Thyzakos. "Sir, whatever you have been told, I must remind you of my loyalty and devotion to you."

"Your loyalty is to your family," Falka said sharply. "Do not disrespect my father by pretending otherwise."

Well, Lexos thought. He couldn't argue with that. At least Tarro wasn't saying anything. Tarro was almost never without words, and perhaps he was, for the moment, withholding judgment. After all, he had known Lexos for so long, and in fact probably knew Lexos better than he did Falka.

"Let us hear your charges, then," Lexos said, throwing as much confidence into his voice as he could, "if only so that I might refute them. I have conducted myself with the honor befitting my station."

"You do not deserve your station," Falka said, but Tarro held up a hand.

"Now, now," he said, and Lexos couldn't help the rush of relief, his knees buckling slightly. "There's no need for that sort of talk." He came forward, close enough that Lexos could make out a rip in the rich, glistening fabric of his shirt, the edges of which were dark with dried blood. "Tell the boy what he stands accused of."

He would get Tarro on his side. He had to. No matter what Falka said next, she didn't stand at the center of all this. Tarro did.

"Not long ago," she began, her voice echoing stridently in the hall, "a man matching your description broke into my father's quarters and attempted to take his life." Her green skirts billowed out behind her as she took a few purposeful steps forward, sending Lexos stumbling back. "He left something behind. Do you know what that might be?"

Lexos had a sinking feeling that he did, and that there was no way out of this left to him.

"A dagger," she said, not waiting for his answer. The guard nearest to her produced it from the folds of his armor, and she took it. It was unmistakably Lexos's; there the leather-wrapped grip, there the pommel with the Argyros crest stamped clearly in the metal, its arcing olive branches crusted over with blood. The sheath hid the small, perfectly balanced blade, and its surface was smooth, designed to slide into its pocket without catching on any stitching.

"Do you recognize this?"

Lexos let out a long breath. She had planned everything. There was no point in lying. "Yes."

"And does it belong to you?"

He couldn't exactly pawn it off as somebody else's. He was the only Argyros in the country. There was nobody else to take the blame.

"Yes," he said, holding his chin high. Let Tarro see he had no guilt within him. Let Tarro see he was unafraid. "That dagger is mine. Indeed, it has been missing from my person at least since last night." He glanced at Falka with narrowed eyes, and then—she was unimportant in this, after all—turned fully to Tarro. "Sir, you know I hold no malice for you in my heart. It seems there is some game afoot."

"You consider an attempt on my father's life a game?"

He ignored Falka and stepped forward. The guards drew their swords, and immediately two blades were crossed between him and Tarro, but at least Tarro was looking at him now, with a cool, curious gaze.

"You must have seen your attacker," Lexos said. "Did you recognize him? Was his face mine?"

Tarro pushed the crossed blades aside and clapped a friendly hand on Lexos's shoulder. "You are wearing his clothes, my boy. And he carried your dagger. I'm afraid that's hard to wriggle out of."

Lexos felt the last bloom of hope wilt in his chest. This was nothing to Tarro. Just another attempt in a long line of them. And he had no real need for Lexos, especially compared to what need Lexos had for him. Without Tarro's backing, Lexos couldn't go home. For him this was ruining everything and dooming his father's rule. For Tarro it was just a bit of entertainment before breakfast.

"Your diplomatic status protects you from our courts," Falka said from behind him. He turned to face her, noticing a curl of distaste at the corner of her mouth. "And protects your life from our executioners. But it does nothing to protect you from the edict of my father."

She held out her hand, and the nearest guard produced a small, neatly rolled scroll of parchment. Falka had planned this out to the very last detail, down to where she would stand.

"Alexandros Argyros," she said, reading from the elaborate script inked onto the parchment, "you are hereby exiled from Vuomorra and from the country of Trefazio. Your feet shall never again step on Trefzan soil; your eyes shall never again see Trefzan sky. Violation of this edict will bring down the fury of the Domina court on your country. May your harvest wither; may your waters run dry; may your life be forfeit."

It was as close as they could get to calling for his execution, and Lexos felt the weight of it come crashing down onto him. No promise extracted from Tarro, and nothing to stop the Rhokeri from moving in on Baba's seat. What was there left to do?

"By the order of the Domina Stratagorra, let this edict be made law," Falka said, and Lexos was about to turn to Tarro, to make one last plea, when Falka held out the scroll to him, and there it was—Tarro's signature, in Domina green ink. This had been decided long ago.

"What now, then?" Lexos asked, voice breaking roughly.

"These men will wait while you gather your things." Falka made her way past him, to Tarro's side. "And then they will see you out of Vuomorra, back to whatever ship you arrived on."

She and Tarro gave him one last look, and turned, heading back down the hallway. Lexos tried to follow, but two of the guards stepped into his path.

"Wait," he called. "Tarro, what about the council? What about peace among the Stratagiozis? You know it won't last if you disgrace me like this."

"It isn't the peace that will not last, I think," said Tarro, smiling apologetically. "Goodbye, Alexandros. Apart from this little business, I've enjoyed your company."

Then they were stepping through the doorway and out onto the sunlit terrace. A servant approached, bearing a tray of champagne glasses, and at the far end of the lawn a pair of Domina children came dashing out of the hedges, their laughter carrying up to the shadowed hallway Lexos stood in.

Life went on for them, unchanged. For him it had all but ended.

The guards watched as he packed; they watched as he dressed in his black traveling suit; they watched as he searched for his dagger before remembering Falka had kept it with her. And when he had finished gathering his things, they watched as he resignedly put everything into his trunk and dragged it out into the hallway.

They kept him at the center of their formation as they escorted him out of the palace. They passed group after group of people: aristocrats, Dominas, and civilians all gaping at the Thyzak second who had tried to kill their ruler. Waiting at the palace gates was a plain, rickety carriage, its driver thin to the bone, its horses poorly groomed. Falka's doing, her dramatic touch evident in every aspect of this whole mess.

The carriage took him slowly through the streets, giving the public plenty of time to gawk. Falka had obviously already spread the word that the Thyzak second had tried to assassinate the Trefzan Stratagiozi. Word would spread through Trefazio, through the world over. Lexos was watching the ruin of his reputation.

At last, they arrived in the harbor, and Lexos hurried onto his ship, its sails marked by the Argyros crest. The crew gave him a wide berth, and it was only the captain who approached with wary steps.

"Back to Stratathoma?" he said gingerly.

"No," Lexos said. He shut his eyes, laid out a map in his head. "To Agiokon."

TWENTY-EIGHT

RHEA

Rhea had expected a bit more to change now that she and Michali were something other than what they had been, but in truth all that marked the occasion was Evanthia's shriek of delight when they'd arrived home from the camp, Michali's fingerprints smudged into the kohl around Rhea's eyes, the two of them standing a good deal closer than they had been when they left.

Since then, in daylight things were much the same. Rhea and Michali made their official visits to the wealthiest families in the city, sipping kaf and picking at small bowls of candied fruit. They attended the opening of the new guild of fur trappers—that particular outing left Rhea feeling a bit ill—and they toured a building, the exact purpose of which she had been hard-pressed to identify. All the while Michali never looked at her for any longer than he would have otherwise, and there was a careful reserve in the way his hand rested at her back, or at her elbow as they passed through the city.

Once the evening arrived, though, and once they were out of his mother's sight (and, she supposed, his father's, although Yannis rarely seemed to leave his chambers in town), there was Michali as he had been on the mountain that day, his smile soft, his touch so careful that Rhea could sometimes barely feel it.

She had been with other consorts, certainly, had even liked some of them. But never so much that she'd been nervous to feel their hands on her hips, her heartbeat turned to wings like the little blue humming-bird's in Nitsos's windup garden. Never so much that in the dark she'd kept hold of them even after they'd finished, eager to stay close.

But it was like that with Michali. It was the way he seemed fasci-nated with the matching marks they bore. It was those moments in the night when he told her how it had been growing up on the island, watching the city and waiting for the day he was old enough to cross the lake. He told her how his mother had cried when child after child vanished from her womb, how tightly she held him to her breast in the days that followed every loss.

And she told him what she could of her own mother, of Aya Ksiga after that title had been buried in the earth. Most of what she knew came from Lexos, rather than her own memory, but she shared it anyway, described the picnics in the meadows, Mama laughing, Chrysanthi cradled tiny in her arms as Rhea and Lexos played with Nitsos. She told Michali about the nursery, its ceiling painted to look like the sky. One night she even told him the story she barely believed herself, of the day of her mother's death, when she and Lexos stole onto the back of a horse and rode as fast as they could, down the beaten-dirt road, heading for somewhere new.

"We were afraid," Rhea said as she finished, and felt the words to be true, though they came from somewhere she did not recognize. "We thought we might have to go with her."

They said nothing after that, but Michali's little finger hooked around hers, and long after he fell asleep Rhea lay awake, a thunder-ing in her ears.

The next morning came slowly, lazily. Michali's side of the bed was already cold. He generally woke earlier than she did, which she supposed made sense—when your life was as long as hers had been thus far, you hardly minded spending more of it asleep.

She closed her eyes and stretched, relishing the pop of her joints

and the push in her muscles. Contentment, she thought. Warm and
sweet like honey, and something she'd never quite tasted before.

Of course, it was ruined not a moment later by a hearty knock on
the door and Evanthia's voice wishing her a good morning. Evanthia
didn't seem to know, lately, whether to call her Rhea or Thyspira,
and so she had solved her problem by simply avoiding calling her
anything.

"Up, up! Breakfast is waiting!" Evanthia knocked once more and
then the door swung open. "There you are! Lying about at this hour
of the morning."

Rhea tried to keep from rolling her eyes as Evanthia winked os-
tentatiously. "Good morning, Evanthia. Thank you for coming to
wake me."

"Oh, it's no trouble. Now come, get dressed and eat. You and my
son have plans this morning."

Of course. She'd heard Michali mention Meroximo before, the
Ksigora's winter festival. Held, as always, on the first day of the lake's
full freeze.

Evanthia swept the covers off Rhea's legs, and Rhea jumped at
the sudden rush of cold. "*Elado*. You and Michali are both expected
to make a showing."

An official one at that, judging by the clothing Evanthia had selected from Rhea's things. She seemed to be planning for Rhea to
wear a number of white wool underskirts, all of which would add
shape and heft to the dress that she was carrying over one arm.

"This was mine," she said, draping it over the foot of the bed. "I
suppose it will fit you well enough."

It was dark crimson, for the Laskaris house, or perhaps just for the
sake of it. The skirt was pin-tucked at the waist so that as it billowed
out, it rippled and folded. Like the bodice, it was embroidered in
blacks and darker reds, a column of curls running down the bodice
to the hem of the skirt. Otherwise, the dress was fairly simple, its
high neck and plain waistband designed not to distract from the
sleeves, which were long and fluid, opening to drape nearly to the
floor before scooping back up to close at the wrists.

"Thank you for letting me wear it," Rhea said, surprised at the softness that stole into Evanthia's eyes as she rubbed the cuff of one sleeve between her fingers. "It's an honor, I'm sure."

It took a few minutes to get it properly on—Rhea kept stepping into the sleeves, thrown by the volume of fabric—but once it had settled on her shoulders, she found that the drape of them hung close to her body, giving her silhouette a sweep that suited her station. And furthermore, she thought, swirling her skirt around her, all this fabric would keep her plenty warm. Which was a good thing, considering Evanthia hadn't pulled out a matching coat.

She sat patiently as Evanthia tugged a brush through her hair and braided the front sections of it back and away from her face. Rhea had learned since arriving in the Ksigora that Ksigorans wore no jewelry in the winter months—too high a chance of having the metal stick to one's exposed skin—and so she was surprised when Evanthia drew a necklace from her pocket and draped it around Rhea's neck.

"What's this?"

"The Laskaris crest," Evanthia answered. Rhea ran a hand over the pendant, strung on a thick gold chain. It looked nothing like the Argyros crest, with its twin olive branches crossing a single blade. Instead, the Laskaris crest was just a field of stars, a few of them joined together in a constellation. Lexos would be proud, Rhea thought, to see his duty memorialized so.

"I know most of my brother's work," she said, holding it where Evanthia could see over her shoulder, "but I don't recognize this one."

"Oh," said Evanthia, and then lightly but with an edge to her voice that said she would brook no further discussion, "that is not one of your brother's making."

This was the sort of light sacrilege Rhea was going to have to get used to. A constellation put into the sky by some hand other than Lexos's, or perhaps by no hand at all. She brushed away the slight discomfort of it and let the pendant rest against her chest.

At last Evanthia was finished, and Rhea had been deemed suitable for public consumption. They made their way through the quiet hallways down to the main room, where a fire was flickering merrily, and where breakfast was waiting on the dining table.

Michali was waiting, too, picking lazily at one of the iced rolls, and he lurched to his feet as Rhea came in, an unchecked smile splitting his mouth. "Good morning," he said. "You look . . . red."

She cocked her head. "Thank you."

Evanthia had already crossed to smack Michali's shoulder and adjust the collar of his matching crimson coat. "You have all the charm of an eel, my son." She gave him one last smack for good measure and made for the kitchen. "Sit, sit," she called over her shoulder. "I'll bring you both some kaf."

Rhea sat down opposite Michali, rooting through the pile of biscuits and pastries to find one with chocolate filling. "Exactly what should I be expecting this morning?"

"It's not bad, Meroximo," he said around a mouthful of bread. Evidently their improved relationship had not come with an improvement in manners. "It used to be for midwinter, but these days the lake isn't frozen in time."

That, of course, was due to Rhea's own triumphs and (more often) difficulties with her consorts, and to Baba's insistence that, to please the Thyzak farmers, winter be brief and sweet. Michali seemed to have forgotten her involvement, and went on without a glance in her direction.

"The whole city will be out on the ice. Skating, a winter market. We'll pay our respects to some of the prominent families, probably buy some children some roasted chestnuts. That sort of thing."

"How picturesque."

Michali raised an eyebrow. "That's quite a lot of disdain for someone who's taken this homeland as hers."

"Is that what I've done?"

"Some might say." He took another overly large bite. "Taking the land of your consort and all that."

Rhea leaned back, crossed her arms. "Perhaps it's you who should take mine."

He got up, brushing crumbs from the front of his jacket. "Indeed, that's the idea." He leaned across the table to kiss her lightly, and Rhea tried to pretend that she wasn't pleased.

That feeling disappeared when Michali helped her into a pair of boots with nails driven through the bottom, creating a spined sole. She was quite sure she would injure somebody with them, and wasn't entirely convinced they weren't meant to be a practical joke of some kind. But then his boots were the same, and once they'd stepped outside, onto ice-slick stone and into air full of sun and loud with chatter, Rhea knew she'd be grateful for them.

Children crouched on the shore of the Laskaris island, packing snowballs together. She was surprised to see them so close to the Laskaris house—Baba would certainly have never allowed something similar at Stratathoma—but then the Laskaris family, even Yannis, had never seemed to mind being stuck in among the people. In fact, that often seemed to be a point of pride for them.

Beyond the children, market stalls were spread out on the ice, draped in brightly colored fabrics and lit with paper lanterns, perfumed smoke rising from the braziers and cookfires that had been lit among them. Rhea could smell something delicious—quite a few things, if the variety of stalls was anything to go by—and even though she'd just had breakfast, her mouth began to water.

Clusters of people were shuffling across the frozen lake, moving from stall to stall, and on the opposite shore, on the promenade, there were more people still, most of them focused on what seemed to be a race between children rolling hoops tied with bright streamers. But more than anything, what Rhea couldn't take her eyes off of were the skaters. She'd never seen it in person before, had only heard descriptions and seen the occasional illustration in a book or two, but there they were, Ksigorans with blades strapped to their boots, skimming across the ice in great arcing paths.

She grabbed Michali's arm as two of the skaters veered perilously close to each other, but they spun away with ease.

"They aren't falling," she said. "How are they managing it?"

He looked bemused. "It's not so hard."

"It isn't? You can do it, then, can you?"

"Well, no—"

"Ah, I see." She watched one of the younger skaters, a girl with twin braids running down her back that whipped behind her as she swept along the shoreline in large spirals. "I'd like to learn, I think."

Michali was quiet for a moment, and then she felt his hand at the small of her back. "Someday, maybe. We'll come back here, and I'll teach you."

"You'll teach me?"

He laughed. "We'll learn together."

They started down the steps to the snow-crusted beach, smiling as the children noticed their approach and came dashing up, hands outstretched. Rhea looked to Michali, alarmed, but he only waved hello and pulled a bag of coins from his coat. When he handed a similar bag to her, she found hers was filled with candy wrapped in thick waxy paper.

"*Ftama, ftama,*" Michali was saying to the children as they gathered around. "You'll each get your turn."

He began doling out a coin to each child, exchanging the traditional Saint's Thyzaki blessing she'd become so familiar with. She followed suit, the Stratagiozi version rolling off her tongue out of habit before she snatched it back. At first the children seemed a bit afraid of her—no doubt their mothers had told them about Thyspira from the west, and to some Rhea now knew she was a saint's mosaic come to life—but when they realized she had sweets to distribute they gathered in close, tugging at her skirts and calling her name (well, calling Thyspira) in delighted voices.

"What do I do when I run out?" she whispered to Michali, who was nearing the bottom of his own bag.

He handed a coin to one child and batted away the hands of a repeat visitor. "Nothing. The first children to spot us get the lot. Why do you think they've been waiting so close to the house?"

True to Michali's word, as soon as their bags ran dry, the children dissipated, dashing back out onto the ice on boots studded with nails, like Rhea's, which gave them a steady grip and kept them upright.

Michali and Rhea followed much more slowly. They made their way down to the beach and stepped out onto the ice, Rhea clinging tightly to Michali's arm even though her steps were sturdy underneath her. Was the ice really thick enough to hold all of these people, all of these stalls? And wouldn't the fires in those braziers melt it? She supposed there were some things that you were born to in the Ksigora, and comfort on the ice seemed to be one of them.

"There are some people we'll have to greet," Michali said, leaning close so that they wouldn't be overheard. "And then Piros will be along."

She jerked back to look at him. "What for?" Was there news? Had something happened with Lexos?

"The last of the plans has been finalized." Michali smiled and waved at someone farther along the ice, and steered their path away. "He'll tell you the rest."

They met a number of prominent Ksigorans, each one with a different flicker of skepticism in their eyes at Rhea's presence. One barely said three words to her, speaking entirely to Michali instead, while another kept peppering the conversation with remarks on how well she seemed to be adapting to the cold despite being a stranger to the Ksigora. Through it all, Yannis drifted in and out, clearly monitoring his son's behavior. Rhea could feel Michali bristling, could hear the tightness in his voice. She knew that feeling all too well.

At last they finished with Michali's required conversations, and he moved them quickly away from the area in which Ksigori's high society was gathered, all warming their hands over the same few braziers and enjoying their spiced tea and roasted nuts. He led Rhea down an aisle between two rows of stalls at the end of which a cluster of children was watching a puppet show. Here the people smiled at them and waved as they passed, but didn't accost them for conversation.

"Keep an eye out for Piros," Michali said.

"He's speaking to us here? In public?" She glanced around them at the other Ksigorans, who, though they weren't staring outright, were clearly watching them. "Isn't that a risk?"

"Of course," Michali said. They drew to a halt by an unoccupied brazier, and Rhea took the opportunity to bend close to the fire and feel some heat spark in her cheeks. "We'll just wait here, and if we happen to run into him, well, we can't control who takes a moment to warm his hands at a public brazier, can we?"

It was a few minutes before Piros was recognizable across the ice, his bulk setting him apart as he wound his way through the crowd. As he neared, Rhea studiously avoided watching him and focused on her fingers, which were red from the cold, despite her keeping them tucked within the folds of her sleeves. Soon Piros settled in alongside them at the brazier with a huff of breath and a great rustle of his coat, which seemed many layers thick and was trimmed in glossy black fur.

"*Efkala*," Michali said, as he had to every other Ksigoran. Piros responded in kind, unable to disguise a gleeful twinkle in his eyes. Clearly he took great delight in this sort of secret proceeding.

"What a fine day for Meroximo, don't you think?" Piros said, winking at Rhea as she glanced up from the fire. "So nice to get a bit of sun."

"Of course," Michali said, "Ksigori shows to advantage in any weather. But we are lucky to have a day like this."

Apparently those were pleasantries enough, because Piros ducked his head and drew his coat farther up around his shoulders, letting his collar throw his mouth into shadow. He looked only like a man shielding himself from the cold, but Rhea supposed he was keeping his words from being read on his lips.

"News from Vuomorra," he said quietly. "I'm afraid things haven't gone well for the other Argyros."

Lexos. Rhea felt a lurch in her stomach, and bit the inside of her cheek, trying not to look too worried. "Is he all right?"

"Oh, he's plenty all right. And besides, things might not have gone well for him, but they've gone well for us."

"Enough," Michali said sharply. "We don't have time for this."

"He's delightful," Piros said to Rhea before digging through his pockets for a scrap of parchment, which he pressed surreptitiously into Michali's palm. "From Falka. She has the details. But suffice to say, the Argyros boy didn't get what he came for."

No promise from Tarro, no troops to help Baba tighten his hold on Thyzakos. Rhea couldn't help a pang of worry for Lexos, who was surely feeling the weight of that failure. She'd written to him after returning to the house from the Sxoriza camp, telling him that there was nothing to be found in the Ksigora—an explanation for when she arrived home empty-handed. But there had been no reply, and she was unsure, now, if it had reached him at all. Still, there was nothing she could do about that.

"Who's Falka?" she asked. They'd mentioned her before, and Rhea hadn't paid much attention, but she was all the way in this now. She wouldn't let any of it pass her by.

"Tarro's new second," Michali said. "She's been with us for a year, nearly. You'd like her, I think." He looked to Piros. "You're sure? Everything's settled?"

"Absolutely. Falka will remain our contact in Vuomorra, and take on some of your duties while you're in hiding. Speaking of which." Piros removed another folded slip of parchment from his coat. "I have made the arrangements. You'll appear to die in a fortnight just as you're supposed to. I'll fetch you from the island myself." He looked to Rhea. "And you'll go home to your father just as you're supposed to."

And then—that was the part she was afraid of. It had been her idea, but that didn't mean she wasn't dreading it more than anything. "I don't think I'll be able to get Lexos to change the tides right away." She wasn't, in fact, sure she would be able to get him to do it at all, but she wasn't about to say so.

"Well," Michali said, "they'll be waiting. Hurry, if you can. And when you have, all you have to do is send a signal."

"Can you get a lantern to the beach?" Piros asked. Rhea rolled her eyes, and he hurried on. "Leave it lit on the night you open the tides to us and wait as near the cliffside entrance as you can. Our soldiers will come up the staircase and take Stratathoma with your guidance."

"Soldiers" was an awfully big word, Rhea thought, and perhaps not the right one if it was meant to describe those people she had seen in the camps. Tired, and hungry, and yes, full of dedication, but not full of much in the way of actual bodily strength.

Still, she was familiar enough with the sort of façade Piros and Michali were putting on now. She and Lexos had done it often enough—pretended to find power where there was none. And this was her plan. It would work because it had to. This was the only way her siblings stayed alive.

"I understand," she said, smiling brightly. "I won't let you down."

Piros nodded to Rhea before clasping Michali's hand tightly. "*Efkala*, both of you."

She and Michali remained at the fire as Piros sidled off into the crowd, and though Rhea kept her gaze locked on the iron curve of the brazier, she could tell that Michali was watching her, studying her with that steady patience she loved and hated in equal measure.

"You're worried," he said quietly, and Rhea did not manage to hold back her laugh. Truly, a staggering insight.

"Of course I am."

"It'll be fine. You heard Piros. Everything's been arranged."

Rhea looked up at Michali, holding tightly to the Laskaris crest hanging around her neck to keep her hand from shaking. "No, you don't understand. I don't know who this Falka is. To be quite honest, I don't really care. But no matter how in hand she has things, you're making a mistake with Lexos."

"A mistake?"

"Yes. You're counting him out, and you shouldn't be."

Michali smiled, its strain betraying his shared worry. "Rhea, I promise you. It's been handled. All of it. You'll see."

"You don't know Lexos. He would rather die before failing our father."

"But sending you here wasn't exactly what your father wanted, no?"

She shook her head. "That's for Baba, too, at the root of it."

Michali frowned, clearly thinking. He was listening to her at least, which was more than she'd got elsewhere. "Well. You'll be at Stratathoma with him soon enough, yes? You can pass word to Falka and Piros if it seems more needs to be done."

"And to you," she corrected. But Michali only shook his head. Until Stratathoma was taken, Piros would be the Sxoriza's first in command, although Piros insisted it was in name only, and Falka would become Piros's second.

Michali slid a gloved hand along her waist, drawing her nearer, and Rhea felt herself blush, even in the cold. They were in public, and though there were no customs that forbade such behavior, Michali hadn't thus far seemed eager to show the Ksigorans how things between them had changed. "Come on," he said. "Let's get somewhere warmer."

He led her across the ice, toward a stall that sold steaming cups of cider. Rhea felt her chest tighten with the sort of joy that bordered on pain. It was all right. Michali would live, and everything would go as planned. And yes, she'd have to face her family. But not today.

Above them, the sky stretched blue and unbroken, and off in the distance, a bird caught the breeze and rose higher, its white wings shining with sun. It was familiar, Rhea thought, and smiled. How at home she was here already.

TWENTY-NINE

ALEXANDROS

It took nearly a fortnight before the rock spire of Agiokon broke the horizon. Much longer than it should have taken, but Tarro's edict had prevented the ship from docking in any Trefzan city to restock their supplies, and bad weather had plagued the rest of the journey. At last, though, two horses into his ride from the coast, Lexos was finally where he wanted to be. There was only the matter of Zita letting him into her house.

The news about the situation in Vuomorra had spread faster than he'd been able to travel. Everywhere he stopped he was faced with whispers about the Argyros boy who had tried to murder the Trefzan Stratagiozi. In Thyzak territory they had stayed whispers; once he crossed the border into Merkher they turned into outright accusations, and he'd even been chased out of one village when he'd stopped to rest his horse.

It would only get worse—he knew that. He had to fix this, and quickly, before the damage was irreversible and Thyzakos's standing, along with Baba's trust, were lost forever. Then there would be time to handle the mess Rhea seemed to be making in the Ksigora.

It was with trepidation that Lexos rode through the streets of Agiokon toward the Devetsi house, where he hoped that Zita would welcome him as she always had. Stavra was certainly no more than a week behind him—she would not have stayed long in Vuomorra without him—but without her presence he couldn't be sure that Zita would put her own reputation at risk to take him in.

She met him at the door, poised in the threshold, her face familiarly impassive as he dismounted and ran his hands through his sweaty hair in a futile attempt to smooth it back. Her expression, at least, was no indication of how welcome he would be. Zita always looked as though she would rather be somewhere else.

"You heard of my coming, I see," he said.

"There are some reports out of Trefazio," she said. "I admit I was quite surprised to hear them."

"I was, as well." Lexos smiled wryly. Zita seemed to be alone, without a flanking of armed guards, and the way she was standing, half in and half out of the house, seemed to his hopeful eyes to be a sort of invitation inside. "I was sorry," he said carefully, "to realize how little weight the truth carries in Vuomorra."

Zita considered him for a moment longer, and then stepped back, clearing the way into the Devetsi house's atrium. "Well," she said, beckoning him in, "there are always traditions we must grow accustomed to when we travel abroad."

She installed him in his regular guest quarters, and graciously proved conveniently unavailable at the time of most of Lexos's meals, sparing him a great deal of excruciating small talk over the three days that passed before Stavra reached Agiokon. At last, nearing sunset on the third day, she arrived, tearing through the city alone on horseback, her carriage left behind some miles back.

Lexos met her at the front of the house as she came thundering in, her horse's coat glistening with sweat. She dismounted with a reckless sort of ease, leaving her horse to stand freely as she came toward Lexos.

"You're all right?" she said in Merkheri, haste slurring her words together.

"Yes. Very well, I promise."

She threw her body against his, arms around his neck. Lexos staggered back a few steps, too surprised to do more than steady them both.

"What about you?" he said, drawing back. "Are you all right?"

Stavra leveled him with a look. "I'm not the one who was exiled from Trefazio. I'm fine."

In the atrium, she cast off her riding cloak and wrestled free of her boots, which were caked with days' worth of mud. Lexos watched her, unexpectedly unnerved by the sight of her bare, spindle-boned feet.

"Are you going to speak with your mother?" he asked. If she was, he wanted to be there for it, if at all possible.

"My room," she said, already starting up the staircase. "I'll talk to her later."

"Can I come?" It was an odd question—he had never been to Stavra's room before—and she raised her eyebrows, perhaps expecting him to retract it. But Lexos only waited for her answer. He needed her advice, and quickly. There was no time to wait anymore.

"All right," Stavra said after a moment, and she continued upstairs, Lexos at her heels.

The corridor at the top of the house opened up directly onto Stavra's chamber. He lingered in the doorway as she continued inside, dropping her boots by the threshold. In his own quarters, after a hundred years at Stratathoma, he kept barely any belongings. Every year that passed only pointed out to him those things he owned that he no longer needed, while Rhea's room, in contrast, was a study in clutter, in sentiment.

Stavra, it seemed, had struck a balance. He watched as she crossed to a tall wooden wardrobe and threw it open, digging through the drawers inside. There was her bed, the sort they'd had in Vuomorra, although decidedly less fancy, and there was a set of shelves stuffed to bursting with books and papers. On the wall hung a large painting of Agiokon, the monastery at the top of the stone tower bursting with color, alive as it had never been in Lexos's time.

"Well," Stavra said, looking over her shoulder as she pulled on a pair of thick socks. "Aren't you coming in?"

"I suppose." It felt odd to get too close to the bed, although he would never have said so. He gave it a wide berth and collapsed onto the divan tucked into the corner of the room, plush with cushions, its embroidery faded from sunlight.

"You," Stavra said firmly, "look a bit wrecked, my friend."

Lexos buried his head in his hands. "I am. I've barely been able to sleep since leaving Vuomorra." She didn't respond, and he lifted his head to look more closely at her, at the shadows under her eyes, at the ragged edges of her fingernails. "Have you been there all this time?"

"For a few days after you left," she answered. She sat down on the bed and began undoing the twists in her hair. "And then to Legerma to finish some business."

"You made good time coming here, then."

"I certainly hope so. I burned through enough horses."

She looked cross. Lexos couldn't think why. Here she was at home, when he hadn't seen Stratathoma in what felt like a month. "Now that you're here, you can help me think of how to solve this."

"I think perhaps a moment's rest might be warranted." Stavra scooted back along the mattress until she was propped up on the decorative pillows. "Your problem cannot get much worse before morning."

"I cannot leave things as they are now," he said, getting up and crossing the room to crouch in front of her. "I must do something." He took her hands in his. "I need you. I need your help. You always know what to do."

Stavra met his eyes. For a moment she looked impossibly weary, as though something deep in her marrow had been wrung out of her. "Please, Alexandros," she said softly. "Can't this wait? Just until to-morrow?"

"I've been waiting," he said, standing abruptly. "I can't any longer. I need to fix this."

"Well, I'm not sure what you expect me to do. I'm a Stratagiozi's

second, same as you." There was an edge to her voice, one he was
unfamiliar with, and it was not without violence that she tore her
hands from his. "Talk to my mother about it, if you must. Talk to
anyone. As long as you're not talking to me."

She threw herself down onto her pillows and was asleep moments
later, her breathing slow and almost ragged. Talk to her mother,
she'd said. And surely she hadn't meant it, but Lexos thought she
might've had the right idea.

Zita proved hard to find, but at last he spotted her in the garden
just off the back of the house, where a number of rosebushes were
growing at odd angles. She was crouched in the dirt, dressed in white
trousers and a matching linen shirt that were, incredibly, unstained.
They stood stark against her brown skin, which served to emphasize
its characteristic Stratagiozi smoothness, untouched as it was by age
or worry—except, notably, for the furrow on her brow, a mark of her
extreme concentration as she plucked a number of deadheads from
the shortest of the rosebushes.

She was well thought of among the other Stratagiozis. To be sure,
she hadn't been in her seat as long as Tarro—no one had—but she
was a fixture on the council, had seen rivals come and go, and now
ruled Merkher with a steady and near invisible hand. If anybody
could help him manage this, it would be her.

"Well," Zita said suddenly in Merkheri, making Lexos jump,
"don't just stand there looking menacing, or I'll start to think those
rumors coming out of Trefazio are true."

The garden was surrounded by high walls, and over them the
sound of the city was trailing in, shouts and the rattle of carriage
wheels, all under the distant ring of bells to mark the hour. This was
all Zita's house had in the way of outdoor grounds, save the stables
off the side of the house, and while Baba and Lexos considered that
a hardship, Zita and Stavra were both so long accustomed to it that
when Lexos had once mentioned to Stavra the idea of seizing city
land to create more grounds for the house, she had called for some
kaf to clear his head.

"Here," Zita said. She handed him a small trowel as he approached. "Help me transplant this cutting."

"I'm sorry?"

"Dig," she said plainly, switching to Thyzaki, as though that were the problem.

It was a testament to how much he needed her help, Lexos thought, that he was willing to get to his knees in the dirt. Zita watched with a mild sort of amusement as he knelt, unable to keep from wincing when the damp of the earth seeped through the cloth of his trousers. He dug a shallow hole as quickly as he could, conscious of Zita's considered and thoughtful stare.

"That's enough," she said finally. Lexos was startled to hear her using an ancient form of Merkheri, one that had long ago evolved into the conversational dialect spoken by most people within her borders. He glanced over her shoulder, to where a servant was waiting, carrying a pitcher of water and a pair of plain wooden cups. Zita smiled as his eyes met hers again.

"Please," she said, still in that stilted, archaic dialect. "Say what you wish to. If we speak like this we may not be overheard. Well," she added as she began situating the rose cutting in the hole Lexos had dug, "we will certainly be overheard, but perhaps not as certainly understood."

He hadn't heard much archaic Merkheri spoken: Stavra had used it once over dinner, presumably to make fun of him, and since then he'd gone out of his way to pick up what he could, but it was still difficult to form the sentences, to fit them together.

"Thank you for your hospitality," he said, stumbling slightly over the pronunciation. He could only hope he was the slightest bit understandable. "I confess I was nervous you might turn me away, after what you must have heard from the Dominas."

She nodded, her eyes fixed on the rose cutting. "I certainly considered it. Pack the dirt more tightly, if you would."

"I went to Vuomorra," he said, setting aside the trowel and kneading at the dirt with his palms, "only for the good of my family, of my father. I had no reason to wish Tarro any harm. His support could save my father and my country both. I would be mad to have risked losing it. Surely you will have noticed my father's seat is not as stable as it has been."

"Indeed. He will be lucky if his seat lasts through spring."

Lexos couldn't help his raised eyebrows. He hadn't expected her to be so frank. But then, she wasn't wrong.

"What is it you want from me?" she went on.

"Not much," he was quick to start with. "You owe my family no loyalty. I know that. And you've done me such a kindness already by welcoming me into your home."

"But?"

"I can fix this," Lexos said. He sat back on his heels. It was difficult to make his case with his face in a rosebush. "If you would call a meeting of the Stratagiozis—my father excepted, of course—I'm sure I can put things right."

Zita chuckled. "I am not sure you understand how gravely the world will take these reports out of Vuomorra."

The rose cutting was firmly upright now. Lexos was grateful when Zita stood, allowing him to follow her. He clasped his hands behind his back, resisting the urge to pick the dirt from under his fingernails.

"If I can just speak with Tarro," he said, "I know I can change his mind. It's his new second, Falka. She's set me up, poisoned him against me."

"You do realize she would be at this theoretical meeting," Zita said dryly.

"Make it Stratagiozis only, then."

"Nobody would agree to that, as you well know." She watched him for a moment, and Lexos knew his frustration was clear on his face. "But consider," she said at last, "a meeting without your father, and without Tarro and this Falka."

"What for?"

And at last, the smile that had been tugging at Zita's mouth spread fully into a sly grin.

RHEA

How strange, Rhea found herself thinking as the days continued to pass, that she was worried more about Lexos than Michali. Only one of them was preparing to fake his own death, but she was far more preoccupied with the other. Lexos hadn't got what he'd gone to Vuomorra for; that was all Piros had been willing to tell her. What had happened? What had this Falka done? And what would Lexos do now that Tarro was no longer an option for him?

He would find some other way to try to preserve Argyros power, certainly. After all, she'd been with Lexos when he'd loaded the two of them onto that stolen horse and ridden for the horizon; she knew what he was capable of, had been part of it herself.

She was still thinking about it as night fell on the day before Michali's scheduled death and the family gathered around the table for dinner. Yannis was there, in a surprise to all of them, but then of all the Laskarises he was the only one unaware that Michali's death would not, in fact, be final. He looked grave as he raised his glass in

a toast, and when he glanced at Rhea there was, in his eyes, an un-
disguised hate that made her recoil and choke a bit on her wine.

"*Efkala,*" Yannis said and took a sip so long he nearly drained his
glass.

Evanthia was beside him, and was clearly conflicted as far as how
to behave. Surely she wanted to console Yannis, to reveal the truth
and assure him that one day they would see their son again, but Yannis remained loyal to the Stratagiozi seat. They'd had no choice but
to keep him barred from their plan. So, instead of knowingly watching a stranger's body be lowered into the ground, Yannis would attend his son's funeral, and Rhea and Evanthia would have to put on
quite a performance.

"Here," Michali said, loading Rhea's empty plate with spiced
rice. Her stomach turned at the sight of it, gray and brown muddled
together like sheep's brains.

"We could've at least had something nice for his last night," Yannis muttered. He'd poured yet another glass of wine, and seemed to
be making quite a bit of progress with it. Rhea couldn't say she
blamed him.

"It's fine," Michali said lightly. "It's what I asked for."

"Rice and rotted pork?" Yannis got up abruptly, his chair screech-
ing back from the table. "Excuse me."

"I do feel awfully bad for him," Evanthia said once he'd gone,
"but if he'd only open his eyes to the state of the world, we might've
been able to tell him the truth."

Rhea shook her head. This business, this pretending that it was
normal and right for her to extinguish a life four times a year. She
had done it for too long, had pushed down every flare of guilt until
she couldn't anymore. Even knowing she was at last doing the right
thing, she could hardly stand it.

"If you don't mind," she said, dabbing at the corners of her
mouth with her napkin before standing, "I'll retire for the night."
She attempted a weak smile. "Big day tomorrow, after all."

Michali was on his feet beside her in an instant. "Of course. Let
me see you back to the room. Mama, you don't mind, do you?"

It looked, actually, as though Evanthia very much did mind, but she kept her mouth shut tight and shook her head. Rhea felt a twinge of regret, sharp on top of everything else. Just another way she was taking Michali from his family.

They passed the atrium on the way back to his room, and Rhea was tempted to stop there, spend the night with Michali staring up at the stars through a gossamer filter of their own breath, but it was selfish, she knew, and shortsighted. There was no escaping what was coming. She might as well get used to it now.

"Tea?" Michali said as they entered his room. He kept a box of herb packets in his wardrobe, and a pitcher of water was always warming by the fire. But he'd never offered it to her before. Stalling, obviously, and Rhea couldn't be too upset about it.

"That would be wonderful."

They were silent as he poured the water into a pair of mugs and leafed through the various herb packets, choosing far more carefully than the situation warranted. When he'd finished, they took a seat by the fire, each in their separate chairs, pretending to drink deeply so as to avoid talking, though the tea was much too hot to swallow.

"This had better be worth it," Rhea said at last, and Michali started, almost as though he'd forgotten she was there.

"My people's prosperity, their freedom? I think that's worth any-thing."

"Not anything."

"Well, if my—"

"I will not," she said harshly, "be the only person in this room who cares about your life."

He set his mug on the table situated between the two chairs. "I understand."

"It isn't brave to not care. It isn't special."

"You're right," he said, reaching out to her. "I'm sorry."

She took his hand and gripped it tightly. "Are you tired?"

"Not really."

She stood up, tugged on his hand. "I rather think you are."

They were careful with each other in the night, and Rhea found herself near to crying as she watched Michali fall asleep, his body curled toward her. He would be fine, and she would see him again at Stratathoma, the two of them together in what might pass for peace. It was only thinking about that, about standing on the stone beach with Michali on a winter's day months from now, that let her drift off to dreaming.

She woke slowly the next morning, her cheek sticking to her pillow as she squirmed closer to Michali. He was cold, oddly, even though the covers were pulled up and she was pleasantly warm. Then again, she'd been the one to put her nightgown back on afterward, while Michali had staved off her attempts to at least get him to put on some socks. Laskaris men were used to the cold, he said. Well, look who was cold now.

"How are you today?" she asked, turning over to face him and tucking her forehead against his still shoulder. There was no answer. He was probably preoccupied with what was to come.

But when she opened her eyes, she saw immediately it was something else. Something wrong. Michali's head was twisted away from her, and flecked across the skin of his shoulder was something brown and flaking.

Blood.

"Michali?" she cried, scrambling to her knees. "Can you hear me?"

Perhaps it was hers; perhaps he was fine. Only he didn't move, not when she threw the covers back and not when she shoved at his arms to tip his body onto his back. It was everywhere, his blood— seeping through the bedclothes, staining her own skin, all from a neat slice along the stretch of his throat, the edges dark and curling.

Dead. He was dead. Someone had killed him in the night. Right there, next to her, as she slept.

Rhea sat back on her heels. Her hands shook, and her whole body felt numb, almost empty, as though she were no longer inside it. This couldn't be happening. He couldn't be dead, not when things were finally starting to make sense. Not when everything depended on him. She'd come as close to loving him as she ever had, and now. Now he was gone. Now it was all for nothing.

From outside the window, she heard the bells in the city begin to toll, their song echoing across the water. It was time. The servants would be in soon for the day to start, and somewhere in the house, Evanthia and Yannis were waiting to say goodbye to their son, and they didn't know their chance had passed, and how was she supposed to tell them when it was still echoing through her, the shock of it so strong she could shatter from it?

Rhea thought she might be sick. She rushed to the washstand in the corner of the room, her stomach convulsing, but nothing came up. There was just her own face in the mirror, clear enough that she could see the blood in her hair. Michali's. He'd lived his last right next to her and she hadn't even known. This was her fault just as it always was with her consorts, but with them at least she'd always held the knife in her own hands.

A sob burst out of her. She'd wanted to save him, but that mark on his palm had doomed him from the start. How could she have been so foolish to think otherwise?

It came again, that wrenching hollowness in her gut. Rhea thought she recognized it now. Grief. And something else, something she'd never quite allowed herself before. Something hot, angry. Because she had planned to save him. She had been on the brink of it. And someone had stolen it away.

Who? Who had snuck through the Laskaris house in the middle of the night, and managed not to wake her as they slit her consort's throat? As far as most everyone knew, she'd been meant to kill Michali today. Only someone who knew her plan to spare him would have any reason to take action. That was a small number. Just her, Evanthia, and Piros, really. But it had to be someone else—Evanthia would never have hurt her own son. And she'd trusted Piros, his devotion to serving as Michali's second too deep to be false.

Rhea caught the bed's reflection in the mirror and felt the swell of a sob. No. Don't let it in, she told herself. Once you do, you will never get it out.

She shut her eyes, splashed her face with water, and went to the window, where she threw the shutters back and let the cold air sweep in. Like her own room, this looked out over the back of the island, where the ground rose in a small, densely wooded hill. Rhea stared into the trees, willing herself to be as still, as calm.

Not her. Not Evanthia. Not Piros. But someone. Someone had known, had overheard. She was in the middle of trying to remember who exactly had been standing near them on the lake during Meroximo when the air was broken by the sharp call of a bird.

Her head jerked up. She knew that sound. She'd heard it somewhere before. But the sky was empty, and the trees were dark in the thin wash of sun. Where was it coming from? Perhaps she'd imagined it.

Again. A three-note song, so familiar she could've sung along. She leaned out the window, squinting against the brightness of the snow. In the trees, there, a white shape in the shadows. A bird, perched on a low branch. Rhea remembered—the grounds at Stratathoma, Lexos kneeling at her side. And his scout, a white bird built just for him.

Now it was here. Watching her from the woods, singing that song he'd chosen for it, on the morning she woke to find Michali murdered.

It had to have been Lexos. Her twin, half herself—of course he would care more that his plan come to fruition than for whatever feelings she might have for her consort. That was who Lexos was, and she had always known it, had always seen him bring that relentless focus to bear on other people. She'd told Michali and Piros that he would do what it took.

She'd been right. He had. Of course, it would have been one of his spies—he was across the country—but that only made it easier to imagine. Like Baba, she and Lexos had both welcomed any opportunity to keep a barrier between themselves and the worst of what they did. For Baba, that barrier was his children. For Rhea, Thyspira. For Lexos, Rhea thought it might well have been her.

How, though, had Lexos found out she'd meant to spare Michali? Had he been watching her since Stratathoma?

No, Rhea thought, feeling ill again. It was her own fault. She'd written him that letter. She hadn't said anything outright, but maybe there had been enough. Enough for Lexos to figure out that she wasn't going to follow through with what he'd wanted.

She turned away from the window, forcing herself to look at Michali, one of his hands reaching across the bed toward the space she'd left empty. She went to the edge of the bed and knelt, brushing her fingers across his marked palm. He'd been so much—safety, and comfort, and promise—and now he would never be any of that. She had let that happen. She had failed him.

She never would again. She had forgiven so many things from Lexos, had borne all manner of hurts; she would not bear this. No, saints burn Lexos. Burn him, burn every person with Argyros blood in their veins. Let the whole federation come crashing down. She would be there to watch it fall.

THIRTY-ONE

ALEXANDROS

After a week of waiting, and of wondering if Baba had heard yet about Vuomorra, Lexos finally found himself standing on a terrace at the Agiokon monastery, Zita next to him. Stavra was a step behind, a frown almost permanently etched into her face. She didn't agree with what he and Zita were planning—a breach in the rules, in tradition, two things Stavra held dear—but she hadn't gone so far as to remove herself, and Lexos had given her a wide berth over the past few days, wary that any stray word would make her change her mind.

"They'll start arriving soon enough," Zita was saying. "And it won't be long before they realize Tarro isn't coming."

"Right."

"Get them downstairs to the meeting room," Zita said, turning from the view of the valley laid out before them, "and don't let them leave until we've begun."

Stavra made a small noise of disapproval. Zita gave her a slow, assessing look before heading back inside. The monks were scarce, keeping mostly to the chapel and to their chambers, bare of anything not used for prayer. Zita had suggested that the council arrive unannounced, and Lexos hadn't missed the alarm on the monks' faces when he and Zita had arrived the day prior and made their demands.

"Well?" he asked. He'd kept his silence long enough, but now that they were here, he had to make sure Stavra wasn't about to ruin everything. "What is it? What's wrong?"

Stavra avoided his eyes, easing back a step. Zita was done up in a red beaded dress, but Stavra had barely been convinced to change out of her regular shirt and trousers. Instead of her usual gown, she was wearing a smart black suit better fit for a Thyzak funeral, and her braids were bound up in a tight, somber bun.

"Come on," he said cajolingly. "Talk to me."

"This isn't right, Lexos." She shook her head, and looked at him at last. He was taken aback by her flat, hard stare. "You know this isn't."

"And what Tarro's doing is? I had nothing to do with that attempt on his life."

She sighed impatiently. "Yes, thank you, I know that."

"I'm just trying to sort everything out."

"You're going about it wrong. Once you break these rules, Lexos, you can't put them back again." She seemed to hesitate, and then continued. "If my opinion is asked, I will not lie. I can't."

He was tempted to keep arguing with her, but she'd clearly made up her mind, as he had. And this was the best he would get from her, really. No matter how she disagreed, Stavra would follow the old rules and not speak out of turn. He could only hope that some tradition held in the face of this makeshift meeting, and that seconds were not addressed.

"I understand," he said, hoping to ease some of the tension before the others arrived. "Come in and have breakfast with me. The monks have made us a flat-baked egg, just like you like."

Stavra looked at him plainly for a moment, and then rested her hand against his cheek. "You're a sweet boy, I think," she said, and there was a finality about it that made him nervous. He was relieved when she broke away from him and went inside, turning left where the corridor branched to head for her chamber.

Back in the dining room, Zita was seated at the low wooden table, a steaming cup of kaf clasped between her palms, her eyes focused on absolutely nothing. She barely blinked when Lexos settled onto the bench across from her and began to serve himself from the dishes laid out by the monks.

"Stavra's fine," he said. Zita blinked slowly, and then took a delicate sip of kaf. "She's just tired."

"You do realize," Zita said, "that I've known my daughter a few hundred years longer than you have."

Lexos chose not to answer that, and instead focused on what he had to believe to be true. "She won't disrupt our plans."

"Of course she won't. I've told her not to." Zita selected a hard-boiled egg, dyed as red as her gown, from the serving bowl and knocked it against the edge of the table, breaking the shell. "Trust me," she said. "I've got you this far, haven't I?"

And she had, but the rest would be up to him.

With neither Baba nor Tarro attending, and Zita already here, they were only waiting for the three Stratagiozis from the north: Nastia and her son, and Milad and Ammar and their daughters. When they arrived, it was almost simultaneously, so closely and perfectly timed that Lexos had to wonder if they hadn't met up beforehand to discuss the situation.

"Thank you for coming," Lexos said when Nastia hauled herself out of the crossing basket and stepped onto the welcoming terrace. Her second had preceded her, and both wore the same skeptical frown as they approached, leaving Lexos to wish that Zita were here with him.

"Enough with the pleasantries," Nastia said, sweeping back her thick blond hair. Lexos was struck by the oddity of the fact that they were both still speaking Trefza, as was custom. "Let's get right to the meeting."

She clearly knew she was the last to arrive. Did she know, too, that Tarro wasn't coming? Had they been in touch with him? Nastia had already started walking, her son falling in behind her as they made for the dining room. There was nothing for Lexos to do but follow.

"Stop eating," Nastia said as soon as she stepped into the room. Ammar and Milad, along with their daughters, looked guiltily up from their breakfast plates. "We're having this meeting now. I want to know what this nonsense is about."

Their benches scraping against the rough stone floor, the other Stratagiozis rose, and Lexos exchanged glances with Zita, who was standing by the door with her hands calmly folded at her waist. She nodded slightly, and gestured toward the door with the elegance of a long-practiced host.

"Please," she said, "after you."

They gathered quickly in the round meeting room, and its doors were left open at Ammar's insistence. His daughter lingered near the threshold, foregoing her traditional second's post just behind Ammar. They were clearly on edge, and wanted a way out (or a way to keep the others in) easily accessible. Lexos couldn't blame them.

"Thank you for coming," Lexos began as soon as everyone was settled, but Ammar waved his hand, his many gold bracelets clacking together.

"Enough," he said in rough Trefza. "What's this all about, then?"

"Where's Tarro?" Nastia added. She was pacing at the back of the room, an unease clear on her delicate features.

Zita had told him what to say, how to broach the subject. For this, at least, he knew the right way to answer.

"I wanted to speak only to you," he said. It would have been even better if he could've spoken Chuzhak to her—a huge show of respect, and his Chuzhak was passable enough—but he had to be sure everybody in the room understood. "When Tarro is here, we must all listen to him, such that I rarely get the chance to hear the thoughts of the rest of the council. Tarro is only one man, and yet his voice speaks far more loudly than any one man's should."

"Have a care, boy," Ammar growled. It would have been frightening if he hadn't had a bit of egg stuck in his thick beard. "You are coming near to sacrilege."

"Let me come closer, then," Lexos said. Be bold, that's what Zita had told him. They would respect him all the more for it. "I have called you here to discuss the deposing of Trefazio's current Stratagiozi and the annexation of its land by this coalition of federated Stratagiozi states."

"What?" said Nastia. Even the seconds, who were meant to keep their expressions plain, could not keep their jaws from dropping.

"Tarro's out," Lexos said simply. "And we're in."

Ammar was watching Lexos with narrowed eyes, which Lexos chose to interpret as a good sign, but next to him, Milad looked horrified, his ruddy face slack in surprise.

"Vuomorra is this coalition's biggest source of trade," he said shrilly. "Prevdjenni exports to Vuomorra keep almost half my people employed. I would be ripped from my seat by my stewards if we lost our preferred trading with Trefazio."

"I'm not proposing we lose Trefazio," Lexos hastened to clarify. "Just that we lose Tarro. All that land, all that money to be made, for just one man? It's not how this council was meant to work." He stepped closer, angling so that he could see Nastia, who had stopped pacing and was now staring at him from the shadows, her second looking uncomfortable to be caught between them. "I was just in Vuomorra myself—"

"Indeed you were," Milad said, scoffing. "We have heard of your exploits there. If you could not take Tarro's life, I see you will settle for his country."

So they had come to it, and to be frank, Lexos was surprised it had taken this long. Most of the conversation, he and Zita had decided, rested on him, but they both knew Lexos defending himself would carry little weight with the other council members.

"You cannot think those rumors are true," Zita said. Every eye turned to her. "It is far easier to believe that Tarro would lie than to believe that Alexandros would break the sanctity of this council in such a way."

Nastia let out a bark of laughter. "Is this meeting not itself a break in sanctity?"

"If it is, you are all participants." Zita's voice was firm, and she seemed to fill the room, her presence so serene and deliberate that even Stavra seemed convinced. "Alexandros has sworn to me he made no attempt on Tarro's life, and I believe him. He puts council before country by coming to you today; he risks his life to protect this council from Tarro's corrupting influence."

"Corrupting?" said Ammar. Behind him his second cleared her throat.

"Truly," Lexos answered. He glanced at Milad before continuing. "I was just in Vuomorra myself. The decadence there—it's unchecked. Unsustainable. Tarro has gotten lazy, has ceased to govern the way Stratagiozis were meant to, and we all know it. Vuomorra should belong to the council, not to an old man in a palace."

"Belong to the council?" Ammar said sharply. "How, exactly?"

"A jointly appointed steward." Lexos was proud of how steady he sounded, how sure. "And the land outside Vuomorra's borders split between us. Equally, as we are."

For a moment nobody moved, and then Milad approached him, peering down his snub nose, and stabbed at his chest with a stiff finger. "Tarro's lived your life five times over, boy. You have no right to pull him down like this."

"I have the same right any man has," Lexos said, brushing Milad's hand aside. "The same right your forefathers had to take their land." They had not, after all, been originally independent under the first Stratagiozi rule, and they knew it; every Stratagiozi but Tarro bore the strange and often unacknowledged shame of having wrested his own country from the clutches of Tarro's ancestor.

"If we were to agree with you," Nastia said suddenly from the shadows, "what would you propose? How would you suggest we take on the largest military and economic power on the continent?"

"A war on multiple fronts," Zita said, and Lexos frowned. Was it a good idea to reveal that the plan was truly hers? "Tarro's resources are great," she went on, "but he cannot last if we press him on all sides."

"You approve of this mad idea, then, Zita?" Milad said.

"Merkher has been caught in the middle of council territory for hundreds of years," she said, stepping forward. "Tarro has used my cities and my people for his own ends since he came to power. For every trade deal he offers you, Merkher does more work for smaller benefit, and my people suffer. With Tarro gone, we will be equals once more."

Ammar had barely spoken, and Lexos was getting nervous. They would need him to make this plan work, need his tightly controlled military, which was loyal to him above all else, to be the core of their attack.

"Equals. It's a lovely thought," Milad said. He'd calmed down a bit and backed away from Lexos, but he still looked skeptical. "I'm afraid getting there is another matter entirely. Ammar is the only one of us with troops directly at his command. How do you expect to wage this war without soldiers?"

"An excellent point," Lexos said, trying to strike a balance between obvious flattery and passive aggression. "We would of course not launch an offensive right away. Not until we've each had time to consolidate our power."

"Consolidate?" Nastia said. Lexos wasn't sure if she just didn't understand the word in Trefza or if she wanted Lexos to quit talking in jargon and speak plainly.

"Indeed," he said, and then, as delicately as he could, "We should all be following Ammar's excellent example."

It was a radical suggestion, perhaps even more so than the idea of removing Tarro and annexing his lands. Stratagiozis had always existed in tandem with each country's regional stewards. Of course, the arrangement varied according to country—in Chuzha, there was an additional tier of nobility, given the vastness of the country, and in Merkher the stewards were all but gone from practical life, with most of their duties handed to Zita—but no matter what, the stewards remained. Ammar's dispensing with them had been a crime against tradition, one that Lexos knew the other Stratagiozis would be reluctant to commit.

Accordingly it had been this bit of the plan that Stavra had balked at the most. Lexos looked at her now, willing her to stay silent. She was biting her lip, shifting from foot to foot, but he knew what Stavra looked like when she was ready for a fight, and it wasn't like this.

"I'm not suggesting anything immediate," he went on, searching out the gaze of each Stratagiozi. "Your stability and prosperity are not to be taken lightly. But if Tarro can turn against me, who might he turn on next? We should move before our next council meeting. We cannot allow this decay to take further root in him, and in Trefazio."

"It *is* unprecedented to exile a fellow council member," Nastia said slowly, and Lexos glanced at Zita. It was time for her to nudge things along.

"Tarro has been poisoned by the success of his country," Zita said softly. "He has forgotten our guiding principle: that we are stronger together than we are alone. He cannot be allowed to forsake the bonds we have worked so long to build." She looked from Nastia to Ammar. "To preserve our seats, we must remove Tarro from his."

It hung in the air, waiting for someone to bat it away, knock it down. Silence, only broken by Lexos's heartbeat racing in his ears. One of them had to agree. Just one. That would bring in the others.

"I agree," Nastia said at last, "that the current situation cannot be allowed to stand."

Well. Not exactly the ringing endorsement Lexos had been hoping for.

"Certainly," Milad said, but that was all, and he looked at Lexos somewhat expectantly.

"I am with you," Ammar said suddenly. Lexos felt practically woozy with relief, and let out a long breath, but Ammar held up his hand. He hadn't finished. "If, and only if, you can promise me Amolovak ownership of the Vitmar."

Lexos felt his relieved smile freeze on his face. He'd prepared for some back and forth, but nothing of this size. The Vitmar conflict had stretched on for generations. Ammar couldn't possibly expect him to get Nastia to relent. In fact, perhaps he was counting on that; he'd look good agreeing to the plan, but when Lexos failed to hand him the Vitmar, he'd have a practical reason to back out.

Nastia was already shaking her head, exchanging incredulous smiles with her son. Lexos had to move quickly before this fell apart.

"Ammar, I'm not sure this is the place to be discussing such—"

"Why not?" said Ammar, grinning wolfishly. "We're discussing border adjustment, aren't we?"

Nastia muttered something unintelligible in Chuzhak, and Ammar shot back with a phrase Lexos did understand, one composed of vividly foul insults. Decorum during these negotiations had long since gone out the window, and Lexos could only be thankful neither had produced a weapon, which he was sure both were secretly carrying.

No, Nastia wouldn't relent, but neither would Ammar. As much as Ammar's gambit was a natural continuation of an ongoing conflict, it was a test of Lexos's resolve, of his ability to maneuver among the council. It would be a mistake, he realized, to engage with this, to try to convince Nastia. That was not the way to get what he wanted.

"Ammar, remind me," he started. "What are your primary objectives in annexing the Vitmar?"

"Bringing my people back into their homeland," Ammar said declaratively, as though there were more of an audience here than just the other council members. "The Amolovaks living in Chuzha deserve to be under the rule of their sovereign leader."

"That," Nastia said, crossing her arms, "is the very thing they came to Chuzha to escape."

"Think what you like about my policies," Ammar said, his voice turning grim, "but the Vitmar is nearly entirely Amolovak. That alone is reason enough—"

"What, am I entitled to rule Agiokon because a Chuzhak has set foot here? You might as well—"

"I am speaking, obviously, of a situation in which the population is a significant—"

"You are *speaking* of greed, pure and simple, Ammar. They don't want to be Amolovaks. They left their country to get away from you, and—"

"Friends, please," Lexos cut in, gratified when they actually turned away from each other. "I'm sure there's some accord we can reach."

"If you think I'm giving up my rightful territory," Nastia snarled, "you are madder even than your father."

Hardly promising to hear his father so poorly thought of. Lexos held up his hands in surrender. "Of course. I wouldn't dream of suggesting such a thing. But perhaps there's another way."

"Yes, because in two hundred years we haven't considered other options," she said snidely.

Lexos ignored her and took a deep breath, picturing a map of the continent in his head. What Ammar really wanted was to expand his territory, and to gain a metropolitan center, a city like Vashnasta in the Vitmar that, as well as being one of the most ancient cities on the continent, was decently wealthy with the potential for further growth. Ammar liked to present it as a question of sovereignty, but Nastia was right—it was greed, and ambition, and not much more.

"What if," he said slowly, "you could get that land from somewhere else?"

"It won't be from Merkher," Zita said. Lexos knew she was thinking of her northern border, vulnerable to a push from Ammar.

"Certainly not," he said, glancing her way to reassure her. "But what if Ammar got it from me?"

"What?" Milad, who had been silent for a while, was turning red, and his voice nearly cracked as he spoke. "What can you mean?"

Here it was, a chance to show how committed he was to setting this plan into motion. "Ammar, I'm sure you're familiar with the Ksigora, in the northeast of my country."

Ammar raised his eyebrows. "I am."

"And I'm sure you know that it's lately become home to a number of Amolovak refugees." "Refugees" wasn't quite the right word, and he could tell Ammar was slightly taken aback by the bluntness of his speech, but there was no time to think of a better way to say it, and certainly not in Trefza. "Not equal, perhaps, to the number living in the Vitmar, but certainly significant."

"So?"

"You can't be serious," Nastia said, looking so unsteady that Lexos had half a mind to ask someone to fetch her a glass of water.

"I very much am," he replied. "Ammar, Thyzakos would be open to negotiating the transfer of the Ksigoran mountain territory from Thyzakos to Amolova."

It was unheard of, a perhaps worrying display of weakness, but Lexos knew he would gain just as much as he lost; he would pay in territory, but Ammar would crack down on the Sxoriza and bring the whole region under order. Ammar would essentially be a soldier for hire. It didn't matter that Thyzakos would never get that land back— how much had it really been worth in the first place? Of course, then there would be the matter of telling Baba, but first things first; Ammar had yet to agree to this whole thing anyway.

"Really?" Ammar said, looking genuinely surprised. "You would offer your own land?"

"For this cause? Certainly." He risked a sidelong look at Zita, expecting a concerned frown, but she seemed thoroughly comfortable with the path he was taking. If he could win over Ammar, the others would follow. "I would rather see Thyzakos sacrificed for a worthy cause than ripped apart by these pernicious rumors and by Tarro's fanciful accusations. But the fate of Thyzakos—indeed the fate of this council—is yours to determine, Ammar. We are depending on you."

Ammar considered him with narrowed eyes, and then at last he nodded. "You promise me the Ksigora, and I promise you my support."

Lexos held back a smile of relief as he clasped Ammar's proffered, heavily ringed hand, the man's palm rough against his own. The rest of it would all fall into place. He'd got what he'd come here for.

"You'll need Merkher as a pass-through for these maneuvers," Zita said. "Can I also expect a piece of Thyzakos to ensure my cooperation?" There was a pause—a bit too long, and Lexos was beginning to feel uncomfortable—before she laughed, showed her teeth in a wide smile. "Nonsense, my boy. I am dedicated to the cause, to the integrity of the council. Merkher is with you."

"Prevdjen, too," Milad hurried to add. It wouldn't do to be the last one in.

Lexos looked to Nastia, who was still lingering in the shadows behind her second, her arms crossed and lips pursed. She was no doubt torn between resentment and gratitude—the former because she would not be given the same consideration as Ammar, and the latter because the Vitmar was now safe from his grasp. But if he let the expectant silence press on her, it would do his work for him.

Finally, she sighed and uncrossed her arms. "Chuzha will be in charge of drawing up the agreements for splitting Trefazio."

It was a last grab at some sort of power. Of course the rest of them would be able to shape the agreements however they liked, but with Chuzha in charge, at least Nastia would have a slight advantage. It was one Lexos felt he could afford to give her.

"Very well," he said, and looked to Ammar. "A fair trade, no?"

"Fair indeed." Ammar extended his hand to Nastia, who took it gingerly and shook it once before letting it drop.

"We are agreed, then," Lexos said, and felt his cheeks flush with joy. Telling Baba would come later. For now, this was a victory worth rejoicing in.

There were no documents to be signed, no seals to be stamped on official agreements; they couldn't leave any evidence that this pact had been made. But as Lexos watched the others shake hands with one another, a slice of blood running down each palm, he knew the bargain had been sealed. He would return home and work to consolidate power under Baba in time to launch a naval attack on Vuomorra while the others took their positions along Trefazio's northern border.

"A word, Alexandros," Ammar said. "I'm afraid we cannot proceed without discussing the matter of your father."

Ah. They were probably worried that Lexos was here without

permission—which was true—and that he was making a play for his father's seat. He would not have been the first second to try such a coup, although he didn't think any had ever been quite this brazen. To get around the issue, Zita had said it would be best to lie, to pretend that all of this was being done in Baba's name.

"He sent me in his stead," Lexos said smoothly. "What I have said to you here may be taken as having come from his own mouth."

Ammar and Milad exchanged glances. "Indeed, that's what I was afraid of," Ammar said.

"Pardon?"

Neither Zita nor Nastia appeared surprised by this turn of conversation. Had they discussed this without him? Why hadn't Zita warned him?

"What Ammar is saying," Nastia supplied, taking a lazy step forward, "is that it might be best if we didn't involve Vasilis."

He swallowed hard, dread building in his stomach. "How so?"

Nastia tilted her head. There was a glee in her smile, a nastiness that Lexos did not like. "Perhaps you should consolidate power yourself, so to speak."

"You want him out?" He should have been expecting this— Baba's behavior at the last meeting had been unacceptable to the others—but it still hit like a punch, left Lexos fighting to keep his voice steady and even. He had spent his whole life in service to that man, had grown up at his shoulder, had tasted his meals, saddled his horses, carried his flag. Never once had he considered taking his place. Perhaps that had simply been naïve.

"Do you think it's really necessary?" he said. His fists were clenched, and he forced himself to relax. "I know my father doesn't always show to advantage, but—"

"He's past his limit," Ammar said dismissively. "No shame in it. Not everybody's made for this seat. But you are."

"I'm not sure I understand," Lexos said, stalling as best he could. How could he make this work? What way was there to change their minds?

"Let me put it even more plainly, then." Ammar frowned, leaning in. "If you want this plan of yours to go forward, it will only go forward with you in the Thyzak seat. Remove your father and Tarro both, or neither."

Nastia was nodding, and Milad was standing just behind Ammar, taking the place usually occupied by his second, who was instead inching toward the door as if to keep Lexos from leaving. Lexos turned to Zita, but she looked back at him with a cool expectance. Was this her doing? Lexos was certainly using the council to protect his family and his country. Was the council using him, too? How much, really, had the other council members known upon arriving here?

Behind her, Stavra watched, pity in her eyes, and Lexos set his shoulders, let the sight of it ignite an anger in his chest.

"Surely you are not expecting me to remove my own father," he said, sharpening the edge of his voice.

"He is your father. Who else would do it?" Ammar said, and when Lexos opened his mouth to answer, he held up his hands disarmingly. "We've made it clear what we require from you. It's your decision, Alexandros."

As important as it was to not show any weakness, to keep his show of strength, to never break, Lexos couldn't help it. He turned, showing the others his back, and shut his eyes tightly, tried to ignore the pounding in his temples. If he said no and stayed true to Baba, Tarro's accusations would ruin their international standing and would only embolden the stewards, who would hasten to tear them down. Baba and the country both would fall into ruin.

If he said yes, though—if he removed his father and took the seat for himself, the council would oust Tarro. Thyzakos would prosper, and the Argyros family would be strong once more.

His father or his family.

Both, Lexos thought, and faced Ammar. "You have a bargain," he said. What was one more lie?

THIRTY-TWO

ALEXANDROS

It should have been a three-day ride back to Stratathoma, but Lexos made it in two. The west country slid by him, his world reduced to the dust thrown up by the wind and to the pounding of his heart. He would find a way to keep from following through on what he'd promised the council—he had to—but the farther he got from Agiokon the harder it seemed to be to come up with a solution.

By the time he arrived home, it was late, the sun long since set and the stars slow in coming out. He'd neglected his duties somewhat since leaving Vuomorra; the stars and tides could do without him for a few days before they stilled entirely, but he would need to spend the night in the observatory, setting things back into motion. Luckily, Baba never went up there anymore, and Lexos could be assured of at least a few hours of peace. That was, if Baba wasn't waiting for him at the entrance, news of the situation—that was what he preferred to call it—in Vuomorra having already reached his ears.

Inside, Lexos found his bed unmade, just as he'd left it (and just as he'd asked the servants to leave it). He smelled of horse and sweat, so rank he could taste it, but there wasn't time yet to wash, nor to sleep. He undid the clasps on his trunk, which Stavra had kindly sent back early to Stratathoma, and drew out the fluid length of inky silk and the empty tidewater bowl. He'd rest when the work was over.

Morning came, and with it a deep dread. Baba surely had to know he was home, and the fact that he hadn't barged in at first light to give Lexos the reprimand of his life was a disturbing sign. Lexos far preferred Baba at his sharpest; it was those attacks that Lexos's armor was best equipped to deflect.

He rose stiffly, joints seizing from so long in the saddle, and dressed, carefully choosing an Argyros blue shirt and eschewing anything that even hinted at Domina green. Let Baba remember that everything Lexos did was in service to this family. Even the promise he'd made the council.

Across the hall, the door to Rhea's room stood open, and he lingered there, closing his eyes briefly and imagining her looking back at him. What a relief it would be when she returned. It wasn't right for them to be apart so long, so often. She was half of him, and he of her; perhaps when everything had been settled with Tarro they might find a way to pass her duties to Chrysanthi, and allow Rhea to stay at home.

Chrysanthi herself could be heard still snoring in the room next door. It was a shame—he was hungry and her breakfasts were far better than anything he could put together himself—but Lexos left her undisturbed and made for the kitchen, taking the north staircase and the long servants' passage that cut across the back of the house to avoid running into Baba. He'd yet to determine how to convince Baba that his trip to Agiokon had been for the best, and there was nothing worse than arguing with Baba while unprepared.

The kitchen, to his great surprise, was not empty when he arrived. Nitsos was sitting at the stone counter, a steaming mug of kaf waiting next to him while he sorted through a tin of kymithi that Rhea had made and left behind, examining each one with narrowed eyes. He was, in fact, so preoccupied with this task that he didn't notice the first time Lexos cleared his throat, nor the second, and it was only when Lexos said his name very loudly that he looked up with a start.

"Oh," Nitsos said, his cheeks flushing pink. "You're home."

They stared at each other for entirely too long, until at last Lexos shuffled in awkwardly so he could pat Nitsos on the back in what barely passed for an embrace.

"Hello, then," Nitsos said.

A hundred years, and they had never got very good at this.

"Thank you." Lexos gestured to Nitsos's kaf. "Is there any more?"

Nitsos looked practically poleaxed by the suggestion that he might have prepared kaf for anybody beyond himself. Of course. Younger siblings were always this way, Lexos thought, and sidestepped Nitsos to make some of his own.

"How has it been at home?" he asked over his shoulder. It was much easier talking to Nitsos if he didn't have to also look at him.

"Fine, I suppose."

"I hope Baba didn't give you too much trouble."

"Not as much as he's about to give you," Nitsos said, and there was such a snide sting to his voice that Lexos turned to look at him. He was hunched over the counter, tumbling blond curls obscuring his eyes.

"What?"

"Did you think we hadn't heard about what a mess you made in Vuomorra?" Nitsos took a leisurely sip of kaf. "Baba's furious. Those of us lucky enough to stay at home got to bear the brunt of it all."

He stood up, and Lexos found himself startled. Nitsos was tall. Had he always been so tall?

"Anyway, welcome back," Nitsos said. "I suppose I'll see you later."

It was not the most he'd ever heard his brother say, Lexos thought as he watched him leave the kitchen, but it was close.

After breakfast there was no more delaying to be done, and Lexos knew he had to go and find Baba. At least if Baba had already heard about Vuomorra, Lexos was saved from having to deliver the news himself.

Baba wasn't in his study, nor was he stretched out in front of the fire in the great room, where he could often be found asleep, having never made it up to his room the night before. It had not always been like that—back at Lexos's childhood home, Mama had been there to pull Baba away from his work and from his wineglass—but in the years since, Baba rarely spent the night in his own bed. Respect, Chrysanthi called it, for their dead mother; she was far too charitable.

It took him a while, but at last he found a servant still in possession of half his wits who pointed him toward the veranda, where he said Baba was having breakfast. Nerves weighing down his every step, Lexos trudged down the house's central hallway, staring at the stone floor and pointedly avoiding making eye contact with the end of the corridor, where the view opened onto the veranda and the sea beyond.

It had to be done, he told himself, repeating it over and over with every step. It had to be done. A bargain had to be made. He'd tried.

Outside, winter was starting to loosen its grip, and the air off the sea was brisk but bearable. Baba was at the railing, leaning against it while picking at a tray of figs wrapped in grape leaves. He hadn't caught sight of Lexos yet, and so Lexos took a moment to study him.

Deep circles cut rings under Baba's eyes, his age weighing more heavily on him than Lexos had ever seen before. His skin, tanned and usually lit with a flush of life, seemed drained and looked alarmingly pale in contrast to the black jacket he wore buttoned up to his chin.

"Enough," Baba said suddenly, and Lexos jerked back, flinching as Baba's stare flicked over to him. "Either come and face me or leave my sight."

Lexos took a breath, ignoring the uncomfortable way it caught in his chest, and started down the stairs onto the veranda. The tables had been cleared out, and a thin film of ice covered the reflecting pool. As he passed it, he could see designs traced on it in sunlight—Chrysanthi's work, and her favorite part of the season.

"Well?" Baba said as Lexos approached. "How was your trip?" He smiled, too wide to be genuine. "I heard you encountered some trouble."

"I—"

He cut off as Baba struck him, the back of his hand cracking against his jaw and sending him staggering. The pain dizzying, rattling through his bones. He cradled his cheek, blinking back sudden tears. Baba had never hit him before. Never, not in all their years, not even after his first council meeting, when he'd mistakenly spoken Thyzaki instead of Trefza.

"Stand up," Baba said, sounding bored, "and explain yourself."

Lexos could already feel a bruise forming, his heartbeat throbbing in the tender skin of his cheek. "I am glad," he said, "to have this chance to apologize to you."

It had worked before, and he'd been hopeful it would work again, but Baba let out a noise like a snarl and lunged for him, grabbing a fistful of Lexos's shirt and hauling him in close.

"Do not ply me with pretty words," Baba said. Lexos could smell the sour tang of his breath. "I am not a steward you can wind around your finger. I am your father. And you should be kneeling."

He dropped Lexos to the floor. The sun was behind Baba, throwing his face into shadow, and for a moment he looked truly like the saints of old, a golden ring shimmering around his head.

"I sent you to Vuomorra," Baba said, his voice echoing in the emptiness of Lexos's chest. "I sent you in my name. What did you do, boy?"

"Nothing," he choked out. No blade held to his throat, but it felt like that all the same. "Only what you bid me."

"What I bid you?" Baba sneered. "Your attempt on Tarro's life, Alexandros? Was that on my order, then?"

"Lies, Baba." He had to understand. Lexos had to make him understand. "Spread by Tarro's second."

Baba shook his head. "I think the liar here is you, boy."

Lexos was through with having his loyalty questioned, through with having it poisoned and turned into something else. Everything he'd done had been for Baba. For the family. That had to be enough.

He stumbled to his feet, satisfaction blooming hot in his chest at Baba's poorly concealed surprise. "What cause would I have to kill Tarro? What good would that do?"

"The Dominas—" Baba started, but Lexos had had quite enough.

"You think the Dominas are our friends," he interrupted. "Our allies. But they will see us deposed before they help us hold this country. I did what I could, what I had to."

"Oh," Baba said, folding his arms across his chest, "and what is that?"

It would be smart, Lexos thought, to back away. To get out of Baba's reach. But he could not stomach another retreat. He was an equal here, in a way he never had been before.

"I went to Agiokon," he said, his voice steady. "I called a council meeting. And I've come back to you with a way to save your seat, and Thyzakos along with it."

Baba had never looked so old. His anger, which usually lit him up and sent power thrumming through his veins, this time had left him unsteady. The tendons of his body stood out sharply, his skin sagging around them. "You did what?" he said, barely a whisper.

"I met with the council," Lexos answered. He straightened, set his shoulders. Let Baba see that he was not groveling, that he was proud of the bargain he'd struck. "Zita, Milad, Nastia, and Ammar. We've come up with a plan. They've agreed to join us in removing Tarro from his seat."

"Removing Tarro?" Baba's breath was rattling, his hand grasping at the veranda wall.

"And taking Trefazio for ourselves. We'll annex it, divide it up."

For a moment, nothing, and then Baba turned, looked out over the ocean. When he spoke, it was only the breeze carrying his words back that allowed Lexos to hear them. "And you say the others have agreed?"

"All of them. Nastia, Milad, even Ammar."

"How quickly they forsake Tarro," Baba said, his back hunched. He was gripping the stone wall so tightly that his knuckles were blanched white. "Just so, they will be quick to forsake each other."

Baba was right. It was a risk, all of this, and Lexos couldn't be assured that the plan would hold together. But Baba had to understand that they were out of other options.

"When they do," Lexos said gently, "we will be ready for it. Until then, I fear this is the only solution. The stewards will be placated by the war abroad, by the wealth we gain from Trefazio. We can promise them territory in the annexed land."

Baba nodded, and when he faced Lexos again, he'd gathered back some of his usual stature. "Indeed, a great victory," he said, a mildness to his voice that left Lexos uneasy. "Tell me, with what have we paid for this support from the council?"

He'd known it was coming. Braced for it, practiced in his head giving Baba this particular piece of news. But there was nothing that could have truly prepared him to look Baba in the eye and say that it was his life they would pay with.

"The others," he started, "are worried about the security of our family's hold on Thyzakos."

"Our family's hold," Baba said flatly. "Meaning, of course, mine."

Lexos ignored the temptation to point out how heavily Baba's hold relied on the gifts of his children. He knew Baba better than that.

"They have suggested," he went on instead, "that for the purposes of this campaign against Tarro, someone else serve as the country's formal leader."

"How finely you speak," Baba said. He was closer now, crossing the distance between them with measured steps, the violence of his earlier outburst drained away. "They want you, don't they?"

Lexos swallowed hard. "Yes."

"And?" Baba smiled knowingly. "They want something else, too, don't they?"

Best to just say it outright. "Yes," he said. "Your life."

Baba's face didn't change. Lexos had been expecting shock, or at the very least a raised eyebrow, but Baba only nodded, gaze fixed somewhere in the distance between them.

"Baba?"

He looked up. There was an emptiness to him, a melancholy. "And you agreed, did you?"

"Only to convince them of my sincerity," Lexos said hurriedly. "Only to get what we want. But I know we can find a way around it. Perhaps if we let word spread that you have died, or that—"

"No." Baba shook his head ruefully, looking disappointed. "It would not do to lie to our friends. Death belongs to the Thyzak Stratagiozi, doesn't it? So it must belong to you."

"What?"

"They have asked you for my life, and you have promised it to them. A bargain struck." Baba was so close now that Lexos could see the fine lines gathered at the corners of his down-turned Argyros eyes. "You would be no son of mine if you did not carry your end of it."

He reached down, grasped Lexos's hand and pressed the palm of it to his chest, right over the beating of his heart. Lexos tried to pull back, but there was no wresting himself from Baba's grip.

"*Elado*, my boy." Baba touched his forehead to Lexos's. "Now's your chance. Where is your will?"

"Baba, I never meant to," Lexos stammered. "I made what bargain I could, but I never once thought to follow through."

"Never?" Baba took a step backward, dragging Lexos with him. "Not even in your most secret dreams?"

"I promise."

Another step, and another. "You have never wanted my seat? I see the looks that pass between my children. I am not some doddering fool."

They were pressed against the stone wall now, the edge digging into Lexos's ribs and the sea crashing below. Lexos licked his lips, trying to stay as relaxed as he could. "Let's go up to your study," he said. "I'll explain everything."

"What more is there to explain?" Baba's voice dropped, an urgent whisper in Lexos's ear. "Take your seat, *kouklos*. Do what every Stratagiozi before you has done."

It would be easy. Easy to take Baba's head in his hands and dash it against the stone. The matagios, along with its power, would pass to him, the eldest, and the family would be safe. Rhea could live in peace. They all could.

"No," Lexos said. It was almost an apology. "I can't."

Baba let go of Lexos and shoved him back. *"Mala,"* he spat. "Your mother could not have given me a weaker son."

Well, Lexos thought dazedly, she did give you Nitsos. But it hardly seemed the time to point that out.

Baba straightened his dressing gown. "Inside," he said. "We'll discuss this plan of yours."

Lexos followed him off the veranda, shame burning hot in his cheeks. Strange, to feel sorry for having left his father alive. Maybe Baba was right; maybe this was weakness. He supposed they would find out soon enough.

THIRTY-THREE

RHEA

The ceremony was held on the island, at the crest of the small rise behind the house. The prayer sung by the mourners spilled down from the hill like fog, its words well-known. It was spoken at funerals across the continent, but Rhea was most familiar with it as the prayer Baba spoke every night to end the lives of whomever he'd chosen. Words meant something more when you had the matagios on your tongue.

The Laskaris family buried its bodies the way the saints had done, rather than burning them according to Stratagiozi mandate, and so Rhea had to watch as Michali's body was lifted from its birch bier, placed in a coffin, and lowered into a deeply dug grave. She'd barely been able to tear her eyes away from the line of his profile, clear despite the cloths wrapping him. Her hopes, her future, all buried with him.

Thinking about it now, in her carriage as it flew through a crisp field of dead grass, the whole thing seemed like one of the puppet shows she'd seen put on for children during Meroximo, more performed than the funerals of her other consorts, at which she'd bowed her head and sung. The mourners had gathered around his grave, and of them all, Rhea herself and Evanthia were the only two who knew just what a surprise it was for Michali to have died. Evanthia had blamed Rhea at first, had called her son's death a Stratagiozi plot. And it was, Rhea had tried to explain. But Lexos's, and not hers. She still wasn't sure how much Evanthia believed her, but all that was behind her now, laid to rest in Ksigori under a layer of fresh snow. Here, an afternoon's ride away from Stratathoma, it was only just cold enough for Rhea to see her breath in the cab of the carriage.

She settled into her seat and closed her eyes. When she woke again, the house was clear on the horizon. The way she'd left things with Baba, she'd be lucky—or perhaps unlucky—if he said a single word to her, but better to be ready than caught unprepared. It was, however, not Baba who was waiting for her in Chrysanthi's wild courtyard. It was Lexos, standing in the doorway like he always was when she came home from some consort's house abroad.

It had been lying dormant in her chest, muffled by the shock of the funeral, lulled into a sleep by the miles and miles of travel, but now it woke with a snarl. Lexos. He'd taken Michali from her. He'd ruined the only thing she'd ever built for herself, and now she was here, facing him again. What did he expect? That she would be grateful? That she wouldn't care? She supposed they'd spent their whole lives like that: Lexos pulling her along behind him, Lexos telling her how things should be. He must have thought it would always be thus.

But it couldn't. It had changed, to the very bottom of things. She had bargained for his life, and even when she'd given up on Baba, she hadn't let go of him. Until she'd woken up next to Michali's corpse and decided that Lexos should burn right alongside their father. He didn't deserve her protection anymore. More than that, he didn't deserve her love.

Enough, she thought, pressing her shaking hands to her thighs as Eleni and Flora came hurrying out of the house to help her. She would keep her anger in check, keep things easy between her and

Lexos so that, when the time came, he would do as she asked. Michali was dead but the Sxoriza cause was not, and she still had work to do.

When she climbed out of the carriage, it was with a smile firmly pasted on. Lexos came toward her, circles under his eyes, and the stink of horse detectable under the scent of soap from a fresh wash. There was a bruise on the side of his jaw, too, faint enough that Rhea supposed it was fairly new, but its color already rich enough that she knew it went right to the bone.

Baba. It could be from no one else.

"Rhea," Lexos said and opened his arms.

For a moment she only looked at him. She had forgotten what it was to be here with him, to be not just his sister but his twin, half his body and half his blood. His face built with the same sharpness, his hair the same deep brown, the same weight and curl. How would she ever break the thread linking them? What if she couldn't manage it, even after what he'd done?

He wrapped her in his embrace then, and she forced herself to relax against him, one hand resting limply on his back while her other clenched into a tight fist, nails biting into her palm.

"Are you all right?" he said as he withdrew. "You look dreadful."

"That's not a very nice welcome." Meaner than she'd meant to sound, but it was a relief to let some of her anger out. Had he known how it would hurt her when he'd ordered Michali's death? Had he cared?

"Sorry." He shook his head, sagging against the wall of the house. "It's good to see you, *kathroula*."

"In fact, if anybody should be asking after anyone, I should be asking after you." She stepped past him and through the house's double doors, into the great room. It was cold, the hearth empty, the floors covered in a thin film of dust. Above her, even the sunlight streaming through the small, high windows seemed paler than she was used to. "I heard about your trouble in Vuomorra."

He followed her inside. " 'Trouble' is a delicate way of putting it. Baba and I have had words."

"Words and perhaps a bit more," she said, nodding to the bruise on his jaw. "Did you earn that for anything in particular?"

"When has Baba ever been so forthcoming?" Lexos answered. She could hear the strain in his voice, the effort it was taking to sound as blithe as he did. "It doesn't matter," he went on. "I think I've found a way to resolve this entirely."

"You think that's possible?" From what she'd heard, Tarro's second Falka had made a thorough enough mess of Lexos's plans that the situation was unrecoverable.

"Not without work," Lexos said darkly, "and not without sacrifice."

She knew what was expected of her—to ask what he meant, to find out the details of his plan and report them back to Piros, whose rank had risen from second-in-command to first after Michali's death. But she could barely look at him without seeing Michali's face laid over his, wide staring eyes and the blood crusted all down his throat.

She needed to rest. She needed a moment to herself, and more than that if she was really going to get Lexos to open the tides for her.

"I want to hear more," she said, brushing his clammy hand with hers briefly, "but I'm afraid I need to freshen up. I'll see you later."

Eleni and Flora had been in her room, and the air was scented with lavender, her bed cushion by the window draped with clean linens. It felt like years since she'd been here last. This room had been her refuge. Now she couldn't wait to leave.

She'd meant to ask Lexos where Baba was, but the idea of spending any longer than necessary pretending to be fine was beyond unappetizing, especially when she had such work to do with Lexos later. She would look in the study. Whether she found Baba or not, there would be something useful there.

Quickly, she peeled off her traveling suit and changed into a simple gray dress, its shape similar to those worn by the maids. It wouldn't do much, but perhaps it would keep her siblings from noticing their sister sneaking into Baba's study.

It was strange, though. Besides Eleni and Flora she had yet to see any other servants. Had Baba become so volatile that they were stay-ing out of sight? Or perhaps he'd become so paranoid that he'd sent all of them away.

The door to Baba's study was open when she arrived, the room inside just visible. Lamps were lit, casting long shadows, but Baba didn't seem to be inside. She pushed the door farther open, and leaned carefully in. Empty, with only a still-smoking candle to sug-gest that someone had just been there.

The desk was layered in parchment, sheaves of it spilling onto the floor. Pushing aside thoughts of the last time she had been here—the feel of Baba's glove hitting her cheek still fresh in her mind, the sight of Lexos's face, empty and blank as he struck—she stepped inside, careful to keep her tread light. If Baba found her here she would tell him she'd only been looking for him to pay her respects, the way any returning daughter should.

She sidled in front of the desk and began to sift through the doc-uments laid out across the top of it. Piros had briefed her, told her what sort of information they were looking for: troop movements and supply stores of the other Stratagiozi countries. Were they sup-pressing word of the Sxoriza, and were there recruits to be had? Of course some information would only be known to Baba, which was part of why Piros had agreed with Rhea in the first place that keep-ing him alive would be best. Now Rhea wondered if it might have been better to send her home with a knife and instructions on where to stick it.

The top layer of documents seemed to be nothing relevant, just a collection of reports on the latest harvest, and she moved those to one side, careful to keep them in their order. More tax documents, and a few letters from the steward to the south who'd been petition-ing Baba for a reprieve for a few seasons now. Perhaps it was all worth something to someone, but not to Rhea.

What did seem to be worth something were the notes she found underneath, scrawled in Lexos's familiar handwriting. He wrote in a shorthand, her brother, one he'd developed when they were children as a way to write notes to her that their tutor couldn't decipher. He used it still, and as she lifted the top sheet of parchment to the light, each trimmed word unfurled before her eyes.

Agiokon. He had been to Agiokon and called a meeting of the Stratagiozi council. This was practically a transcript of what had been spoken there; Lexos's memory was sharp and he'd spent years learning just what to pay attention to at meetings like this. There was Nastia's name, shortened to simply Chuzhak N, and there were the others: Ammar, Milad, Zita. But Tarro's was absent, and instead Lexos referred only to the seat at Vuomorra.

But a few lines down, it became clear: the reason for everything, the objective Lexos had obscured with shortened phrases and hurried notation. The Stratagiozis had decided to oust Tarro.

Rhea kept reading, skimming the pages for the most important details. This was exactly the sort of thing Piros had told her to look for. Lexos would call this simply a reorganization of the federation, but to the Sxoriza this was the first step toward its dissolution.

The notes would have to stay in the study, so Rhea slid open one of the desk drawers in search of a clean sheet of parchment. She could copy it out, translate it for Piros and the rest of the Sxoriza. She would be worth something that way.

She'd only made it through one of Lexos's pages when there was a noise in the corridor. Rhea shoved the parchment up the sleeve of her dress and, with shaking hands, returned everything else to its place before hurrying to sit in the chair on the opposite side of his desk. If Baba caught her in here, she could pretend she was waiting to see him. As long as he didn't find her in the midst of copying down Lexos's notes, she could talk her way out of it.

It was only a moment until the door opened, and Rhea leapt to her feet as Baba came in, a frown creasing his forehead as he pored over a wrinkled letter, which looked as though it had been folded several hundred times before being dunked in a trough of mud.

There he was. Months away from him, months spent picking away at the gilded image she carried of him in her heart, and now he was real again. Everything she'd let go of, wrapped up in one man.

She found, looking at him, that she didn't regret it at all.

It was difficult to imagine him alongside a saint. It had been hard enough before, when the trouble had been with putting together a true picture of her mother, but now it was nearly impossible. Could he really have been ignorant of it? But then, if he'd known, why hadn't he told his children? If not Nitsos and Chrysanthi, at least her and Lexos.

She would get no answers today, Rhea thought. What she wanted to know of her mother lived in the Ksigora, not in a house Mama would have died before entering.

"Keresmata," she said, and Baba stopped short. He looked up at her, a moment of blank confusion sweeping across his face before recognition sparked.

"What are you doing in here?"

"I only just arrived home." She crossed the room and kissed him on each cheek. "I wanted to pass on the well wishes of the Ksigoran steward."

"I have no need of well wishes from a fool," Baba snapped. "Off with you."

She could stay, Rhea thought. Try to thaw Baba's heart, try to coax some last morsel of love from him. But she had had enough of all that.

There were still a number of hours before dinner, but Rhea had already made up her mind not to attend. Instead she went back to her room, anxious to copy down what she could remember from Lexos's notes. She would have to sneak back into Baba's office to gather the rest of the information, or else pry it from Lexos himself. As it was, neither option seemed particularly appealing.

It was horribly cold in her bedroom when she arrived, almost as though she were back in Ksigori, and with a shudder she tugged twice on the rope by the door, which rang a bell somewhere in the servants' quarters. Someone would be in shortly to light a fire in the ash-covered fireplace, to burn away thoughts of Michali and the life she'd left behind. In the meantime, she sat at her vanity and tried to elaborate on the notes she'd copied at Baba's desk. Not much, in the end, but altogether more than she'd expected to find on her first day home.

It was Eleni who arrived a few minutes later, slightly out of breath, a flush rising on her cheeks. It was startling to see such color on her skin, to see anything that reminded Rhea that Eleni was in fact as human as she was herself.

Rhea said nothing, only pointed to the fireplace and began unbuttoning her own gray dress, a near twin of Eleni's. In the presence of a servant, it felt wrong to be wearing it. Almost a mockery, and for all the times Rhea had taken her servants for granted she had never meant to demean them.

It was early still, but Rhea was exhausted, and by the time Eleni finished building the fire she had settled onto the bed, the cushion cover familiar in its roughness underneath her. Rhea waited for her servant to exit silently, but instead Eleni stayed by the hearth, a hesitant expression on her young face.

"Yes?" Rhea said, trying not to sound impatient. All she wanted was to go to sleep and hopefully wake up in a world that looked somewhat less like the one she found herself in now.

"I'm so sorry, *kiria*," Eleni said. "I didn't mean to disturb you." And then she was hurrying out of the room, her skirts swirling around her as she fled.

How odd, Rhea thought, and she sat up. She was almost ready to go after Eleni—had she offended her somehow?—when she noticed a small spot of white on the floor where Eleni had been standing. In the firelight, it looked almost like parchment.

And in fact it was. Rhea got up from the bed and crossed to crouch in front of the fire. The note had been folded up many times, and intricately so, layers tucked under and over one another such that as Rhea tried to unfold it she found her fingers prying at unmovable corners. Pulling didn't seem to be working, so instead, she cupped the whole thing in her palms and cradled it, pushing in slightly. The parchment almost seemed to catch before it released, unfolding like a blossom.

We are with you, it said, in Saint's Thyzaki. *Even if Michali is not.*

Rhea sat back on her heels, ignoring the sob trying to climb up her throat. How long ago had Eleni joined their household? How long had it been since she had begged Rhea to take her to Stratathoma? And why had Rhea listened? Now that she thought about it, she couldn't quite remember.

It seemed that up in the north, the Sxoriza had been planning for years, waiting and waiting for something. Waiting for Rhea.

THIRTY-FOUR

ALEXANDROS

Rhea did not come down to dinner, and Lexos was doing his best not to be worried about it. She was usually eager to spend time with him, and with Chrysanthi, after she came home from one of her trips—Nitsos was another matter—but he'd thought she'd seemed strange upon her return from the Ksigora, and this only proved it.

"She must be tired," Chrysanthi had said when he'd mentioned it as they gathered outside the dining room before the meal. "It was a long trip, after all."

Lexos thought it was a great deal more likely that Rhea was tired from whatever confrontation with Baba she surely must have had by now, but he held his tongue.

Now he and his siblings were standing at the dinner table, waiting for their father to arrive so they might begin the meal. The food had already been laid out, in fact, but nothing had been touched, and would not be until Baba joined them.

That, however, did not seem to be likely to happen anytime soon.

Even as the light coming in through the windows grew dimmer and the steam coming off the tureen of vegetable soup began to thin, Baba's chair remained empty, and the house beyond the dining room remained still.

"Can we sit at least?" Chrysanthi said finally. "He couldn't be angry about that."

Lexos scoffed. "He very well could."

"It's just that we've been standing for so long, and I—"

"Enough."

Lexos and Chrysanthi looked in surprise at Nitsos, who had spoken gruffly and was sitting down, reaching for the basket of rolls.

"What?" he said, when he realized they had gone quiet. "Aren't you hungry?"

Chrysanthi glanced at Lexos, looking practically pitiful. "It is only dinner."

"Excuse this today," he said shortly, "and who knows what you will be excusing tomorrow." He was overreacting, and attempting to punish his siblings for his own betrayal of Baba, but knowing that did nothing to keep the flare of self-righteous anger in check. "If we cannot follow this simplest of rules, cannot give our father this simplest measure of respect, then what—"

"Oh," Nitsos said suddenly, "and I suppose your meeting with the Stratagiozi council was a measure of respect, was it?"

Lexos felt his whole body turn cold. "How do you know about that?"

"Did you honestly think you'd be able to keep such a thing a secret?" Nitsos shook his head, poking at his soup with his spoon. "Agiokon is full of people happy to share what they've heard."

He didn't seem to be referring to the sort of gossip that passed idly between people. No, there was a certainty to his voice that left Lexos equally sure that while he had been traveling, trying to piece together a future for Thyzakos, Nitsos had been up to something of his own.

"You have your own sources, then?" he asked.

"Well, it wouldn't do," Nitsos said bitterly, "to waste all of my time in my workshop, would it? I had to find something better to keep me occupied."

Those were Baba's words coming out of Nitsos's mouth. Lexos had heard them tossed about carelessly at dinners, had seen them strike home in Nitsos's heart. And here they were, come to life.

"Whatever will you do?" Nitsos went on, leaning back in his chair. His yellow hair was dusted with soot, presumably from some attic experiment, and though he certainly looked no older than he had the day before, Lexos was struck suddenly by the shape of Nitsos's face—the bones so close to the surface, the roundness of his childhood vanished from his cheeks. "Is that perhaps why our dear father has not joined us? I'm sure you've shared your indiscretion with him." Nitsos tilted his head. "To be frank, brother, I'm surprised to find you living."

It was unwise. Lexos knew it even before he opened his mouth. But Nitsos was sitting there, judgment curling his lips into a smirk, and he had no idea, no idea at all, of the pressure that came with being a second. Or, more particularly, with being Baba's.

"I have a plan," he said hotly, "and Baba has agreed to it, if you must know."

Nitsos frowned, and sat forward. Next to him, Chrysanthi was looking longingly at her own chair, but Lexos ignored her and watched instead as Nitsos broke a twig off the cypress branch centerpiece and began to bend it into a new shape.

"What plan is that?" Nitsos said, glancing sidelong at Chrysanthi. "The council has asked for something from you that Baba cannot be happy to provide."

So he knew even that. Lexos supposed he should be grateful that Nitsos was sensible enough to not discuss the details in front of Chrysanthi, but it was hard to remember that in the face of the knowledge that his younger brother—little Nitsos, who Lexos could still picture as the puffy, solemn child who hated to leave their mother's arms—had sources so deep within the council that this most secret detail had found its way to his ears.

"What are you both talking about?" Chrysanthi asked, and she looked neither surprised nor upset when Lexos ignored her, only resigned.

"Baba and I have found a way to solve that problem," Lexos said. Nitsos snorted, not looking up from where he was cutting into the cypress twig with his fingernail.

"Oh, you have?"

"We have."

"Then I suppose," Nitsos said idly, "you have considered the matagios."

"Of course," Lexos said, but it was a reflex more than anything else, because the truth was that he had in fact not considered the matagios at all. And if Lexos meant to tell the council that he'd killed his father, certainly they would ask to see the matagios as proof.

Nitsos stood up. He looked, Lexos thought, horribly satisfied with himself, and on the table in front of him rested the twig from the cypress centerpiece, finally shaped into a perfect circle.

"Well done, then," Nitsos said. "You've thought of everything."

He was out the door before Lexos could find the words to reply.

Chrysanthi sighed. "If you would be a bit nicer to each other," she said, "I think we might all have a much better time."

"It's not a question of being nice." Lexos scrubbed at his eyes. He was so tired. Had he slept since coming home? He couldn't remember. "There's quite a lot you don't understand."

"I might understand," she said, "if anybody ever told me anything. But I suppose that's not likely." She reached over and took a roll from the bread basket, tearing out a large bite. "Enjoy waiting for Baba," she said, her mouth full. "You're the only one left who will."

She hurried after Nitsos, her skirts trailing behind her, and soon Lexos was alone. Around him the air grew colder, and the candles guttered in the draft from the windows. But Lexos remained, his hands resting on the chair in front of him. He would wait for Baba, as long as it took. Baba would see how loyal Lexos was.

The matagios couldn't be passed through ritual. Instead it would pass to Lexos, the eldest, only once Baba died, or at least that was the prevailing wisdom. But there had to be a way for Baba to give it to Lexos the way he'd given his children every other gift. They would find that way together.

It was much later when the doors finally slammed open and Baba came thundering in. Usually, he could be expected to change for dinner, as he required his children to, but today he was still in the sort of jacket he preferred during the day: black, with a collar that skimmed his jawline. If he had done it to intimidate his children, Lexos thought, he had done well, although it might have worked better had there been more than one child left remaining to observe its effect.

"Well," Baba said, a servant scurrying in behind him to pull out his chair. "More than a hundred years of looking after my children and I see they cannot be bothered to do so much as break bread with me."

Lexos wondered, sometimes, if Baba had only bothered fathering children so that he might have an audience for the pronouncements he so enjoyed making.

"Rhea was feeling ill," he lied, anxious to spare her whatever bit of Baba's anger he could. "I sent her to bed early."

He was not surprised when Baba did not ask about Nitsos and Chrysanthi. Baba rarely referred to them as individuals; rather they were "the children," part of a unit he only ever considered in rhetorical terms.

"I wonder, though," Lexos went on as Baba took his seat and waved over a servant to pour his wine, "if we might take this time to discuss our dealings with the council."

Baba did not answer, but Lexos was prepared to consider that a victory. He went to Baba's side and knelt there as Baba speared a large chunk of fish and dropped it onto his plate.

"Don't you think," he began, ignoring the slight spatter of oil that hit his face as Baba began to carve the fish into bites, "that our plan would be best served by as great a degree of authenticity as possible?"

"Authenticity?" Baba growled. "This is good fish."

Lexos blinked. "I'm glad. But I mean your gift, Baba." He took a long breath, and hoped that his voice sounded steady as he said, "The council will know you're alive if I don't show up to the next meeting with the matagios."

At first Baba hardly seemed to understand, but then he set down his fork, and Lexos watched anxiously as his grip on his wineglass tightened until his knuckles were white.

"Excuse me?" Baba said. Lexos immediately wished very hard that he had not knelt so close.

"Only for the sake of appearances," he hastened to clarify. "The power would still belong to you, of course, if not in . . . execution."

Baba turned to stare at Lexos. The candlelight flickered, throwing distorted shadows across his face, exaggerating the curl of distaste at the corner of his mouth.

"This," he said quietly, "is not how a strong son takes his seat. Not by asking permission."

Mala, Lexos thought. Why couldn't Baba see that he didn't want that? "Baba, that's not—"

"Out," Baba growled. "I can't stand to look at you."

He pushed to his feet. There was no sense arguing. Baba had already bent enough in agreeing to Lexos's plan—bending any further would break him, and he would never allow that, not even if doing so was required to make the plan actually work.

Lexos left Baba then, and found his feet tracing the familiar path up to the observatory. It was the highest room in the highest tower, and it was the only place in Stratathoma that Lexos truly considered his. Even his bedroom belonged to Baba, belonged to the servants and to the other Stratagiozi children who had lived there before Baba took the seat, but the observatory was of no use to anybody but him, and though Lexos's duties had been granted to him by Baba, they had immediately thereafter fallen out of Baba's memory, and the dust collecting in the corners of the round stone room was proof that they had also fallen out of everybody else's.

The observatory windows looked west out over the ocean, and when Lexos had climbed the last stair and shut the door behind him, he was greeted by the sea below, lit rosy and burning by what remained of the sunset. It wasn't nearly time to begin the evening's work, so he dragged the room's lone chair over to the window and slumped down into it. It was markedly cooler up here, with the breeze buffeting in off the water and the stone soaking in the chill, and Lexos felt some of his frustration leach out of him, replaced by a soothing calm.

Baba would not pass him the matagios. When Lexos returned to the council, they would know that he hadn't held up his end of the bargain. And they would not turn against Tarro, and the family would suffer, and Thyzakos, as well.

No, there was no choice, he thought. It had to be done. He remembered the crack of Baba's palm against his cheek, remembered the way the veranda wall had pushed relentlessly into his back. Take it, Baba had told him. And there had been such a palpable disappointment in him when Lexos had refused.

Very well. He would do what his father wanted. For the family's sake, he would kill Baba.

THIRTY-FIVE

RHEA

Rhea left the note turning to ash in the fireplace and went to bed. She lay awake as she heard Chrysanthi come stomping upstairs, and she lay awake listening for Lexos, for the tread of his step, which she knew as well as anything.

Barely a day back at Stratathoma, and being so near him was already more than she could bear. She wasn't sure how she would manage to be the sister she needed to be in order to get him to open the tides. She knew it had to be tonight, though. She would never be better able to pretend.

But it was too early in the evening still. Baba would be prowling the house, and she and Lexos would likely be caught on their way out to the beach. Never mind that as Argyros children they had the right to go wherever they pleased—that meant nothing when Baba was like this.

So she waited, anxiety curdling in her stomach, until the clock that Nitsos had made for her room showed that it was nearly midnight. Baba might still be awake, but he would be dulled by whatever he'd had to drink, and it would be easy enough to avoid him.

Rhea pulled on her boots, made her bed, wrapped a shawl around her shoulders, and snuck out of her room. Lexos's door was opposite hers, and was only just open, the shift of sea light sneaking through from his window to paint the corridor in blue and white. She peered into the shadows, but there was no shape curled in his bed.

Still, she whispered his name, her voice sounding too loud in the night. Nobody stirred, so she eased the door open, stepping through. The room was empty, which meant Lexos was still awake, still in the house somewhere.

Rhea's stomach dropped. What was he doing? Something to do with his spies, perhaps. Or planning yet another way to break her heart.

She pushed the image of Michali's empty face out of her head and left Lexos's room, following the corridor to the staircase that would lead her up to his observatory. The tides still needed to be opened. If she had to, she would do it herself, no matter the consequences. Better that than to remain here in this cage a second longer.

She'd been to the observatory before, but never so late, and never alone. After a wrong turn she found herself winding up the back staircase, almost as if she were taking the route to Nitsos's attic. It felt wrong to be treading these stairs without Lexos ahead of her, to be opening a door that had only ever belonged to him. But hadn't he done the same thing with her? He'd used her gift as it suited him, and now it was her turn.

When she reached the room at last, the muscles burning in her legs, it, too, was empty. A chair had been pulled up in front of the tall, arching windows that cut through the stacked stone, the upholstery still warm. Lexos had only just left. It was a wonder she hadn't passed him on the stairs.

Resting on the seat of the chair was a white handkerchief—Lexos's, of course—that had been stained lightly with blood. She frowned, picking it up gingerly. Strange, that even after all the hurt he had dealt her, it worried her to think he might be hurting.

She crumpled the handkerchief in her fist. She couldn't afford to care about that sort of thing anymore.

Through the window the sea was flat, as was the water in the bowl of tides that sat on its pedestal at the center of the room. Rhea went to stand in front of the bowl, the ends of her hair dipping into the water as she leaned over it to look closely. She didn't know exactly how it worked, but she'd seen Lexos use his gift before, and it seemed simple enough—tracing patterns, and watching them form under the water. She just hoped it would respond to her. Chrysanthi's paints did, but with barely half the effect they had in Chrysanthi's hands. If something similar happened here, that was fine. Rhea did not need the tides to hold for very long. She just needed a chance. So she dropped her shawl to the floor, set her shoulders, and slid her fingers into the water.

It was cold. So deeply, wrenchingly cold that she gasped, the air seeming to expand in her chest until she could not breathe it out again. The water closed around her wrists as she pressed her palms together.

Open, she thought, and swept her hands apart.

Rhea was not sure exactly what she had expected, but it had not been for the water to suddenly turn as thick as mud. She could barely move her fingers, could practically feel the water pushing back against her skin, resisting the command she'd given. She was the wrong Argyros.

There had to be a way around it. She took her hands from the water—that at least was easy—and stepped back, shutting her eyes, tilting her head so the cool air drifting through the window hit the skin of her neck.

Something was pricking at the back of her mind. An image of the river in the Ksigora, the Dovikos. Of its water, that startling blue. The saints had held power over it once. Maybe they still did.

She kept her eyes shut as she dipped her fingers back into the water. Slowly this time, and she waited until they went numb, until her whole world was there in the cold break of the water against her skin.

"*Efkos efkala,*" she said.

And Rhea knew it wasn't true. Knew that she was hearing things, knew that she was only hoping so hard for an answer that she'd crafted it herself, but she would have sworn the water in the bowl whispered, *"Efkala,"* right back.

She couldn't say "open" in Saint's Thyzaki. So instead she said, "Please," and dragged her fingertips through the water, the beach held in her mind's eye. She imagined the waves that crashed there endlessly receding, imagined them turning flat as the blade of a knife. Imagined Sxoriza boats sidling along the coast and climbing up onto the pebbled shore. "Please," she said again. "Do you see?"

No answer, not like she'd heard before, but in the air Rhea could feel a charge, a sort of shimmer that seemed to gather around her fingers as she withdrew them from the water. She opened her eyes, dried her hands on her dress, and went to the window.

The beach wasn't visible from here, but that didn't matter; she could see already that the ocean was changing. She'd asked for something and been answered.

Now she had to hurry and make good use of it.

She grabbed her shawl and made for the back staircase, which would take her away from Baba's rooms and wind around the side of the house before depositing her in the great room. It was deserted when she at last hit the ground floor, not even a fire burning in the hearth and only a single lantern to light the hallway. She snatched it up and went on.

Still no servants to be seen, and her footsteps echoed in the empty great room. Stratathoma had always felt alive to her, brimming with the energy of those who lived inside it, but tonight it felt stifled inside. Practically dead, if houses could be such a thing.

Outside was another matter. When Rhea pushed open the double doors to step into Chrysanthi's wild garden, the air was alive with wind, the open sky above a riot of stars. Usually the view was clouded by mist off the sea, but tonight the air was clear and sharp.

Had she done this? Had what she'd asked of the water ricocheted up into the world? It should have felt wrong. She'd dabbled with Chrysanthi's paints now and then, but one Stratagiozi's child wasn't meant to take on another's gift, not to this degree. Instead Rhea had the distinct sense that something was far more awake than it had ever been before.

And there was something else, too, in the air, a smell that she couldn't quite put her finger on. Not the scent of snow, which she'd become quite familiar with in Ksigori, and not the tang of salt that always whipped up over the side of the cliff. It was crisp, almost sweet, and it brought to mind the taste of kymithi, of memory. She wished, suddenly, that she'd made one of Michali. Of how safe she'd felt, how full of purpose to be alongside him. Would she ever feel that again?

The breeze was tugging at Chrysanthi's roses, and the leaves on the solitary olive tree were blown with their gray side up, only barely hanging on to their branches. Rhea's hair caught on the wind, billowing out behind her in a great dark stream, and as she hurried across the flagstone, to the doors that waited on the other side, for a moment Stratathoma didn't look like Stratathoma at all.

Out, through the double courtyards, and then Rhea was pushing open the last set of doors and stepping into the grounds beyond. She kept to the paths, her shawl nearly ripping away from her as the wind continued to howl. Surely a storm was coming, she thought, but there were no clouds in the sky. When at last she passed Nitsos's windup garden and reached the top of the stairs that cut down the cliff to the shore, her view of the ocean was startling, the color of it where it met the pebbled beach both surprising and familiar.

She'd seen that clear blue in the shallows of the Dovikos River. It wasn't reaching out into the depths of the water here—beyond the cliff, the ocean was the same deep shade as the eyes of every Argyros child—but it was unmistakably there.

Whatever she'd done up in the observatory, it was more than she'd realized. But Rhea didn't have time to wonder. She had to signal to the Sxoriza.

She started down the path. It was easy enough at the top, but the farther down she got the more slick with sea spray the steps carved into the cliff face became. But though she hadn't gone down these steps in years, her feet still knew the way, and so she found herself on the pebbled beach, alone and damp from the wind.

The tide was high, higher than she'd ever seen it, and the water was almost unnaturally still, so much so that when she bent to flick at the surface of it, she could watch the ripples continue out for what felt like miles. The Sxoriza had their way in. Now she had to let them know.

It felt a bit ridiculous, leaving this small lantern to beat against the vastness of the dark, but Piros had said they would be waiting, watching. She climbed to the highest point of the beach, stones clacking together under her boots and tumbling down the steep slope as the water pulled at them. She had loved that sound once, when she was small.

But so many things had changed since then, and Rhea felt no guilt as she set down the lantern and turned to see its firelight glancing out across the water, no guilt as she went to the staircase and began her climb back up the cliff. And why should there be? She was certain that everything had been leading her here.

THIRTY-SIX

ALEXANDROS

He pricked his fingertip that night, bled onto the inky silk as he stitched a new set of stars. Though Lexos knew it was impossible, he still half expected to see a red spill rippling across the sky. Not an omen, he told himself firmly as he stirred the tidewater in its gleaming silver bowl, blood eddying in the spirals. Omens were for weaker people.

He left the observatory, water still dripping from his fingertips, and took the stairs back down to the main house slowly. What was it Baba had always said? Death belonged to the Stratagiozi, and so it belonged to him. One day, Baba had told him, it would pass to Lexos, and Lexos would feel it running in his own veins, both the thrum of life and his right to take it.

Well, he would take it. And Baba would pay—but for a heartbeat, before it was over, he would be proud.

He'd never got his dagger back in Vuomorra. Perhaps that was for the best. Perhaps this was something a man should do with his own two hands.

The hallways were dark as he made his way through a set of un-used apartments and past his siblings' rooms. He tread lightly past their closed doors. With any luck his siblings were sleeping soundly, and Lexos hoped it stayed that way well into the morning, until he had time to sort out what he was about to do.

Baba's bedroom was set apart from his children's, across an atrium whose ceiling opened to the sky. It was an odd thing, Lexos thought as he passed through, the flagstones starting to darken as humidity gathered in the air. His mother would have liked it here. She'd never wanted any part of the Stratagiozi world, but Lexos could picture her in this house, reading her books and brushing her children's hair, and worshipping her saints when nobody was look-ing. If only she'd had a chance.

Out of habit he paused at Baba's door but caught himself before he knocked. He stepped back, took a breath. The sky overhead was studded brightly with stars, their shine so vivid that it looked as though Chrysanthi had taken her paints to them.

Lexos closed his eyes and settled his nerves. Death belongs to the Stratagiozi, he thought, and so it belongs to me.

The door opened easily. Inside no candles were lit, and there was only the moonlight that slanted through the large window on the op-posite wall to show Lexos the way. Baba's room overlooked neither the mountains nor the sea, but rather the main atrium of the house and the fountain burbling at its center. A defense strategy, that's what Baba had said a hundred years ago when they'd chosen their rooms. Meant to protect him against those outside the house. But today the threat came from within.

Baba was in bed, seemingly asleep, and when the door creaked slightly as Lexos shut it again, he did not stir. Was that better or worse? Lexos wasn't sure.

Across the warping floorboards, then past the low table cluttered with half-drunk mugs of kaf. Lexos had only been in this room a handful of times, but even so he could tell that it had fallen into a level of disrepair. Dust coated the floor, rising in motes that caught in every shaft of moonlight. Hanging from the window were bundles of

dying flowers, arranged in a strangely familiar way, their order picking at some distant memory until he could finally place it—a children's rhyme, from their life before Stratathoma, meant for protection.
Their mother had sung it to them, helped them make hangings like
this of their own, until Baba had torn them down and let the Stratagiozi seat consume his every thought.

Lexos approached the window and reached out with a shaking
hand to brush his fingers across the ragged hems of lavender and
therolia. The doubt he'd been pushing back all night was hot and
frothing in his gut, making him wish for a glass of water or a bucket
to throw up in.

"She used to hang them in our bedroom," came a voice from
behind him, and Lexos turned, startling at the gleam of Baba's eyes
in the dark. Baba was sitting up and he sounded tired, rough, as
though his voice had been torn from his body and poorly stitched
back in.

Lexos felt the familiarity of Baba's silhouette puncture his chest.
It had been easy enough, up in the observatory, to decide this needed
to be done. Now, faced with Baba in the flesh, what had felt like simply the next move to be made felt alive and wriggling under his
hands.

I'm sorry, he wanted to say. We have made mistakes, and I have
to fix them.

"I remember that," he said instead, coming toward Baba to kneel
by the edge of his bed. He couldn't ignore the pang of love in his
chest—love, or perhaps pity—as Baba's lined face came into view in
the dim light. They said that Stratagiozis didn't age, and perhaps they
didn't, but that had not kept Baba from growing old.

"Your mother," Baba said, trailing off, his gaze fixed on the open
window.

"What about her?"

"Was she beautiful?" Baba sighed, rubbing at his eyes. "I can't
remember."

"It's been a long time," Lexos said, although he could still picture his mother's face. In fact she had not been beautiful, or at least

not to anybody but her children. Neither had she been kind. She had been, Lexos thought, something better—constant. Always the same, always with the same things held close to her heart. Or perhaps that had only been because she hadn't been given time to change.

But Baba didn't want to hear about that. "Yes," Lexos said. "Very beautiful."

She had died only a month before Baba's campaign for the seat began in earnest. Lexos remembered their empty house, remembered being looked after by a rotation of faceless, voiceless women until Baba returned, bloodied and bent, and took them to Stratathoma. He and Rhea had wept the whole carriage ride here, and had only been lured into the great room by the promise of choosing their own bedrooms. They had been young enough then that Rhea had still asked after their mother, still wondered when she would return.

He hadn't, though. He'd known she was dead, even though Baba had done his best to disguise it in pretty words and promises. How had he known so certainly? Even now, Baba had never said what exactly happened.

"Baba," he said slowly, "how did Mama die?"

Baba looked back at him and then, after what appeared to be some consideration, said, "Neatly."

Lexos gripped the edge of the bed tightly, a splinter biting into his palm. "What is that supposed to mean?" But he knew. He remembered now. Baba, breathing heavily as he stood over Mama's still body, her eyes and mouth open, spit slick down her chin and bruises already vivid around her neck. He'd seen it. And when he'd realized what it meant, he'd stolen a horse and taken Rhea with him as he rode far away from the man who'd killed his mother.

"We put her back in the earth afterward," Baba was saying, "like one of her saints."

"Why?" Lexos barely managed to get it out past the lump in his throat.

"It's what she wanted. I owed her that much, I suppose."

"No, why did you kill her?"

"Oh," Baba said blithely, "well, that's what I wanted. She was against my campaign for the seat, and that was of no use to me."

Lexos pushed to his feet, pacing away. There they were, the thoughts he'd been honing to sharpness. That his loyalty was to his family, and that Baba had done enough damage that he could no longer be considered part of it.

With one last glance at the garland of herbs, swaying lightly in a gathering breeze, he turned and strode toward Baba's shadowed figure. One step after another, and it was easy, once he put the right name on it, to push Baba back onto the mattress and lock his hands around his throat.

Baba didn't struggle. Even though the dark lay over his face like a curtain, Lexos was sure he could feel Baba watching him as he bore down, his arms trembling with the effort as he leveraged one knee on the bed and leaned.

It was taking so long, and the small, wet sounds as Baba began to choke were filling his ears, pounding loud as a heartbeat. And for all Lexos's fire-beaten resolve, he could not seem to press hard enough to take the last little bit of life.

With a cry he fell back, scrubbing his aching hands over his face, his chest tight as he teetered on the edge of tears. Not an omen, he'd thought earlier, but what was this, then? He would be trapped in this room, in this moment forever. Always deciding, killing Baba over and over again.

"I said you were weak," Baba rasped from the bed. "I always said. You have your mother's blood in you, after all. But today at last you do me proud."

Lexos looked up in surprise. Baba had pushed himself to sitting, and in his hand was something Lexos recognized. Baba's own dagger, the hilt stamped with the Argyros crest. A twin to the one Lexos had left behind in Vuomorra.

"Take it," Baba said. "No sense stopping once you've begun."

The blade trembled in the moonlight as Baba's hand shook, and there was a true weariness in what Lexos could see of his face. "Baba—"

"Boy," he said plainly, "you have always been on your way here."

And he was right. There, the Argyros crest, its two olive branches gleaming softly. He'd spent his entire life in service to this family, spent year after year trying to earn what Baba was giving to him right now. The natural order of things, Lexos thought, and he reached for the dagger.

The blade cold against his fingers, hilt snug against the black mark on his palm. The choice had already been made. When the dagger sank deep, it scraped against bone, sending a shiver up the blade that seemed to sing back to him. Beautiful, Lexos thought, and went on.

It was very possible, he thought once he had finished, that he had overdone it. In the dark he couldn't see how much blood was seeping into the bed linens, but there was a wetness against his knees from where he'd knelt over the body, and he knew when he got into the light he would find blood settled in all the lines on his palms. How many times had he stabbed Baba in the end? He couldn't remember, couldn't force his mind to fix on the happening of it. No, rather it was as though somebody else had done it, and he could not say he altogether minded.

He stepped back from the bed and let go of the dagger. It clattered to the floor, tremendously loud in the night, but there was nothing to worry about. Let the others wake up. Let the servants come running. This was his house now, his country.

He held up his left hand and tried to examine his palm in the midnight gloom. Would the mark there fade now that he was Stratagiozi? Or would he have it and the matagios both? For that matter, had the matagios been transferred to him already?

Over his shoulder, Baba's body was making slight sounds, gurgling a little as it emptied. Perhaps it was a matter of burying the body. He would feel better, regardless, without Baba's sightless eyes staring at him, even if Baba had given him what passed for permission.

Lexos wiped the sweat from his brow. Baba had buried Mama in the ground, like one of her saints. Like she wanted, Baba had said. It had been a kindness to her, then. He fetched the dagger and slid it into the hidden pocket in his trousers. It would be no kindness to Baba when Lexos buried him.

The sky was unnaturally clear as he carried Baba's body out into the grounds, the moon so close that Lexos thought he might reach out and touch it if his hands weren't full. Baba was light, frail and stiff as though he were only a shell, and he felt like nothing in Lexos's arms. Perhaps this strength came with the matagios, Lexos thought. Or perhaps it was only that Baba had been lesser than he'd ever let on.

He kept going along the path, through the olive groves and between rows of cypress trees. He was heading, he realized, for Nitsos's windup garden, and though he had only been there a handful of times before, it seemed fitting. He would bury him there, in the midst of every creation Nitsos had built that Baba had never given any value.

He laid Baba's body out under the beaten copper cherry tree at the back of the garden, ignoring the crunch as delicate glass flowers broke under the body, ignoring the brush of the tiny fabric snowflakes that drifted down in clockwork routine. The soil here was thin and loose, much of it dug out of the garden to make room for Nitsos's mechanics, and Lexos could tell it would be easy enough to clear out a few layers with the dagger, its blade crusted over with blood. All Baba needed was a shallow grave.

He knelt at the base of the tree and began scraping dirt away in a long trench. One stroke, and then another, until the feel of the dirt, dry and crumbling under his hands, was all that remained. Lexos could see the glint of machinery as he dug, the metal tracks Nitsos had laid to gather the still-falling snow becoming clear.

At last the trench was large enough, and Lexos stood, letting the dagger fall to the ground. He'd kept from looking much at Baba's body, but there was no getting around it now. Baba's eyes were open, his neck gaping from a wound that slashed down the length of it and continued onto his chest. But the worst part, the part that made Lexos turn away as his stomach clenched uncomfortably, was that Baba was wearing a nightgown. A simple, woolen thing like what Lexos himself often wore to bed, and it was so ordinary, so familiar. It ended below Baba's knees, baring his legs and feet, which were thin and corded with muscle, bristled with hair. It was nearly impossible to put this Baba together with the one who had killed Mama, with the one who had let the family fall apart. And though Baba had handed him the dagger, Lexos felt a stinging guilt begin to crawl up his throat.

No. No, that would not do. Bury him, Lexos told himself, and you will never have to face this again.

He balked at the idea of once again lifting Baba to his chest, of carrying him the way he supposed one carried an infant, and instead took hold of Baba's arms. Dirt kicking up around them, Lexos dragged Baba toward the fresh grave and, with a grunt, maneuvered him in.

He took a step back and closed his eyes. Though everything in this garden was mechanical, Nitsos had somehow managed to make it smell like the flowers that grew elsewhere on the grounds. If Lexos focused on that, he could almost forget the blood under his fingernails, the feel of Baba's body going limp under his hands.

Nitsos's snow was still falling, and it was soft and somehow cold as it grazed Lexos's cheeks. The breeze, which had hovered on the edge of a storm all evening, was softening as dawn began to wake below the horizon, and threaded through it, Lexos heard birdsong, as soothing as the black of his closed eyes. The tune of it sounded familiar, one he remembered echoing down from Nitsos's attic workshop. He opened his eyes and searched the trees, gaze skimming over the translucent birches and the willow with its draping fabric leaves to land on the cherry tree.

There, by the lowest branch, flitting about in its regular pattern. A hummingbird, wings gilded in deep blue.

"Lexos?"

He jumped and looked toward the low stone doorway. Rhea, just come up the staircase from the beach. Mouth open, shawl hanging off her shoulders.

"Lexos," she said, "what have you done?"

THIRTY-SEVEN

RHEA

For a long moment, he only stared at her. She had never seen him like this—his composure gone, and in its place something stranger, something wrong.

"He was ruining everything," he said at last. "Rhea, he killed our mother."

Their mother. Did Lexos know what she had truly been? Did he deserve to? And whether he did or not, none of that changed what he was saying: that their mother, their saint, had died at the hands of their father.

It made sense, in a way. She had survived a thousand years, and of course, it had been Vasilis Argyros to bring her down.

But any further thought vanished, because there, there on the ground, Rhea saw the dagger, bright and bloody, and she saw the wounds, saw the slice torn down Baba's throat. Just like what Lexos had ordered done to Michali. And nothing—not the impending arrival of the Sxoriza, and not even Baba's body at the base of the cherry tree—nothing else mattered.

She lunged for the dagger, ignoring Lexos's shout. Dirt in her mouth, anger burning the fog from her mind. The hilt was crusted with blood, flaking off as she gripped it tight. Lexos backed away from her, skirting the trench where Baba's body lay.

"What are you doing, *kathroula*?" he said, his voice fond and nervous.

She held the blade out, aiming it for his heart. No, she'd never had the training Lexos had, but she'd killed enough consorts to know what needed doing.

"Payment in kind," she said, proud of how level she sounded, how steady her hand was. "I'm taking from you what you took from me. From Michali."

Lexos looked genuinely confused. "Michali?"

He didn't even remember. It had meant so little to him that Michali's name had already slipped from his head.

"My consort," she said, and a sob began to crackle in her chest. She had married so many times, and it had never meant what it did now. "My consort, who you killed."

Lexos let out a bark of surprised laughter. The sound raked over her, and Rhea threw herself at him, a wail bursting from her lips.

"*Mala*, Rhea," Lexos said, catching her by the wrists. "What's all this about? I never killed any of your consorts. That's your doing."

"You're lying." She shoved him away, sending him staggering back against the copper trunk of the windup cherry tree. "I woke up next to his body."

She was shaking, her breath coming fast. This sort of anger felt unsettled in her body, as though the whole world around her were moving too slowly, as though she were too big for her skin. But Lexos seemed his regular self, his face placid, the only sign of distress his raised hands and widened eyes. It only infuriated her more. Men, men and their detached, patronizing calmness in the face of anyone else's anger.

"I promise you," Lexos said, "I have no idea what you're talking about. Have I ever hurt you, *kathroula*? Have I ever treated your life as less important than my own?"

A thousand times, she wanted to say, but that wasn't the point. Was it possible he was telling the truth? Was it possible he hadn't ordered Michali killed?

"Explain it, then," she said, dropping the dagger a fraction. "He wasn't supposed to die. You were the only one I told."

There was still that confusion twisting his mouth, and Rhea knew he was struggling not to ask again for some explanation. It was a very good act, she had to admit, though he'd never felt the need to act with her before.

"I remember your letter," Lexos said slowly. He'd edged away from the cherry tree and now stood on the path that ran through a patch of stiff fabric grass. He was still in his clothes from the night before, his black jacket and trousers askew from carrying Baba's body. Compared to him, Rhea knew she should have felt vulnerable in her nightgown and unlaced boots, but she didn't. She didn't need those trappings anymore, didn't need the armor she used to wear.

"You seemed to be enjoying the Ksigora," he went on. "And I knew you were . . . regretful. But I would never have taken such matters into my own hands, even if you were planning to—"

"To what?" she said, her voice rising sharply. "To forsake my duty? To abandon my family?" Those were, she knew, the highest of crimes to Lexos.

"To spare him," he finished, frowning. "And yes, all that, as well."

"But if you meant to take no action, why bother watching me at all?" she said. "I know you were. I saw your scout."

"My scout?"

It came as if called. The white bird, its three-note song echoing in the air, dropped out of the sky to perch on the high garden wall, and Rhea felt a burst of fury in her chest. She had been right. How could Lexos deny it now?

"See," she said. "It followed me to Ksigori. It's yours."

"It is," Lexos said. "I never sent it north, though. Rhea, I swear."

"That's a lie," she spat, but some of the heat was gone from it. Baba was dead, and Lexos was Stratagiozi now. Why would he need to keep lying to her?

"It isn't." Lexos came toward her, and she fumed at how easily she relented as he pushed the dagger down to her side. "The scout must have gone back to its old pattern." He took her free hand in both of his. "I had nothing to do with your consort's death."

This was half her heart staring back at her. So earnest, so sincere, his dark blue eyes a mirror of her own, her blood running in his veins. It would be so easy to forgive him and pretend nothing had changed.

After all, Baba was dead. And wasn't that what the Sxoriza wanted? He was the one hurting the country. His policies, his rule. Lexos would be different. Rhea could help make him different.

"I don't know what happened," Lexos went on, his grip on her hand tightening. "What I do know is that none of it matters now, *koukla*. Baba is dead, and with him die all his mistakes. I have his seat now. I will protect it, protect this family." He leaned in, touched his forehead to hers. "Protect you."

No. Lexos would be no different. The federation had always served him, and he would serve it in turn. He would hold the Stratagiozi seat just like Baba, and as much as he wanted to be different, he would fail.

She and Michali had resolved that Stratathoma would come down stone by stone, and the rest of the federation, too. She couldn't go back on that now, no matter who had ordered Michali's death.

"It's too late for that, I'm afraid," she said, laughing a little.

Lexos straightened, easing back to look her in the eye. "What do you mean?"

"You want to protect the Thyzak Stratagiozi seat."

He nodded. "I do."

She had to do it. Now, now, there was no other time. "Right." She stepped back, heard a delicate crunch as a clear glass fern broke underfoot, and she dropped his hand. "And I want to tear it down."

For a moment Lexos did not react, only looked at her with that same sincere bewilderment. And then she saw it, the crumpling of his brow, the wounded drop of his jaw. "What?"

"The federation, the council. All of it. This is just the start, Lexos." She swallowed hard. "It isn't anything to do with you." But she knew it was pointless as soon as she said it. Of course it was.

"What for?" Lexos asked, shaking his head. He seemed to be having trouble finding the right words. "With everything you have gained. With all the privilege you have been afforded. You have lived a good life here."

"Perhaps," she said. She had thought so once. But the feeling of one's life in one's own hands—that was worth almost anything.

"Not good enough, it seems," Lexos said wryly. "Rhea, what did you do?"

"I didn't murder our father," she snapped.

"No, you're only working to destroy everything he held dear."

It was, Rhea thought, a ridiculous conversation to be having while they stood practically over their father's dead body.

"You don't understand," she said. "Baba was different with you. This whole world was different for you."

"I am not sure I agree with you, but Baba aside," Lexos said, which seemed rather bold of him considering the blood still on his hands, "this isn't just a betrayal of him."

It was a betrayal of Lexos, too. A repudiation of the Stratagiozi seat was a repudiation of Lexos, whether she wanted to admit it or not.

"I know," she said firmly. "It pains me. Truly, it does. But not enough to make me change my mind."

There it was. Clear and undeniable. Rhea and her twin brother, on opposite sides of what she was sure was shaping up to be a war. Rhea was surprised to find she felt better for saying so.

Lexos, on the other hand, looked as though she'd taken him apart. She could just about hear it, the endearment—*kathroula*, mirror, reflection—falling from his lips as he begged her to stay.

But what came out was something else.

"Mathakos ala," Lexos said, his voice dropping to a hiss. "After everything I've done for you."

"Lexos—" she started, not quite knowing where she was going, but he held up one hand. Eyes cold and unrecognizable, and no longer hers. Somehow with all her planning and plotting, she had never truly reckoned with the loss of her dearest sibling. With what it would mean to be against him for the rest of what lives they had.

Maybe there was a way to fix it, a way to bring Lexos across this bridge with her. She'd thought it was impossible, had never even considered he might be swayed, but Baba was gone now. That had to make a difference.

But there was no time to find out. Lexos stormed toward her, grabbing her arm so firmly that she was nearly jolted off her feet. The dagger fell from her grip as he marched her along the path toward the door of the garden, a sturdy steel rosebush tearing her shawl from around her.

"Wait," she said, but he wasn't listening.

She strained against his hold as they approached the door, digging in her heels, throwing her weight back toward the cherry tree. No, no, if he took her away from here she would lose everything. At least in the garden she still had time. Time to change his mind before the Sxoriza came, or at the very least protect him from the destruction she'd welcomed in. She could have everything. She could make Lexos understand. She could, she knew it.

"Elado, Lexos," she said, trying to keep her voice kind as she wrested herself free. *"Kathroulos,* we can—"

"Don't," he said sharply, throwing her to the ground. Pain rushed up her spine like fire, and she scrambled back, the shards of broken glass flowers slicing into her palms. "How dare you."

Lexos advanced on her, his figure dark and looming against the soft morning sky. Above him the white bird took flight, streaking into the sunlight. Rhea felt her breath hitch. She had never been afraid of Lexos before today. But then, he had never looked at her the way he was now, like she was an ant that had found something of interest in his breakfast.

"I'm sorry," she said. Apologies had always meant something be-tween them. They'd never had them from Baba, and so had always given them generously to each other, had always assigned them a particular weight and power. But Lexos did not seem moved.

"So should you be" was all he said. He knelt before her, one hand going to rest on her outstretched leg. Nearly friendly, but his hold was so tight she knew it would leave bruises. "Rhea, I cannot let you take the path you have chosen."

"Take it with me," she tried, but he was already shaking his head.

"This family is the most important thing," he said. His gaze fixed on hers, his dark hair sweeping across his brow. "I will protect it and what we have achieved, no matter what."

"At what cost, Lexos?" She pushed herself close to him, took his face in her hands. There was her straight nose; there were her down-turned eyes. "What good is loyalty when there is nobody left to be loyal to?"

Lexos didn't answer. He only looked at her, and she could see it behind the glaze of his expression, could see a decision being made. She had watched it happen a thousand times before, as he made plan after plan that altered her life, all without asking what she thought, what she wanted.

"Goodbye, *kora*," he said, and he leaned in to kiss her on both cheeks.

For a moment, Rhea didn't move, afraid that if she so much as twitched she would break the calm that had spread over them. He was letting her go. He really was letting her go.

She thought so, at least, until he began reciting the mourning prayer. The one so old it was in Saint's Thyzaki, the one she'd heard from her father every night at dinner.

"Aftokos ti kriosta," Lexos started, his voice shaking but growing in strength. *"Ta sokomos mou kafotio."*

These were the words the Thyzak Stratagiozi spoke to draw the life from someone's body. The words that Baba had always said could not be used like this, like an arrow aimed at one person's heart. But here was her brother, lifted to the seat by his murder of their father, using them on her.

"*Ftama,*" she said, lurching painfully to her feet. "Lexos, *ftama.*"

It was for nothing. He kept going, repeating the prayer as Baba had every night before him, his eyes squeezed shut as though to keep from looking at her. "*Aftokos ti kriosta, po* Rhea Argyros. *Ta sokomos mou kafotio.*"

"It won't work," she said, and clutched at his bloodstained shirt. "That's not how this works, Lexos."

But when he opened his eyes, Rhea recognized their feverish gleam. This was the Lexos of her childhood, the Lexos in front of her on that horse as they fled from home. He would do what Baba had never been able to. The matagios would bend to him; everything always did.

Rhea could feel a panic rising in her, could feel her breath coming quick, but suddenly it was all very far away. Over it all, like a sheet of crusted snow, lay a glittering calm. It was going to happen. There was no point in fighting.

She had never seen somebody die this way. She had never been there when Baba's words drew the life from someone as though it were poison in a wound. Would it be painful? She held her hands up in front of her, flexed her fingers gently. It wasn't yet. Not for her, at least, but Lexos's face was screwed up in something like anguish, and he seemed to be shaking.

There was no need for all that. Didn't he know she understood? This was kinder than a knife between her ribs; this was better for both of them. And she'd have done the same to him, if she'd had the chance. There was nothing more like love than that.

"*Aftokos ti kriosta,*" Lexos finished, his breath a rough catch she could hear. "*Ta sokomos mou kafotio.*"

The last of the prayer rang in the quiet, seeming to echo through the small garden. Rhea held her breath, waited for a coldness to seep through her limbs. If these were the last things she ever saw, this garden, twinkling with glass and metal, and her brother's face, so

dear even now, it would be all right. She had done what she could—
she would bear her death as gracefully as she could manage.

Only, it didn't come. And when Lexos opened his eyes, Rhea saw
his surprise as he realized that she was still standing in front of him,
blood dripping down her fingers from the cuts on her palms.

She could hear her heart, could feel every brush of breeze against
her skin. She was not dead. No, if anything she was more alive.

THIRTY-EIGHT

ALEXANDROS

Rhea looked as surprised as he felt. There she was, standing there as if he'd never spoken in the first place. It had cost him everything to get the words out, only to have them fail. Had he said them wrong? Or maybe Baba had forgotten to teach him some crucial part of the ritual. Yes, he knew the matagios wasn't meant to be used this way, but power was power—it was meant to bend to its wielder. And now that he was Stratagiozi, this gift was his to command, and its rules were his to break.

Rhea took in a long, shuddering breath, and Lexos met her eyes. No matter the reason, it hadn't worked. He would have to face his twin sister for the rest of their lives, both of them knowing he had tried to end hers.

"Rhea?" he said uncertainly. Please, let this have changed her mind. Please, let her have already forgiven him. *"Kathroula—"*

"You're not supposed to be in here without me," came someone's voice from the doorway. Lexos jerked back, startled, and there, over Rhea's shoulder, was Nitsos, standing at the threshold, looking rumpled and cross, his inventor's apron dangling from one hand, a lantern from the other, shining through the blue dawn.

"What are you doing up so early?" Lexos said, but Nitsos didn't pay him any mind, and only frowned as he set down his lantern and took in the damage they had done to the garden: the flowers that had shattered, the trench dug at the foot of the cherry tree with Baba's body inside it. Lexos recognized the look on Nitsos's face, the way he was biting his lip as his brain sorted through a thousand different ways to solve the problems presented to him. He had worn it since they were children, since he had first learned that something could be made from the sum of small parts.

"Nitsos," he said, *"elado."*

Nitsos waved a dismissive hand. "Yes, yes." He crouched by the nearest of the broken plants, a set of delicately fronded ferns that had cracked underfoot. "Wait just a moment, will you?"

It was true that Lexos had only just finished with trying to kill Rhea, but some things were too hardy to ever be broken, and he exchanged a weary, vaguely incredulous look with her as their brother did what he did best and avoided participating in the conversation for as long as possible.

Nitsos ran a finger down the curl of the fern still intact, and looked about ready to fuss in the pockets of his inventor's apron when Lexos finally cleared his throat. The longer the garden sat in silence, the closer the whole thing was to falling apart. Lexos knew he and Rhea could only ignore what they'd done to each other for so long.

"You could have taken a bit more care," Nitsos said as he stood. "Do you know how long I spent building that?"

"What are you doing here?" Rhea asked.

Nitsos slipped his inventor's apron on, tying the strings around his waist. "Fixing the situation. I'm sure you'll agree it's got a bit out of hand. And I have to look after my creatures."

Nitsos held out his hand. Lexos watched as the hummingbird broke from its pattern and sped toward him, alighting on his fingers.

The bird. The bird with its familiar blue-tinted wings and down-turned eyes. Argyros eyes, Lexos thought, and the gears began to click into place.

"Your creatures?" Lexos said warily.

Nitsos set the hummingbird on a nearby cluster of roses, pausing a moment as it whirred to life and flitted back to the cherry tree, then stepped farther into the garden. "The plants, the animals." He tilted his head, looking at Rhea with an examining sort of interest that made Lexos uncomfortable. "You."

Lexos wasn't quick enough to stop Rhea as she lunged toward Nitsos, grabbed hold of his shirt, and pushed him back against the wall of the garden. "I am not your creature," she said, spit flying onto Nitsos's cheek. "I am nobody's but my own."

Nitsos blinked owlishly, and looked over Rhea's shoulder at Lexos, as though asking for his help in removing her. "I don't suppose we could have this conversation some other way, could we?"

Rhea yanked Nitsos down by his hair, forcing him to look at her. "Explain yourself. What did you do to me?"

"I'm not suggesting that I built you," Nitsos said, peeling her hands off him and sidling out from between her and the wall. "That is still much too complicated for me."

Lexos felt as though the answer were on the tip of his tongue. Something had been going on here, for much longer than anybody had been aware of. What had Nitsos been doing while nobody was looking?

"But?" he said. The dagger was glinting in the dirt at the corner of his eye. Rhea was closer, but he could still get to it first—to kill Nitsos or keep Rhea from killing him, Lexos wasn't sure.

"I may," Nitsos said, "have had some influence."

"Influence?" Rhea sounded calm. But Lexos knew that, with her as with Baba, that only meant the worst was coming.

Nitsos pointed to the hummingbird, which had returned to the lowest branch of the cherry tree. "I only have to wind it up when I want something done. Of course, I can't control everything. But I can set it in motion. I can arrange the right conditions. Usually, that's enough."

Lexos watched as the bird cocked its head. He'd seen it. The day of the choosing, he'd seen it there in the courtyard. Rhea, set in motion.

"The bird," she said. "It's me, isn't it?"

The markings and its eyes: Nitsos had built his sister in miniature, in the only way he knew how. Like every creature he'd ever built at Stratathoma, a symbol for one in the world beyond. And somehow, here was one for Rhea.

Nitsos grimaced. "It's more complicated than that. I hate to hear my work reduced to such—" Rhea took a threatening step forward, and Nitsos held up his hands. "Yes, I suppose you could say that it's you."

"How?" Lexos cut in. "Your gift isn't meant to work with people."

"And what would you know about it?" Nitsos said, sounding suddenly so bitter that Lexos was quite unnerved. "Baba gave you both everything." Rhea scoffed. Nitsos's eyes turned to her, bright and eager. "And as he was so fond of saying, he gave me a child's toy. So I took it and I made it into real power. After all, our gifts come from Baba's matagios, no? Every gift, out of life and death. Why shouldn't I be able to make them my own?" He paused, and then tilted his head. "Well, to a point."

"Not any longer." Rhea shoved Nitsos, sending him staggering back against the wall, nearly knocking over the lantern. "I'm destroying that thing. I'm ending this."

"That's actually an interesting point," Nitsos said, so happy to explain, to share, that Lexos felt a pang of affection. "Destroying the model won't remove the influence. It will only . . . what's the word? You will stall, I think is how I would put it."

"That's nonsense," Rhea said, striding toward the cherry tree, but Lexos caught her around the waist. Nitsos was not lying. In fact, Nitsos had never, Lexos thought, lied in his whole life. It was only that nobody had ever asked him any questions.

"Why did you do this?" Lexos asked. Rhea was struggling in his grip, throwing her weight against him, but he couldn't let her go, couldn't risk letting her make things worse. "What could you need Rhea for?"

Rhea, and not me, was what Lexos was leaving unsaid. But Nitsos only smiled, and Lexos knew he'd heard it anyway.

"You're very predictable, Alexandros. I hardly needed to manage you at all. Rhea, on the other hand, is something else altogether. It's quite a compliment, I think."

"A compliment?" Rhea cried, but Lexos was focused on some-thing else. Something that set dread blooming in his gut, bitter and queasy.

"Manage me for what?" he said.

"I wanted what you had," Nitsos said as though it should have been obvious. "Baba paid you attention. He listened when you spoke, whereas at times I am not sure he remembered my name." He glanced over Lexos's shoulder to where Baba's body lay half-buried, frustration twisting the corner of his mouth. "I wanted to be his sec-ond."

Lexos felt a rising anger that he was sure belonged also to Rhea. Baba's attention had never been the gift Nitsos thought it was.

"So why not kill Lexos and be done with it?" Rhea spat. Nitsos seemed surprised by it, and Lexos was, too. How could she suggest that so readily? "If you really wanted to be his second so badly."

"I have no stomach for that sort of thing," Nitsos said, as though just discussing it was making him sick. "And why do myself what you could do for me? Setting you against Lexos was sure to get you both out of the way. Baba would have no choice but to look to me."

Everything Rhea had done, all of her betrayals—they had been Nitsos all along. Lexos released her and urged her around to face him, eager to see his own relieved smile mirrored on her face, but she was rooted to the spot, her mouth dropped in something Lexos could only call horror.

"Rhea?" he said. She barely moved, as if she hadn't even heard him.

"When?" she said softly, staring past him at Nitsos. "When did it start? Your manipulation."

"A season or two back," he said evasively. "I tested it first for your autumn consort."

The delay in Patrassa. That had been Nitsos's doing. A test for what would follow, with no regard for the anger it would bring down on Rhea from Baba. And, Lexos thought, remembering that homecoming, what about Rhea's odd, dreamy sort of question to him, about the worth of a life. Had that come to her on her own? Given everything she'd said to him in the last day or two, he rather thought it might've.

"First," Rhea said. "So what came next?"

"I told you," Nitsos said, and Lexos could tell he was starting to get agitated—for all his patience with machinery and mechanics, he had far less for people. "It's a windup sort of gift. I could only set you in a certain direction and create an environment in which your path might take the hoped-for course."

"And what direction did you set me in?"

They all knew the answer, and Lexos wished desperately Rhea would just let it drop. But she seemed to need to hear Nitsos say it.

"I aimed you toward Michali," Nitsos said. "I knew he would take care of the rest."

For a moment there was only stillness, and then Rhea crumpled against Lexos with a muffled sob. Lexos only just caught her, levered an arm around her waist to prop her up against his hip.

It was, he thought, a bit of an overreaction.

Rhea was saying something, but he couldn't quite make it out, and it was only when she'd scraped the tears from her cheeks and repeated herself that it became clear. "Did I love him?" she asked. "Was it real? Any of it?"

Nitsos threw his hands up, making an exasperated noise. Lexos thought that he was probably longing for his workshop, where none of his creatures were flesh and blood. "How am I supposed to know that?" Nitsos said, his voice rising sharply. "Isn't that your job?"

"You took my heart from me," Rhea said, her feet steadying under her. Anger had lent a flush to her cheeks, and stripped the weakness from her limbs. Lexos knew how that felt, and wished he had some of it for himself.

"It doesn't matter anyway," Nitsos said. "He's dead, just like he's supposed to be, and you're with the Sxoriza, just like you're supposed to be. Baba dying is a bit of a problem, I will admit." He shrugged. "Lexos, you surprised me. I never thought you would kill him."

"But I have," Lexos said, setting Rhea aside and stepping in front of her. "Baba is dead, and there is no favor of his left to be won. What will you do now, Nitsos? What point is left to any of this?"

Behind him he could hear Rhea working to settle her breathing. She had to know that he had the best chance of setting things right. Nitsos would never listen to her, not with her anger running wild. "Release us," he finished. "Release her."

Nitsos at first said nothing, and only looked at him impassively. "You are right," he said at last, "that I cannot win Baba's favor. But as it happens, that is not all I want. To release our sister would be a waste, I think."

And it bothered Lexos that he knew exactly what he meant. He and Rhea were still opposed—they had not fulfilled the fate that Nitsos had created for them. Rhea was still of use to Nitsos as long as Lexos was alive.

"Listen," he started, but suddenly Rhea was scrabbling in the dirt for the dagger, clutching it tightly and making for Nitsos.

"It was you," she said. "You had Michali killed."

"I did," Nitsos said, oddly undisturbed by the dagger in his sister's hand as she advanced. "I knew you meant to let him live, and that couldn't be borne."

"But how?" Lexos cut in. How had Nitsos known? And how had he managed to get Rhea to think her own twin had done it?

"Your spies have more than one master, Alexandros. I'm the one who built them, after all."

Lexos was about to answer when Rhea raised the dagger to strike Nitsos, and instead halted, her hand stuck in midair, her mouth opening and closing.

"See?" Nitsos said, practically beaming with pride at his own ingenuity. "She recognizes her maker. None of my creatures can harm me, I'm afraid."

Rhea stumbled back, crashing to the ground, almost gasping for air. She cursed loudly, a string of words that Lexos did not know—she had always taken more interest in that area of their education than he.

"I'm going to kill you," she said then, looking up at Nitsos. Lexos knew her voice well enough to recognize when she was making a promise she would not break. "Somehow."

"All right," Nitsos said mildly, "but that's not what I would be focusing on at the moment, if I were you."

"What?"

Nitsos glanced over his shoulder. "We have guests."

Rhea let out a laugh from where she was sprawled on the earth. To Lexos it sounded incomprehensibly triumphant. "Yes," she said. "I know."

But Nitsos only shook his head. "Not those, I'm afraid."

"Will one of you tell me what is going on?" Lexos asked as Rhea's eyes went wide.

Nitsos gestured to the door of the garden. "Go and see."

The wind was fierce outside the walled shelter of the garden. When Lexos stepped out, Nitsos and Rhea just behind, he could at first barely see through the tangle of his hair. Nothing seemed out of the ordinary in the grounds—just the same rows of trees, and somewhere in the house, Chrysanthi, still thankfully asleep—so he made for the top of the nearby staircase that cut through the perimeter wall.

There, the gulf spread blue and glimmering out beyond the cliff's edge, and the dawn-lit sky bent down to kiss the horizon, an endless line broken only by a fleet of masts. Masts. Ships. Somebody was crossing the gulf, heading for Stratathoma. And in great numbers, if the distance wasn't blurring Lexos's view.

He swallowed hard. The insignia on the sails was too small to see clearly, but the sails were a color he'd recognize anywhere: Domina green.

"You made an excellent effort," Nitsos said from behind him. Lexos turned, breathing as evenly as he could. What was this? Had Nitsos set this invasion in motion just as he'd set up Rhea?

"Did you call them?" he asked. "Would you really risk the whole of Thyzakos for the sake of a petty siblings' quarrel?"

Nitsos held up his hands. "I cannot claim the credit here, brother. I am afraid it belongs entirely to you both."

It was all right. Everything would be all right. Lexos always drew the tides tightly around the cliffs, kept the waters too rough and clever for any ship to pass safely through them. "We're protected," he said. "We will hold."

"As it happens," Rhea said, "we won't." When he turned to look at her she was so pale he could almost see through her to the other side.

"Rhea," he started, trailing off as she clutched her stomach and swayed to one side.

"I thought . . . It wasn't meant to be them."

Nitsos made a small noise of amusement, but Lexos ignored him and stepped closer to his sister. She looked ill, her eyes fixed on the forest of masts that covered the sea.

"Explain," he said. "Or I will wring it out of you."

"I laid the tides open," she whispered. "For the Sxoriza. They said they'd be waiting."

A shake rippled through his body as he grabbed Rhea's arm and dragged her to the top of the staircase. It was too much; he was holding on to her too tightly. But he couldn't let go, not when she'd ruined everything out of sheer selfishness. "Look at this," he hissed in her ear. "Someone in your Sxoriza has betrayed you."

"No," Rhea said, trying to break free of him, but he only took hold of her jaw and held her still.

"Those ships would not be here if they didn't think their way in was clear." He could have laughed. How foolish she'd been. "You have brought this country to ruin, and for what?"

Baba would have punished her, would have brought her back under the family thumb no matter what. But Lexos had spent years watching him waste time and strength holding on to things that never did an ounce of good. Rhea was one of those things—family, and his sister, and half of his heart, but a liability, too. Better to cast her off, along with his anger, and fix this himself.

He let go of her, ignoring her startled cry as she staggered away, and started toward the house, refusing to look back at what he was leaving behind. It was too late for him to undo whatever Rhea had done, and after his failure to master the matagios, it seemed, for the moment, too dangerous to rely on anything but his wits. No, his duty now was simply to survive the Domina invasion and establish a Stratagiozi seat in exile, where he could build his strength anew and retake the country. He had the council on his side; he would get word to them and soon enough their troops would aid him in defeating Tarro.

He began to run, dirt coating the black shine of his boots as he tore through the cypress trees and careened through the double doors into the outer courtyard, its neatness stark against the tumult he had spent his morning immersed in.

Chrysanthi was waiting there, at the doors to the inner courtyard, still in her nightgown with a shawl pulled tightly around her. She seemed half asleep, but there was a baffled frown on her face. She knew something was wrong.

"Get inside," he barked before she had time to open her mouth. "Get dressed, pack everything you need. We need to leave as soon as possible."

"What for?" she asked through a yawn.

Lexos felt a little bad for her—nobody would ever be able to explain to her what had happened in the windup garden, not really—but there was no time for coddling. "Go to your room," he said, "and take a look out your window. I think you'll be able to guess."

He left her there, stunned in the courtyard, and made for the stables on the southern half of the grounds, planning to saddle only a horse each for himself and Chrysanthi. Rhea and Nitsos could find their own escape, and though he could pretend otherwise, he hoped they did. But they were no longer his responsibility.

They kept the horses out in the grounds, free to roam for the most part on the southern half and brought into the stables by the grooms during bad weather. They were beautiful things, tended carefully to by Chrysanthi and her set of paints, and nearly wild. Nitsos didn't bother with them the way he did with the other creatures on the grounds—the Stratagiozi before Baba had ordered them built, and Lexos remembered Nitsos saying they were of a different mechanism that he could not understand.

He pushed open the outer courtyard's double doors and was veering to the right, toward where the horses would be pastured, when he stopped short. A rider was coming up the path. And only a member of another Stratagiozi family could make those outer doors open without permission from Baba. Or rather, permission from Lexos himself now.

Stavra. He'd know her posture anywhere.

Had she brought troops with her? Had the council come to rescue him?

"It's good to see you," he called in Merkheri as her horse came thundering up the gravel path, juddering to a halt a few yards away.

Stavra had clearly been riding hard. Mud was streaked up the legs of her mount and splattered all over her boots and trousers. She was breathing hard, sweat collecting in her hairline, worry drawing her eyes wide.

"You're all right?" she said. She was speaking Thyzaki, but in her haste her tenses were muddled, and Lexos couldn't help a slight smile. "They haven't arrived?"

He shook his head, reached out to help her dismount. "You're just in time."

He expected relief, maybe even one of the rare smiles Stavra kept hidden away. What he got was a shake of the head and her averted gaze as she swung down from the saddle.

"Come on," he said. "Help me get the horses. We'll fall back behind your troops."

"I'm sorry, Alexandros," Stavra said, looking at him at last.

"What for? You did bring troops, didn't you?"

"Ammar's soldiers," she said impatiently. "But, Lexos, listen to me. They're not here to help you."

Of course they weren't, Lexos wanted to say. But she wasn't talking about Tarro's ships, was she?

"What do you mean?"

"Your plan with the council," she said. "It was never real, Lexos. They set you up."

There was a ringing in his ears. He thought perhaps he hadn't heard her correctly. "Excuse me?"

"I didn't know," Stavra said, taking his hand. "But after the meeting in Agiokon my mother told me. The council went to Tarro. They played you, used you to get rid of your father. And now they're here with the Dominas to annex Thyzakos, just the way you were planning to annex Trefazio."

"No." Lexos pulled his hand free of hers and took a shaky step back. "No, no, we had an agreement."

"They were lying."

"They can't just—"

"They can." Stavra looked over her shoulder, scanning the path. There must be others behind her, Lexos thought. Coming to rip this country from his hands.

"And you're here for what?" he asked, voice curdled and sour. "To gloat? You were right, after all. I shouldn't have gone to the council."

"Don't be silly," she said, turning back to him. "I came to get you out. I cannot spare your father from the council but I can at least spare you. Where is he? Still in the house?"

Lexos couldn't keep the confusion from his face. "He is dead," he said plainly. "I did what I said I would do, after all."

Stavra's face blanched. "Oh, Lexos."

"I had a promise. I had the support of the council. What did you expect from me?"

"You are Stratagiozi now, then?" she said, and she closed her eyes, as if afraid to see the answer written on his face. "You should have waited."

"For what?"

She didn't answer, instead backing away and returning to her horse. "I could rescue you when you were only his second. That was a difference enough that I could keep from breaking my oath to my mother."

Lexos followed after her. "And now?"

She stared intently at her horse's saddle as she adjusted the stirrup. "I'm sorry. I wish I could."

He snatched the reins from her hand. "Your oath means more to you than I do?"

"My oath is constant," she said. "I have seen your kind before, and I will see your kind again, but my oath, my duty—they are with me always." She swung up into the saddle and her horse pranced backward, yanking Lexos forward a step before he let go of the reins. "They're coming," she said. "Best to face it with some dignity. It's the only gift I can still give you."

She was gone before he could say anything, wheeling her horse around tightly and cantering back toward the gate, where he supposed she would be meeting the rest of the council's troops.

There was no escape by sea, not with Tarro's ships already so close to shore. And of course he couldn't expect to ride past Stavra and the troops. The only way out left to him was one of the secret entrances built into the perimeter wall, but what then? He would be free, but with no resources, no power. Barely more than a dagger to wield against the combined forces of the council. How would he build up any sort of force to take back his country?

There was another way. There was always another way.

It was with that thought racing through his head that he went back into the house. And when the council's soldiers entered Stratathoma, Tarro at their head, they found Lexos sitting in an armchair by the hearth in the great room.

Lexos had ordered the servants to attend, each carrying a serving tray loaded with freshly poured glasses of wine. He hadn't had time to think of Rhea or Nitsos—they would be captured or they wouldn't be, and at least this way he didn't have to handle them himself—and with any luck Chrysanthi had seen the ships on the horizon, heard the noise as the troops burst through the courtyard doors, and hidden herself away. No, Lexos could only look after himself now—himself and Thyzakos.

"Welcome," he said as Tarro stepped through the house's double doors into the great room. "Please, won't you join me in a glass of wine?"

Tarro was dressed oddly for the occasion, in a pair of trousers and a loose jacket that seemed better suited to a stroll through Vuomorra's regimented gardens. Behind him, Stavra and Zita waited, Stavra watching Lexos with anguished eyes, and alongside them were Ammar, Milad, and Nastia, each with their seconds standing nearby. Nobody was dressed for battle, but Lexos knew not to let that fool him. Beyond the doors, there were surely soldiers waiting in ranks, their armor gleaming in the sun.

"Alexandros," Tarro said. "How lovely to be in your company. I had hoped your banishment from Vuomorra would not impede us from seeing one another again."

Tarro certainly would not have come without Falka, who had designed his banishment, Lexos thought, and he searched the invading party for her face. It was only after a second look that he recognized her, lingering at the back of the group, her expression eager and expectant. Waiting for her moment, he supposed.

Lexos stood and beckoned one of the servants closer. It was a young woman, one of Rhea's maids. Eleni, or something like that, and she looked terrified, her serving tray trembling in her hands. "Thank you," he said, taking a wineglass and sipping from it delicately. "I'm thrilled to play host," he went on, turning back to Tarro. "I don't believe any of you have been to Stratathoma. At least not during Argyros rule."

"Speaking of Argyros rule," Tarro said, waving Eleni away as she offered the tray to him. "Where is your delightful father?"

Lexos raised his wineglass to the light. "Dead," he said, inspecting the vivid color as it played with the light. "You will have been expecting that, though, if your companions have been honest with you."

"Indeed," Tarro said lightly, but Lexos could see a sparkle of interest in his eyes.

"So that leaves you in your father's seat?" Ammar said. Tarro let out a small huff of annoyance, presumably at being forced to share the stage with another player. Lexos ignored Ammar, and addressed his answer to Tarro.

"It does."

"And your siblings?" Tarro gestured to the gathering. "Why don't they join us?"

"I'm afraid," Lexos said, "that I have no idea at all where they are."

Tarro paused for a moment, presumably wondering whether or not Lexos was telling the truth. Let him pry if he wanted to. There was nothing left inside Lexos for him to get at.

"A shame," Tarro said at last. "But we'll get along without them, I think."

He turned away and snapped his fingers. Maryam, Milad's second, and Ohra, Ammar's second, crossed to Lexos, their faces solemn, strides matching. If they were going to kill him, Lexos thought, he had rather not spill wine on himself in the process, and so he drained his glass and set it down on Eleni's proffered tray before lifting his chin and summoning all of the calm he could find.

As it was, they did not kill him, and only took a firm hold of his arms. A hostage, then, Lexos thought. Which was, in fact, what he had hoped for.

"Falka," Tarro said. "If you would."

It occurred to Lexos that he had never learned what her particular inherited gift was while he'd been in Vuomorra. She would not have taken on Gino's—there were no gifts that passed with the title of second, and rather the administration of such things was left to each family to handle as they pleased.

"She's very good," Tarro was saying as Falka approached, her dark eyes serious, her hair pulled tightly back. "It shouldn't hurt. She may make it hurt anyway, though, if she likes."

Make what hurt? Was it Falka who was going to kill him, after all?

Maryam and Ohra forced Lexos to his knees, their hands still locked around his arms. Lexos looked up at Falka. She was carrying no weapon. But perhaps she meant to do it by sheer force of will.

"Give me your hand," she said at last, after a moment of quiet so long and deep that Lexos thought he could hear her heart beating.

He was so startled that he found himself asking, "Left or right?"

She smiled gently. "Left, if you don't mind."

The willingness had gone out of him, but it was no use. Maryam yanked his arm out toward Falka. He clenched his hand into the tightest fist he could, the black mark on his palm beating in time with his pulse. Falka only shook her head and peeled back his fingers one by one as though it cost her nothing.

"The gift I have is quite unusual, apparently," she said as she ran her fingers along the lines of his mark. It tickled, and though Lexos tried to wrest himself from her grip, she was too strong. He relented, relaxing his hand completely. "There are so many things that need doing, and only so many children. But I'm sure you know that the Domina family has an excess of those. Which is how I find myself of great use at this particular moment."

Slowly, she dug her thumbnail into his skin, and Lexos gasped at the sharp prick of pain.

"We cannot let you keep your gift," she went on, "and certainly not the matagios—not if you are to remain alive." She smiled confidingly at him. "And I think you would rather remain alive. So I'm going to take them from you."

Lexos went rigid. He could feel his hand trembling, but even as he tried to curl his fingers in to hide his mark from Falka, Maryam and Ohra leaned in, and there, the cold press of steel against his neck.

"You will let me do this," Falka said. Her friendliness, if Lexos could really have called it that, had vanished, and the threat of Maryam's knife could be heard in her voice.

It wasn't worth a fight, Lexos told himself. The matagios had failed him with Rhea—what good was it, really, if he could not use it? And if he refused, kept his gifts and died here, they would all belong to the Dominas eventually, whether by ritual or by blood. Falka would get what she wanted no matter what. Better she leave him living in the process.

"Very well," he said, and he had no sooner finished speaking than Falka had bent over his palm and begun to dig at his black mark with her fingernail. Lexos watched, shock sizzling through him, as the black filling the lines of his palm, the black that had years and years ago become part of his very skin, scraped away like powder until a clump of it had collected on the tip of her finger.

"What will you do with it?" he asked hoarsely.

"Keep it myself," Falka said, as though he'd asked a ridiculous question. She let go of him, Maryam and Ohra still holding him tightly, and tipped the black powder she'd gathered into the palm of her hand. "It's simple, really."

As he watched, Falka began to press the powder into the lines of her palm, and though some of it fell away, as if Lexos's gift was reluctant to pass fully to her, enough of it clung to her skin that soon the mark on her palm, the mark that identified her gift as given to her by Tarro, had taken on a new shape.

A gift was meant to pass with bloodshed. That was how it had been since the age of the saints. This, this strange process—it was unnatural. It was wrong.

Lexos shuddered as Falka smoothed her fingertips across his now blank palm. "There, now," she said. "That wasn't so bad, was it? Now for the matagios."

Her hands were steady and warm at his jaw, and Lexos waited for her to pry it open, but she only tapped one finger on his chin. She wanted him to give in. She wanted this last surrender.

Fine. Fine, he would do what had to be done. He would lose his seat now for the chance to take it back later.

He opened his mouth, holding his breath as Falka leaned in and peered at the flat of his tongue. For a moment she said nothing, the silence around them so thick and cottony Lexos thought it could almost certainly be spun into some sort of fabric. And then Falka let go of him and straightened up.

"Well," she said. "That's odd."

"What is?" came Tarro's voice from over her shoulder.

"You wanted me to take his matagios," she said. "But he's never had it in the first place."

Twins, was Lexos's last thought before he fainted.

THIRTY-NINE

RHEA

H e left her on the clifftop. Left her there with Nitsos, Baba's body half-buried in the garden behind them. How easy it was for him to walk away as though everything that had come to light barely mattered to him. And perhaps it truly didn't—she was the one, after all, who was suddenly a stranger in her own life.

It had felt real. She'd loved Michali slowly, and only really after things changed and they'd been honest with each other. But she couldn't forget it now—how she'd made her choice that day in the great room of Stratathoma. How she hadn't known who to pick even as she came down the stairs. How Michali's name had come out of her mouth, surprising everyone including her. She'd waved it off, barely considered it for a moment, but now it made sense.

And beyond that, beyond what she'd felt for Michali, there were the Sxoriza to consider. No, Michali hadn't been responsible for her change of heart, but she wasn't naïve enough to discount the role he'd played. Her dedication to them had come piece by piece, and it might never have all fit together without Michali.

Could Nitsos have really set all of it up? If not for the humming-bird perched on the branches of the windup cherry tree, would she have ever found herself here? Here, looking out at the enemy she'd let into her father's house.

Lexos was right. Somebody in the Sxoriza had to have told Tarro Domina their plans. She'd wondered if perhaps Nitsos was to blame, but he'd shown no hesitation in claiming his deeds. Why keep this one last secret? No, there had been a traitor in the Sxoriza, someone Piros and Michali had trusted enough to tell of their plans, and Rhea thought she knew who. One name, coming back to her over and over, with only the shadowiest hint of a face attached: Falka, Tarro Domina's daughter and now his second.

Piros and Michali had trusted her to handle Lexos. And in a way, she had. But she'd handled them, too. Rhea almost wanted to meet her, to see what sort of woman could spin things just so.

Well, if she stayed here, she would meet Falka, and presumably her own death, as well. There was no time for dawdling.

She slid the Argyros dagger into her boot, all too aware of Baba's blood still crusted on the blade. It was lucky, she thought. Baba had gone to his death never knowing that she'd betrayed him, never knowing that she'd learned the truth about her mother. She should be sorry, she knew. After all, surely some of the answers she wanted had died with him. But he never would have told her the truth, never would have allowed the choices she made to stand, and so Rhea found that she was glad he was gone. To Baba, she had always been a dutiful daughter, and she could bury that part of herself in the ground with him.

Nitsos's hummingbird stared at her from its perch on the branch of the cherry tree, its eyes unblinking, the gloss of them unnervingly liquid. It was more alive, somehow, than the other creatures of Nitsos's she had seen. Certainly more alive than Lexos's scout, the one she'd disassembled with her own hands. The one Nitsos had used to watch her and implicate Lexos both.

She couldn't leave it behind, not if it was truly tied to her the way

Nitsos said it was. Even the barest scratch could leave her stalled, and though she had no real idea what that meant, she also had no real wish to find out.

"Go ahead," Nitsos said from behind her, and she closed her eyes briefly. "Take it. It will come when I call it anyway."

She hardly needed his permission, but at his words she picked her shawl out of the dirt and shook it clean before holding out her hand. The bird hopped from the branch to balance on her finger, and she let out a sigh of relief. Carefully, she wrapped it in her shawl, bundling it up before tying the shawl around her waist.

"Why are you still here?" she said, turning around reluctantly. Whatever had passed between him and Lexos, it had done nothing to upset Nitsos, if his appearance was anything to judge by (although, she was learning it perhaps was not at all).

Nitsos gestured to the garden around them. "I wanted a last look at my work. I'd say we'll have to bid farewell to Stratathoma before the morning is out."

The ships, rocking gently back and forth in the cradle of the ocean. "They came with so many," she said. So many, and she'd opened the tides to all of them. It was her fault Domina power was spreading, her fault the federation seemed to be turning into something that would be harder than ever to pick apart. Michali would have been so disappointed.

"Stratathoma would have fallen to half the number," Nitsos said. "But this fleet is not meant for just Stratathoma."

The ships were close enough that if she listened hard she could hear the faintest ring of their cries carry across the waves. They were coming not for Stratathoma, but for the whole country.

"Baba is gone. There is no favor left to win," she said, stepping closer to Nitsos. He was polishing the lenses of his magnifying glasses with the edge of his shirt, his inventor's apron hanging slightly askew. Her brother, who made things with his hands—he couldn't have any wish to see Thyzakos fall apart. "This can't be what you want."

"It didn't used to be." Nitsos folded up his glasses and tucked them in his trouser pocket. "But this system, this federation. It has done nothing for me. In fact, it's long outlived its use. Past time for it to be torn down, don't you think?"

"Don't pretend we're on the same side," she snapped. "If you wanted a better world, Michali would be alive right now." She and the Sxoriza were fighting to replace the old order with a new one, with independence, with freedom. That was a sight better than burning something down just for the sake of it.

"I suppose that's one way of looking at it," Nitsos said. "But either way, it's past time I was off." He sounded awfully cavalier, but then, that seemed to be his way.

"Oh?" she said.

He nodded. "And you should be, too."

There was a noise from the front of the house, the clatter of hooves on the gravel path that led through the grounds. Somebody was here, and if the approaching ships were anything to go by, it was nobody friendly.

"Well," she said, dusting herself off. "Goodbye, then. I'll see you."

"If I wish it."

She narrowed her eyes. He didn't realize, did he? "No. If I do. I may be your creature, but you will never make another like me." Part warning and part pride. Whatever link that still existed between them, it bound him to her just as much as her to him. And she would use it to kill him. She'd promised him that, for herself and for Michali.

Nitsos only smiled. "Perhaps," he said, and the last she saw of him as she ducked through the garden doorway was his little white teeth.

The best way out of Stratathoma, she thought as she hurried between the cypress trees, was one of the secret doors built into the perimeter wall. They were only built into the southern half of the wall, given that an exit through the northern half of the wall would only have led off the cliff and into the sea, and to get there she couldn't very well go around the front of the house—there were certainly soldiers there on guard from whatever delegation had come riding up the front walk.

No, it was safest to pass through the house itself. It was too big for invading soldiers to learn all of its secrets in time to catch her. She could use the northern servants' entrance, cut through the servants' quarters, and come out the other side, and nobody would be the wiser.

The question, of course, would be what to do once she'd got free. Were the Sxoriza still coming? And could she still rely on them, given that they'd so obviously been compromised?

The servants' entrance was near the rear of the house, close enough to the veranda where she'd first met Michali that Rhea felt a pang in her chest. It was a low, crooked door, built from an aged, warped wood, and when she opened it, it revealed an empty corridor, the torches guttering low. Stratathoma was designed so that sound was funneled from the family chambers to the servants' corridors, so that the servants could always be right where they were needed. Of course, the first Thyzak Stratagiozi had also been sure to build in pockets of privacy, which as a Stratagiozi's daughter Rhea had been grateful for. Now she wished she could eavesdrop on the whole house.

There were voices, though, echoing faintly, and she thought she recognized one of them. Lexos, speaking with that tone she hated, with its irritating calm and barely hidden snideness. She ignored her urge to join him—she would have to excise that permanently now—and continued on, following the winding path of the corridor toward the kitchen. From there she would take another hallway and find her way out.

One turn, and then another, and at last she could smell the warmth of something baking, could see the opening into the kitchen up ahead. She slowed, tried to get the best glimpse she could of the room without stepping out of the shadows. There was someone in there, and not a servant, if the smell of them was anything to go by. Rhea could only see the muddled shape of them where they were (oddly enough) crouched under the extending ledge of the stone counter.

She squinted. "Chrysanthi?"

The shape let out a muffled squeak, and then unfolded itself and clambered out from its makeshift hiding place. It was indeed Chrysanthi, her golden hair spilling out from under the hood of a ratty old cloak she had to have stolen from one of the servants.

"Rhea," Chrysanthi breathed. "*Mala,* am I glad to see you."

Rhea came into the kitchen and pulled Chrysanthi in tightly, burying her face in the crook of her neck. Here was her last remaining sibling, the only one in her family who was still who she had been the day before.

"Lexos told me to pack," Chrysanthi whimpered. "I can't find Baba anywhere and there are people in the great room. Something's gone wrong."

Rhea released her and stepped back. "We need to get out of this house as soon as we can. Do you have everything?"

Chrysanthi lifted a small bag. "I only had time to get my paints."

"That will do." Rhea took her hand and led her toward the opening at the other side of the kitchen, where another hallway branched off. "Come with me."

They were nearly through when there came the sound of somebody clearing their throat. Panic closing in, Rhea turned, only to let out a sigh of relief. It was just Eleni.

She looked terrified, sweat beading on her upper lip and a tray of empty wineglasses trembling in her hands.

"Yes?" Rhea said. Eleni had passed on a message once. Rhea could only hope she was here to do it again.

"South wall," Eleni said. "He's waiting." And then she was gone, hurrying back out toward the great room, having snatched a fresh tray of glasses from the kitchen counter.

She hadn't been left behind, after all. Rhea could have cried with relief.

"Who's waiting?" Chrysanthi said. "What's going on?"

There was no time to explain. Rhea dragged her sister into the shadowed hallway and hoped that a familiar face would be waiting for her at the other end.

Chrysanthi wisely kept quiet. She would descend into tears later—Rhea couldn't blame her, and might in fact join her there—but as they moved briskly toward the south of the house, Chrysanthi's face turned grim and her steps were steady. Rhea felt a rush of fondness for her sister. Argyros women were good at nothing if not making the best of situations for which they had been woefully underprepared.

At last, the southern servants' entrance, and beyond, more olive groves than cypress trees, which provided ample cover as Rhea led Chrysanthi through them at a near run. Before long they were at the secret door built into the perimeter wall, visible only from inside the grounds and crafted so carefully that Rhea had to run her fingers across the wall for a few meters before she finally found the hinge and was able to push it open.

Eleni had been right. Someone was waiting on the other side. Tall, with a thick beard, and warm eyes that crinkled when he smiled. Piros, Michali's second, and perhaps the only person Rhea was prepared at that moment to trust.

"You made it," he said. Rhea saw Chrysanthi's eyes widen at the sound of his Amolovak accent. "I was worried. No doubt you've realized things aren't quite going according to the plan."

"I have." Rhea reached out to shake his hand. "Thank you, Piros."

Piros waved off her thanks. "And you've brought a friend?"

"My sister, Chrysanthi."

"Delighted," Chrysanthi said, sounding anything but.

"You are lucky I brought Amolovak horses," Piros said, gesturing over his shoulder to where two brown geldings were waiting patiently. "The strongest horses on the continent. You will ride with me, and your sister will take the spare."

Before long they were mounted, and Piros was spurring his horse forward into a charge, Chrysanthi close behind as they galloped south. They would follow the line of the coast until they were well clear of Stratathoma, Piros explained. As they rode, Rhea's thighs already cramping, he told her what had happened—how the council had gone to Tarro behind Lexos's back and agreed to invade Thyzakos. Worse than that, according to Piros, was the betrayal of the Sxoriza. Piros, too, suspected Falka Domina, and though it was impossible to be sure without asking the woman herself, the Domina crest visible on those sails left little doubt in Rhea's mind.

"She was for her father the whole time," Piros said, his anger audible even over the noise of the wind.

"Indeed, it seems that way." And it did. But Rhea had been a daughter, and more than that, she had been a Stratagiozi's daughter, and she was not sure Piros was entirely right.

They rode for most of the day, their destination one of the Sxoriza camps in the mountains, only slowing when the sun began to dip low in the sky. Piros had plenty of supplies stored in the saddlebags, and they stopped in a cluster of orange trees that would shelter them and keep the light of their fire from being seen.

"You're with the Sxoriza," Chrysanthi said as they dismounted. "I see things changed while you were in the Ksigora."

Rhea didn't know what to say. How could she explain everything that had passed? How could she explain her own reservations, especially now that she knew the truth about their mother? "Yes," she settled for. "They did."

She supposed she would have to tell Chrysanthi, she thought as Piros tied the horses to one of the orange trees. Inside the grove, the grass was brown and cracking, but the oranges were just ripening, their weight bending the boughs low. Michali had died by a hand other than her own, Rhea thought, trailing her fingertip along one branch. Was that keeping spring from taking full root?

She sat down heavily, her legs trembling from the day's ride, and Chrysanthi collapsed next to her, nearly squashing the hummingbird where it was still tied around her waist. Rhea was already shivering, the breeze only just broken by the trees.

"You should have dressed more warmly," Chrysanthi said, drawing her cloak around both of them. Piros knelt near the center of the grove, digging clear a spot to light a fire.

"I was a bit busy," Rhea said, before remembering that Chrysanthi had no idea what had passed in the windup garden. "Your brothers, *koukla*. We have to let them go, all right?"

Chrysanthi frowned. "What do you mean?"

"I mean that Baba is dead. Lexos killed him." She pushed on, ignoring Chrysanthi's gasp. "And Nitsos has done far worse. It's only us now."

"But Baba—"

"Do not," Rhea said sharply, "mourn him. He deserves nothing from you." She turned, her knee knocking against Chrysanthi's. "Who was our mother? Do you know?"

Chrysanthi's eyes were wide, and she could do nothing more than shake her head.

"She was a saint," Rhea said. The time for tact had long since passed. Best to get it over with. "And Baba killed her." That was what Lexos had said in the garden. And for everything else he'd done, Rhea did not think he'd been lying.

"If our mother was a saint," Chrysanthi started, her voice wavering, "how come our gifts are only from Baba? Shouldn't we have . . . something else? Be something else?"

"No," Rhea answered, even as Piros snorted, and said, "You poor girl."

Rhea quite liked Piros. But he was taking his life into his hands, speaking that way to Chrysanthi.

"It's like with a Stratagiozi," she explained to her sister. "If a saint dies and no rite is performed, their gifts pass back to the earth."

Piros looked up from where he was building the fire with a bundle of dry sticks he'd pulled from his saddlebag. "Blood and dirt. Where do you think your rituals come from?"

Rhea fell silent. She knew that beside her, Chrysanthi was remembering the same thing she was—the feel of Baba's fingers, calloused and firm, as they packed the mixture of earth and blood into the lines of their palms. Rhea folded her left hand into a fist. She would not look.

"So our mother," Chrysanthi said. "When she died, her gift went back to the ground?"

Piros nodded and fussed with the flint and tinder, striking twice before a spark leapt to catch.

"If only Baba's could have done the same," Rhea said darkly. "It might have saved us all a lot of trouble."

"You don't want his gift?" Piros asked.

The fire was growing, too small yet to give off much warmth, but Rhea inched closer. "I certainly don't, but that, at the very least, isn't my problem."

For a moment Piros said nothing, his head tilted as he studied her. "I am not sure," he said at last, "if you are joking. Thyzak humor escapes me sometimes."

Rhea frowned. "What are you talking about?"

"The Stratagiozi's black spot. What do you call it?"

"The matagios," Rhea said, but she wasn't listening anymore. Lexos had killed Baba, and so the matagios had surely passed to him. They were twins, but Lexos had been born first. Hadn't he?

She hadn't seen the matagios on his tongue in the windup garden. And it hadn't worked when he'd recited those words and tried to take her life.

No, Rhea thought. Please, no. Except Piros was looking at her almost sadly, and Rhea knew, certainty sitting like stone in her gut, that her father had told her more lies than she'd ever expected.

"Chrysanthi," she said hoarsely, "it's there, isn't it?"

The firelight playing across her sister's face, a black mark traced on both their palms, and when Chrysanthi nodded, Rhea shut her eyes.

Death belongs to the Stratagiozi, she thought, and so it belongs to me.

RHEA

I n the mountains, snow fell long into spring. Crocuses bloomed under thick drifts of powder; with them came the stench of rot, and their petals withered before they could fully unfurl. Above, the sun shone with a fresh strength, but it did nothing to beat back the chill that whipped in with every gust of winter wind, so bitter and sharp that it was almost as if the season hadn't changed at all.

Rhea didn't mind. In her tent, there was always a well-banked fire waiting for her to warm herself by. Other tents went without food, rationed themselves to starving, but Rhea never went a day without a bowl of fresh cherries not an inch from her hand, and when she slept it was comfortably, under a pile of blankets that might have, in her absence, belonged to several other people.

No, she thought as she rose each morning, it was not exactly fair. But she had cast off her mother's name, and they called her Aya Thyspira now, for the things she had done. She had stopped correcting them. She would take what comfort she could get.

Things in Thyzakos were still settling in the aftermath of the sacking at Stratathoma. At first, Rhea had made suggestions, had followed Piros from tent to tent with ideas on how to pull the council apart by the seams, how to win Thyzakos back from the Dominas and claim independence. That was, after all, the Sxoriza's goal, and with the loss of Falka Domina, it had seemed that they would need Rhea more than ever.

But since then nearly a month had passed, and until they found a way to strike at the council—until her sources across the continent found Nitsos—she had better things to occupy her time. Thinking of Falka, for one, and trying to assemble the various descriptions she'd heard of the other woman into a mosaic face. Few people seemed to have a firm impression of her, and even fewer had actually met her, but Rhea could feel a sort of tug at the back of her mind whenever she dwelt too long on Falka's name. Another Stratagiozi's daughter, another child scratching her way past her father toward something resembling power.

She was busy, too, with worship, great stretches of time where she sat at a makeshift altar and allowed people to kneel before her and kiss her cold hands. And with looking after Chrysanthi, though Chrysanthi seemed to be adjusting to being a saint's sister far better than Rhea was to being a saint.

There was one such worship service this morning, and that was where Rhea was headed, dressed in a black, fur-lined gown, the mechanical hummingbird perched on her shoulder, a smear of her own blood dabbed across her forehead as a mark of her power. The matagios, Piros had said, was not enough, was too associated with the Stratagiozi. She needed to give the people some other reminder of what she could do.

And what she could do was changing. They had been mixed up in her already, life and death. The seasons were always a braid of both, each new season bought with the death of the old, but the power in Baba's matagios had turned her gift into something else entirely.

Truly a saint. That's what Piros said. Rhea wondered if her mother would say the same thing.

The camp's altar was set up on clean-swept ground at the edge of the tents, sheltered by a lean-to. There was no portrait hung like the one she'd seen in the church that day—there was no need for one, after all, since they had the real thing—but there were candles lit no matter the hour, and the air around the lean-to was powdered with snow and incense.

Waiting for her there today was a collection of newcomers to the camp, their faces dirty, their clothing riddled with holes. They had presumably traveled some ways to meet her. News had spread that the Sxoriza had a saint on their side, a real live saint, and more were joining their number every day.

She would receive them in a moment. First, Rhea turned her attention to the figure standing beside the altar. Familiar, beloved, and entirely hers. Obscured in the shadows, but as she approached, clearer, and clearer still when he stepped into the sunlight and knelt in the snow. Michali.

It had only taken a few days after arriving for Rhea to wonder if she might be able to bring him back. There were stories of such things happening during the reign of the saints. And Rhea was no saint—not really, not the way people thought she was when they worshipped her—but perhaps she was close enough for this. Though she hadn't been sure how she might accomplish it, she'd remembered how easy it had been in Lexos's tower to ask the water for what she wanted. Maybe it was as simple as that.

Piros had nodded, eyeing her warily, and sent men to bring Michali's coffin up to the mountain camp. And after a week of what Rhea supposed someone else might call prayer, of resting her palm against Michali's mottled skin, she had opened her eyes to find her consort, breathing and bound again into his body.

He smiled now as she approached, his eyes fixed on hers. Behind him, the worshippers were whispering, pointing. Across the continent it was a rumor, she knew, that she'd raised Ksigori's favorite son from the dead. Today they knew it to be true.

"*Keresmata,* my love," Michali said. His voice was the same as it had been before he'd died, if perhaps a touch hoarser, although Rhea supposed that was no surprise. It had gone a long while without use, after all.

She said nothing in response, and only leaned down until their lips were just touching. This close, she could see the flickering dark at the center of his eyes that nobody else seemed to notice. She could feel the answering stirring in her chest. Something had come back with Michali, and made a home in them both.

Let it, she thought, and kissed him.

ACKNOWLEDGMENTS

Thank you to my editor, Sarah Peed, and to Cat Camacho as well for the thoughtful feedback and support. To my agents, Kim Witherspoon, Jessica Mileo, and Daisy Parente, a huge thank-you, as always. I count myself very lucky to work with all of you.

Scott Shannon, Keith Clayton, Tricia Narwani, Alex Larned, Anne Groell, Bree Gary, and the entire team at Del Rey—thank you for welcoming me to the Del Rey family so warmly. To the publicity and marketing teams, it has been such a joy to get to know everybody. Thank you especially to David Moench, Jordan Pace, Ada Maduka, Julie Leung, Ashleigh Heaton, Sabrina Shen, Megan Tripp, and Matt Schwartz.

Thanks also to Catherine Bucaria, Rob Guzman, Ellen Folan, and Elizabeth Fabian on the audio team for all your incredible work. And to Jo Anne Metsch, Tim Green and Faceout Studio, and the production and design teams at Del Rey, thank you for creating such a beautiful book inside and out.

I owe a particular debt to my mother for her help with translation from Greek to the fictionalized language that appears in the text, and I owe thanks as well to my long-suffering friends and family, my early readers, and everyone who helped me direct my research.

ABOUT THE AUTHOR

RORY POWER lives in Rhode Island. She has an MA in prose fiction from the University of East Anglia, and is the *New York Times* bestselling author of *Wilder Girls* and *Burn Our Bodies Down*.

itsrorypower.com

Instagram: @itsrorypower

ABOUT THE TYPE

This book was set in Baskerville, a typeface designed by John Baskerville (1706–75), an amateur printer and typefounder, and cut for him by John Handy in 1750. The type became popular again when the Lanston Monotype Corporation of London revived the classic roman face in 1923. The Mergenthaler Linotype Company in England and the United States cut a version of Baskerville in 1931, making it one of the most widely used typefaces today.

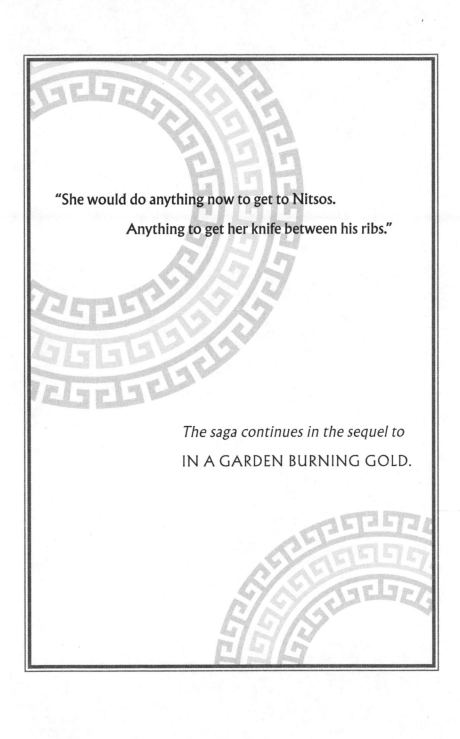

"She would do anything now to get to Nitsos.

Anything to get her knife between his ribs."

The saga continues in the sequel to
IN A GARDEN BURNING GOLD.